THORNE OF BLOOD

THE HUNTER GAMES

BOOK THREE

ARIEL DAWN

NAUGHTY NIGHTS PRESS LLC • CANADA

Thorne Of Blood

The Hunter Games

Book Three

Copyright ©2024 Ariel Dawn

ISBN: 978-1-77357-622-0

978-1-77357-623-7

Naughty Nights Press LLC

Cover Design by Willsin Rowe

THORNE OF BLOOD

An Omega on fire. Three potential mates. An unexpected twist.

For Clementine Srirocco, her heat is all consuming.

To make matters more complicated, the mate she longs for is a hunter, and her pack mate has been helping her cover it up for a year. With her Alpha away on pack business, and her mate out of reach, Cleo isn't sure she will survive the heat much longer.

When a vampire attack on the Thorne Estate lands her ally in the hands of the enemy, Cleo will stop at nothing to rescue her prospective mate. Even if it means seeking out the aid of Malcolm and Alaric, both of whom will stop at nothing to claim her for their own.

Will Cleo be able to fight the bonds of fate? Or will her heat devour more than just the feisty Omega?

THORNE OF BLOOD

Thorne of Blood is book three in The Hunter Games series, filled with hungry hunters, vicious vampires, wicked werewolves, and other supernatural creatures.

1

"JUST A LITTLE harder," Rocky groaned.

Cleo could see the sweat starting to form on his brow.

"I can't go any harder, Rocky," Cleo huffed as she collapsed against the tree.

"Yes, you can. You need to keep your strength up, or this heat will consume you."

Cleo pulled her knees to her chest, burying her face in her arms as she focused on trying to catch her breath. She was burning up, and it wasn't just because of her daily sprint with Rocky.

Nearly a year and a half ago, she'd fallen into heat after arriving in Mahoning to live with the Thorne brothers, a strong, good pack in need of an omega like herself.

She'd gotten out of her childhood home in the nick of time too, just in time to evade the vampires who'd attacked her town, who were searching for *her*.

An omega who hadn't fallen into heat yet.

Though the natural born enemies had always stayed away from her kind in an unspoken truce, it seemed there was one particular coven who was most interested in taking supernatural prisoners for their own gains; the Boracelli coven, fronted by a sadistic, twisted queen who held no qualms about breaking unspoken bindings.

Though at the time, Cleo thought perhaps something had been wrong with her, for once she had arrived at the Thorne's estate, it seemed there was no heat.

Day in and day out, she waited for a heat she thought would never come, wondering if somehow there had been a mistake, and what would her fate have been then if it was a mistake?

Would she be sent back home with her tail between her legs, a failure?

If she wasn't an Omega, who would she have been?

Still, the truth and details surrounding her heat were murky at best, despite the fact she had fallen into it just as the seer had told her she would.

It will happen in Mahoning, she had said, and Cleo held onto that notion, even as the days trudged along on without one of the Thorne brothers doing so much as to rustle any sort of animal need in her.

And then suddenly, it *did* happen, but it wasn't the Thornes who stirred her heat, despite the fact Rocky *insisted* to everyone in the pack, even his brothers, that it was him.

He knew the truth, after all—that a *human* had stirred Cleo's heat. A hunter, no less.

And that complicated everything. Though Cleo found herself growing more attracted to the Thornes by the day, she couldn't bring herself to cross the line with any of them. *Especially Sawyer.*

Not when her mate, Malcolm Crowley, had *rejected* her, left her alone to wither away with the mad heat, in the privacy of her isolated quarters. Left her on her own to hunger after a bond she wasn't certain she would ever finalize, despite how often she spoke with him on the phone, and even those moments were few and far between.

But a phone wasn't the same as being with him in the flesh.

After Malcolm had left to hunt

whatever it was that called him, Cleo had resigned herself to her quarters, mourning the human and his touch. The further away he was, in the beginning, was downright sickening.

And then Alaric had disappeared without so much as a goodbye, off on some urgent pack business that not even his brothers were privy to, taking with him the spark that had festered in her stomach, in her heart.

The one that told her maybe, just maybe, she could choose him... if she wanted.

Her room had gotten rather crowded from all the sweet, cozy omega gifts that arrived nearly daily from him in his absence, but they only made her feel worse.

Alaric had been upfront with her, he'd told her he would have given her everything, anything she wanted, if she would only ask.

But Clementine could not bring herself to ask Alaric for the one thing she wanted the most, because she knew not even the alpha of the pack could bring her to her moon; Malcolm Crowley.

Sawyer did not try to coax her out of her room, nor did he drop off gifts as his eldest brother had.

Instead, he'd only shown up to her room, drunk, nearly every night, begging for forgiveness before running his hands down her arm, or sliding his thick fingers in her hair in a way that made her skin crawl.

Night after night, she refused Sawyer's advances, telling him to leave her be, shoving the man away, tossing him on his ass before locking her door to wallow once more that nothing would fix the hole in her heart. Everything was a stark reminder of what was missing.

Her only light in the darkness of the aftermath of Malcolm's rejection and

Alaric's absence was Rocky Thorne. The many days they'd spent with the Thorne pack children, or the nights they spent relaxing reading or watching movies, and of course, their daily runs, were a respite from the maddening heat. Though to be fair, Rocky had been her ally since the day she arrived on the estate.

Where his brothers hadn't been the gentlest of hosts, treating Cleo as if she was a fragile doll or a *thing* to be kept, Rocky had offered her friendship, and alliance. He also happened to be the only one who knew the truth about who Malcolm was, and what had really transpired between them.

He'd agreed in a heartbeat, no questions asked, to protect Cleo and this truth, and not once did he push her or expect favors in return. In fact, it was the opposite.

While Cleo fought her way through a multitude of stuffed animals and blankets, Rocky was the only one who provided her comfort. He did not try to woo her or push her.

Instead, he looked at her with understanding and asked her to fight.

Fight the heat, fight the desire to let the rejection pull her under, and Cleo relented.

She'd need to return to "normal" if only to placate the rest of the Thornes who seemed to think her isolation was due to her pining for Alaric, and they'd only been a quarter correct.

She *did* miss Alaric, but she missed much more than that. She missed her freedom, and Alaric was the key to it.

Who's off on official Alpha business because the pack always comes first...

She also needed to keep with the fabricated lie she and Rocky had spun, that he was the lucky Thorne who had stirred her heat. Eventually, she'd have to do something. She couldn't put off the instinct to mate forever.

She couldn't deny she felt something for the Thorne alpha, but she couldn't quite pinpoint what it was. It wasn't the same as what she felt for Malcolm, that she was certain of, and it definitely differed from what she felt for the youngest Thorne brother, but with as much as Alaric seemed to be off on "pack business" these days, the spark had dwindled to an annoying ember. Not ready to die, but not strong enough to ignite on its own without ample oxygen and attention.

Cleo had long heard that putting off "nature", fighting the mating bond itself, was damn near torture. Omegas were built to breed, after all.

It was natural, primal. Failure to do so could cause an Omega to go practically feral.

But Rocky had assured her she was strong enough to fight the heat until she'd made her decision. That despite what was *natural*, she still had a choice in the matter. She didn't have to give in so easily, if it wasn't what she wanted.

If they aren't who I want.

Training, fighting, and even relaxing with Rocky had been the one thing in her endless days she'd found herself looking forward to, if only because it was the one time she could be free of the memory of Alaric's worried gaze every time he left, or Sawyer's lustful one every time she passed him in the hall.

With Rocky, Cleo could just... be.

She could be free, honest. With Rocky, she didn't have to hide or lie, and there was a beauty in that she couldn't deny, though she knew it was just who Rocky Thorne was.

He was caring, understanding, loyal, and most of all... he was comforting.

"Or I can just... give in. Stop fighting," she said as her breath caught in her throat.

Rocky sat down next to her, offering her a bottle of water like an olive branch from the backpack they'd packed.

Cleo looked up from her spot in her lap. Rocky shook the bottle, a hint of a smile tugging at his lips.

Like his older brothers, he held the same features; dark eyes and hair, tan, toned skin.

But there was a light in his eyes that didn't exist in Sawyer's or even Alaric's.

Cleo's shoulders loosened as she unfurled herself like a flower, reaching out to take the bottle from his warm, long fingers. Her heart skipped a beat, the icy cold of the water bottle against her palm a welcome contrast to the heat that plagued her.

The touch of his fingertips against hers sent a shockwave through her body, directly to her groin, and she had to grind her teeth to keep the moan threatening to escape her throat at bay.

This is happening more frequently.

She brushed the feeling, the thoughts, aside as she popped the cap and took a long, refreshing drink, practically swallowing down more than half in one gulp.

"Is that what you want? To give in?" Rocky asked, his voice even, devoid of any emotion one way or the other.

He was always like that with her, though. Where Alaric had difficulty showing his actual emotion, Sawyer seemed to not be able to think first before acting. But Rocky was always ground zero. Neutral.

At that moment, as their eyes met, she understood by the briefest flicker, the shimmer of desire and hope that flashed in his eyes, that he was fighting just as hard as she was to remain neutral.

He was fighting too, though she could not be sure what his beast of burden was.

"Sometimes I think it would be easier," she said as she licked her lips, which had already gone dry despite the cold drink.

The sun shone down on the two of them in the open field, which was miles away from the estate.

Out in the mountain forests, they could be free. Cleo loved it. The wind, the sun, the surrounding woods that felt more like home than the Thorne estate ever would.

As long as the vampires stayed at bay...

"To just let nature run its course, let the heat take over and just... mate. Form a bond and do what I'm supposed to do."

"But?" He shot her a raised eyebrow.

Cleo drained the rest of her water, setting her hands in her lap. She looked to her side, taking in the sight of Rocky; of his toned, sweat-slicked skin, his wet, dark hair hanging in his eyes. The sharp cut of his eyebrows, his jaw.

He truly was breathtaking for a young man.

"But my heart wants *him*. And I know it's dumb to wait for someone who might never come back but..."

"You still want him. I know." Rocky's voice softened, his eyebrows furrowing as his gaze fell. His long lashes stood out against his skin, and he hung his head in defeat as he took his own sip of water.

Cleo sighed as the clouds moved in front of the sun, blocking the light. The air smelled like rain and earth, and she knew a storm was coming.

"We should head back," she said, wanting to make it home before it started pouring. She could always shift and run, but she hated doing so in stormy weather.

For starters, she didn't like the mud.

"Of course," he said, his breath catching in his throat. He shrugged off whatever was on his mind as he drained the last of his water bottle, discarding the empties in the backpack before zipping it up and tossing it on his back.

"Want to race back?" she asked, wanting to dissolve the weird tension that had somehow formed between them.

"I thought you'd never ask," Rocky said with a grin, as Cleo rose.

"On the count of three," she said.

The clouds moved in, and just as Cleo counted three, the rain came, and as she ran through the rain, Rocky Thorne beside her, keeping her pace, she closed her eyes and let the water wash away all thoughts of hunters and alphas. Instead, she focused on the wolf beside her, chasing her to the edge of the estate like he longed to catch her, and her heart beat faster.

Because, for a startling moment, Cleo wished to be caught.

2

ROCKY FOLLOWED CLEO like a moth to a flame. He'd been told all his life about mating bonds. Being the youngest in a line of purebred powerful shifters, he was not as beholden to tradition as his older brothers, but the expectations were placed on him nonetheless. To be strong, powerful, and obedient to his pack. Though truth be told, he hadn't put much thought into ensuring his pack's future, not when the omegas typically mated with the alpha or beta of the pack.

And Rocky was neither alpha, nor beta.

He was just, quite frankly, the baby brother, and being the baby of the bunch had its advantages. But everything changed the moment Clementine came to the estate, all blue-green eyes and wavy hair, smelling like fresh cut lilies and sunshine.

In human form, he was still quite fast, and so it did not take him long to catch up to the speedy little Omega, but he was certain nothing would have prevented him from catching her. Ever.

He would run circles if she asked him to, not just because she was *the* Omega—Thorne pack's omega—but because there was something about her that spoke to him on a deeper level than anyone ever had.

The desire to be *hers*, whatever it was she needed, a friend, an ally, a lover, was a groundbreaking thing for him. The desire to wrap his entire being around her was a heat all its own. And Rocky Thorne knew the moment he saw her, it was over for him. No one would ever compare to her. Not ever.

Cleo's legs picked up their pace as she all but leapt toward the entrance of the estate's courtyard, underneath the terrace. Rain drenched the rhododendrons, turning them into sopping wet balls instead of the fluffy, prim-petaled beauties they were in the daylight.

Jumping in front of her, he grinned as she stopped, her chest heaving with breath as the rain continued to fall.

Cleo let out a laugh.

"What's so funny?" he asked, running a hand through his hair. Thunder boomed in the distance, beyond the edges of the forest.

"You just can't help yourself, can you?" she said with a laugh, running her hands through her hair, pulling it from her face.

The rain came down harder, but neither of them moved from where they stood. Instead, they only laughed, soaked to the core.

He tugged at his backpack, his fingernails digging into the leather straps, seeking grounding as he dropped it into a lounge chair.

Rocky's heart raced, from adrenaline, and from the sight of a drenched Cleo, her white tank top clinging to her breasts, her naturally wavy hair darkened by the rain. Her dark, thick eyelashes stood out against her scarlet cheeks.

He shifted his stance, if only to quell the sudden thickness growing in his pants, his breath rapid as the scent of lush, fertile omega made his fangs *ache* to push forth.

It was a tragedy that neither him nor either of his brothers, no matter what he insisted, had stirred her heat.

It seemed fate was more than cruel. He'd been there, witnessed the human, the hunter—Malcolm Crowley—awakening her heat. Even now, he could remember the mouthwatering smell, and all the blown pupils of the wolves in their proximity.

Despite Cleo's heat, he wasn't sure about the human responsible for it. He was, without a doubt, the enemy. His kind *killed* creatures like them, and would do so in the blink of an eye if given the chance. Anything they deemed a *threat* was nothing but fodder for their one-sided agenda. To a hunter, they were monsters. Like the vampires.

But Malcolm had done the opposite. He'd *saved* Cleo on more than one occasion, despite knowing what she was.

But could he trust the hunter?

Could he let her go, if it meant she was out of reach?

How could his brother do such a thing

time and time again?

Because he knows she is in good hands with you. That you will take care of her in his absence.

Rocky looked at her in the gray haze, wondering if Alaric was standing there, in his place, what he would do.

Charge in and command her?

Tell her to cease these games because she belonged to *him*?

Certainly Sawyer would have puffed up his chest to play big bad wolf, until she'd submit to his voracious instinct to rut, until her resolve had thinned enough she would give in to such demands, if only to quiet the animal inside, but Rocky was not like his brothers.

In the presence of Cleo, he only wanted to *soothe* her turmoil. To warm her heart and give her everything she desired.

Even if what she desired was someone else.

Even now, in the rain, she smelled the

same as she had the first day she'd arrived on their doorstep. Like fresh cut lilies, like summer rain, like sunshine drenched linens and citrus.

Ripe, intoxicating, and... *aroused*.

The animal inside of him rallied at the pheromones she was giving off, making his cock swell and his throat run dry.

It's just the heat, nothing more. It doesn't mean she wants you... It's nature. It's instinct. She needs to mate, to solidify her bond. A bond that is not with you.

Rocky swallowed his harsh truths as he approached her. Cleo seemed frozen in place; the only motion to suggest she hadn't turned into a full on icicle was the rise and fall of her chest, the sparkle in her eye.

"I don't know what you mean," he said. It took so much concentration on his part to hold back. But Rocky was not like his brothers. He would not force his affection, his nature, on the bright, beautiful omega because he understood more than anyone that fate had already divined her mate.

Though the time would come and Cleo would have to make a choice, Rocky wished to free himself from the pain of that choice. The pain of knowing that she would choose *Malcolm* inevitably. He was the one who stirred her heat, who was fated to be hers. Who she would no doubt mate with when all was said and done, and it was he and his brothers who would have to shoulder the shame of her choice. It wouldn't be easy, for humans were not capable of breeding with them, but if Malcolm Crowley was what she wanted, what she needed, he would back her up. He would stand against Alaric and anyone else who dared to hurt her in any way.

Rocky's heart thudded in his chest so loudly he thought the booming thunder was coming from his chest.

Anything else—any touch, any stolen moment would be only that. Stolen.

Like their kiss at the bar, the one he claimed stirred her heat. He hadn't thought, only acted.

The desire, the need to protect this omega—*his* omega, against the pack, the vampires that threatened to take her away... and perhaps even against the darkest parts of himself—was more than a desire. It was nature.

A basic, primal instinct.

"You do not let me win," she said with a grin as he pushed some stray, wet hair behind her, twisting his hand around her braid.

He offered her a soft smile. Her hair was soft against his palm, like moist silk. Another puff of arousal perfumed the air between them, making his cock throb. The memory of her kiss, sweet like peaches and cream, made him ache to taste her again.

Cleo fought her heat with all that she was, and he envied her. For the amount of concentration and strength it took for him to drop his hand, swallow his words, and stifle his cock was agonizing.

"Because I have faith in you, Cleo. I know you can beat me." he said warmly. "You just haven't figured out how, yet."

Cleo breathed him in, her eyelashes fluttering as water trickled down her cheek, over her perfect, flushed pout.

Rocky watched as she breathed deep, biting her lip. Up close like this, he could smell her intoxicating arousal, her heat, just as he could feel the fire brewing between the space that separated them.

"You smell really good," she sighed, opening her eyes. "Like fresh baked cookies," she murmured lazily.

Rocky's lips turned up in the corner of his mouth.

"What kind of cookies?" he asked, leaning closer to breathe her in. Thunder boomed loudly, but it was white noise to them.

Cleo settled her hand over his shirt, which was clinging to his chest like it was a second skin.

"Chocolate chip...." she said as she ran her nose up his neck, sighing.

The sound of contentment sent a shiver through Rocky's spine as he closed his eyes, pretending for the moment that there was no Malcolm Crowley, or alphas who sent a plethora of stuffies, or meddling pack business.

There was only him, and his omega, the woman he was deeply in love with.

Together, as it should have been.

"My favorite kind," she said, her voice a faint whisper on his skin.

Her hand on his chest was warm as she relaxed her fingers, clawing at the sopping fabric that separated her true touch. Rocky slipped his hand around hers, holding it where it lay, giving in for the briefest moment as he nuzzled his face in her hair.

"Cleo..." he murmured. "I can't," he said, trying his hardest to be noble. To be the man she *needed.*

A friend, a confidant. An ally.

"Rocky..." she purred, sliding her hand up his chest, settling it around his neck. She tugged slightly, forcing him to open his eyes, to look at her.

"Are you rejecting me?" she asked, her voice small.

"No," he said hurriedly, settling his hand on her hip, his eyebrows furrowed. "God, no. I could never—"

"Then why are you fighting *me*?" she asked, her fingers teasing the edges of his hair on his neck.

"Because it's not me you want. Not really." His voice was soft, and the pain was evident. "You said so yourself..."

Cleo ran her fingers across his cheek softly.

"You said you had faith in me, Rocky. You have not doubted me before... do you doubt my choices now? Here, outside your home? *Our* home?"

Rocky closed his eyes, a contented purr leaving his throat as he slid his hands up her sides, his thumbs hooking underneath the flimsy, wet hem of her shirt. Her skin against his fingertips was cold, moist.

He stroked the cool surface with his thumb. To hear her refer to the Thorne estate as *theirs...* it settled something deep within him.

As the youngest of the governing Thorne pack, Rocky could have bedded or wed anyone of his choosing. His relationships would never be under as much scrutiny as that of his brothers, who were expected to do little more than breed their prize omega to ensure the longevity, the strength of the pack.

But even without consequence, Rocky had never felt inclined to mate or rut with anyone.

Ever.

Not until Cleo showed up looking like everything he'd ever wanted, everything he'd ever dreamed of.

And to hear her say the words, *ours.*

It was enough to drive a sane man mad.

Enough to push him over the edge into oblivion.

Rocky stole her lips like a thief in the night. And just as she had the night her heat had awakened, she tasted like peaches and cream, like hopes and dreams, and absolute perfection.

Cleo sank in his hold, snapping in his grasp. What once was strong and vigilant was now frail and flimsy, needing support.

The sweet, melodic sigh meddled with a deep purr of her own as she pulled him closer.

The cool rain against their bodies washed away all pretenses and worries, leaving nothing but pure, unfiltered heat in its wake. Cleo kissed him with hunger, with need, her hands traveling down his chest as she grabbed onto his soaked shirt for dear life.

Mine.

The word echoed in his brain, hanging on the tip of his tongue. But he could not say the words, not when Cleo caressed his tongue with hers, stealing it away, swallowing it down into the pit of her stomach like it was nothing more than candy.

But their stolen moment would be short lived, as the thunder clashed and the rain washed in a new scent; one that chilled Rocky to his bones. He broke away hesitantly, his inner animal on high alert as he scanned the edge of the estate, the forest for the foul scent he'd know anywhere.

The scent of *vampire.*

3

"CLEO, GET BEHIND me," Rocky's voice was solid and unwavering, and the seriousness cut through the hazy heat, striking her down to her core.

"Rocky, don't..." she said as she pushed away from him, her gaze settling on the black-haired vampire who stood, hands in pockets in the center of the field just mere feet away. She could see two more flanking their leader on the edges of the forest. With their agility, it didn't matter that they were on the outskirts of the woods. They could have just as easily sprinted to their oily-haired leader in a human heartbeat if it was needed.

They were truly outnumbered three to two.

Rocky's body rippled with shifting energy, the hair on his arms standing at attention as he bared his *fangs* at them, pushing her behind him.

"When I tell you to run, Cleo, you run. You run and lock the fucking door, okay?"

"Do not be absurd, Rocky. I will not leave you alone, I—"

"Cleo, please..."

But Cleo did not like to be told what to do. Not anymore.

"This is our property," she bit out as she took a step forward, toward the vampire. Her body flared with heat, her inner animal baring its teeth.

"Cleo, stop..."

"By right, you are walking on dangerous grounds," she said, stopping just on the edge of the courtyard.

The tall, languid vampire looked at her with a sinister grin, his eyes vacant.

"Yes, well, desperate times call for desperate measures and all. It seems you are a hard bitch to pin down, Clementine." He sneered.

Rocky was beside her in an instant, wrapping his arm around her, his fingernails digging into her side.

He was *scared* of these monsters.

But she was not.

"What do you want?" she asked, her inner animal rising to the surface.

The man looked from her to Rocky, then back again before speaking.

"Why, I want what everyone else does, my dear. You."

"Well, I hate to break it to you, asshole, but you're not my type," she said, crossing her arms. "So you can take your little gang of bloodsuckers, and turn around or—"

In the blink of an eye, his hand was around her throat, crushing her airway.

Shifting energy rippled through the air as clothes flew and Rocky shifted in an instant, lunging at the vampire.

His grip only tightened on her throat as he kicked Rocky. A yelp echoed in the air as the other vampires ascended.

The vampire stared at her with soulless eyes.

"Eden said to bring her back *alive,* Octavius." The redheaded vampire snuffed.

"Yes, well, she did say to use force if it was necessary," he snapped, loosening his grip only slightly.

Cleo called her own shifting energy, but it was no use. Whatever grip the vampire had on her... she was unable to shift.

What the fuck?

He threw her down on the ground, hard. She attempted to stand, but slipped in the mud, her leg aching with fresh pain. She tried desperately to shift again, to stand, but it was no use. Cleo could barely move.

Rocky yelped once more as the brown-haired male vampire bit him. He managed to knock the creature off, but it was plain to see he had been hurt. He shook off the hit, but she didn't miss the blood seeping out of his hind leg.

"Rocky..." She reached out for him.

The red-haired vampire woman tried to grab her, but Rocky attacked, jumping in front of her and clamping his teeth down on the vampire's arm.

"You fucking dog!" the woman roared, shaking him off, but the damage was done. Thick, rivulets of black blood seeped down her arm, followed by shrieks and pain.

"Now, play nice and perhaps I will let your little mangy mutt live," Octavius said as he held up his hands.

All around her, Cleo could feel an energy; a dark, encompassing energy that vibrated her very being. The shifting energy did not come, and she was paralyzed. She knew vampires were powerful, but she'd never heard of any having the power to immobilize someone.

Rocky yelped as the other vampire sank their fangs into him, and soon his yelps turned to screams.

"Cleo, run!" he screamed, but she could not move.

"Cleo! Rocky!" Sawyer's voice cut through the air, like a prayer.

Tears prickled at the edges of her eyes as she tried to move her leg.

As she tried to save him, her *mate*.

Rocky...

Octavius wrapped his arms around her waist, pulling her up from the ground, but he would not take her.

Not on this day.

Sawyer hissed, fighting back against

Octavius.

"Get her the fuck out of here, Sawyer!" Rocky screamed as the vampire bit his flesh.

Cleo could see the streams of blood along his naked body, the pain in his kind, amber eyes.

Octavius was distracted by his cries, and there was only one, small minute moment. But it was enough for Sawyer to wrap his larger arms around her, hoist her over his shoulder, and run.

"Rocky, no!" Cleo struggled in Sawyer's grasp as the vampire looked up at her, dripping blood from her fangs.

"Take him, Darla. He could be useful to us... To Eden." He sneered. "Or at the very least, he'll make a delicious snack on our way to Kentucky."

Octavius's words were the last Cleo heard before the pain took her under, into a land of nightmares.

For Rocky Thorne was gone.

And it was all her fault.

4

CLEO STRUGGLED TO move her limbs as they felt like deadweight. Sawyer's grip was tight, and she hated that it provided her a sense of comfort.

The rain had stopped, as it no longer pitter-pattered on the glass.

Or had she imagined it?

Warmth surrounded her, and she burrowed against it. It didn't smell like fresh baked cookies, but it was still a pleasing smell nonetheless.

Spicy, earthy. Like burning cedar and

moss.

Fingers stroked her hair, and for a moment she wondered if it all had been a terrible dream. Fingertips traced warm lines down her arm, causing her hair to stand on end and goosebumps to form. Her stomach flipped, her inner animal resistant to such an *intimate* touch that did not belong to her mate...

Mate.

All at once, reality came back in a flash as Cleo opened her eyes to find herself curled around Sawyer Thorne.

In bed, wearing nothing but her bra and panties.

She scrambled away from him, grabbing the dark blue comforter to cover herself, panic racing through her as she realized he was *on top* of the covers, shirtless, but otherwise clothed in thick gray sweatpants that hung deliciously off his hips, showcasing a deep, pronounced V accenting a dark smattering of hair around and below his navel.

Like his brothers, he shared the same sun-kissed complexion, with dark hair and eyes. Though Rocky's amber ones were warm and inviting, Alaric's reminded her of fiery flames. But Sawyer's eyes carried flecks of green along with his hazel-brown, like murky water that covered up dangers beneath.

Sawyer rubbed his eyes, his voice groggy.

"And the princess is finally awake," he grumbled, sitting up.

Cleo watched as he ran a hand through his hair, mussing it up.

"What the hell are you doing here? Why am I half-naked? Why are you not—"

"Easy, Cleo. One thing at a time, baby."

Rage encapsulated her at his words, his nonchalant tone. His brother was *hurt*, or worse.

"I am *not* your baby," she growled as

she scrambled out of bed, taking the comforter with her. It smelled like some heady mix of Rocky, Alaric, and Sawyer, and settled her nerves only a fraction.

Because it smelled like him.

Rocky.

The one who settled her storms.

"Your clothes were covered in mud. I undressed you and had the staff take them to the facilities. Should be done before the night is over," he grumbled.

Memories flashed in her brain of the attack, the sliding and pain of the ground. But it wasn't the attack that she found herself replaying in her mind, no.

Moments before it had all gone to hell, before the vampire, Octavius, had shown up, something shifted between her and her friend.

The storm had unearthed something... new.

The animal inside reared its wolfish desires, the heat rising within her like a mercury thermometer. Perhaps it was the way Rocky *chased* her, through the woods, through the valley. Something about the chase, the run, the feeling of being *prey* ignited a spark within her wolf she hadn't felt since she first laid eyes on Malcolm, the day he stirred her heat.

And Rocky had been there for that too.

Just like he was *always* there for her. Guiding her as a friend, an equal, a confidant.

He hadn't rejected her.

He'd *kissed* her.

Tender and warm, slow and deep. It was spellbinding.

Cleo brought her fingers to her lips, touching them as if to remind herself it was real.

Malcolm Crowley was her mate. He had stirred her heat, and she was *certain* he was meant to be hers, and she his. But her wolf longed for the youngest Thorne brother as if he *too* belonged to her. As if he was made for her, and she for him. As if his wolf belonged to her wolf. Which made no sense.

While there could be a difference between the one who stirred her heat, and the mate she chose to bear children with, it wasn't often that such a thing occurred. Most of the time, omegas mated with their alpha, or in some cases, the beta. They most certainly did not mate with two different men, let alone mate with *humans* and other wolves.

Sawyer swung his legs over the side of the bed, leaning his defined arms on his knees as he looked up at her through disheveled locks that framed his face. Against the gray haze outside, he looked positively menacing, but somehow also... quite attractive.

It's just good genes, Cleo.

The same as Alaric's and Rocky's.

It doesn't mean you like the guy.

"How are you still sitting there, so

calm?" she bit out, tightening the comforter around her like a fortress.

Her body was warm, and she could feel a chill between her legs, where the moisture of her heat had subsided. Her insides *ached* for the touch of her mate, but there was no mate to be found in Sawyer Thorne's bedroom. She narrowed her eyes at him.

"Well, we all can't go off half-cocked after the vampires and leave this place defenseless."

"I was not—"

"Oh yeah? I saw you go after those vamps. You baited them. If you would have just listened to Rocky, like a good little girl—"

Cleo's fist balled at his words. Fire burned behind her eyes as she shouted,

"I was not going to leave him on his own to fight three vampires."

"Three vampires who were after *you.* Rocky knew what he was doing. We were raised to protect our pack. What makes you think you are capable of fighting off *one* of them, Cleo?" Sawyer growled, standing as he took a step toward her.

"You're an *omega.* It's not in your nature to *fight.* Your nature is to be a good, obedient wolf and provide your pack with heirs. That's it, baby. You get a life of luxury. Soft nests and hard dick. That's *it.*"

Cleo took a step toward him, baring her fangs.

How dare he!

"You don't own me, Sawyer. None of you get a say in who I am and what I do."

Sawyer growled, the sound causing fresh warmth to blossom between her thighs.

She hissed, glaring up at him. "Especially you. You're not *my* alpha."

"*Baby,* I am the fucking beta. You belong to this pack whether you like it or not, and with alpha Alaric gone, I am the one calling the shots," he snapped.

Cleo realized as she gazed up at him that he was close. So close she could bite him. Sink her fangs into his skin and show him who really called the shots. But she also knew Sawyer wasn't worth her venom. There were more important things at hand.

Like rescuing Rocky.

"You're not my fucking beta, Sawyer. You're just a shadow to Alaric. That's *it.*"

Sawyer snarled as he fisted his hand in her hair.

"You didn't think I was a fucking shadow when I chased you in those woods. When you nearly let me..."

"Nearly. Because I'd just had my heat awakened by—"

The words died on her tongue. The truth was, no one but Rocky knew Malcolm had stirred her heat that night. As far as everyone knew, it had been Rocky.

He'd covered for her, and now he was gone.

Because of her, and her heat.

The vampires were here for you.

Because of your heat.

"My idiot brother who wouldn't know where to put his dick if you had a neon sign?" Sawyer chirped.

Cleo's eyebrows furrowed.

Was he insinuating that Rocky was...

A *virgin*?

"Those vampires came onto your property because they aren't scared of *you.* Fucking beta."

"You are not to leave this fucking house, Cleo. Not now, not until we have those damn vamps incinerated, do you understand?"

Cleo grabbed him by the throat, her fingernails digging into his skin. She watched as a gleam filled his gaze, his lips turning up in a smirk.

"Careful, baby. You might wake the

beast." Sawyer ran his nose up her neck, his fingers tightening their grip in her hair as he let out a deep growl.

"*You* are my fucking omega, Princess. Whether you like it or not. You are my top priority. And if you know what's good for you, you will obey *me*."

Cleo shoved him away, dropping her hand, her fist shaking as she brushed past him toward the door.

"Where the fuck you think you are going?" he growled. But he did not stop her.

"Nowhere that concerns you."

She took a deep breath, dropped the comforter at his door, and ran down the hallway.

Fucking run and lock the door, Rocky's words echoed in her brain.

And that was exactly what she did.

5

ALARIC BRACED HIMSELF against the rustic wooden balcony of the Mayfield's guesthouse cabin, taking in the sight of the lush green hills and forests. Sweat formed on his brow, in crevices he didn't even know he had until he'd arrived in Mayfield, Kentucky three weeks prior. It was a stark difference from the crisp, cool mountain air of home.

I hate the fucking heat... he thought, running his hand over his face.

Once upon a time, Alaric hadn't

minded traveling to distant cities and towns. After growing up in Mahoning, a small town hidden in the Blue Ridge Mountains, the vibrancy and beauty of the world that awaited him as an alpha was a temptation that was damn near irresistible, not to mention the beauty and exoticness of new pussy.

After all, women *loved* a good looking, stoic alpha wolf.

But all of that changed the moment his parents told him they'd secured an omega.

He'd always known the day would come, where he'd have to step up and do as every other alpha in his pack had before him. Rise to lead and protect his pack, and keep their pristine, strong bloodline going.

At the time, before her arrival, he'd prayed Cleo would overlook him. After all, he was the oldest of three, and at the age of thirty-two he wasn't quite sure he was ready to give up his comfortable rogue alpha life.

Until he saw her, that was.

Alaric knew the moment he laid eyes on Clementine Srirocco, she was *his* omega. Nothing and no one would ever compare to her. His wolf was practically salivating at the sight of her, not to mention the startling pain of his alpha's knot swelling for the first time nearly took his breath away.

It took everything in him not to grab her and steal her away into his den and mark her as his, to quiet the *instinct* to bite, to breed. The overwhelming desire was too much, and so Alaric did the only thing he could to keep himself and his wolf in line. He left for his den of his own accord, locking himself inside to take care of his maddening, swollen knot so that he could think straight and do what was *needed*. And when he emerged, he kept his distance, if only to quiet his wolfish desires, so he could concentrate on protecting his pack and doing his job.

Because with Cleo came the threat of something much, much greater.

Vampires.

Primarily, vampires who were just as interested in his omega as he was, for their own twisted reasons. Reasons that he could never let come to fruition.

Alaric vowed to protect Cleo, and his pack, and he was not about to break that vow. Not now, not ever.

Though it was getting harder and harder to deny the magnetic draw between them, to leave her presence even if she wanted nothing to do with him. Just being near her... was enough.

Wasn't it?

The very thought of Clementine, even now, after being apart from her for nearly a month, caused his cock to twitch, his knot to tingle. Since that day she showed up, he hadn't even looked at anyone else, let alone desired them.

"Fucking hell," he murmured as he adjusted himself, even though he didn't need to hide. He was the only one staying in the prestigious guest cabin built for five, if only as a sign of the respect the Mayfield's held for his *esteemed* pack. Such a large house only made him long for what he didn't have. What seemed to be out of his reach.

Imagine all the laughter and love that could fill a place like this. It would make a beautiful nest.

He breathed a deep sigh, imagining Clementine among all the blankets and pillows in the master bedroom where he slept alone, settled into the plush round bed, hair sprawled beneath her, the light of the fireplace lighting up her fair skin.

Safe, warm, and in my arms where she belongs.

He closed his eyes, daring to imagine a future he never thought he wanted, but that his heart ached for, all the same.

Tiny paws and feet smacking the hardwood, giggles and howls filling the air as they tore through the halls. Like he and his brothers used to do.

Alaric grunted in frustration as his thoughts strayed to the Thorne estate, and the testy omega.

Fate was a cruel mistress, it seemed. Despite the deep, unrelenting need to mark Cleo as his, in every way possible, it would appear that Cleo did not share the same strong feelings.

His youngest brother, Rocky, had stirred her heat, and Alaric was jealous.

It should have been me. I am the alpha, for god's sake!

His cock throbbed as he imagined himself in his brother's place, imagined Cleo's lips on his, the sounds she would make beneath him if he touched her. Despite the draw he could feel between them, it would appear that Clementine was *rejecting* him, though she hadn't officially said the words and he dared not ask.

No one rejects a fucking alpha!

Her actions were enough. When he walked in the room, she didn't notice.

She gravitated toward Rocky, like a magnet. Clung to his side like ivy. The two were practically inseparable, no doubt due to the fact he was the Thorne who stirred her heat, who brought about the maddening *desire* for the Omega to mate.

Though as fate would have it, Cleo hadn't given in to temptation on any account yet, and that was the sliver of hope Alaric held on to.

Perhaps there is still a chance...

His knot ebbed with need as his cock pulsed at the thought of such things. No matter how he tried to banish such thoughts from his mind, it was no use. Nature and instinct were just as cruel to him as fate was.

He growled as he squeezed his hardness through his jeans, to the point his knot twinged in pain. No one could understand his pain, the deep cut of rejection. What it felt like to know she was meant to be his, but kept out of his reach, just close enough to torment him.

If he'd been at the bar that night, instead of Rocky…

Would it have made a difference?

The sound of his phone ringing pulled him from his torturous thoughts.

"Hello, Sawyer."

His brother's breath on the other end was heavy with anger, with fury. It caused Alaric's jaw to stiffen immediately.

"Sawyer, what's wrong?" he panicked. "Is it Cleo? Is she—"

"Cleo's fine. A bit of a pain in my fucking ass, but she's fine. It's Rocky."

Alaric breathed a sigh of relief. Although he detested his brother calling the pack omega a *pain in the ass,* he could tell by Sawyer's furious voice there were much bigger things to settle.

"Vampires attacked. Rocky shifted, and—"

After getting hit by a car; a car which belonged to the hunter Cleo seemed to have been smitten with—Malcolm Crawley something or other—Rocky hadn't been the same. Though he put on his best face for Cleo, Alaric knew the truth of the extent of Rocky's injuries. He'd been advised not to shift, for doing so could cause more damage to his right leg, which had barely healed properly as was, even with their accelerated healing abilities. From the outside, Rocky looked right as rain. But due to the nerve damage in his leg, Jennika, the Thorne's best healer, had advised Rocky to refrain from shifting for the time being.

Alaric pursed his lips, pinching the bridge of his nose. "Fuck, this is bad."

"Yeah, tell me about it. Stupid kid

shifted because of her, and now the vampires have him and—"

"The vampires... have Rocky?" Alaric could feel his blood boiling.

"Yeah. I got Cleo and put her ass in line but—"

"Why is there always a *but*?" Alaric huffed.

"She went off half-cocked on those vamps, and then on *me* because I didn't run after Rocky. I swear, Alaric, it's getting harder and harder to hold my temper with her."

Alaric sighed in frustration. "She's in heat, Sawyer. Until she mates, she's going to be all over the place, you know this."

"You got a lot of nerve, Alaric. You're not *here*. It's getting worse. Today she got up in my goddamn face. Inches away from me. I was practically drowning between her scent, and her attitude."

Alaric's fists balled at his brother's complaints. While it wasn't unheard of that omegas sometimes picked the beta as their mate, Cleo had shown little to no interest in his beta brother.

A part of him couldn't blame Sawyer for being keyed up in her presence, but he also knew as his beta, there was no one better to protect Cleo in his absence.

"I don't know why she's so fucking resistant to what's natural," Sawyer sighed. "She and Rocky have been practically attached at the hip since he stirred her heat, but he hasn't done shit. What a fucking waste. Maybe if he had, maybe he'd still fucking be here, and she'd be a lot more docile."

Alaric hung his head in despair as he tried to push such thoughts out of his brain. A part of him had been relieved his youngest brother hadn't acted on the impulse to mate. He'd hoped the space would be enough, that eventually Cleo would see reason and choose him, as it was supposed to be.

He'd promised not to push her, but if he had... If he had made more of an effort, perhaps they would have all been better off.

"This is my fault, I should have been there..." He sighed.

"Nothing you could have done that I didn't already do, Ric."

"Everyone locked down?"

"Yup. Including the royal pain in the ass. She got all pissy and stormed off, but she's not going anywhere. Locked herself in her room just to get the fuck away from me."

Alaric couldn't help but understand the pain of rejection in his brother's voice, and he felt rather conflicted about such things.

"How are things going down there? Negotiations any closer?"

Alaric sauntered back into the living room, closing the sliding glass door to the patio. He collapsed on the micro-suede couch, the soft cushions a relief for the moment.

"Well, things would be going a lot smoother if the damn vampires weren't such a fucking nuisance."

"Still no sign of their omega?" Sawyer asked.

Alaric grunted in frustration as he closed his eyes. "Nope. Vamps are getting smarter. Covering up scents, spreading out their attacks. We haven't been able to pinpoint their base yet, and every time we think we're close..."

"They misdirect." Sawyer sighed.

"Yeah. Makes it really fucking hard to find a pregnant omega in the middle of a haystack, you know?"

"What do you think they want with the omegas, anyway?" Sawyer asked nonchalantly.

Alaric wasn't entirely sure what to tell his beta. Though he trusted Sawyer, he knew sometimes it was best to keep pertinent information to himself.

Only tell him what he needs to know.

"Hell if I know, Sawyer. I don't understand the minds of monsters."

Sawyer sighed. "Me either, man."

"What are we going to do about Miss Priss?"

"What about her?"

Sawyer let out a deep sigh. "She isn't just going to sit back and twiddle her thumbs while she's all riled up over Rocky. She was practically seething when she woke up and found out we hadn't rescued him."

"We can't afford to lose any more wolves to the vampires. Especially her."

"I know. Personally, I think it's pointless to go after him. That's what they want. For us to leave this place unprotected. He's fucking bait now, she doesn't get it."

Alaric's heart ached at the truth of his brother's words. Because deep down, in the depths of his soul, Alaric knew Sawyer was right. Vampires had always been smart, but the Boracellis were another breed. Their queen was always ten steps ahead, which made capturing the bloodsuckers much more difficult.

As much as he wished he could run after Rocky, he knew the best option was to focus his attention on securing an alliance with the Mayfields. They could not take down the coven alone. He would need allies. Expendable ones and valuable ones.

"I'll talk to her," Alaric said, licking his lips.

"Good luck," Sawyer said with a huff. "Maybe her alpha can talk some sense into her."

6

ALARIC'S HAND HOVERED over the little green button, his heart in his throat. Even after the three glasses of whiskey it had taken for him to get up the courage to call, he still felt like a nervous teenager. Only Clementine Srirocco could make an alpha such as him come completely undone.

And only she can put me back together again.

He tapped the ominous green button, holding his breath. The phone barely rang twice before she picked up.

"Alaric?"

Alaric's shoulders instantly relaxed as he leaned back into the couch, fighting the desire to let out a sigh of relief. The sound of his name on her tongue was like a balm to his soul, and he hated how it melted his entire being like the sun melts the snow.

"Cleo," he breathed, trying to keep the control in his voice. "It's good to hear your voice," he proclaimed, instantly hating how *desperate* he sounded. A growl escaped his throat as he chastised himself.

He didn't miss the tiny, minuscule *whimper* that escaped her throat in response.

"Yeah," she sighed. "I guess it is."

He closed his eyes, trying to catch his breath. With his eyes closed, he could pretend she was there, with him. Next to him.

"You sound surprised," he said, his voice dark and tinged with drink. A part of him relished the ease of talking to her like this.

"You sound... different," she said, her own voice tinged with darkness.

Alaric licked his lips.

"Oh yeah? How do I sound?" he said, getting comfortable on the couch.

"You sound... relaxed, I guess."

Alaric couldn't help the dark chuckle that escaped his throat.

"That's probably the whiskey talking, sweetheart."

"Oh. I guess that makes sense. You never call me, so..." she said softly.

"Sawyer called, he said—"

"Of course. That's why you're calling," she replied, her tone shifting to one much more cold.

"Why else would I be calling?" he asked, defensively.

Cleo grunted an angry sound that

made him sit up straighter.

"I suppose there isn't any other reason. This is an alpha call."

Alaric growled in response to her bitter tone.

"When my pack is attacked, it is my business."

"Well, I wouldn't know what your business *is*, would I, Alaric? It's not like you're here. You're always somewhere else, taking care of *business.*"

"That's not fair, Cleo. You know I would be there if I could—"

"No, I don't. Not to mention even when you are here, you avoid me like the plague. "

Alaric could feel his blood boiling from her sudden attitude.

It's just the heat, nothing more...

Did she not know all she had to do was ask?

All she had to do was say the words and he would give her *everything* she desired. Everything she deserved...

How could she not understand the pain she caused him every time she looked at Rocky instead of him?

Every time she *touched* him instead of...

"There are things you don't understand, Cleo. Things I can't tell you, or Sawyer," he grumbled. "I need you to understand that I am doing what is best for you. For all of you."

"And what about Rocky?" she snapped.

"Excuse me?"

"Rocky protected me today. Not you, and certainly not Sawyer. Rocky protected me from those vampires, and I would have protected him too, had I not been thrown over Sawyer's shoulder like a rag doll and hidden in the fucking Thorne Palace, and no one seems to even care that he's out there, and..."

"You could have gotten yourself kidnapped, or worse, Cleo."

"You don't get it, do you, Alaric?" She huffed, her angry voice making his cock twitch.

It seemed in his absence, Cleo had gotten bolder. She was no longer the quiet, shy omega that showed up on his doorstep a year and a half ago.

Alaric growled in frustration, shifting his weight on the couch.

Omegas were supposed to *obey*. They were certainly not supposed to talk back, especially to their alphas.

But a part of Alaric *liked* this side of Cleo. Her attitude caused his cock to twitch and his blood to boil, his knot to tingle...

Cleo responded with a shaky sigh, her voice trembling as it darkened.

"I am not some... some princess that needs to be kept in a tower. I am a wolf. I am—"

"Mine," he growled, drunken fury and desire lacing through him.

"Excuse me?" she bit, but he could hear the desperation as she breathlessly responded to his brash words.

"I said, you are *mine*. You are my omega, my pack, and I will do whatever I have to do to keep you safe, sweetheart," he said, his body shaking with his admission.

"And Rocky is *mine*," she growled in return.

Alaric stiffened at the sound, the solidness of her tone. Almost as if she was not an omega, but an alpha herself.

A strange mix of desire and anger flooded him as his cock throbbed, his knot starting to swell.

"And I will stop at nothing to protect what belongs to me," she said.

"You will do as I say," he hissed. "You will not set foot outside that estate, and you will wait until I come home, when we will deal with this situation *properly*."

Cleo's voice was full of venom.

"Goodnight, Alaric," she snapped, hanging up the phone.

Alaric let out a frustrated grow. Sawyer was right, the woman was *maddening*. But she was not stupid. Emotional, sure, but Cleo knew the danger of the vampires better than anyone, considering they were the reason she'd been moved to the Thorne Estate so quickly.

And after the last attack, the night Rocky stirred her heat... Surely she would not go off half-cocked after his brother. Surely, all she needed was a good night's sleep.

Alaric brought up his text messages, texting her good night. He would not let her have the last word. Though Cleo did not respond, he could see she viewed the message, and for the moment it was enough.

He adjusted himself once more, switching gears as he brought up his security cam footage of the terrace. He watched quietly as a rain-drenched Cleo and Rocky entered the frame of the footage of the terrace, smiling, laughing.

He hated to see how *free* she was with his brother. How she smiled and laughed as if they were the best of friends. He'd seen a lot of such behavior between them, and therefore it was nothing new.

Until it was.

He watched as Cleo's pupils *dilated*, her nose twitching and her breath heaving.

Rocky's entire body stiffened like a livewire, and Alaric was sick to his stomach.

Yet, he could not turn away.

He watched as Rocky set his hand on her hip, as Cleo leaned against his chest, falling into him like a star. Watched as Cleo snaked her hands up his chest, into his hair.

His cock throbbed as he watched her, the way she parted her legs easily for his brother, the sight causing his knot to ache with need. Tears prickled at the edges of his eyes as he watched his omega offer herself to his brother.

Who turned away.

The vampires came.

He straightened himself, focusing on the events that happened next.

Cleo took a step closer, Rocky flanking her side. The vampire she spoke to, a tall, pale, and dark-haired creature, bared his fangs as Rocky turned to Cleo, but he could not make out the words. They were too far away from the terrace to pick up sound.

And then the creature struck Cleo, and Alaric watched as his younger brother shifted in mere seconds, lunging forth to attack the monsters that threatened *his* omega.

Stifling a sob in his chest, he remained vigilant. He needed to see what happened, needed to see what they were up against.

He watched as Cleo fought against the vampires with determination. She put up a good fight, but Sawyer was right. She was no match for three vampires, and his brother wasn't in the best of shape to shift, let alone fight.

Alaric pursed his lips as he watched the vampires strike Cleo, watched them sink their teeth into Rocky's bad leg.

His gaze focused as he watched his brother shift back to a bloodied, beaten human form, screaming in silence for Sawyer to take Cleo.

Alaric swiped right on the surveillance once he'd watched the vampires carry his brother off into the woods. He noted the house was quiet as he cycled through the live feed cameras in the hallways, the common areas. It was rather late, and he knew mostly everyone was in bed for the night. Except, perhaps mouthy omegas who needed a swift reminder of who actually ran the pack.

Alaric swiped right once more, to the last room, the updated live feed showing. The Thorne estate itself was massive, a straight up mansion in the mountains. But being the primary pack and one of the largest in the neighboring areas, meant the place needed to be not just indicative of their stature as a pack, but big enough to house multiple family members and staff.

Thorne estate was home to his parents, his brothers, and his aunts, uncles, cousins... And one day, it would be home to his—and his brothers—wives and children too.

Just as he moved to swipe out of the live footage, he noticed a shadow. He sat up straighter, panic lacing through him. Though when he saw the familiar face on the screen, a part of him was relieved.

Cleo slipped out of a plush bathrobe, just in front of the hot tub.

At this hour, with everyone in bed, the

pool house was empty, but during the day, it was always packed, and the families often coordinated with one another so they could have uninterrupted spa time, especially with the kids. After all, the estate housed almost sixty people, staff included.

But for the moment, it was just Cleo. Standing front and center in a white, crochet-patterned bikini.

Alaric swallowed harshly as his cock throbbed, his knot still tingling with desire. The bikini top only accentuated the swell of her breasts, showing off their true size, the bottoms cut high to show off her thighs. Normally, she was always under several layers of clothing, her tank tops and kimono wraps among her jeans and skirts, hiding her natural curves.

Her wavy hair was pulled back in a ponytail, instead of her trademark braid, and he couldn't help but salivate at the sight. She looked different.

He knew he should look away. But like the moment she'd shown up at Thorne estate, he couldn't tear his eyes away from her.

With his free hand, he attempted to adjust his erection. But the touch did nothing to quell the frustration, the desire prevalent in his heart and his knot.

He watched as she turned around, and he could see she was on the phone, talking to someone as she stepped one foot at a time into the bubbling waters.

Cleo's grin widened as she closed her eyes, leaning her head back against one of the neck rests, biting her lip. Her body relaxed in the water, and she rolled her head to the side. She shifted herself right over one of the powered jets.

For a moment, his glazed eyes stared into the abyss of static and black and white, as he watched her expressions on her face. He watched as she slid her own hand down beneath the waters, down her stomach as the bubbles increased.

Her entire body stiffened, her mouth forming a small 'o' as her shoulders tensed, eyebrows furrowing, and he realized all at once, what was happening.

What he was watching...

"Fuck!" he said as he hurriedly swiped out of the footage, slamming his phone down.

It wasn't like he was purposefully watching her. After all, the pool house was not a private room.

Heat enveloped his body as he tried to catch his breath. His cock ached, his knot heavy with need.

"It's just the heat, it's... nothing more. It's... I mean... fuck!" He pounded a fist into the pillow.

He felt partly to blame, for such things. While Rocky had stirred her heat, and it looked to be that they were progressing, much to his dismay, it had been a year and a half.

When an omega came into heat, resistance was usually futile. Most chose a mate within weeks, or sometimes months, but most of the time, the process was completed within three months, tops.

But Cleo hadn't chosen *anyone* to mate with, and Alaric realized as her image filled his brain, that perhaps the heat was getting to her as well.

Jealousy shot through him as he remembered the way she parted her legs for Rocky, how she kissed him...

Perhaps Cleo was close to giving in to fate.

Alaric grunted as he tried to push the thoughts from his mind of his *brother* and the woman he was desperate for.

Had he not made his affections clear?

Had he not given her enough space to decide what she wanted?

Had he somehow pushed her further away when all he wanted was to hold her close and...

His cock throbbed as guilt racked him, her words echoing in his brain.

You're never here.

You avoid me like the plague.

Perhaps, in his noble attempt to give the omega space to make her choice—a choice which he valued the utmost, even if she did not chose him—he had done more harm than good.

The image of her breasts filled his psyche, along with her hand disappearing beneath the waves, the way she bit her lip...

Coupled with the sound of her *whimpers* from earlier, Alaric could not fight his desire. He slid his hand beneath his jeans guiltily, his fingers brushing along his sensitive shaft until he settled on his knot. It was still a strange, new feeling; the bulbous swell that formed at the base of his cock every time he was aroused, now.

It would appear, that Cleo wasn't the

only one with a maddening instinct to fight.

He'd always known one day the knot would come, once he was presented with an omega. Only alphas had this unique special feature that would quite literally *lock* him into his mate until...

Alaric groaned as his thumb brushed over the swollen, hard knot. He swallowed harshly as his hips rocked of their own accord, his cock needing the friction, the release.

He closed his eyes as he gave in to the maddening sensations. The touch of his hand, the sensitivity of his full knot. It didn't take long for him to reach the pinnacle of release.

He turned on his side, his cock throbbing as he emptied himself into his hand. Tears streamed forth as his chest heaved, his heart breaking once more as the world converged on him all at once.

All the guilt, the shame, the pain, the

loss, the heartache.

I should have been there.

For her...

To save Rocky, to save Cleo...

To protect them all.

But Cleo was right. He was not there, and because he wasn't, his pack had paid the price, and his brother had been kidnapped, just like the Mayfield's omega.

Cleo was cross with him, and rightfully so.

Rocky was his blood, his responsibility. But there was no way he could risk the alliance with the Mayfields, or risk losing anyone else in the pack to the vampires.

Not to mention, he was no closer to finding the Mayfield's omega or the vampires that threatened to steal his precious Cleo from his grasp.

7

CLEO PACED BACK and forth in her room as she contemplated what to do. It seemed that Rocky's brothers were perfectly content to sit around and do nothing while the vampires did God knows what to him. She could not understand for the life of her, why she was the only one worried about the youngest Thorne.

Because he is your mate.

The word settled in her psyche, but she could not comprehend its truth.

Malcolm was her mate. She knew it in the depths of her soul, in the shadows of her isolation. He'd awakened her heat, for goodness sake!

But there was no denying the same spark, the same pull had made itself known on the edge of the terrace, only hours earlier. Underneath Rocky's amber gaze, she felt the unmistakable cord, the bond between her and her accomplice.

And then he'd kissed her, and the vampires came, and...

They all just... let him disappear, locking themselves in Thorne estate, including her.

They should be out there, looking for him, hunting for him.

Alaric's words reverberated in her brain.

You are mine.

He'd said the words no doubt as her alpha, not as her friend.

Were they friends?

No, we are not friends, she thought, stopping as she stared at the phone that lay on her bed. For a moment, when he'd called, she'd thought perhaps the distance had finally gotten to him.

Malcolm always called her, told her how much he missed her. How he couldn't wait to see her again, when he'd finally settled his scores. When he found the prey he was currently hunting—his former partner who should have been dead.

But even with the distance between them, when they spoke on the phone, she felt like he was close. And if she closed her eyes, if she focused on the sound of his voice, sometimes it felt like he was truly there, with her.

Her heart ached at her last memory, standing outside the Thorne estate.

When he'd told her he had to leave. She'd asked him if he was rejecting her, because it felt so painful. The stab in her heart, knowing he was leaving without her.

Knowing that she could not run away with him as her heart wished.

You're mine.

Alaric's words echoed in her thoughts like a heartbreaking curse.

In Malcolm's absence, she had crumbled, and like Malcolm, Alaric had just left.

You're never here.

Her own words danced a macabre waltz with Alaric's.

The growl in his voice, the unwavering clarity when he said those two words, even when she was furious with him.

You're mine.

Cleo hated that it soothed something inside her tumultuous soul when he said them. Heat bloomed between her legs as her insides twisted, the animal inside of her reacting to something much more primal, much more instinctual than her human self could understand.

Cleo *whimpered* once more at the memory, the way his growl laced through her skin, even though he was miles upon miles away.

How the sound of those words made her breathless.

She'd closed her eyes, soaking in his attention for the moment, her inner wolf surging forth. For one miniscule moment, she wondered if the spark between her and Alaric she'd felt so long ago existed still, buried beneath ash, waiting to be uncovered.

They'd shared a moment once, a kiss a year and a half ago, after Alaric *rescued* her from the clutches of what he thought was an evil hunter.

The *evil hunter,* Malcolm Crowley, her *mate.*

But her relationship with the Thorne alpha was shaky at best, as it was hard to have any sort of connection with a man who ignored you and left more than he came home.

I'm doing what I have to, to protect you.

You are mine, you are my pack.

Why did such claims anger her so?

As an alpha, it was his birthright and duty to *protect.*

Hadn't Malcolm told her the same thing?

That there was *unfinished* business he needed to take care of, before he could come home to her. Before they could be together again, and solidify their bond.

Cleo felt on edge, and she hated it.

Perhaps a dip in the hot tub will relax my frayed nerves.

She'd always loved to swim in the lakes back home, when she was upset. Being in the water always helped clear her mind.

She changed into her bathing suit—one of the many items Alaric had sent to her from his varied outings—a white, crocheted bikini that was soft and comfortable, even if it was much less fabric than she was used to.

Once she'd dressed, she grabbed her robe and phone and headed down the quiet hallway, past Sawyer's room. Her skin prickled with goosebumps as she thought about his words, about the warmth of his skin against hers.

For a moment, she'd imagined he was someone else, and when reality broke, she felt sick to her stomach.

The night Malcolm stirred her heat, she'd almost given in. Despite knowing what was expected of an Omega when they came into heat, she hadn't been prepared for the amount of sensory overload she felt when she'd shifted, or the animalistic desire that overtook her human self.

She relished in being *chased* by Sawyer, her animal intrigued by the strong, *virile* beta. His scent was overpowering, and so was his cocky nature. In human form, he was every bit an asshole, and the same cockiness he held as the Thorne beta was much more prevalent in his shifted form.

The overwhelming *need* to be mated was strong that night, but Cleo managed to grasp the reins of herself.

But even now she couldn't deny that it felt *right.*

The chase, the submission.

But it wasn't Sawyer she wanted then, and it wasn't Sawyer she wanted now.

As if the object of her desires could read her mind, her phone rang. Cleo slipped her hand into her robe pocket easily, answering on barely one ring.

"Mal?" she asked, stopping in her tracks, just at the top of the grand staircase.

"Hey…" he said, his voice low and tired. He sounded like he hadn't slept in days.

Knowing Malcolm, that's probably accurate.

"Is... everything okay?" she asked, her body tensing.

"I, uh... feel like maybe I should be asking you that?" he said awkwardly.

"What do you mean?"

"I mean, I had this weird fucking dream, and I just... needed to know you're okay."

Cleo could hear his breath catch in his throat, and her heart ached. It had been almost a month since Malcolm had called her in the aftermath of a nightmare. He never divulged the terrors he saw, but Cleo could hear the fear in his voice, and she knew they must have been awful. And given the horrors he'd experienced recently, she supposed the nightmare's return was inevitable.

She wished she could soothe his demons, the way his voice soothed hers.

"I'm okay, Mal," she breathed, leaning

against the banister. All the strain, the stress of everything threatened to fall away at the deep timbre of his voice.

"I just needed to hear your voice," he said softly. "I needed to know."

"I know," she whispered as she sauntered down the steps.

"But? I sense there's a *but* in there somewhere," he said, his voice gravelly and dark, but somehow still full of his patented sarcasm she loved so much.

She didn't wish to burden him with her troubles, but it was as if his words had unlocked something inside of her. The tone made her insides warm, and she could imagine his smirk.

"Where are you?" she asked.

Malcolm scoffed. "Some dive in the middle of bum-fuck nowhere. Mayfield, Kentucky, I think."

"On a hunt?"

"Something like that," he said, his tone relaxing a bit.

Cleo opened the door to the pool area, which was dimly lit and most certainly empty as she had hoped.

"This wouldn't have anything to do with that friend of yours? The one you've been looking for..." She searched her thoughts, trying to remember the name.

"Dallas, is it?" she asked.

Malcolm let out a deep sigh. "I can't ever keep anything from you, can I?"

His words were not menacing, nor were they accusatory. There was a peace in his admission, for Cleo knew Malcolm showed vulnerability to no one.

His words were soft and full of *relief,* as if just saying his name out loud, in the space between them was enough to soften his pain, to let go for a fraction of a moment.

Days ago, Malcolm had been on a hunt. While he rarely divulged details of his hunts to her, he'd called her crying that night. Because a routine hunt had taken someone dear to him, his partner, his friend. His brother in arms. He'd watched as his comrade died, taken his sister, and left the scene of the crime, solid as a stone. Malcolm Crowley was strong, vigilant. But he was also human, and everyone had a breaking point.

He rarely talked about his sister, Ava, his parents, or his hunter allies. But that night he'd crumbled, if only for a moment. She could still hear the pain in his voice, echoing in her memory.

She'd wanted nothing more than to soothe his ache, to wrap her arms around him and hold him until the pain subsided. Instead, all she could do was listen until he'd cried himself to sleep.

Despite the distance, even now she could feel his despair, like it was her own.

Could he feel hers as well?

Could he feel how her heart and body *ached* to be near him?

To be held and touched, to kiss his lips

one more time.

Her insides twisted at the thought of his lips on hers, of his warm skin pressed against her own. She closed her eyes for a moment, sighing deeply.

"Cleo?" he asked, his voice full of warmth.

"Hmmm?" she asked, disrobing. The cool air kissed her exposed flesh, causing her nipples to stiffen.

"What's wrong?" he asked.

"I—"

"Something's wrong, I can feel it. You're upset. What happened, did Alaric do something? Did he—"

"Alaric is only doing what is best for his pack," she said, placing one foot in front of the other and entering the hot water.

"That's a good thing, right?" Mal asked skeptically.

Cleo sat down, letting the water cover her like fire. "I don't want to talk about

Alaric, or the Thornes," she said, her heart in her throat.

"Cleo..."

"I just... wish you were here. That's all."

Malcolm's heavy sigh echoed across time and space, vibrating her soul.

"I wish I was there too," he breathed. "Where are you exactly?" he asked, his tone mischievous.

"I'm in the hot tub, why?" she asked.

Malcolm let out a dark chuckle. "They have a hot tub?"

"Indoor pool house, actually. It's pretty nice, but I don't come down often unless I really need to relax."

"Rough day, baby?" he said, and the words elicited a soft *whimper* from her throat. Hearing Malcolm use such a term of endearment was almost tantamount to the feeling of Alaric calling her *his*.

"Something like that," she whispered.

Malcolm let out another dark chuckle.

"You naked in that hot tub or…"

Cleo let out a laugh, and it felt good. "You wish, Malcolm Crowley," she teased.

"No one calls me by my given name, you know," he said, his voice no longer soft and scared, but full of mischief and lust.

Lust that caused fresh heat to blossom in her core, and her wolf to awaken.

"Legally, I changed it when I started hunting. All my shit says Malcolm Reynolds. You know, like the Firefly captain." His voice was lighter, and she could almost hear the ghost of laughter in it. "And everyone usually just calls me Mal, but–"

"Oh, I'm sorry, I—"

"No, I like it. You calling me by my real name. You might be the only one I like calling me by my full name," he said softly.

"It's a lovely name, Malcolm," she said, her own voice softening.

It was almost as if he had given her a piece of him no one else possessed. The dark timbre of his voice was smooth on the other end of the phone as he responded.

"Mhmm. So is Clementine Srirocco. Spicy."

"No hot tub at the Kentucky motel?" she pressed as the jets blew bubbles against her skin, beneath the expanse of her bottoms. The sudden rush caused an influx of desire to swell, and she nearly moved away. But instead of moving, Malcolm's voice pinned her to her spot.

"I wish. I'm in bed, if you really want to know. Long freaking day here too."

Cleo's mind wandered to the first time she'd woken up in a motel room with her mate. He'd saved her that night when her heat was stirred. Taken care of her. He'd even bathed and clothed her.

She could still remember the *need*, the ache in her soul as she stared at him, knowing he was *hers*. She'd wanted to sink her fangs into his neck and make him her *mate* forever. Without thinking, she groaned at the memory.

"What are you thinking about, baby?" he purred, his voice laced with darkness and lust.

A part of Cleo knew what she was doing was wrong, but she didn't care. For the moment, there was only her and her mate.

No vampires, no kidnapped mates, no broody commanding alphas.

"You," she murmured, closing her eyes as she let her hand travel down her stomach, past her navel. She only meant to adjust her bikini bottoms, but instead found her touch only accelerated her desire.

She could hear some shifting on the other end of the line, Malcolm's breathing hitching as he continued his dark deluge of desire.

"Oh, yeah?" he purred. "Tell me what I'm doing."

Cleo's heat raged inside of her, her pussy throbbing with need as his words settled on her.

They'd never done *this* before, but something about the impulsivity of the moment only spurred her curiosity. She liked hearing him like this.

"Kissing me," she whispered.

Mal chuckled. "Just kissing, Clementine?" he teased, letting out a groan. "Because when I think about you, we do a hell of a lot more than *kiss.*"

"*When* you think about me?" she asked, sliding her fingers beneath the siding of her bottoms. She gasped at the sensitivity, the rush of heat inside of her body as well as the heat from the water.

"Yeah," he breathed, his breath catching, and she knew. She could hear the faint sounds of the squeaky bed through the phone.

Knowing he was touching himself only added more fuel to the fire in her loins. Her wolf was salivating with renewed desire.

"Malcolm, I—" Her heart raced as she slid one finger inside, as he groaned on the other end of the phone, spurring her insides to tighten with need.

But it wasn't enough. She needed more.

She needed her *mate.*

"Shhh. I know, baby," he purred.

"I don't know if I can fight this much longer," she cried, tears pooling at the corners of her eyes.

Malcolm breathed a shaky breath. "Then don't fight it, Cleo. Give in," he said, his breaths labored. Though his voice was tinged with lust, there was something else hiding behind it.

Hope, perhaps?

Was Malcolm tired of fighting too?

She slid a second finger in, and the

pressure was blissful. Closing her eyes, she pretended it was him, touching her.

"Malcolm..." Her breath caught in her throat.

"Come for me, Cleo," he said, his voice solid and full of command, heavy with need.

Cleo's head fell back as her orgasm rocked her core. The frustrated whimper that escaped her throat had Malcolm cursing on the other end. And for a moment, all Cleo could feel was utter *bliss.*

His ecstasy entangled with hers, in cyberspace, in magical space.

And she felt *exhausted*, but relieved.

All the tension left her body as she slid her fingers out of her sensitive entrance, as the world sharpened from the hazy blur it had been moments ago.

"Cleo," he breathed her name like a prayer.

"Malcolm..." she purred as she rose

from the hot tub, her wolf pushing her to find her nest. She needed soft pillows and blankets and *mate.*

"I—" His voice trailed off into the shadows as Cleo hurried through the corridors, her insides still twisting in delicious knots.

When she got back to her room, she locked the door, collapsing on her bed. She positioned herself into a curled position, grasping onto the large body pillow she slept with nightly.

The silence between them was palpable, and for a moment she thought he was going to apologize. Tell her he'd gone too far, even though she could not deny she felt *better* than she had in ages. Malcolm always had a way of settling her storms, it seemed.

"Yes, Malcolm?" she asked sleepily as slumber tugged at her consciousness.

"I'm glad you're okay," he said, his tone full of exhaustion as well.

"You make everything okay," she murmured as they both fell asleep to the sound of one another's breathing.

8

THE FOREST LOOKED dark and never ending. Cleo stalked through the brush, her bare feet sinking into the moist soil as she carefully made her way. The sounds of the night were skittish, and she could feel a presence, as if she were being watched. The scent of blood and wolf was prevalent in the air.

This land beholds death, she thought.

So much death.

A fresh sheen of sweat covered her skin as she came to a clearing. Set against the hills was a large, ominous looking house.

It looked haunted, or abandoned maybe, but somehow she knew it wasn't. She was drawn to it, like a moth to a flame. Her heart ached, her wolf antsy.

Cleo took one step forward, then another, until she was on the front step. The door was open wide, shadows blanketing the inside, and she was on the edge of a precipice. She had to make a choice.

Do I go in, or do I run?

The smell of blood was strong to her senses. She looked down at her feet, seeing the darkened spatter decorating the porch floorboards, some dried into the wood, some glistening as if they were fresh. The moon was high, and her wolf was on alert. In the distance, she could hear a howl, but she could also smell the overpowering scent of vampire mixed in with the metallic scent of blood.

This is where the vampires are. I know it, even though I do not see a vampire in sight. But that doesn't mean they aren't here...

Cleo turned to look back at the forest, its never-ending blackness blanketing the landscape behind her. Her insides twisted with anticipation, her heart thudding so loudly in her chest she thought it may echo in the ominous cavern.

I am in danger. I know this. My omega instinct knows we should run.

But there was a stronger instinct beneath her omega nature.

A primal instinct to protect what was hers.

And that instinct, that throbbing echo in Cleo's heart outweighed all self-preservation.

She stepped into the darkness, nearly gagging at the scent of blood, fur, and death. Her stomach roiled as she held her hand up to her mouth.

Run, baby, run.

The words echoed in her head, but she ignored them.

Every step she took led her further into darkness, into danger.

But the echo, the ache in her heart, only grew stronger with each step. The halls were empty, broken portraits hanging haphazardly on the walls. Cobwebs and dust piled in the corner, and Cleo thought perhaps she was alone, that there was no one there. That perhaps it was some sort of a trap.

Until she saw the footsteps in the dust.

She followed them without hesitation, her blood boiling, her skin flush with heat.

She froze at the base of the ornate mahogany staircase. Her mouth watered as the appetizing scent of chocolate chip cookies filled her lungs. She grasped the banister, grounding herself as warmth and desire blanketed her. Her eyes fluttered closed.

That scent rocked her to her core.

Cleo's wolf salivated, her instinct taking over. She followed her mate's scent up the stairs, down the hallway. She stood at the top of the staircase, and there he was.

He sat at the far end of the hall, outside a closed door, the skin of his knees peeking through ripped holes in dark, tattered pants, brought up to his chest, his arms wrapped around them.

"Rocky," she breathed his name, and he looked up. His gaze softened, his shoulders loosening upon her voice. He was pale and bruised, but he was alive.

He's alive...

She didn't waste a second as she ran down the hall, her bare feet hitting the wooden floor with resounding determination.

Within seconds, she was kneeling before him, pulling him toward her. Rocky fell against her weakly, burrowing his face in her neck, in her hair. He breathed her in deep, sighing as his fingers twisted in her hair.

"Cleo," he whispered. His voice was strained, but still the sweetest relief.

"I'm so sorry, I—"'

Rocky's lips crashed against hers, quieting her cries as she fell into him like a shooting star.

He fell back against the dusty wooden floor, bringing Cleo with him, a deep groan escaping his throat. Cleo's wolf lunged forth, pushing her body forward to straddle his hips.

Outside, thunder clapped, causing the floor beneath them to rattle. The scent of blood was everywhere, mingling with the delectable scent of chocolate chip cookies.

Rocky settled his hand on her neck, his hardness brushing against her heated core. She could feel the tips of his fangs against her tongue, and she was hot.

So fucking hot...

Cleo removed her shirt, her chest covered in sweat. Her white, soaked bra stuck to her like a second skin.

Rocky's hands slid down her back, settling against her ass. He didn't push her or pull her, almost as if he was afraid. Instead, he gently ran his fingers over the curve of her ass delicately, reverently.

In the distance, she heard a door slam, but she didn't care.

The only thought in her brain was her animal.

Mate.

Almost as if he understood her thoughts, he arched his back off the floor, thrusting himself against her heated, sweat-soaked core with an uncharacteristic grunt that only fueled her desire further. She'd never heard such sounds from him before.

"Cleo..." he breathed, his voice full of lust and... fear.

Clementine's fingers trailed over his wet shirt, resting at the waistband of his jeans. She dipped her fingers beneath his soaked shirt, trailing tiny touches along his waist, through the trail of hair beneath his navel. His skin was warm, flush against hers.

"Rocky," she breathed his name as she kissed him, grinding herself against his rigid erection. Feeling him against her, knowing he wanted this... that he wanted her... caused her pussy to throb.

Instinct was strong, and all Cleo could think about was how desperately she wanted to feel his skin against her own, how her heart and her wet, aching pussy longed to feel him in every corner of her body, mind, and soul.

My mate...

Rocky wrapped his arms around her waist, like he did on the terrace.

Lovingly, achingly.

As if she were as delicate as glass.

Protecting her.

He gazed into her eyes with sadness, his amber eyes watery.

"I can't..." his voice was strained. "You shouldn't be here..." he said, biting his lip. His cock throbbed against her, protesting his claims. He pushed Cleo off of him.

He is rejecting me...

"Are you... rejecting me?" she asked, her heart in her throat. Between his rejection and the pungent scent of blood, she thought she was going to be sick.

"God, no. Cleo. I meant what I said, I... Rejecting you would be a fate worse than death," he said, closing his eyes. His expression was pained. He leaned his forehead against hers, his chest heaving.

"I want you more than you even know, but..."

"Then what—"

"You need to go, you can't be here," he said painfully. "I need to protect you. I won't let them take you."

Cleo held him in front of her, gazing into his warm amber eyes. The circles underneath marred his naturally golden skin tone, and she wanted to kill whoever had done such things to him.

Whoever has hurt my mate... they will pay.

"Where is here?" she asked, her fingernails digging into his shirt, trying to hold on as his image flickered, fading before her like a ghost.

"Mayfield, Kentucky, I think. That's what the other omega said."

Clementine's heart froze at his words.

Other omega... is he...

"Cleo..." he kissed her, taking her bottom lip between his teeth, pulling her from her possessive, jealous thoughts.

"You are mine," she whispered against his lips as she slid her tongue in his mouth. The groan that escaped him echoed as his fingers twisted in the strands of her hair tightly. Possessively.

"Come on, we need to get you out of here."

Cleo couldn't stifle the whine that escaped her throat. She didn't want to let go.

"Come with me, please, if we leave now..."

Rocky pulled her close, his lips at her ear. They were warm, soft, and caused fresh wetness to bloom between her thighs.

Cleo's insides ached for him.

I need him, my mate.

"I can't, Cleo. Not yet."

Her heart broke. "Why?"

Rocky traced his fingertips down her soft cheek, letting his thumb gently brush over her lip.

In the distance, Cleo could hear the faint sound of a baby crying. Of children laughing.

"It's too dangerous."

Rocky started to fade like a ghost, and she reached for him.

"Rocky!" she called out, but the world dissolved into something else.

Somewhere else.

Cleo looked around, realizing she was no longer in the haunted house with Rocky, but that she was still soaked to the core, her feet soiled from her run in the forest. Her exposed skin was clammy from sweat. But now she stood on dry beige carpet, under buzzing amber lights.

Malcolm sat shirtless on the bed in front of her, sharpening his knife. Cleo watched as his dark hair hung in his eyes, fresh from a shower. He smelled like whiskey and tobacco, mixed with the heady scent of mate. She watched the way his muscles corded in his shoulders with every motion as he methodically sharpened his weapon.

"Malcolm?" she called out, her heart still racing.

He looked up at her, dark brown eyes alive with fire. His smirk reached his eyes as he handed her the knife, the handle toward her. Like it was a peace offering.

"You ready to hunt, baby?" he said with a grin.

Clementine took the knife from him, noting it was heavy in her hand.

She watched as he got up, coming over to where she stood, bridging the gap between them. He was not as tall as Alaric, or Rocky, and certainly not as defined. But the way he looked at her, the hunger in his eyes would have rivaled any wolf.

"Hunt? What are we hunting?" she asked as she looked between the knife and her mate in front of her.

Cleo's body flushed with heat again, and she could feel fresh moisture coating her thighs. Her insides twisted as she looked up at him, his mischievous smile that said 'trouble.' She swallowed harshly.

It baits me and my wolf, and it is irresistible.

"More like *who* are we hunting," he said, reaching out to run his hands through her damp, bronze hair.

"Dallas," she said out loud with understanding. His friend, who had been attacked, left for dead. Who'd suddenly disappeared.

"Rocky," he said solidly.

Rocky....

The name ignited a fire within Cleo.

"What do we do when we find them?" she asked, her voice shaking.

Malcolm wrapped his hand around hers, which was holding the handle of the blade he gave her.

"What we have to, baby," he said softly, his fingertips smooth against the back of her hand. He picked her hand up so that Cleo held the tip of his blade pressed against his chest.

"I don't know if I can..." she said, her

voice small.

"You are stronger than you know, Cleo," he said, his voice smooth, blanketing her in heat. He pressed himself against the tip of the blade, and the moment she saw blood, she flinched, dropping the knife.

"I hurt you," she said, feeling panicked.

"You can't hurt me, baby. Promise," Mal spoke, grinning.

Cleo's wolf salivated at the sight, the scent of her mate's blood like warm cherry pie. Her breath hitched, her insides twisting as she took in the sight of him before her, shirtless, pale, a trail of vibrant red blood dripping down his chest, down his abs, permeating across his skin and the hair beneath his navel.

She didn't think twice about licking him clean, driven by an animalistic need she couldn't describe.

"Fuck," Malcolm cursed, sliding his

hand over her hip, his fingernails digging into her sensitive, flushed skin, pushing her against his arousal.

When Cleo came to the mark, the source of the blood on his chest, she looked up at him.

In his eyes, she saw his awe, his desire.

For Malcolm looked at her as if she was everything. As if she could do anything.

In Malcolm Crowley's eyes, she was not an omega.

She was just Clementine Srirocco, and that was enough.

Clementine took his lips like a thief, his tongue against hers, the taste of his blood still prevalent in her mouth only driving her desire, her need to feel him, to covet him and keep him all for herself. She let her hands travel down his smooth skin, her fingers twisting with the buttons on his jeans.

He grinned against her lips as he pulled away. When he looked at her again, her lips still swollen from his heated kiss, thighs still wet, he handed her the knife again.

"I said, are you ready to hunt?"

Before Cleo could take the knife, before she could answer him, he disappeared, just like Rocky had.

Cleo reached for him, but it was no use.

She cried out, "Yes!" But there was no one there to hear her.

The hotel room faded into a scene expansive forest and hills, the air sticky and warm. Which did not nothing to quell the heat boiling beneath the surface of her skin.

She stared at the hills and forests beyond her reach, thinking of her mates. The pain in her chest was unbearable.

Anger and frustration ebbed throughout her body.

She was hot, sweaty, covered in her own arousal, and half-naked. Her wolf was just as furious, and together they let out a deep, furious growl.

"Cleo..." A solid, dark voice caressed her, causing her to freeze once more.

The omega inside of her reared her head, wanting to kneel. To submit to that voice.

The voice of an alpha.

But the human side in Cleo wanted to fight.

She turned to see Alaric standing there in nothing but a pair of black tight underwear, his defined muscles on total display. Like Rocky, he boasted a golden sun kissed complexion, but he looked almost bronze in the light, save for the dark smattering of hair across his chest, trailing down his solid abdomen, drawing stark contrast to his defined hips that bore a perfectly chiseled v like arrows, guiding her gaze. On display as he was, it was impossible for Cleo to deny what he was.

An alpha.

His height, frame, his fiery gaze. His commanding, stoic nature.

Her wolf wanted nothing more than to let him in, to let him touch her, own her. Breed her.

She sucked in a deep breath, biting her lip, fighting the instinct, the primal urge that blanketed her as she looked at him.

His dark hair was longer, a testament to his absence. But Cleo could not deny it was a rather attractive look for him. His facial hair was longer too, but unlike his hair, he seemed to have kept it trimmed.

Still, after not seeing him for over a month, he looked like a stranger. A hot stranger.

I think I need some air...

"This is your fault!" she wailed as she stomped over toward him. Anger and pain echoed within her.

She only wanted to escape the pain. She'd been so close to her mates... so very close, and yet they'd disappeared, slipping through her fingers once more.

"My fault?" he growled.

"Yes, you! If you wouldn't have left, Rocky would still be here!" she screamed at him.

Alaric did nothing but stand there, taking her words like knives as she threw them at him.

Cleo could feel the tears at the edges of her eyes as she held herself tightly. The vision of Rocky's bruises, of his weakened state, made her feel as if she could throw up. She'd been so close to him.

Alaric bared his fangs at her.

"I was needed in Mayfield! I can not fight this war with the vampires and keep you safe without a fucking army, Cleo, don't you understand that?" he bit back. "I need allies."

"Why? Why am I so fucking important to the vampires? I'm a nobody, I'm a—"

"You are an omega, Cleo. You are the magic that keeps our bloodline strong," he said reverently.

"I am more than some... some... incubator, Alaric!" she bit back, her wolf protesting with every word.

Sawyer's words rang in her brain.

"It's all soft nests and hard dick for you."

"I am a person! I am a fucking wolf!" she cried, anger flooding her veins.

Cleo bristled as she stood tall, despite being five foot four. She was more than an omega. She was made to do more than just mate for the rest of her life.

I was made to fight.

"Of course you are, but the vampires don't care about that," he growled in frustration. "They only care about what your blood can provide them..." he growled.

Her blood.

It was her blood that brought upon her fate. It was her blood the vampires wanted, her blood that meant she was to be given to the Thorne's, for no other reason than what Alaric had stated.

To ensure a strong, healthy bloodline of wolves for years to come.

It was her blood that boiled under Alaric's fiery gaze, under Rocky's adoring touch.

And it was her blood that brought her to the Thorne estate, that spurred her heat when she looked at Malcolm.

Cleo pushed Alaric, angry with him and everything this cursed life brought with it.

"Malcolm," she breathed as she realized without any of it, she would have never found him.

The memory of his words as she watched him drive off in his red Chevelle were a wound that was still fresh, despite the time passing.

Watching her mate *leave*.

"If you hadn't rescued me that night from Mal, he'd still be here!" she said with realization as she looked up at him. In Alaric's amber eyes, she could see they were rimmed in gold with shifting energy, her burning reflection staring back at her.

"Malcolm Crowley? What does he have to do with shit?" Alaric bit, getting in her face.

Shifting energy coursed through her from his venomous tone, her wolf wanting to rise to the surface, warring with the desire to drop to her knees at the feet of her alpha.

"He is my mate!" Cleo yelled, balling *her fists against his chest as she fought the desire to submit, to give in to the shift.*

For Cleo knew if her wolf took over, resistance would be futile.

"He is a human! Rocky is your mate. You can not—"

The world came crashing down around her as the events of the last year and a half, the lie she'd been living, threatened to take her under once more.

"Rocky lied!" she cried, tears coming to her eyes. Her words echoed in the space between them, sharp like swords.

Alaric's silence spoke volumes, the heat of his gaze transfixed on her.

"What do you mean, he lied?" His voice was barely a whisper.

Cleo's body heated like a flame as tears slid down her cheeks. Her heart ached for Rocky, but he was not here.

He was trapped, and she had been so close...

Her heart was in her throat as the words fell out of her mouth, as the tears came like a waterfall.

"It was Malcolm. Rocky only did what he's always done, what you claim to do, but have not done since day one!" she said, her tone full of venom.

Her heart hurt. Everything hurt.

She wanted them. Rocky, Malcolm. Her mates. She longed to feel their touch, their love, their acceptance.

Alaric grabbed her fists, holding them tight, his gaze unwavering as he captured hers.

"Oh yeah, and what's that?" He sneered. His own eyes were glassy and full of hurt.

Cleo looked up at him, at his fiery gaze, and it reminded her of Rocky.

But it was darker, harsher, full of pain and anger like her own.

Alaric's gaze raised a wildfire inside of her, decimating barren lands.

"Protect me!" she cried as the tears ran down her cheek. Her fangs forced their way through her gums, aching to bite, to attack.

Alaric broke apart her fist, intertwining his fingers with hers. The touch was a mixture of force and softness, and she dug her nails into the back of the skin on his hand, between his fingers. Hard enough, she knew she could draw blood, but he did not flinch. Instead, he only held her gaze, standing tall like a monument of strength.

"You can not have two mates, Cleo, that is impossible," he said, tightening his grip.

She knew he could break her hand if he wanted, but he only dug his nails into her skin, his thumb brushing over hers, a sliver of gentleness among the pain.

Clementine looked up at him, relishing in his harsh, desperate touch. She bared her fangs at him, growling as the fire in her blood heated every part of her. Her insides ached to be filled, and she was so wet.

Realization struck her as she loosened her grip, feeling the heat of his skin on hers. It sparked a hunger in her, one that was much different than the hunger she felt for Rocky or Malcolm.

It was desperate.

Cleo sucked in a breath as his grip loosened, as his nails in her skin eased up, and she wished he hadn't.

The rush, the pain he brought also brought a sort of relief. It felt good.

She was desperate for his touch, for his love. Cleo gazed up at Alaric, noting the same hunger she felt echoed in his own gaze.

He, too, was starving. For *her* touch, her pain.

She could feel it in the depths of her broken, heated soul.

Alaric was wrong. She didn't have two mates.

She had three.

Cleo looked up at him, overwhelmed with truth and fate, and her entire body was set aflame with this truth. She burned, like a five alarm fire under his touch, his gaze.

Alaric Thorne was hers too, but for some reason he chose to reject her, despite never saying the words.

She broke free of his hold, the animal in her taking over once more. Cleo jumped on him, and he caught her with ease as she wrapped her legs around his solid hips, his hands settling on her thighs as she kissed him.

And all the fire came rushing back full force.

A deep growl escaped his throat as his hands held her tightly against him.

Alaric dropped her against something soft, something plush, and the world was a blur. A blur of rough hands, and fire, and heat.

So much fucking heat...

Her wolf let out a contented growl as instinct overwhelmed her.

Beneath the pain, there was bliss.

She arched her back as his lips caressed her neck, his fangs grazing against her skin. A strained, desperate whimper left her throat, her insides twisting as her orgasm started to culminate.

"You are mine," he growled. His cock throbbed against her through the fabric that separated them, his breath hot on her skin. "You belong to me."

His words sounded like someone else, someone who angered her, someone who saw her as nothing but a hole to fill.

"You are my omega," Sawyer sneered in her head.

Alaric's lips trailed fire over her skin, but Sawyer had poisoned her brain. She pushed against Alaric as the fury mingled with her heat.

"I belong to no one!" she cried, her wolf angry for her protest, her heart so heavy it felt as if it may break.

Alaric held her hands in his as he pressed himself against her, into the soft cushions, blankets, and pillows.

Into her *nest.*

The realization satisfied her wolf, who was practically preening underneath her alpha. Her thighs were slick with arousal, and her skin was flushed as she tried to catch her breath.

"You belong to him," Alaric growled. "Malcolm fucking Crowley. To that fucking idiot human." He settled her fists beside her hand, his hands loosening their grip only slightly.

"To my god damn baby brother." The jealousy was unmistakable in his voice as he tightened his grip around her wrists, grinding his erection against her, making her see stars. It wasn't enough.

She knew she could break away from his touch, but it was his words that held her like chains.

"Why not me, Clementine?" His voice was full of anguish.

Jealousy, pain.

And love.

His teeth grazed her neck as he let go of her wrists.

Cleo could still feel the warmth where he'd held her.

Her heart wanted to break at his words, and the emptiness she felt when he stopped touching her was agonizing. Her body moved of its own accord as she wrapped her legs around his hips, pulling him closer, brushing against his sizeable hardness.

She gripped his shoulders, tears pooling in her eyes as she ground herself against him, her fingernails digging into his skin. She held onto him like he was her lifeline.

She didn't want to let go of him. She didn't want to lose him, her alpha.

Because she knew it was all a dream.

Alaric wasn't really there. He was never there.

But I wish he was.

A tear slid down her cheek as she

secretly wished for the life of her, that he would walk through her bedroom door and say those three words.

You are mine.

That he'd grab her, throw her down onto her bed, and breed her like she truly was his omega.

The realization was harrowing, arousing, and terrifying for her, dream or not.

Something about his words ignited her, and she remembered her own words earlier.

"They are mine," she growled as she pushed back against him. "They belong to me. And if you're not going to save your pack, then I will."

***

Cleo stood in the Thorne's rather large garage, staring at the blue sedan.

"This is where it all started," she murmured to herself, holding her chilled arms. The haziness of her strange dream still hung over her like a ghost.

She could still remember the moment like it was truly yesterday and not a year and a half ago. When Rocky had propositioned her to sneak out of the Thorne Estate for some fun, at the local bar. Howlers.

Where Mal had been on a hunt.

The rest was history.

"This is probably a bad idea," she said, shaking her head, twirling Rocky's keys in her hand.

Surely Alaric will kill me for this.

Her wolf protested, but Cleo was strangely calm.

The vampires may kill Rocky if I don't, and I will never see him again.

Cleo tugged on her backpack, or rather Rocky's backpack; the one he'd left in the midst of the attack. Sawyer had left Rocky's things in his room, not bothering to lock the door.

An oversight of course, because with him gone, who would truly need to go in the youngest Thorne's bedroom?

Aside from his *mate* of course.

She twirled the keys in her fist, letting out a deep breath.

The dream she'd had felt so real, almost as if she were truly there, wherever Rocky was.

Wherever Mal and Alaric were.

Though visions and premonitions were not uncommon among Omegas, she refused to believe in such things. After all, she'd never had a vision or a premonition before, and dreams were simply just that. Dreams.

But somewhere in the depths of her soul, she knew without a doubt, Rocky was alive, and he was in Mayfield, Kentucky.

And so was Malcolm.

And Alaric.

Cleo bit her lip as she shoved away the

thoughts of the looming alpha from her dreams. Her insides twisted at the very thought, and she fought against it.

Her wolf perked up at the memory of her dream, at the way Alaric grasped her fists, at the fire in his kiss. The rigidness of his muscles, his warm skin. It had felt so real, and even as she stood in the chilly garage, she could not deny the heat the mere *thought* of him brought about.

But Cleo only stubbornly ignored her wolf, instead focusing on unlocking Rocky's car.

She threw the backpack into the backseat, settled into the driver seat, and closed the door. She placed her hands on the wheel, her heart in her throat. Methodically, she unlocked the garage door, hoping the mechanical sounds would not wake Sawyer or anyone else in the house.

As the garage door slid open, revealing the expanse of the night, she held her breath. Not a soul in sight was outside at this hour, and she did not wait. She turned the car on, did one cursory glance behind her, if only to make sure she was not in the process of being discovered, and then she left.

She simply put her foot on the gas, closed the garage door with the opener attached to Rocky's visor, and sped off into the shadows, toward Mayfield, Kentucky.

Toward Malcolm Crowley and Rocky Thorne.

9

THE ALARM ON Malcolm's phone sounded with astounding clarity.

Mal groaned as he reached for his phone on the nightstand, fumbling until he brought it close, his eyes focusing. He wiped his eyes, his vision sharpening as the numbers came into view.

Eleven thirty-five pm.

"Fuck," he grumbled as he swung his legs over the side of the bed, tossing the phone to his side. He ran a hand through his hair, cursing himself. He'd had every intention of getting up at eleven, if only so he could eat something before engaging on his hunt.

But that dream was too fucking hot.

He adjusted himself as his thoughts threatened to fall back to *her.*

Cleo.

Hunting on an empty stomach was never a good idea, but hunting your best friend on an empty stomach…

Mal sighed as he stood, heading to his duffel that sat on the other unused bed.

Once upon a time, he and Dallas hunted together, staying in places just like the nameless motel he was in.

And now I'm hunting him.

Mal tried to push the emotional thoughts and feelings aside.

This wasn't personal, he told himself.

It's business.

Finish the job.

He pulled out a fresh shirt and pair of jeans, sighing as he tried to think of anything else except what lay ahead.

If his calculations were correct, by the data he'd been tracking, Dallas was in Mayfield, Kentucky. And where the Djinn were, the vampires wouldn't be far behind. It was only a matter of time before Amora Medici, vampiress and leader of a rogue Djinn faction, sank her claws into his partner.

Former partner.

Granted, he and his sister, Ava, had gotten out unscathed from the Marquis, along with the human they'd gone to save, and the pain in the ass vampire, Cassius, but it hadn't been without its challenges.

Mal knew, like most monsters, Amora would regroup. And when she did, he would be ready for her.

But first I'll get what I need... answers, and perhaps a bit of revenge.

Mal dressed in a fresh pair of jeans, sauntering toward his discarded phone. He picked it up, noticing the call log, which must have queued up when he'd thrown it down. He stared at the ending time, noting it was several hours ago. He stared above those numerical digits at the name that graced his screen,

Baby.

Mal's heart ached as he remembered their conversation in the faint glow of the light casting from his phone.

No wonder that dream was so fucking hot.

He sighed, remembering the beautiful, Clementine Srirocco, his....

Well, he wasn't sure *what* she was, truly. He was a hunter. It was his sole purpose in life to eradicate the world of the monsters that threatened his kind. To prevent travesties and tragedies such as the ones he'd experienced. He *killed* creatures like Clementine, monsters without blinking an eye, and yet...

She'd claimed they were mates, but she was a werewolf, and not just *any* werewolf. An omega, a prized breed of wolf built specifically for breeding and ensuring strong pack bloodlines. A prized wolf the vampires were interested in as well, though he could not understand why. Vampires and werewolves had been enemies for eternity, but until a year and a half ago, they'd honored the land treaties in Mahoning, where Cleo was.

Until they hadn't.

Until he'd showed up, laid eyes on Cleo at Howlers bar that night, and stirred her heat, some legendary *mate bond*, and because of such, the vampires had tried to take Cleo for themselves.

Over my dead body.

Though despite the overwhelming desire and *need* to protect what belonged to him, Malcolm couldn't bring himself to terms with being anyone's mate. Not when he knew that it was a death sentence.

Love was nothing but a curse for a

Crowley.

His parents had proved that. They'd left their life as hunters to have a family. But even the years of familial bliss had been stolen from Peter and Lenore Michaels—changing their family name should have been Malcolm's first clue his parents were *hiding*.

And despite doing such, the bloodsuckers still found them, still destroyed everything they'd built together.

No, it was much easier to *pretend* with Cleo, because then he could never hurt her, let her down. And if he kept his distance, if she was miles and miles away, then perhaps he *could* have his cake. He just couldn't eat it.

But I've tasted it, and that is enough.
Isn't it?

And so for the last year and a half, that's what he'd done.

He called her frequently, if only to quell the ache in his chest that persisted when he'd tried to *fight* the need to hear her voice, just the teeniest bit of frosting to sate his hunger.

A lick here, a crumb there. As long as the cake was intact, he could get by.

Just the sound of her voice could soothe his nerves, and it had done so plenty of times over the course of their... relationship?

"It's not a relationship, asshole. You can't have a relationship with someone you never fucking see." He told himself this as he picked up his blade—the one Dallas had given him when they started hunting together. One that used to belong to him when he was a novice hunter himself. Everything else the man once owned, was now left to him, including his home in Albright, Ohio.

Malcolm turned the blade in his hand, looking at the scratches and marks on the leather handle, the pristine sheen of the blessed silver. Of all the weapons he'd ever bought or used, nothing served him as well as his first blade. He slid it into his back pocket, checking his phone for the time, cursing again to see it was now eleven forty-five.

He often lost track of time when he thought of Cleo. Of her big, blue-green eyes that reminded him of stars speckled in a summer night sky.

Mal sighed as he grabbed his keys, heading out the door into the sticky night air. While he was no stranger to heat, he preferred the crisp, cool air of autumn. It reminded him of home, in Salem.

He fired up the engine of his candy-apple red Chevelle, tearing out of the Econo Lodge parking lot like a bat out of hell toward the Mayfield Motel.

It was the most recent hit he'd gotten on Dallas's credit card, after all.

A part of him hoped he was wrong. That somehow, someway, this trip would end up a wild goose chase. That perhaps, somehow he'd been wrong and his best friend really was dead.

What kind of deranged asshole wishes their friend was dead?

He sighed, focusing on the road as he murmured aloud, "A fucked up one, that's who."

The engine roared as he flew through the darkness down the winding road. He turned the radio up, leaning back in the driver's seat as the unmistakable riffs of Kansas's *Carry On My Wayward Son* filled the air.

He let out a deep breath, knowing resistance was futile. It was his father's favorite song, and one of his favorites to perform in his band, Blood Of My Enemy.

The band which now is lacking a front man.

The singer droned on about masquerading as a man with a reason, and Mal sang out in unison as the singer expressed disappointment, claiming to be a wise man whilst never truly knowing, letting the music fill the crevices of his tired, aching soul.

He let his thoughts wander to his father as he flew down the road. It was hard not to think about the man, when he suffered from nightmares.

Nightmares in which he'd come upon the bloody corpses of his parents, laying in a pool of blood that stained the beige carpet crimson and black. The memory of their cold, lifeless eyes, open, gaping at him, still made him want to throw up, even seven years later.

His memories had been poisoned. No longer could he think about playing drums while his dad strummed away on the guitar, no longer could he think about working on their pride and joy, his '67 candy-apple red Chevelle, and his father's black '69 Impala that now belonged to his sister, Ava.

All of his best memories had been

soured and ruined by the sight of their bloody, vicious death.

That was the night Malcolm Crowley truly died. The night he'd discovered the truth about his parents, about his own heritage.

Malcolm felt the beginnings of tears beckoning to be freed, but he would not cry, not in the privacy of his car, and certainly not when he had more important things to do, to hunt.

He still felt remorse for crying the other night in front of Cleo. The fact she hadn't mentioned such things gave him hope that perhaps she would forget such a mishap, such an anomaly on his otherwise spotless record of emotional breakdowns.

Crying is for pussies.

I'm not a fucking pussy.

For he was a Crowley, and Crowleys endured.

He pulled into the parking lot of the

Mayfield Motel, turning off his lights. He wasn't certain what he would find, if he found anything. But the ever-present feeling in his gut told him he was exactly where he was supposed to be.

The motel parking lot seemed to be quite packed, with an RV, a boat load of motorcycles, and an array of cars and trucks.

Could one of them be a stolen one for D?

Or perhaps he hitched a ride somehow.

For a hole in the wall, the place was busy.

He watched as a group of women, twenty-somethings, strolled past his car, but they did not head for their rooms, no.

Instead, he watched as the tall, beautiful group sauntered toward a... bar?

Malcolm sat up straighter as he watched the crowd gather outside the porch of a building that looked less like a bar, and more like a town hall, but the presence of bikers, women, and the sound of brawling was one he knew all too well.

Malcolm twisted his lips. He had come to observe, to stake out the Mayfield Motel, but he also knew Jake Dallas better than most.

Just like him, he was a creature of habit.

Motels, bars, shows, rock music, fine ass, fine cars...

That was life.

At least, it was until he'd met Cleo.

Malcolm couldn't remember the last woman he looked at and felt anything for.

Once upon a time, he'd reveled in the differences, the newness, the spontaneity of not knowing who he would go home with, especially on nights he performed.

Or slayed.

When he was high on monster kills, drunk on whiskey, or running away from his nightmares.

But now, it seemed he'd lost his appetite for even the most beautiful of women. It was like his brain had been hijacked. Nothing sated his desire anymore.

Nothing except the *thought* of Clementine Srirocco, that was.

Mal opened the car door, letting the warm southern air kiss his skin as he watched the crowd mingle about the bar. The sounds of breaking glass and hollers accented the loud music he could hear as he shut his door, walking closer.

The smooth, familiar sound of Freddie Mercury carried as he got closer. Mal hummed along to the song, sinking his hands into his pockets. The guitar riffs of *Crazy Little Thing Called Love* echoed in the space as he made his way indoors. The bar itself was packed with people, drinking, dancing, singing.

Mal stood off to the side, casually sweeping his gaze over the room, looking for his prey.

It was hard to believe only eight days ago, he'd been running through a labyrinthine masquerade, chased by vampires and Djinn.

The memory replayed in his mind over and over. It had been so sudden.

Dallas pushed him and Ava out of the way.

It was one split second. One second that changed the course of everything.

Malcolm made his way through the crowd of people, watching, waiting.

But he would not find Dallas in the crowd, or at the bottom of his whiskey glass, like he had hoped.

The bartender called for last call, and Malcolm sighed. He tossed his money on the bar, somehow feeling a mixture of relief and of uncertainty.

Dallas was not here.

Perhaps, he'd been too late, and now it was nearing two am, and he hadn't anything to show for his stake out.

"I should've stayed in the fucking car," he mumbled as he shoved his hands in his pockets, ambling out of the bar.

He'd barely touched his whiskey, worried that at the drop of a hat everything would change and he'd need to be ready for an attack.

Because if Jake Dallas truly was a monster, it would be his life or…

The parking lot had thinned out, except for a handful of motorcycles, the RV, and some trucks.

The inhabitants who were likely staying at the motel.

Malcolm got in the Chevelle, the radio blaring with Duran Duran's *Hungry Like The Wolf*. He rolled his eyes, but alas, he did not have the heart to change it. Instead, he only focused on the familiar words, singing in a whisper about being on a hunt.

As he drove, he couldn't help but think

that perhaps he truly was chasing ghosts.

Dallas, his parents.

The answer to breaking Ava's vamp claim.

He was tired. Tired of coming up short, tired of failing those he loved, who he was supposed to protect.

He stared at his phone in the passenger seat, noticing a missed call from *Baby*.

That's odd.

He picked it up, checking the time.

Two-thirty am.

His blood chilled as he worried what a two am call from Cleo meant. Surely she wasn't in any trouble; surely it was just an accident, a butt dial, something.

Without thinking, he called the number back, but the call failed. One look told him he was in a dead zone.

"Fuck," he cursed, pushing on the gas harder, hoping and praying to whatever god would hear him that he could get some damn reception.

When he'd made it back to his motel, he was far too tired. It seemed the years hunting, performing, and running were catching up to him. He got out of the Chevelle quietly, queuing up his phone again, vehemently searching for a signal as he twirled his keys in his hand, heading to his rented room.

"Malcolm."

He stopped dead in his tracks, his blood rushing all throughout his body, heating him like a flame. He looked up instantly, to see the mirage of Clementine, standing against a blue sedan, her bronze and gold hair blowing in the breeze. Under the harsh streetlights in the parking lot, she looked almost angelic.

He blinked furiously, thinking perhaps he truly was experiencing a psychotic break.

Stress can cause a lot of shit.

But when she moved the slightest

toward him, the undeniable scent of *fire* wafting off of her, he knew.

She was no mirage.

The magnetic pull to her even now was strong, like gravity. He moved toward her, without conscious thought, as if it was the most natural thing in the world.

"My darling Clementine," he said, his lips twisting into a smile. "Is that really you or do I need to check myself into the psych ward?" he asked.

Cleo's eyes sparkled as the tiniest *laugh* escaped her throat.

"I just drove seven hours straight from home to here, so I can assure you, you are not the crazy one," she said, tucking some golden waves behind her ear.

Malcolm stood only inches away from her, reaching his hand out to brace himself on the car. The very real, cool, steel of the car was like a bucket of cold water to his system.

He felt as if he was overheating.

Cleo moved gently, inching her fingers toward his, her captivating golden-rimmed eyes the only thing that gave away her non-human abilities. All wolves had that same, golden tone, especially when they were about to shift.

Something about that knowledge both terrified and intrigued him. While their first introduction had been in the aftermath of Cleo's first shift, and he'd certainly seen enough wolf action since to last him a good while, just knowing that she could change at any moment, that she could become something much more vicious, much more dangerous, caused his blood to rush, his cock to twitch.

He knew it was wrong to want such things, to *favor* monsters. After all, his job, his life was about slaying creatures like the beautiful woman before him. But when Malcolm Crowley looked at his darling Clementine, he did not see a monster.

He only saw the woman he shared his darkest secrets with, the woman whose voice had pulled him back from the brink barely even a week ago, and so many other times.

The woman who soothed his nightmares.

Malcolm did not think twice as he set his hand on her hip, pulling her to him like a drowning man clings to a life raft.

"I beg to differ," he whispered as he kissed her.

Her lips against his were silky, smooth, and she tasted sweet, just like he remembered.

Cleo slid her hand up his neck, her palm resting on his cheek as she deepened their kiss, *whimpering* as her body melted against his.

Heat engulfed him as he brought his left hand to her hip, turning them both around. His hands coursed over her smooth, exposed skin, underneath her tank top and fringy kimono, fingers tangling in her wavy hair as she pulled him against her, her nails digging into his skin as she wrapped her leg around his hip. Her heartbeat was loud in his ears.

Wait, what...

Malcolm felt flush from head to toe, his cock throbbing as he settled against her hot form, making him groan as her tongue danced with his.

Mate.

The voice in his brain was not his. It was someone else, something else...

Something *animal.*

"Cleo," he spoke, trying to gather his bearings. His cock ached, his heart beating rapidly in his chest. His breath was labored as he tried to breathe. The overpowering scent of fire mingled with something else, something he couldn't quite place, but that smelled divine.

It smelled like...

Like the lake where he gazed at

constellations in the sky, like the crisp autumn air of Salem.

She smelled like *home.*

Cleo bristled beneath his body, her grip on his hair loosening, her leg sliding down between his as she gazed up at him with a look of wonder and awe, the gold dissolving into pure, glassy bluish- green.

"Malcolm," she breathed his name like a prayer. Like a wish, and somehow it settled the storms, the pain inside of his chest.

He ran his fingers through her hair slowly, taking in the sight of the magnificent creature in front of him.

When he gathered himself enough he was certain he wouldn't expire on the spot, when her breath had returned to normal, he spoke.

"What the fuck are you doing here?"

10

CLEO FOLLOWED MALCOLM into his room, her heart beating so loudly in her chest she thought it may leap out.

He was here, really *here*. In front of her, and the reality was overwhelming.

The whole way from Mahoning to Mayfield, she'd gone over her plan. Arrive in Mayfield, find Malcolm Crowley, and ask him to help her *hunt* down Rocky and rescue him. After all, hunting was what Malcolm did best. He'd made that more than clear.

If Alaric and Sawyer weren't going to take things seriously, someone had to.

And Cleo was certain Malcolm would take her offer seriously, if it meant he got to stake some vamps. The man had an unsettling joy when it came to killing the fanged nuisances.

Because they've taken everything from him, just as they've taken everything from me.

Mal sat on the edge of his bed, motioning for her to sit across from him.

"Have a seat in my office," he said with a smirk, and she did as asked, though she could not deny her wolf, which let out a petulant sigh.

She longed to be *near* him, but after the overwhelming *heat* she'd experienced against his car, when he'd turned them around, pinning her beneath him... his tongue in her mouth...

Cleo pressed her legs together as she set her hands in her lap. Perhaps some distance was good. She needed to be able to think clearly, to be able to speak properly.

"Thanks," she said, tucking some hair behind her ear as she took in the sight of him. Time had not affected him. He looked every bit as enticing and handsome as the moment she'd laid eyes on him at Howlers a year and a half ago. And for the moment, as she stared into his deep brown eyes, she felt safe.

Soothed.

Malcolm slid his knife out of his back pocket, and Cleo had the strangest feeling of déjà vu. She watched as he set it beside him.

"So you want to tell me why you decided to leave your tower, Princess? Or am I going to have to use more unsavory methods to get you talking?" he said the words tauntingly, and a part of Cleo wondered what sort of *unsavory* tactics Malcolm would use to get her to talk.

Her mind threatened to wander to that strange dream, and she pressed her thighs tighter together as the heat demanded to return, as moisture begged to blossom in her core once more.

Focus, Cleo!

"I wasn't honest with you earlier, on the phone," she said, biting her lip.

Malcolm leaned back on his palms, raising an eyebrow. "Does this have to do with your guard dogs?"

Cleo scoffed at his remark, but Malcolm only grinned. "They are not my *guard* dogs. They are my pack."

"Yeah, well, they must not be so great if you're sitting here in my hotel room."

"It's Rocky. The one you... hit. With your car." Cleo let out a sigh as Malcolm remained stone-faced.

"I'm not paying his vet bill."

Cleo wanted to be angry, but the sarcasm in Malcolm's tone only made her laugh. She shook her head.

"I'm afraid it's a bit more serious than that," she said, her smile fading.

Mal sat up straighter, leaning his arms over his black, jean-clad knees. His dark gaze captured hers, and in his dark brown eyes, she could see flecks of amber. They reminded her of the color of freshly turned leaves in the mountains.

It was in his gaze that she found the courage to come clean.

"The vampires attacked us. Rocky and I."

Malcolm nodded for her to continue.

Cleo wrung her hands together as she relayed the events to Malcolm, including Sawyer's words, and Alaric's order to stay put. When she was done, a tense silence formed between them, like a bridge. She almost thought he was going to tell her she was crazy, to leave, and that the pack was right.

But instead, Malcolm only got up, and planted himself beside her. He hooked his knuckle under her chin, forcing her to look at him. His face was inches away, and his thigh pressed against hers.

"I will fucking kill Sawyer Thorne," he said seriously. "If he hurt you."

Cleo melted under his gaze, the heat of his touch burning through her skin, just from his fingertips that traced her skin. The declaration of her mate fueled her desire, her heat, and she forgot how to speak.

In Malcolm Crowley's presence, there was nothing but *heat.*

"He didn't," she said softly, reaching out to run her fingers through Malcolm's silky hair.

"Good," Malcolm breathed out, his voice gravelly and dark. "Now, that that is settled, how do you expect to find Rocky, hmmm?" he asked, his voice still tinged with the remnants of anger.

"I was hoping that was where *you* could help me." She sighed, her gaze never leaving his. She did her best to look *pleading*, which was not difficult given her natural omega instincts.

"Mhmmm. Give me one good reason why I should help you find your little boy toy," he said.

Cleo smirked, pulling him closer, letting her fingernails trace his cheek.

"Because I asked nicely," she purred with sarcasm of her own.

Malcolm leaned into her as she settled on the bed. "Not nice enough, I'm afraid," he said with a sheepish grin, and he kissed her.

Cleo sank into the flimsy pillows as she kissed him back.

"You are a monster, Malcolm Crowley," she murmured, her voice tinged with the beginnings of laughter as he kissed her jaw.

"So I've been told," he said as he slipped his arm around her waist, settling himself between her warm thighs. "Give me another reason," he purred, his breath hot against her neck, baiting her wolf to the surface.

Cleo's eyes fluttered as heat ebbed throughout her. "Because there will be vamps for you to kill," she purred back, her voice thick with lust as his lips traveled to her collarbone.

He pulled at the edge of her kimono, exposing a bare shoulder, and she could feel his hardness against her warm, moist jeans.

"Now you're talking my language, baby," he said, biting at her flesh.

Cleo held onto him for dear life, her entire body thrumming with desire from just his lips on her skin.

"Is that a yes?" she asked, breathlessly. "You'll help me?"

Malcolm tore his lips away from her flushed skin, his dark gaze holding hers as they lay there, entangled together. His lips were slightly swollen from kissing her.

"Of course," he said seriously. "What, do you think I'm going to tell you *no* after you drove seven hours to ask me for *my* help? How could I tell you no, baby?"

Cleo bristled in his grasp, needing to feel him and his weight against her, pinning her, keeping her in place. For she feared she may drift up to the heavens if he did not hold her.

"You left once before, it was a risk."

The pain on his face broke her heart.

"I left because I had to, Cleo. You know that."

"I know, but it doesn't mean it didn't hurt."

Malcolm sighed, his forehead falling against hers. His breath on her skin was warm and smelled faintly of whiskey.

"I never wanted to hurt you," he whispered.

"I know," she whispered back. "But now you're here, and it hurts less."

"I know the feeling," he admitted, his

voice shaking as he brought his lips to hers.

Malcolm kissed her softly, smoothly at first, his tongue caressing hers.

Cleo sank back into the pillows once more, hooking her leg around his hip, drawing him closer.

"Malcolm..." She sighed, her body warm and buzzing like a livewire. Her wolf preened from his admission, from his touch, his kiss. She thrust her hips against him, seeking the friction of his hardness against her core.

"Yeah, baby?" he breathed, his voice heavy with lust, with hope.

"I need you," she whispered, every ounce of her being rattling with the truth of those words. She did need him. She needed her mate in every sense of the word, to soothe her storms, to solidify the bond of fate.

To quiet her heat.

A part of her worried her admission

would send him for the hills, make him regret his agreement. But instead, Malcolm slid his hand beneath her shirt, over her stomach and up, until his fingertips brushed the underwire of her bra, and he breathed into her mouth with vulnerability.

"I need you too, Cleo. I don't want to hurt anymore either."

His words were like an unsung prayer, and she crashed her lips against his once more, her fingertips making quick work of unbuckling his belt.

Malcolm pulled at the hem of her shirt, and she let him take it off, her breasts chilled from the sudden air. She slid his pants down over his ass, and he quickly unbuttoned her jeans, until they were both in nothing but their undergarments, skin flushed with heat.

Malcolm slid his fingers beneath the straps of her panties, his dark gaze causing her heart to catch in her throat.

"I don't want to hurt anymore either, Malcolm," she said as she took in the sight of him above her, the outline of his arousal a most enticing silhouette. Her nipples stiffened from the chill in the air as he gently slid her panties down, exposing her heated core, her slick thighs to him.

The overwhelming desire, the *need* for release, was maddening. She was burning up.

"Make it stop," she cried, her voice rimmed in lust. "Take the heat away, please..." she whimpered.

Malcolm knelt between her knees, his gaze holding her in place.

It wasn't the first time they'd been down to their underwear, and it certainly wasn't the first time they'd gotten close. But those moments were moments they'd *fought* against the mate bond. Those moments were peppered with blood, and fighting, and feelings neither of them understood.

Cleo looked at Malcolm as he gazed upon her like he had the night she'd woken up in his hotel bathtub so long ago.

Like she was everything he wanted, everything he needed too.

Malcolm leaned down once more, sliding his fingers inside of her, and the sudden pressure was like letting off a steam valve.

It was *a relief.*

Cleo let out a moan full of ecstasy.

"Is that better?" Malcolm quipped, that sarcastic tone still coloring his deep, sexy voice.

Cleo squirmed as he slid a second finger in, rocking her hips against him.

"Yes, but—"

"There's always a but with you," he bit.

Cleo smiled as his torturous fingers stroked her slowly. "Don't tell me *this* is all you think about doing when you think of me," she bit back.

Malcolm snickered, removing his fingers from her channel and leaving her feeling empty once more.

"Mhmm. Is this why you really drove from the mountains?" he taunted her, settling his free hand beneath her exposed cheeks. His grip as he *yanked* her, settling her ankles around his neck, was startling, but exciting.

Cleo gazed up at him, his playful tone baiting her.

"You think I would drive seven hours for a... booty call?" she teased.

But Malcolm would not respond to her with words.

Instead, he only ran his tongue along her sensitive clit, sucking it into his mouth and making her see stars.

"Oh fuck, Malcolm..." Cleo felt as if she could burst into a thousand pieces as his tongue probed her.

The familiar swirling in her abdomen

returned, her orgasm like a building cyclone.

She tightened her legs around his neck as his fingers returned to her entrance, his teeth nipping at her clit. He curled his fingers inside of her, and it was no use.

Her orgasm ripped through her, along with shifting energy. A strained whimper left her throat, mingling with euphoric ecstasy as she tightened her legs around his neck, feverishly grinding herself against his tongue.

She expected him to drop her, now that he'd taken care of her heat, and was surprised when he did no such thing.

In fact, he only seemed to double down on his strokes, his licks, and his groans.

Soon, Cleo found herself building once more as he feasted on her. Like an animal.

"Please," she strained, shifting energy vibrating within her as the heat culminated in her core again, a second coming brewing like a storm.

"Please what, baby?" he asked, his voice husky as he licked and sucked her toward another orgasm.

Words were difficult as she tried to focus on anything other than his talented tongue ministrations.

Cleo herself was no stranger to sex, but since coming into her omega heat, she had not given in to the pleasures of sex. Not until her wolf had decided its mate, until her instincts told her *who* to mate with.

The reality was both startling and full of relief, as she *knew* what she needed.

Or rather, *who* she needed.

Her words came of their own volition, spurred by desire and bond.

"I need more, I need... you, Malcolm. Please..." She writhed on the bed beneath him, a sheen of sweat covering her from head to toe. Her eyelashes fluttered as she watched him take leave of her pussy, which throbbed with need from the sudden emptiness, aching to be filled.

Malcolm stared back at her, wrestling his cock free.

Her gaze settled on his length, shadows falling from amber light across his abdomen, making the dark hair beneath his navel stand out prominently. His dark brown hair fell in his amber eyes, lips swollen from his fiery kisses, chest heaving as he caught his breath.

Fire tore through her veins, her blood, as she let out an audible gasp.

He truly was a hunter, and under his gaze, she knew she was *prey*. But her wolf did not feel threatened by such notions, no.

Her wolf pushed against her, salivating at the sight of their mate, naked, glistening with arousal before them.

Cleo moved back against the bed, slinking away playfully as Malcolm crawled over her, stalking her like a starving wolf, finding her lips once more, his tongue pushing into her mouth with a deep groan.

She could taste the sweetness of herself on his tongue, and responded with a groan of her own.

"Fucking hell, Cleo," he murmured her name against her lips as his right palm held her still. His eyelashes fluttered against her skin as he hooked her leg over his hip with his spare hand.

"You're going to be the death of me, baby," he whispered as he breached her entrance, slowly at first.

The heaviness of his breath was not lost on her, and she worried for a moment if he too was so riddled with overwhelming pleasure that he would not last. But all concerns dissipated as he kissed her once more, devouring the remnants of her sanity, washing away desire and leaving nothing but primal instinct in its wake.

As he settled into her, she felt a startling pressure, but it was not painful or worrying. It felt like she'd finally found a part of her that was missing, like she was finally *whole.*

A soft whimper left her throat as Malcolm sank himself into her, bottoming out, his hips flush with hers.

Cleo rocked against him, her hands exploring every inch of her mate. She kissed his mouth, his jaw, his collarbone. Her fangs pushed through, and she wanted to bite him. She grazed them along his neck, and he cursed.

"Christ, Cleo..." His voice was strained.

Cleo licked the spot on his neck, her fangs teased him and Malcolm picked up his pace, his thrusts coming faster, and harder than before.

A strange thought pervaded in her brain.

A thought that did not belong to her, but that only fed her desire more. Desire fueled between them as she nipped at his flesh again, eliciting another ecstatic curse from her hunter.

She settled her hands on his throat as he pulled her breasts out from their brasserie prison.

His fingers on his right hand tugged and pinched at her sensitive nub before he took it into his mouth.

Cleo gripped his hair tightly as she fell into his rhythm, rocking her body to meet his thrusts as they both chased one another's desire, her entire body aflame.

And then it happened.

Her vision went white as she came, calling out her mate's name in bliss.

Malcolm's curses echoed in the air and he stilled inside her.

Her insides clenched him tightly as he filled her, his fingernails digging into her flesh like claws holding her in place, with every twitch and pulse of his cock inside of her.

She kissed his sweet lips with fire, like a shooting star across the night sky. Malcolm devoured hers in response as she poured every ounce of herself, her truth into his mouth, her body melting into the bed beneath him.

Malcolm kissed her back with a heat of his own, his body collapsing against her as he slowed his thrusts, his fingers sliding through her damp hair, gently caressing her neck, and it was only then that Cleo realized she was no longer burning up.

She tightened her hold around his hips as the tremors of release rang through her, through him, whilst they both lost themselves and found themselves all over again in their kiss, their bodies melding together as one.

When they broke apart, the only sound that could be heard was their heavy breaths. Malcolm's breath shook as he continued to empty himself inside of her.

His dark eyes lightened, shimmering with a mixture of emotion as he gazed down at her, his chest heaving with breath.

Panic and anxiety laced through her, but it was not her own.

Cleo ran her hands up his chest, over his shoulder, her palm settling over his fast-beating heart.

"The heat is gone," she murmured against his lips, the euphoria of their bond emanating through her.

Somewhere in the corners of her brain, she could have sworn she heard his voice, echoing, cursing, overwhelmed by the magnitude of *feeling*.

Of love.

Perhaps she truly was spent from climbing such great heights.

Malcolm slowly removed himself from her body, letting out a shaky sigh.

Oh shit, the voice rang in her head. *I didn't mean to... fuck.*

Malcolm rolled off of her, but his hold

did not relent, and she could feel the faint panic lacing her own euphoria.

The heat was *gone.*

Because she and her wolf had *chosen* their mate, and they had simply completed the bond.

They'd *mated,* in the truest sense of the word. Which was why she could hear him, his panic, in her brain. It was why she could feel his anxiety threatening to pull him under.

The realization was as beautiful as it was harrowing.

Delirious with ecstasy, she pulled him closer, and he buried his face into her hair, his labored breaths laced with anxiety.

"Fuck, Cleo, I—"

"It's okay," she sighed, trying to find the words. "Everything is going to be okay," she said, pulling him closer.

Malcolm tightened his grip on her, breathing deep against her.

She ran her fingernails up and down his back as he twisted his leg through hers. Cleo curled closer to his chest, burrowing into the comforter.

"Now that you're here, with me. Now that we're mates." Her voice was tinged with the oncoming of sleep, and her muscles felt like jello.

Somewhere in her consciousness, she was aware of the remnants of their bond slipping down her thighs. Her wolf preened with the knowledge, ecstatic that their mate had *accepted* them in the most instinctual, primal way.

Cleo's entire body melted against the hold of *her mate.*

Malcolm buried his face in her hair, his breath shaky as his grip on her tightened like he was afraid to let go of her.

It only soothed her wolf, confirming that despite his thoughts, despite his *fear*, he needed her too, to soothe the storm raging inside of him.

"It's okay," she purred, clutching him to her body like a second skin. "I'm not going anywhere," she whispered.

Malcolm let out a shaky breath. "Promise?"

They held onto one another for only a small moment, but it felt like eternity.

"I promise," she whispered back. The warmth from their bodies pressed together was a different kind of heat, but one Cleo never wanted to fade.

"Mate," she purred as she settled into his warmth.

Malcolm's lips left soft kisses in her hair, and she could feel the faintest touch of moisture on her forehead.

Malcolm sighed as he curled himself around her protectively.

"Yeah... mate," he whispered shakily as slumber dragged them both under.

11

ALARIC SAT DOWN at the kitchen table with a fresh cup of coffee. Despite his early bedtime, he felt nearly exhausted. Though a part of him knew it was because he hadn't slept well. Not after that feverish dream in which Cleo had jumped on him, practically ripping his clothes off.

He sighed as the memory made his cock twitch, of the contented omega whimpers and her blinding hot heat as she touched him, rubbing herself against him with need.

He growled, knowing that it was just a dream. Which was why in the space of his own consciousness he could say the things he could not aloud.

Why not me?

The dream itself had awakened him, his knot so swollen it was painful.

So naturally, he'd done the only thing he could do to calm his alpha instinct, and it didn't take much.

Afterward, he'd fallen back into a sound sleep, but he did not dream again.

Though he wished he had, if only to erase the pain of the perfect one that haunted his memory now.

He sipped his coffee as he cued up his surveillance footage, checking on the pack back home, or at least that was what he told himself. He noticed Rocky's car was missing from the garage as he cycled through, which he thought quite odd.

He cycled back the footage, watching

and waiting to see if his brother had taken Rocky's car as he suspected, and nearly spilled his coffee when he noticed it was *not* Sawyer who had gotten into the car.

"Fucking hell," he cursed, his blood heating at the sight. He immediately queued up his touchpad, speed dialing Sawyer.

"What the fuck, Alaric, it's like six am, man," Sawyer drawled groggily on the other end.

"Where is she?" he grit through his teeth.

"Who?" Sawyer yawned.

"Clementine. Where the fuck is she, Sawyer?"

His brother grumbled on the other end of the phone, "Locked up in her fucking room, your majesty, where else would she be?"

Alaric laughed, but it was not an amused laugh. "You fucking idiot, she is most certainly *not* in her room."

"What?"

"She left the house, at seven thirty last night. You going to tell me you didn't know?"

Silence befell his brother on the other end. "That's impossible, I—"

"She was last seen in the hot tub at five thirty."

Another strained silence embroiled his blood.

"How would you know where she was at five thirty..."

"Because apparently I can not trust my *beta* to keep tabs on my omega."

Sawyer growled on the other end.

"She isn't *yours* yet, Alaric. She hasn't made a decision." Alaric did not miss the tone of possessiveness in his brother's voice, or the way it called his own wolf to the surface.

Shifting energy coursed through him, and he grit his teeth together.

Sawyer was a *threat.* A threat to his precious omega, a threat to his dominance, and a threat to his wolf.

"Which is precisely why she should not be gallivanting off to God knows where in *heat.*"

Sawyer cursed on the other line, and he could hear the garage door opening.

"Fuck, she took Rocky's car."

Alaric grinned, but it was not happy. It only solidified his understanding that his brother had fucked up royally.

"Go to her room," he ordered.

"What, why?"

Alaric slammed his fist down on the table. "Do not question your alpha!"

Sawyer bristled. "All right, all right. Jesus."

Alaric could hear his hurried footsteps following the closing of the garage. He focused on his breath until he heard the soft sound of a door opening.

"I need you to tell me if she left her

phone."

Sawyer grumbled something unintelligible as he tore through Cleo's belongings.

"I don't see it anywhere," he muttered.

Alaric closed his eyes, breathing a sigh of relief. A part of him relished that he should call her. Ask her what happened, why she'd left. Perhaps if he could just talk to her... maybe they could sort out whatever had gotten into her lately. But the alpha in him would not settle for *talking.*

She needed to be protected. She needed to listen.

It wasn't natural for omegas to deny their submissive nature, as Cleo had for the past year and a half, and she was not strong like he or Sawyer. If the vampires got a whiff of her scent...

"We will settle this matter when I return, Sawyer, but do not think you are off the hook. I trusted you to keep her safe, and you let her drive right off the fucking property."

"Alaric, I—"

He would not hear Sawyer's pleas. Instead, he queued up the tracking device he'd placed on Cleo's phone, for emergencies such as this.

It took a long, agonizing moment before the little green dot blinked with a location.

The Econo Lodge in Mayfield, Kentucky. Only ten miles away.

His blood ran cold.

She was here, in Kentucky...

Had she come for him?

For his aid?

Alaric did not have time to think, he only acted as he got up from his chair, sliding the phone in his pocket as he reached for the keys to his BMW. Once inside, the radio blasted with the sounds of Foreigner, crooning on about being hot-blooded. He sped off from the ostentatious guest cabin, past the Mayfield motel, toward his destination.

Toward *her.*

He did not care for speed limits, flying down the highway as his blood boiled with anger, frustration, and worry.

He hoped when he found her she would be all right. That she would be safe.

He flung his car into an open parking spot, not even caring that he was taking up two spaces. Storming his way toward the room, he followed the green dot on the screen until he came to the door marked thirteen.

He knew he should have knocked, but he couldn't risk doing so if she was in trouble. So he kicked the door open, announcing his arrival with a resounding "Cleo!" that echoed off the walls.

All the air left his lungs as the smell of sex assaulted him.

And not just sex, but...

Omega heat.

Sweet, hot, heat, and seed.

Shifting energy coursed through him as he laid his eyes on Cleo, fury bubbling like an overflowing laundry tub.

There she lay, with her legs wrapped around a bare-assed *Malcolm Crowley,* both of them locked together, kissing, moaning, and writhing against one another in pure heat.

Alaric let out a furious growl as Malcolm cursed. Cleo cried out in an ecstatic heat filled haze, and his vision went red.

He grabbed the hunter by the back of his neck, hauling him off of Cleo as he roared, throwing him to the ground like he was nothing more than a rag doll.

"Fuck!" Mal cursed, scrambling to his feet, covering himself.

The scent of his release was prevalent in the air, and it only made Alaric more furious as realization struck him.

No, no...no...

I'm too late.

"Alaric, stop! Don't hurt him!" Cleo called, wrapping herself in a sheet.

"You..." Alaric threw a punch to Mal's face, which was quickly reciprocated.

"The fuck is your problem!" Mal bit as his fist connected with Alaric's jaw.

Alaric slid his hand around Malcolm's throat, throttling him.

"Asshole.," Mal spit at him through his strained choking. Malcolm kicked his legs as Alaric tightened his grip, watching as the hunter's face turned a lovely shade of pink.

"Get in the fucking car, Cleo, now!" he roared at her. Pain laced through him, giving way to anger, fury, and an innate desire to *kill.*

His wolf was hungry for blood, but the scent of Cleo's arousal warred with his animal instinct as she came closer. He glanced at her, clutching the beige sheets to her chest, her lips still swollen from kissing Malcolm.

The sight enraged him, but was also strangely arousing to him. His cock twitched as he bared his teeth, his fangs aching to tear out Malcom's neck for what he'd done.

What he's taken from me.

He wanted to destroy the man who'd taken what belonged to him, but he also wanted nothing more than to throw Cleo down onto the bed and dominantly breed his omega until he'd erased all remnants of Malcolm from her body, mind, and soul.

Despite the fact humans could not breed omegas.

Still, the ever prevalent desire to assert his dominance to this pain in the ass hunter was a force all its own.

"Put him down!" she roared, and it was like déjà vu. Her eyes glistened with shifting energy.

They'd been here before, almost two

years ago, when she'd gone into heat that fabled night.

Malcolm kicked his way out, his foot connecting with Alaric's ribs, making him gasp.

He dropped the hunter to the floor.

Malcolm raised a blade over his head, as Cleo yelled once more.

"*Both* of you fucking knock it off!" she roared, and Alaric stopped at the levity of her *roar*.

It was not the submissive cry an omega usually carried, no.

This was a roar of *command.*

Like an alpha.

It was enough to stop them both dead in their tracks. His gaze settled on her as he caught his breath. Her hair was free of her normal braid, long waves cascading over her exposed shoulder, her normal ocean colored eyes now full gold. Her beast was just below the surface, and he could see her fangs glistening.

His wolf wanted to challenge her, and his cock throbbed in his jeans from the adrenaline, from her scent.

The words from his dream reverberated in his head as she walked toward *Malcolm.*

Protecting him. Her *mate.*

"Get. In. The. Car. Now," he said, trying to hold onto whatever slivers of power and sanity he still had.

Because the sight of Malcolm next to her was causing a war within him, and he could not process anything but *her.*

She'd chosen a mate, it would seem, and that made the ache in his chest tear further.

It wasn't him, or Rocky. It was a *hunter.*

"She's not going anywhere with you, *Al,*" Malcolm's voice bit as he stepped in front of Cleo. Malcolm said his name like a curse.

"Malcolm, stop," Cleo said softly,

tugging his arm down. Cleo's gaze met Alaric's.

"Get in the car right now, so help me God, Cleo, or I will drag you there myself," Alaric said, his voice shaking. He had never felt so powerless in all his life, and he could not let them see him falter. He could not let Cleo see how much her choice hurt him.

"Over my dead body," Malcolm bit, his hand wrapped tighter around a rather sinister looking knife.

Alaric rose to his feet, standing tall over both of them. "That can be arranged," he said, showing his teeth.

He wanted nothing more than to sink his fangs into this pain in the ass mortal, but it was the look on Cleo's face that kept him from doing so.

If Malcolm was truly her mate, he could not break her bond. Doing so would cause her an immense amount of pain, worse than the pain of her rejection.

Cleo set her hand on his biceps, the touch sending sparks through his entire being, soothing the hurt, the pain that ebbed through him.

"I'll go with you," she said, her lips still swollen and pink from *kissing* Malcolm.

Her words placated his ache, if only a fraction. He wished they were true. That she would come with him, leave this mortal nuisance behind.

"What?" Malcolm bit as Alaric let out a sigh of relief.

He knew what she would say. Her heart belonged to her mate, and she would go nowhere without him.

"Under one condition," she said as she stepped away from Mal, clutching the covers to her. She took small steps forward until she was inches away from Alaric.

This close he could smell the hunter's *seed* all over her, and it made him want to howl in pain.

How could she do this?

To me?

To the pack?

He focused on steadying his breath, on trying not to shift. All he wanted was to run, to howl in agony that he had been rejected, that he was not worthy of being an alpha if he had no omega to serve. No one to love and cherish, and bond with, to bear children with.

He had lost her.

But still, he ached to give his omega everything she wanted. Even if it wasn't him.

He'd promised her that the first night he'd pulled her from Malcolm Crowley's bed, hadn't he?

"Anything," he said, tears begging to be set free. But Alaric Thorne would not cry in front of her, or her mate. But it did not make the words Clementine breathed hurt less.

"He comes too," she breathed, her tone

solid and unwavering.

Alaric could not fight the desire to touch her. He let his fingertip trace her jaw, feeling the soft skin beneath him, taking in the sight of her flushed lips, her disheveled sex hair.

Her vibrant, deep eyes. They were filled with hope, with a glimmer of something he couldn't quite place.

She nudged her cheek against his palm, her eyes fluttering closed as a soft whine escaped her throat. He dropped his hand, if only because the sound went straight to his cock, then to his heart. His broken, battered heart.

"Fine," he growled, turning his back on both of them.

"Get dressed," he ordered, his gaze flashing to Malcolm, who was putting his shirt on, wearing a bemused look.

"We have much to discuss."

12

ROCKY WAS THANKFUL for the sun, if only because it meant most of the vampires were subdued, sleeping off the daytime until sunset.

Only Daywalkers guarded the abandoned house they'd brought him to.

But even with the low number of guards, Rocky knew he was no match for them. He hadn't been a match for them at the Thorne estate, and he was certainly no match for them now, in his current state.

He pulled his good knee up to his chest, while resting his bad one. Though he hadn't remembered dressing himself in the aftermath of his shift, and he felt a strange mortification for whoever had clothed his nakedness.

He rolled up the baggy gray sweatpants, noting the bite marks from the various vamps were still pink and swollen, the skin still tender where they bit him.

Vampire venom was toxic to werewolves, and he'd sustained more than enough to kill a werewolf.

So why had he not perished?

He leaned against the wall, rubbing his sore leg and trying to massage the tight muscles. He was as good as dead if he could barely move.

"You made it through the night, they must have some use for you," a soft, sweet voice spoke.

Rocky turned to look at a woman who

was rising from one of the five beds in the room, her sullen blue eyes and pale skin shimmering in the stream of light peering in through the curtains. Long, messy golden waves framed her round face. Coupled with her pale skin, she looked like an angel. But Rocky knew she was anything but.

His heart lurched as his gaze fell to her swollen belly, her scent wafting toward him.

Omega.

He swallowed as his wolf stood at attention, his mind wandering to another omega who was not present.

One he feared he would never see again.

"Who... who are you?" he asked warily.

"My name is Ashley," she said sweetly as the other prisoners awakened from their beds. "Ashley Mayfield."

The other inhabitants were much smaller than Ashley, the biggest looking to be about ten or eleven.

Kids.

They have kids trapped here... why?

What the hell do vamps want with kids?

Ashley rubbed her pregnant belly, smiling. "And this here is Petunia," she said.

"How long..."

"Eight months. I've been here for about a month and ten days."

"Where is here?" he asked.

One of the children swung their legs over the edge of their small bed. She had dark brown hair, and vibrant red eyes.

"Here is home," she said apathetically, her voice tinged with the darkness of trauma.

She was a child, but she did not speak like one.

Rocky's heart broke for the terrors that must have aided such an adult voice.

"I think we're in Kentucky, but I lost

track," another voice, a smaller, younger male voice, echoed from behind the red-eyed little girl. "Places blur together sometimes," he said sadly.

"I'm Emma, and that's Daniel," the little brown-haired girl said, pointing to the boy behind her, then to the two beds across from her. "That's Taryn."

A smaller girl, with bright red hair and freckles waved, but did not speak as Emma continued. "And that..." She pointed to a small room with a closed door. "That's where Henry sleeps. But we don't see him very much."

"Who's Henry?" Rocky asked, taking in the sight of his new roommates.

Ashley climbed out of bed, and he could see her in her entirety. Her honey-colored hair and blue eyes reminded him of *Cleo*.

The thought of her name caused the onslaught of memory to push forth.

It was only yesterday they'd been

together, when she'd *chosen* him.

He could still remember the taste of her kiss.

And that dream...

He touched his lips, remembering the beautiful dream where Cleo had come for him.

She'd called him her mate.

But it was only a dream, and one that could not come true, if his or her life depended on it.

"Henry is why they brought me here, I'm pretty sure," she said as she stretched, heading over to the other side of the room where there was a dressing partition.

Rocky watched as she made her way, her nightgown catching the light to illuminate her silhouette underneath, before she disappeared behind the partition.

His body ached, and he was tired, despite the fact he'd been out for hours, that much he knew. The last he saw sunlight was yesterday, before the rain came.

"What do they want?" he asked, looking from the partition to the children who were now out of bed, and making their way across the room.

He watched as Daniel followed Emma toward the door. Toward where he sat.

"When I came, Henry was quite malnourished. Latched onto me right away," she said as Emma shot Rocky a wary look. She stopped in front of him, wrinkling her nose.

"Ashley, this one smells," she said bitterly.

Taryn giggled as she ran to Daniel, who was also watching him skeptically.

Rocky's eyebrows shot up as he glanced between them. They reminded him of his younger cousins, who lived at the Thorne Estate.

"I beg your pardon?"

Ashley *laughed,* and the sound was like windchimes.

It reminded him of the way Cleo laughed.

His heart broke as he remembered the look on her face when he'd been bitten. When his brother had carried her to safety.

I couldn't keep her safe.

The one thing I was born to do.

Because I'm broken.

He fought back tears, turning away from the young girl's impenetrable crimson glare.

"That's because he's like me, sweet pea. He's a full-blooded werewolf."

Emma twisted her lips, raising her eyebrow.

"Whattaya think Daddy wants with him?"

Daddy?

Who the hell was this kid's father?

Surely it was not the man who'd taken

him.

"Emma here is part werewolf. Part vampire. A miracle in her own right."

Rocky's eyes widened as he took in the sight of the little girl.

A hybrid?

He'd never heard of such things.

As far as he had been told, werewolves were only capable of copulating with their own kind. It wasn't unheard of that vampires could mate with humans, though the results of those unions were far and in between, to his understanding.

But a vampire and a werewolf...

God, what was next, werewolves and *mortals?*

Ashley came out from behind her partition, pulling his attention. She was dressed in a much more form fitting dress. The black fabric bunched at the waist, drawing attention to her ample cleavage and pronounced bump.

She tousled her hair loose, smoothing

it over her shoulder. In the sunlight she looked almost natural, healthy even.

But her eyes were glassy, the bags underneath them telling a much different tale as she came to stand beside Rocky. She also had several bite marks bruising her slender neck.

"I'm not sure, Emma. You know we shouldn't question things," she said, setting her hand on the girl's shoulder.

Emma scoffed as she headed toward the door where Daniel and Taryn stood waiting.

Rocky looked Daniel over, noticing he had the same red eyes, and that they looked strangely... alike.

Like siblings.

The thought made his heart ache, as he thought about his own. Alaric would kill him for putting Cleo in danger, if he did not kill the vampires who'd taken him first.

"Be careful, and stay away from—"

"I know, I know..." Emma drawled, grabbing Daniel by the hand, and they disappeared around the corner, Taryn chasing after them.

"Are you injured badly..."

"Rocky," he said, licking his dry lips. "And yes, but to be fair I was busted before I got here," he said through his teeth as he tried to stand.

Ashley knelt beside him, placing her hand on his thigh. He jolted from the contact, surprised.

"Can I take a look?" she asked gently, her touch on his leg soft, soothing. "It looked pretty rough last night."

Rocky flushed with embarrassment as he realized this omega was the one responsible for his care, his clothing. The realization made him feel vulnerable. Though he could feel the sweetness of her omega nature like an echo. It was nurturing.

Up close like this, the light caught

fragments of gold in her eyes as the sun lit her up like a halo.

His wolf trusted this woman, this Ashley, and therefore, he nodded.

"Sure," he said shakily. She poked at his flesh, and he sucked in a breath.

"Are you in a lot of pain?" she asked.

He shook his head. "Not as bad as it was," he lied, sliding his shirt up to reveal the peppering of bites all across his chest and abdomen. "But these ones itch like a bitch."

Ashley's eyebrows knit together in consternation. "You shouldn't even be alive with that many bites," she murmured, her fingers tracing over his chest.

He twinged in pain as her fingertips smoothed over his skin. His wolf twisted them away from her. The touch felt *wrong*.

It did not belong to his *mate*.

"You're bonded," she whispered in awe.

"What?" he asked as he pulled his shirt back down, and she pulled her hand back.

"I can sense it. Do you... have a mate, Rocky?"

He looked away, at the expansive room and the five beds in the room, only one made, trying to focus on anything but Ashley's blue eyes that reminded him of Cleo.

"Yes," he said as images flooded his brain, along with Cleo's words.

"Are you rejecting me?" she asked, her eyes full of pain.

"God, no," he told her.

And then he had kissed her. He'd given in for the fraction of a moment, and the vampires came.

He'd dreamt of her after passing out from the venom, the pain.

In his dreams, she came to him, to rescue him, to *mate* with him.

His cock twitched at the very thought

of such things. He'd never even come close to mating with anyone before, though he knew one day he would. Yet the thought of doing so caused a fresh bloom of concern and excitement to form in his stomach.

What if he was terrible at it?

What if the experience was unpleasant for Cleo because he didn't know what he was doing?

His cheeks flushed with embarrassment as his fears and insecurities resurfaced.

His brothers both had reputations of being expert lovers, even if it was talked about in whispers in the community, but their prowess came from their rank as well as their confidence.

Rocky was not a beta, or an alpha.

He was simply just... Rocky.

Another wolf in the pack.

No, he did not know the first thing about mating, about having a mate.

He'd already failed miserably to protect Cleo from harm, how could he *please* her?

If he ever made it out of his prison.

Ashley pulled his face back to her, her sapphire eyes pleading with him. Her scent was overpowering, and wolfish instinct to placate and care for this *omega* mingled with the thought of his own omega, swollen with *his* child.

Despite his insecurity, his lack of confidence, Rocky could not deny the instinct within him to *breed* was strong. To give his pack and Cleo what they deserved.

The thoughts, as well as the emotion and the sudden arousal, were too much for him, and so he fought to bury them down, deep in the confines of his soul where he'd kept his love for Cleo for the last year and a half.

"Can you stand?" Ashley asked, and he swallowed harshly.

"I haven't tried... yet," he said as she

offered him her hand.

"You need to try," she coaxed. "If you can stand, I can get you cleaned up a little better."

Rocky did not wish to obey this omega, but he had no choice. She was right. He could not very well lie on this dirty wooden floor and wither away.

Not if he wanted to see Cleo again.

The very thought of seeing her again gave him strength he didn't know he possessed, as the images of his dream resurfaced.

Of Cleo pinning him to the floor, grinding herself against him, her lips biting at him as she whimpered above him.

Of her words, breathed against his skin.

"You are mine," she whispered.

Those three little words were all the reminder he needed, to remember he needed to *fight*. He needed to fight to come home to Clementine Srirocco, if it was the last thing he did.

He nodded as he pushed himself up. The pain was blinding and he growled as Ashley wrapped her arm around his waist. In the distance, a baby wailed.

"Come on now, almost there," she cooed as he finally put weight on his leg.

It hurt something fierce, but he was upright.

"That's Henry," she chuckled as she led him over to an unmade bed. The distance from the floor to the bed was not far, but Rocky was relieved when his rear found the soft mattress. He was quite winded and sore.

Ashley tucked some strands of hair behind her ear as she gave him a warm smile. Without the halo lighting of the sun, he could see the wet spots forming on her breasts, and he blushed with embarrassment.

Though he'd aided several of his family members with the deliveries and births of their children, there was something strangely *intimate* about being privy to such things.

"Sit tight. I'll feed Henry and then we can get you cleaned up a bit. Emma and Daniel should have something to report soon enough," she said as she headed for the closed door, where the wailing seemed to be coming from.

Ashley opened the door, and did not close it. From where he sat he could see her in the doorway. Within seconds he could see the silhouette of a child latching onto her, the wails softening to light sounds of sucking.

Rocky fell back against the bed, his body heating as a form of sweat formed on his skin.

"Emma said *Daddy*. Is her dad—"

"He is a hybrid, like her. But she is of no interest to him. She is marked, just as the rest of us are. As you are now."

Rocky gave Ashley and Henry privacy

as he stared at the ceiling.

"And Daniel?"

"Daniel is her half-brother. He's part Djinn," she called out.

"Someone's not getting Dad of the Year," Rocky chimed.

Ashley sauntered over, clutching Henry as she ran her hand up and down his back.

The sight made Rocky miss his younger cousins. While his brothers were busy *ruling* the pack, alongside his retired parents, being an average wolf had its advantages. It meant he got to spend much more time with his rather large and extended family.

Neither Alaric or Sawyer seemed remotely interested in the births of their pack, nor did they show any inkling of interest in *childish* activities like decorating cookies or playing Marco Polo in the pool, or even hide and seek in the oversized estate.

But Rocky loved spending time with his young cousins, almost as much as he loved spending time with Cleo, who tried her best to be a part of the festivities, despite her own feelings.

And he'd cherished those moments spent alongside his family, with her by his side, even if they were only pretending for the sake of her truth. They were not mates, but to the Thorne's they played pretend.

And in those small, slivers of moments, Rocky wished it could be true.

That she could be *his.*

His mate.

Then she'd done the unthinkable. She'd made her choice *known* the moment she asked if he was *rejecting her.* She'd chosen him, and he'd failed her.

"How old is he?" he asked cautiously, forcing the anxiety deep below. His wolf whined and chortled in pain, knowing he'd fucked up.

Ashley bounced Henry around as she smiled. "Under a year. I don't know what happened to his mother. All I knew was, when I got here... it was needed."

"You said we're all *marked.* What did you mean?" he asked.

"How much do you know about vampire bloodlines?" she asked quietly.

"I know that sometimes they can breed with humans, but that's rare."

Ashley frowned. "Breeding among themselves is even rarer. At least nowadays."

"What does that have to do with us?" he asked skeptically, feeling as if the picture was on the edge of his grasp, but somehow out of reach.

"Queens need heirs to keep the bloodlines going. Just like we omegas need offspring to keep our packs strong."

Rocky's blood chilled at her words. "They brought you in to take care of Henry, you said?" He swallowed harshly.

Ashley nodded. "Well, that, and the obvious," she said softly as she shifted Henry in her arms, removing her long hair from the side of her neck where fresh bites stood out, pink and red against her pale skin.

Rocky's heart broke as he laid his eyes on the bright red puncture marks. They looked fresh.

Of course, that explains her coloring, her eyes...

They're draining her.

"And the kids? What do they want with the kids?"

Ashley's eyes glazed with sadness. "To control them of course. Can you imagine what they could do, if left unwatched?" she said, her voice shaking. "Emma is small, but she is powerful. I've seen her take down a newborn vamp. Just because she's *hungry*."

Rocky felt as if he was going to be sick.

"And... Daniel... Djinn can manipulate

the mind, and vampires have thrall... his powers are just starting to come to light. There's no telling what he will be capable of."

"And Taryn?"

Ashley frowned. "Mortal, I'm afraid. But, she has witch blood in her. Her powers are not as strong as Emma or Daniel's. It drains her. I'm not sure what use she is to them, but I do not question it. As long as she lives, that is a victory in my book."

Rocky's body heated once more with fire, his leg throbbing.

"And me... what do you think they want with a injured werewolf? Why wouldn't they just kill me?"

Ashley bounced Henry back and forth, and the tiny child turned to look toward Rocky, dark eyes rimmed in red. He could see the beginnings of fangs in the child's gums. He surmised like the others, he was some sort of vampiric hybrid as well.

"You're bound," she said, sniffing the air.

"Freshly bound, which means you haven't solidified your bond yet. Your omega will not be able to keep away."

Rocky's jaw tensed as he remembered his dream, remembering Cleo who had come to save him. He'd told her to stay away, worried that his rescue would only cause her more danger.

Because he knew... somewhere deep down his wolf and he knew that he was nothing more than bait.

"Your blood will be potent, what with all the mate bond chemicals flowing through you," she said, her own eyes glistening with golden shimmer.

The unmistakable scent of *desire* perfumed the air as she pressed her lips together.

Rocky's breath was labored as he tried to process the information from all sides.

Including the sudden arousal cresting

between his legs.

"Mate bond chemicals?" he asked, trying to focus.

Ashley's scent was thick like a fog, despite her keeping her distance.

"When did you accept? The bond, I mean."

Rocky's eyebrows furrowed. Though he hadn't rejected her, because he would have rather *died* by vampires a thousand times than deny Cleo access to his heart, he hadn't said the magical words.

You are mine.

Her dreamy voice echoed in his brain.

"I—yesterday, I think."

"And you didn't seal the deal, correct?" she asked, stepping back toward the door as Henry laid his head on her shoulder.

Crimson eyes pinned him to the bed where he sat, feeling as if he would combust into flame. A sheen of sweat broke out on his forehead.

"No," he shook his head, his cheeks

flushing with warmth. "I, uh... haven't mated with *anyone*. Like ever..."

Ashley's voice carried from Henry's room. "The mate bond chemicals are the most potent for the first few days. They drive your instinct to breed. If you don't solidify the bond, it can be... harmful. To the both of you."

"How harmful?" he asked as he adjusted his erection, cursing under his breath, waiting for the flames to die down.

He closed his eyes as the memory of Cleo filled his vision, and he held onto it. Onto the thought, the *hope* he would find a way out of this prison, back to *his* mate. No matter what obstacles lay in their way, he knew it would be worth it.

Cleo was worth it.

Ashley's words carried a weight that was heavier than anything he'd ever heard.

"If you don't mate with your bonded Omega before the full moon in six days,

Rocky, you will die."

13

AS MALCOLM SAT in the passenger seat of Alaric's car, he was certain of two things. One, was that he'd had a true psychotic break, and lost his damn mind, and the second was that he was without a doubt, absolutely certifiably insane.

Because despite the fact the lumbering alpha had thrown him around to the point the muscles he didn't even know he had, were sore, it wasn't enough to stop him from helping his... girlfriend?

Girlfriend didn't seem like the right

word, but the word that echoed in his brain, the *m* word he'd uttered last night—or rather at two thirty in the morning—made him skittish.

Sitting next to a pissed off alpha werewolf was much less frightening than admitting to himself that the bond he felt with the omega werewolf in the backseat of the alpha boyfriend's car was the truest *love* he'd ever felt.

It wouldn't be the first time.

When Alaric pulled past the Mayfield Hotel onto a large hill, into the driveway of a rather large ,rustic-looking cabin, Mal did not blink.

"You know, usually I like to be taken out to dinner first before my date takes me home, but for you, Al, I'll make an exception," he quipped.

Alaric shot him an angry glare, his amber eyes rippling with golden shifter energy.

"This is not a pleasure call, Malcolm,

so do not get cocky. The only reason I have not ripped your dick clean off your body is because *Cleo* would be upset."

"Alaric!" Cleo bit as Alaric opened the door, heading to open Cleo's.

Though as timing and luck would have it, she opened the door, smacking Alaric right in the—

"Son of a bitch!" he growled as he grabbed his groin.

Mal snickered as he shook his head, pulling Cleo toward him. "Karma is a bitch, ain't it, Al?"

Cleo smacked him in the chest. He turned to look at her with a soft, pleading expression.

"What?"

Cleo pushed away from him as she sauntered over to Alaric. "I'm sorry, Alaric. Are you all right?" she asked, giving Mal her back.

A strange ripple of *rejection* flowed through him as a thought entered his brain.

I'm not some prize to be won.

Mal blinked, looking back and forth. "What did you say?" he asked as Alaric stood up straighter, focusing on Cleo.

"I didn't say anything," she said.

"I'm fine, Cleo. Now come on, let's go inside where we can *discuss* what you have done."

He brushed her off, leaving them both in his wake.

Cleo's voice escalated. "Excuse me?" she said as she chased after him.

Mal chased after her. "Yes, you did, you said 'I'm not some prize to be won,'" he bit. "I heard you."

He grabbed Cleo by the arm as Alaric opened the door. She shook him off, but the heat that bloomed between their skin was like literal sparks. His cock awakened from the jolt of electricity, and he felt strangely *hot*.

"I said no such thing," she said as her

pupils dilated.

Alaric grabbed her, moving her out of Malcolm's reach. He growled as he shot Malcolm an angry glare.

"You, over there," he said as he pointed to a large fireplace. On the opposite side of the room.

"What the fuck, Al? We're all adults here, we can—"

A sweet, thick scent bloomed in the air that made his mouth water. It smelled like *home.*

Like crisp fall leaves and sunsets in Salem.

"Stay the fuck over there," Alaric growled. "For five fucking minutes, keep your dick to yourself."

Malcolm flicked the werewolf off as he sauntered off cockily to the fireplace.

"Fine. Better, Daddy?"

Alaric let out another growl, and Malcolm watched as he *gently* sat Cleo down on the kitchen chair.

"I am not your *Daddy*. And you will show me the respect I deserve. Lest you have a death wish, hunter."

Malcolm only rolled his eyes as he watched Cleo smack the lumbering alpha.

"He is not the enemy, Alaric."

Alaric gazed upon Cleo with warmth and adoration, and Mal did not miss it.

A thought pervaded in his brain, he was certain was not his.

Why does he have to be so difficult...

"Which one of us are you talking about?" Malcolm asked, pulling both their attention.

"What?" Cleo asked, her eyes widening in surprise.

"I'm not—"

"You can hear her, can't you?" Alaric asked, his tone serious.

Malcolm felt nervous under the steely alpha's gaze. He shifted his weight.

"That is crazy. I'm not telepathic. I'm a lot of things, but psychic ain't one of them."

Alaric crossed his arms, his gaze holding Malcolm in his place.

"It's a side effect of mate bonds. You'd know that, if you knew *anything* about our kind."

Cleo's gaze fell upon him, heating him like a flame. She moved slightly, but Alaric held his arm out, barring her from doing so.

"This...." he said, looking down at her. "This will need to be dealt with, but for the time being we have bigger issues. Such as your safety, Cleo. What were you thinking?"

Cleo pushed his arm down as she got up, standing up against Alaric like she was much taller than five foot something.

"I did what you couldn't do," she bit.

Mal's lips twisted into a smirk.

That's my girl.

Cleo's cheeks flushed scarlet as she turned with wide eyes to Mal, and he understood she had heard him.

Oh, shit.

I didn't know you could hear me...

Cleo pursed her lips as Alaric cried out, "Excuse me? Who do you think you are talking to, Clementine? You might get away with talking to my brothers like this, but I am your *alpha*. You are supposed to obey me."

Cleo crossed her arms. "And you are supposed to take care of your pack, not leave your brother out there to die!"

Understanding dawned on Malcolm as emotion and memory flooded him.

Cleo in the rain, with another man.

A dark haired, softer version of the one before him.

Cleo kissing *said man, and wolfish instinct riddling her to* mate *with this man.*

Jealousy prickled Malcolm's subconscious, but he could not fault her for her feelings.

He'd stayed away from her, and

though he could not deny their *bond*, not then, and certainly not now, he also had not expected her to stay celibate.

She was *in heat* after all, and he knew she was in better hands with her own kind.

As much as he cared for Cleo, he knew that their differences were just as dangerous as their similarities.

The memories of their previous trysts echoed through his thoughts, pushing aside any jealousy and rearing their possessiveness.

Her legs wrapped around his hips as he thrust himself inside her.

Her fangs against his neck, spurring his maddening release.

Heat flooded him as he remembered just how warm and wet she felt wrapped around his cock, as he came.

And the panic took forth, just as it had that morning, when he remembered what he'd done in the heat of the moment.

In all the years he'd traveled, the years he'd spent hunting, he was always careful, and so was Dallas. It was safer, better, if they had no attachments, least of all attachments that came in the form of crying, squirmy creatures with ten fingers and ten toes.

But in the year and a half since he'd met Cleo, he hadn't *wanted* anyone else, and as such he'd stopped packing condoms in his bag.

Anxiety swelled as Cleo and Alaric argued, their voices white noise.

He'd had every intention of apologizing for what had happened, wanting nothing more than to quell his own insecurities and worries, as well as the ones Cleo must have been facing.

But when he'd opened his mouth to speak to his... *girlfriend...* he hadn't gotten very far.

One kiss and the world blurred with Cleo. It was a flash of heat, and desire, and he could not *resist* her, or her soft whimpers, her pleading.

Or how good it felt to be inside her, twitching with release.

Fuck, fuck, fuck!

"You do realize that if you go after him, you are walking into a trap, Cleo?" Alaric bit, drawing Malcolm from his spiraling thoughts.

Cleo brattily cocked her head to the side. "You do realize, that I'm not going to let my *mate* suffer because you're too much of a coward, right?" she bit back.

Malcolm blinked as they both bared their teeth at one another. And that was what pushed him to move, leaping between them without a second thought.

"Hey, back off," he growled at Alaric, who had Cleo backed up against the refrigerator.

She did not even *flinch,* her eyes furious with golden shifter glow.

His palms connected with her chest,

and Alaric's, a shock coursing through him.

I can take him, Mal!

"This does not concern you, fucking human!"

Mal yelled, "Fucking time out!"

Alaric growled as a text notification rang out, echoing in the tense space.

"I need to go," he said gruffly pushing Malcolm away. "You stay the fuck here, do you understand me?" he bit, shoving his phone into his pocket.

Cleo pushed Mal away. "Or what? Huh? Your bark is worse than your bite, Alaric. You don't have the balls to do shit."

Malcolm grabbed Cleo, putting himself between them once more.

"Okay, I think that's enough couples therapy for today, assholes," he said, shooting Alaric a glare of his own.

The need, the *desire* to soothe his *mate,* and her anger was unlike anything else he'd ever felt.

But there was also fury and anger of his own, that somehow he'd ended up in the middle of some crazy wolf mate bond, when he needed to be out there, hunting.

Hunting for Dallas, that was.

"You stay here," Alaric said with finality as he stared at Mal. "Until I get back. I need *her* to be safe."

Something twisted in Malcolm's chest, pulling like gravity. Alaric's words echoed in his brain, in his heart. It was almost as if he could *feel* the alpha's despair, his fear.

And that was what Malcolm responded to as he loosened his grip on Clementine.

"I'll keep her safe. I promise," he said definitively as he watched Alaric storm out of the cabin, into the unknown, leaving him and his *mate* alone once more.

<h1 style="text-align:center">14</h1>

CLEO'S ENTIRE BODY was alive with fire. How dare Alaric just waltz into the room and *command* her like that. How dare he!

He cares for you. That's pretty clear, Cleo.

Mal's voice echoed in her brain, and she turned to look at him.

"You don't need to do that when we're alone, you know," she said softly.

"I know," he said with a soft smile. "If you don't like it, then maybe you don't need to be *fuming* in my brain," he said petulantly.

Cleo rolled her eyes as she headed for the door.

"Where do you think you're going?" Malcolm asked, his voice tinged with the faint sound of laughter.

What was so funny?

"Why must I always be questioned?" zhe bit, fury still lacing through her.

Mal shook his head. "Pissed off ain't going to do you any good. I hate to say Al's right, but you need to calm down. Think about the situation rationally."

Cleo turned her back and headed toward the door. "How is this for rational? You can stay here, or you can follow me. Your choice."

"I believe it was *you*, my darling Clementine, who asked for *my* help," he said, following her.

"And it is you who *agreed* to help me rescue my... boy toy? Is that what you called my *mate*?"

Malcolm sighed, his palm hot against her back, stopping her in her tracks.

She could feel his uncertainty, his panic at that word.

She turned around to look at him, fear evident in his eyes.

Every time the word was uttered, in her brain, or out loud, Malcolm froze.

Though he'd answered her call last night, when they'd mated.

Curled together, he'd called her mate too.

But Cleo knew Malcolm wasn't just having difficulty accepting his new title.

She could feel his anxiety inside of her as if it were his own.

Love did not come easy for Malcolm Crowley, because it was tangled up in death.

This she knew, mate bond or not.

In the shadows of drink, after particularly grueling hunts, or in the aftermath of terrifying nightmares, Cleo could hear the fear in his voice. The worry.

Malcolm feared letting love in, because he feared its loss.

How could she make him understand that there was no death for them?

There was only *life,* and their undeniable bond. They were bound beyond the trappings of the physical realm now. But as she thought such things, she understood that perhaps it was not so simple as she wished.

For even as she looked at him with the knowledge of their bond existing between them, the threads of fate pulled her in another direction.

Into more than one direction, if she was being honest.

Cleo blinked away the anxiety as thoughts fueled her brain from earlier.

The second time she and Malcolm had mated.

Alaric's *growl,* his furious roar... his

hand around Malcolm's throat…

She couldn't deny the sight had thrown her into a second orgasm.

She looked away from Malcolm, not wanting to acknowledge the truth of the matter.

The truth that stared at her blindly in the face as she'd gotten up close with the lumbering alpha who had backed her against the refrigerator.

Wetness bloomed between her legs as the thoughts threatened to pull her under.

Like in that dream…

"I did," Malcolm said as he brought his lips to her neck, pressing his hardness against her backside. The soft touch caused a wave of peace to flood her, cooling her heat, if only temporarily.

His lips were warm, soft against her skin.

She let out a contented sigh as he rubbed the small of her back, as she stood in the doorway, on the edge of a precipice.

Could he pull her back from the edge?

"I'm not questioning your intent here, baby. I'm just asking you to take a minute to *breathe.* You came here for my help, so let me help you," he said softly.

She took a deep breath, as he requested, noting it did make her feel better.

"That's it, that's my girl. Hold on to that fight, okay?" he said, his voice a sexy mixture of lust, and confidence.

He pulled her by the hips backward, and she followed his lead. Once in completely the cabin, he closed the door.

"I can't just stay here *waiting* all day, Malcolm. Rocky needs me, he needs—"

"What he needs is for you not to get yourself *killed* trying to save him."

Her shoulders slumped as she stared back at him.

"I know... I just—" She closed her eyes,

taking another deep breath.

Malcolm took her hand, and his touch was warm, soothing. He wrapped her hand around a leather handle. She opened her eyes to see a blade, the one he'd almost stabbed Alaric with. Her eyes widened as she looked from the blade to Malcolm, a strange sense of déjà vu overcoming her.

"What's this?" she asked.

"It belonged to Dallas. He gave it to me, on my first hunt. It's a blessed blade. It'll kill pretty much anything."

She turned it in her hands, feeling the weight of it as she handed it back to him. He pushed it back toward her.

"Show me what you got, baby," he said as he took a step back, motioning for her to come at him.

Cleo looked at the blade, and back at him as he took his shirt off, draping it over the couch.

"Malcolm..."

"Alaric might think keeping you locked up is the *safe* thing to do, but I know that keeping you safe starts with *defense*."

Cleo sighed.

"I don't... I don't want to hurt you," she said.

Malcolm laughed.

"Baby, this body's taken its share of beatings, I can assure you," he said, cocking his head to the side. His dark hair fell in his eyes, his mischievous grin calling to the hungry wolf in her.

The one who wanted to fight.

"You need to trust yourself, Cleo," he said, his gaze holding her in place as he implored her. "I trust you," he said, his words solid and full of truth.

In the space of their consciousness, she could feel his truth, though she could also feel his nerves.

For a guarded man such as Malcolm, it was as if he *longed* to be heard, to be understood.

To be assured.

He had given her the knife, because he trusted her.

Because he saw her as an equal.

As more than a *prized omega.*

His words gave her strength, and she lunged forth. He blocked her, twisting her hands and arms until he'd locked her against his chest.

"Good first try," he said as he released her. "Go again." He took his stance once more.

"I told you, I—"

"Come on, Cleo, don't stall," he said.

She lunged forth again, colliding with his arms, and once again, he twisted her into a locked embrace, his lips at her neck causing the heat to rise again.

"You're smarter than this, I know you are. Quit playing it safe. You aren't going to win back your boy toy playing it safe," he said, releasing her. "Again."

***

Cleo's body was riddled in sweat as she swung the knife at Malcolm, dodging his attack. She crept up behind him, wrapping her leg and arms around him, the knife finally coming into contact with his chest.

The scent of blood hit her nostrils, and she immediately dropped the knife, letting him go and backing away.

He picked up the knife, turning toward her. A steady stream of blood seeped out from beside his exposed nipple.

"Oh my God, Malcolm, I'm so sorry, I—" She rushed to him, and he pulled her into a warm, tight embrace.

She furrowed her eyebrows as anguish and worry laced through her. Malcolm touched the edge of his blade against her chin.

She froze, worried for a split second of a moment that he would hurt her.

He was a hunter, after all.

He gazed at her with pride. "Well done, young Padawan."

Cleo's breath was shallow as she held it, waiting for his final blow.

Between the scent of his blood, the adrenaline in her body, and the hardness of his cock pressed against her, she could not help but *sigh.*

She rather *liked* being on the end of Malcolm Crowley's knife, at his mercy.

Because deep inside, they were both *hunters* who longed to sink their teeth into their prey.

Cleo's eyelashes fluttered as her chest heaved with breath.

"You're bleeding," she said, her breath heavy as her fangs pushed forth.

Malcolm dropped his knife from her throat, placing a soft kiss against the flesh his blade had touched. His tongue pressed against her throbbing vein, eliciting an irrefutable sigh from her lips.

"How you going to kill those vamps,

baby, if you're afraid of a little blood, hmm?" he taunted.

"Malcolm…" She mewled, bringing her hand to his warm, sweat-slicked hips. "You do not play fair," she said. She could feel his lips turn up into a smile as he trailed his lips up to her mouth, taking her bottom lip between his teeth.

Cleo's eyelashes fluttered, her mouth *watering*. She'd never tasted blood before, not human blood. The thought was thrilling to her, as thrilling as holding a knife and a warm body in her hands.

"Yeah, it's quite a feeling, isn't it?" Malcolm purred, tossing the knife on the couch. He wrapped his arms around her, holding her tight in his embrace.

Cleo realized her thoughts were no longer her own, and part of her relished in the intimacy of such a thing.

She did not need to hide from her mate.

Malcolm understood her in a way no

one else ever could.

"Yes," she purred in response, her fingertips settling across his abdomen, blood pooling against her hand. "But you are hurt," she said softly, looking up at him. "And for that, I am sorry."

He gazed down at her with adoration.

Cleo moved some unruly hair out of his eyes and he smirked.

"It doesn't hurt, I promise," he murmured. "Nothing hurts, when you're here."

Cleo sucked in a breath as she slid her hand along his abdomen. The sun had started to set outside.

Alaric had not yet returned.

A part of her worried he would not. That he would leave her here in punishment, in the middle of nowhere, just so she would *hurt*.

So she would *ache* for him.

She hated that even in her mate's arms, he still occupied her thoughts. That even the mere thought of him could boil her blood, and arouse her at all once.

Malcolm leaned down and kissed her, biting at her bottom lip.

"I need to go," he said, his breath heavy.

"What? Where, Alaric said..."

"I know what Grumpy McGrumperson said," he bit.

"But I'm not a wolf, Cleo. I'm not part of your pack," he said as he walked away from her.

She pouted, her wolf pushing against her with anger.

How dare our mate leave us!

Malcolm shot her an annoyed look. "I'll be back, I promise. I just need to take care of some things."

"Things that involve finding your friend?"

"And your boy toy, baby. I can't hunt if I'm locked up in here with you, and if I'm locked up in here with you, I—" He stopped, blinking as he swallowed his words.

"What?" she asked, tears threatening to erupt as old insecurities resurfaced.

He was leaving. Again.

"If I'm locked up in here with you, Cleo, I'll forget. About everything...." he said as he turned away.

"Malcolm..."

He picked up the knife, handing it to her as he put his shirt on. The scent of his blood still hung in the air, the bright red hue almost black as it dried on the shiny tip.

He handed it to her. "Remember what I said. Trust yourself."

She took the knife from him. "Don't get yourself killed," she pleaded.

Malcolm smiled that sarcastic, sexy smile that was full of trouble, the one that made her wolf and her swoon.

"I'll promise to be a good boy if *you* promise to stay here, so I can find you when I get back."

Cleo nodded. "Yeah, promise," she said as he kissed her once more, this time only briefly.

She hated the feeling of emptiness as he walked away, but she did not chase him. For Cleo knew that it would be dark soon, and the darkness was where Malcolm Crowley lived.

15

ALARIC RUBBED HIS face with his hands as he watched the sun set.

Soon enough, he and Thomas would embark on investigating the claims of another wolf. Claims that the vampires were not the only monsters in their territory.

It seemed that while on a standard patrol of the motel, a collective of Djinn had been spotted.

"What do you think they want?" Thomas wondered aloud.

"Perhaps they are just passing through," Alaric said, but even he did not believe his words.

"Djinn don't usually move in *packs*, though. Clarence said there were at least fifty of them."

"It is odd. Djinn are normally solitary creatures."

"You don't think it has something to do with the omegas, do you? Or the vampires perhaps?" Thomas's eyes widened with fear.

Alaric sighed, watching the sun set behind the trees.

"I suppose there is only one way to truly find out," Alaric said.

"Though what the Djinn would want with another supernatural such as us, is beyond me. They usually only pray on the wishes of mortals."

"Vampires prey on mortals primarily, but you and I both know there are perks to feasting on other supernaturals."

"I'll rally up some backup first. You should check on your omega, make sure she's safe," Thomas said.

Alaric swallowed harshly. Cleo wasn't *his*. Not really, but he didn't question Thomas's assumption. After all, he had told the man *his* omega had shown up, unannounced, if only to ask for more security at the cabin. Perhaps a guard, or two.

Though the request was moot, as Alaric knew the Mayfields numbers were stretched as it was, what with a number of them scouting and hunting for Ashley Mayfield.

But Alaric did not want to think about Clementine Srirocco, who was probably in the throws of heat with her *mate* at this very moment. The memory of her *moan* he'd witnessed earlier, threatened to push through and he fought it hard.

For it was nothing but a cruel reminder of what he didn't have, what he would never possess because fate was a cruel mistress.

"Have you ever... you know... fed on another?" Alaric tiptoed around the question, being as it was a rather taboo subject. The instinct to hunt, to taste blood belonged to their wolf, but even wolfish instinct could take over if you weren't careful.

Thomas smirked as he walked toward the door, Alaric following him with ease. "Only my omega, Ashley."

Alaric raised his eyebrows. He'd expected the man to admit to bloodlust, but had not expected to hear that he'd *fed* off his own mate.

"Don't look so surprised. I'm sure you'll feel the urge eventually with yours. It strengthens the bond. It's completely natural."

"Not where I'm from. Where I'm from, it is the omega who does the biting."

"Biting and drinking are two different

things, you know. And I know you guys do things differently up north. But believe me when I tell you it'll feed you in ways you never thought possible."

Both men traipsed through the Badlands bar, which was barely set up. Some of the chairs were still upside down on top of the tables.

Alaric stopped, for a moment, taking in the sight of Thomas's glassy eyes, his frown. The bartender started refilling the glass racks, and wait staff started to upturn the chairs.

Alaric's heart lurched at the despair on the Mayfield alpha's face. It had been nearly a month since he'd see his precious wife.

Alaric felt for the man. He couldn't imagine being apart from someone so close, not to mention there was an added layer of concern because his wife was eight months pregnant.

"I'm sorry, I didn't mean to—"

"I know, it's just... I don't know how much longer I can take this separation. It's gnawing at me, you know. She should be here, with me, getting ready to welcome our daughter into the world, not..." Thomas turned away, his shoulder blades sharpening as the ripple of shifting energy coursed through him.

Alaric understood all too much the pain of separation. But at least Thomas had a bond with his mate.

A true bond, one of acceptance, of love.

Jealousy ripped through Alaric, and he hated how easy it was to stir such emotion. All Alaric had was a stubborn omega who had chosen a *human* as her mate.

And not *just a human*, but also...

The look of fire in Cleo's eyes earlier, when she'd called him out over his inadequacies, his refusal to save his brother...

It was clear as a bell to him then. The

moment he'd seen on the surveillance cameras only cemented what he'd suspected, what he'd believed for the last year and a half, even if it was true his brother had *lied* to him. To everyone.

Cleo had chosen Rocky too. In the end.

What were the chances the one woman he ached to have would *choose* two mates?

Something so unheard of, and yet...

And yet she hadn't chosen him. He'd been passed over not once, but *twice.*

There was no worse rejection than that of a double rejection.

Could he live a life watching the woman of his dreams build a life and family with his *brother...* and possibly even the hunter, Malcolm?

Could he stand by, wanting, wishing for the rest of his life that things were different?

Because Alaric knew no matter what Clementine *wanted,* he would do his damndest to give her everything she desired, because that was his job. As an alpha, and as a wolf whose paws were tied.

Alaric pushed the thoughts of Clementine out of his brain, even though his wolf nagged at him to leave.

"I'll gather the boys. Meet me on the edge of the forest, on the property behind the Badlands. Together, we will investigate Clarence's claims. If they hold true, we will attack."

"Of course," Alaric said, sliding his hands in his pockets. He watched Thomas leave, and trudged down the steps toward the parking lot, toward his car.

When he'd gotten in, he sighed. He looked up at the hill that would undoubtedly lead him to the guest cabin. A part of him was scared to traverse the damn hill, worried he'd find another devastating scene such as the one he'd witnessed earlier. Though in the privacy of his own car, he could not deny the twitch in his cock, or the way the *thought* of Cleo, legs wrapped around Malcolm, moaning in ecstasy had caused his knot to swell.

He sighed deeply as he turned the car on, drowning out the awful, yet strangely arousing thoughts from his brain. He did need to check on her, if only to make sure she had actually *listened* to him this time. There was no use in ordering her back to Mahoning, and a part of him felt relief that she was here, even if she was causing him distress.

He pulled into the driveway, noting the lights were on in the cabin. He felt a strange pull in his chest, like a magnet drawing him toward the light. Every step felt like eternity. He moved to open the door, noting it was locked.

Good girl, Cleo.

Alaric rationed it was enough to know she was there. And as he turned to leave, the sound of the door being opened froze him in place.

"Alaric." Cleo's voice was soft, even.

Alaric's heart thudded so loudly in his chest, he thought it would echo across all of Kentucky. He slowly turned, taking in the sight of Cleo, who looked freshly showered, dressed in her usual kimono, jeans, and tank top. Her bronze hair looked damp, falling over her shoulders in waves. She usually wore it in a long braid, but the style change was rather nice. Her pale skin seemed to be glowing and dewy, and her bright, green-blue eyes sparkled like an oasis.

And Alaric was suddenly parched with thirst.

"Cleo," he said, his voice dark and dry.

"I wasn't sure you were coming back," she said as she moved aside, leaving the door open.

Alaric looked at the open door, the threshold that separated them. All he wanted was to cross it. To step over the invisible barrier between them, sweep her up in his arms and tell her he was *sorry*.

Sorry that he could not protect her or Rocky.

Sorry that he could not be the man she wanted.

Sorry that he had yelled at her like she was a damn child.

But Alaric said nothing. He only stood on the front porch, still as a statue.

"I always come back, don't I?" he asked, though he wasn't sure if he was asking himself or Clementine.

Cleo gazed up at him, her eyes full of sadness. "Yes, but you never *stay*," she said softly.

Alaric looked in the windows, peeking through the open door. "And what about your mate? Does he stay?"

Cleo's lips twisted. "No, he doesn't." She hugged herself tightly. "Rocky is the only one who never *leaves* me."

Alaric felt his heart break at her words, and he did not think twice as he stepped across the threshold, pulling her into his arms.

She startled at the touch, but soon enough wrapped her arms around him, burying her face into his chest.

Warmth spread throughout him at the *relief* of her touch, the simplest of things.

It was just a hug.

It didn't mean anything, other than the comfort he wished to give.

He shut the door with his foot.

Cleo sank against him, and he felt the lightest shake in her body.

"It's all my fault," she cried, and Alaric sighed.

He ran his hands up and down her back as he purred, "It's not your fault, Cleo. The fault is mine. I should have been there, I should have protected you both."

Cleo looked up at him with glassy eyes.

"Alaric…"

"Everything I've done, Cleo… I've done for the good of this *pack*. For you," he started. "I thought I was doing what was best. Giving you space to make your choice. I told you I'd stick behind you no matter what, and I meant that. I still mean it." He reached out, pushing some golden strands of thick, damp hair behind her shoulder. She smelled of shampoo and sweet honey, mixed with *heat.*

But she'd already *chosen* her mates… the heat should have been gone, unless Malcolm was nearby.

He looked around the living room, sniffing, using his senses to try and decipher another presence, but there was nothing.

Nothing but him and Cleo…

Even with tears in her eyes, she was beautiful.

God, you are beautiful.

"And what about now?" she asked with

a sniffle.

Alaric smoothed his thumb along her cheek, smearing the tear into her skin like a raindrop.

"What about now?" he asked smoothly, his gaze transfixed on her.

He knew whatever she would ask, he would obey her request. For in the presence of his omega, he was powerless to refuse her wishes and whims.

"Do you still think you're doing the right thing?" she asked, her gaze searching his for answers.

"I don't know what the right thing is anymore," he murmured, licking his lips. "I thought I did, but..."

"But what?" she asked softly.

"But then I look at you and I want to be fucking selfish," he breathed, his hands sliding down her hips. "I want to say fuck it all and just..."

Cleo's hands slid up his chest, her fingertips resting on the edge of his shirt collar. His cock throbbed in his jeans as the thoughts and memories resurfaced. Of all the stolen moments and smiles he'd witnessed, given to someone else.

"I want you to fucking *choose me*," he whispered.

Cleo looked up at him, biting her lip as the twinge in his chest ebbed. Like a lightning bolt, his entire soul felt alive with energy.

"Alaric..." she purred, her voice tinged with sadness, but also something else.

Hope.

"But I also know, when I look at you, I know I'd do *anything* to make you happy. Even if it means I have to break down a fucking house full of vampires just to find the man that *makes* you happy. So you won't hurt like I do."

Cleo's eyebrows furrowed as her fingers slipped beneath his collar.

And just like that, the sparks of the past caught flame once more.

Cleo tugged on his collar, pulling him to her lips as she kissed him, tears running down her face.

Alaric melted against her kiss. The energy flowed through him, lighting him up like a powder keg as her thoughts filled his brain.

I want you to choose me too.

Memories of the last time they'd kissed, in his car resurfaced. After he'd rescued her from Malcolm Crowley's hotel room, the night she'd gone into heat and shifted.

I would give you the world Cleo. All you have to do is ask.

Cleo tightened her grip on his shirt, fingers twisting in the fabric as her tongue grazed his, her words clear in his psyche.

I don't want the world, Alaric. I just want you.

Alaric slid his hands in her hair, down her back, across her hips.

Her touch, her thoughts... it was

invigorating. His cock throbbed, his knot starting to swell as shifting energy coursed through him.

He felt *powerful*, as if he could take down a ring of vampires solo.

His tongue brushed against Cleo's fangs, and Thomas's words echoed in his brain.

You don't know the strength her blood could give you.

And that was all Alaric needed to remember the task at hand.

Why he came to find the spellbinding omega in the first place.

"Fuck, Thomas..." he breathed, trying to regain focus.

"Come again?" Cleo said, thrown by his sudden shift in conversation.

"I need to go," he said, turning around, knowing he was already late.

"What? You just got here..."

"I know. But... the Mayfield alpha and I are investigating a claim," he said as he gently pushed her away. "I only meant to stop and make sure you were all right, and—"

Cleo looked up at him with curiosity. "Does this *claim* have anything to do with rescuing Rocky?"

Alaric looked into her eyes, and he could not lie. "I can not confirm or deny that. That's why we're *investigating.*"

Cleo nodded. "I see. Then I'm coming with you."

"Cleo..." Alaric's tone rose only slightly, edged in concern.

"This is not negotiable," she said as she pushed past him.

Alaric breathed deep, his anger starting to rise. How this woman could soothe him and infuriate him within seconds of each other was beyond him. But a part of him *liked* that he could not control her.

Perhaps she is safer with me than alone in this cabin.

Cleo shrugged, looking at him over her shoulder, a smile falling over her plus, kiss-swollen lips. "Are you coming or not?"

Alaric sighed as he closed the door, following after Clementine, silently into the night, to hunt.

16

MALCOLM WAITED AS the phone rang, once, twice. He was about to hang up, when the bitter familiarness of Ava's voice greeted him.

"What?" she nipped.

"Is that any way to greet your adoring brother, Ava?" he drawled with disdain.

"Pffft. We both know the only thing you adore is a bottle of Jack and your car."

He rolled his eyes, letting his hand fall down the steering wheel of his parked car. Though a part of him felt strangely on the spot, even though he knew his sister was not psychic, and therefore could not see him taking up residence in his beloved Chevelle.

"I see you are feeling better enough to bust my balls," he said, watching as hotel-goers and visitors alike arrived at the *Badlands*, the bar he'd checked out only a day prior.

Where Dallas's last transaction had taken place, earlier.

The hunt it seemed was starting to close in on him.

He is here. I know it.

"Yeah, well, I've got better things to do," she nipped.

The sound of shifting movement over the phone drew his attention, the undeniable slide of a body against leather, muffled as if it was nearby.

A passenger was in the Impala, and Malcolm grit his teeth, knowing all too well the company his sister kept in his absence.

"Are you with him?" Ava breathed a sigh of exasperation, as Malcolm bit, "The fucking tick?"

"No," she said too fast, and he knew.

Where his sister went, her pet vampire followed, waiting for his moment to strike.

"Liar," he growled. "I know he's sitting next to you."

"You don't know shit. I told you I have better things to do than—"

"You got one job, Simba. Don't sleep with the vampire."

"And what about you, Captain? I know Dallas wasn't the only one sidling up with monsters, Mal. Unlike you, I know where the line is."

Malcolm's blood boiled, heat ransacking him at her words. There was no way she could possibly know about him, about Cleo. He'd gone to great lengths to keep his connection with the Omega a secret. The only one who'd ever known about her, about *them* was Dallas. As far as Ava knew, Cleo and the rest of the Thorne pack were left in Mahoning, never to be seen or heard from again.

She's deflecting.

"What Dallas did... what I do... it's not the same thing," he grit through his teeth.

Ava laughed sarcastically. "No, of course not. Because only men are allowed to be monster bait."

"Ava..."

"I've got to go, Mal. I've got a vamp to slay," she said, the phone going dead on the other line.

Malcolm pursed his lips as he let the anger run over him. He didn't want her to mope around, upset over the death of his partner... who happened to be her... boyfriend? He wasn't sure what the extent of his partner's relationship was with his sister, being as they'd both clearly kept whatever was going on between them a secret for a while.

There seem to be a lot of secrets going around these days.

While he was glad to see his sister had found her way back to vamp slaughter, he also knew she was trading one vice for the other. For Ava may have been eleven years younger than him, but she was a Crowley through and through. Avoiding the problem by drowning it out with alcohol, blood, and sex was practically a family past time.

But it was her words that cut him deeper than any knife, acting as if his disdain for the vampire who'd *claimed* her was some male chauvinist bullshit that had nothing at all to do with the fact he was *the enemy.*

An enemy who followed her around like a lost puppy, but an enemy nonetheless. Because Malcolm knew Cassius Aurelia was, above all things, smart and patient. Two things he did not like when it came to bloodsuckers. He was also part of an extremely powerful bloodline.

He exited his car, sliding his phone in his pocket as he headed to his trunk, popping it open to retrieve a blessed blade. After all, he'd given Cleo his prized blade, hoping she would be better protected now that she'd had a *bit* of training.

But Dallas's gifted weaponry was not *all* Malcolm possessed. His trunk was full of weapons, from knives to long blades, to wolverine claws, to rope, and even solid silver crosses.

He stared down at the silver cross, which had belonged to his father. He'd discovered it in the aftermath of packing his parent's things, once they'd been burned, as was their wishes. Though he'd never used it, he kept it as a reminder of what he'd lost.

What he was fighting for.

But as Malcolm looked down at the

shimmering cross, he wasn't sure what he was fighting for anymore, or what he was fighting *against.*

He'd have to make peace for the moment, that his sister seemed to be in better spirits, even if those spirits meant she'd traded heartbreak for a stake.

There were worst vices, after all.

Entering the Badlands, Malcolm kept to himself, hiding behind a group of individuals who looked to be Ava's age, early twenties.

And then he saw them.

A group of Djinn. They all boasted the same dark hair and aqua eyes. They parked their motorcycles, all clad in leather like some paranormal biker gang, and Malcolm could not deny they looked sort of... badass.

For monsters.

He slipped past the crowd, sidling around until he reached the front ramp, pulling out his pack of cigarettes and a lighter, casually lighting up as he hung near the rail, shaking his dark hair in his eyes.

The crackle of a catching burn on his cigarette echoed in his ears as he drew in a breath, letting the nicotine coat his nerves for the moment. The first hit felt more than good, it felt like a welcome relief.

With startling clarity, he hadn't realized how *exhausted* and drained he'd been. He'd been running, hunting, and looking for answers on an endless loop, and he was quite tired. But there would be no rest for the wicked Malcolm Crowley.

Not tonight, and certainly not until he'd completed his missions.

"Do you think she'll come through?" one of the Djinn, a woman with shoulder length black hair, asked a rather slim, pale man dressed from head to toe in leather and studded boots.

The man sighed, turning off his bike.

Mal pulled his cigarette from his lips, blowing smoke in the wind as he listened carefully.

"Amora? Of course, she always does," the man said with a shrug.

"If that were true, the Marquis would still be standing and we wouldn't be out here riding from town to town like fucking nomads. That joint was supposed to be our retirement," the short haired Djinn said.

Another woman, a short Djinn with a high ponytail, dark brown hair cascading over her pale, tattooed arms, chimed in.

"If it wasn't for those fucking hunters, we'd probably be rolling in wishes and blood right about now."

Malcolm's body stiffened at their words, and he took another long drag of his cigarette, willing the nicotine once more to fix his anxieties.

Amora is here too.

The memory of his time spent in the vampiress's dungeon—a cell in which he'd been kept like livestock until the race began in her labyrinth—coursed through him.

He'd been the bait then too, at Cassius's request.

Though he would not have trusted his sister in such predicaments, and Dallas had been strangely off his game at the time, being as it was the worst time of year for his former partner in general—the anniversary of his wife's death.

Malcolm hadn't spoken or interacted with Amora other than to be placed in his pen, and released like a prized rat. But he'd played his part in the labyrinth, taking down the vampires who chased him and the other "spots" that had been bought and paid for.

Like fucking animals.

Mal put out his cigarette as the Djinn walked past him, heading into the bar.

While the lure of the kill was tempting, he knew his vengeance on Cassius's Vampire Barbie would have to wait for the moment.

Just as he was about to head in after them, the unmistakable familiarity of Dallas's voice echoed in the air.

Malcolm froze in his spot, hidden by the shadows of the looming porch as he set his gaze across the parking lot. His heartbeat echoed in his chest, his blood cold. For he would know that stature anywhere, not to mention the sun tattoo on his forearm, which he could see. He only had a matching one, after all.

For across the parking lot, was Jake Dallas. Broad-shouldered, lumbering, and ominous, as always, with a woman dressed in all black, with fierce aqua eyes.

A Djinn... he realized.

Malcolm dared to inch closer, careful not to draw unnecessary attention, his hand on his blade.

He was only a mere few feet away, but Malcolm knew he had to be smart. He could not accost the man with so many witnesses, monster or no monster.

"We are to head to the northeast perimeter and gather intel on a property the Boracellis have been guarding," the woman said, her voice full of concern.

"Where is your bitchy little bestie, anyway?" Dallas grumbled.

Malcolm fought to breathe steadily as his insides twisted with panic and anxiety. The need for another cigarette warred with the desire to sink his knife into the man's back, but he stopped, slipping beside a beat up white bronco as Dallas turned around.

Malcolm pressed his body against the side door, straining to keep an eye on Dallas and his Djinn friend.

"Probably wondering where the hell we are. She left like, ten minutes ago," the woman answered, leaning against a motorcycle.

Dallas gruffly chortled, crossing his arms. "And what if I said no?" he asked.

Malcolm watched their exchange with fear and interest.

It appeared the Boracellis were in town, and he wondered for a moment if Dallas was perhaps still the Dallas he once knew.

The Dallas who had been hunting the Boracellis with him up until...

Until he became the enemy.

Though as Malcolm listened to the monster wearing Dallas's skin, a part of him wanted to believe the man he knew was still in there.

What do the Djinn want with the Boracellis, though?

The woman shrugged as he hopped on the motorcycle, casting the woman a deadly glare.

"Well then, I guess I would just have to kill some vampires myself with Rebel. Not like I need your help or anything, but I thought you wanted to have a little fun. Wanted to kill something. Maybe I was wrong," she teased him.

Teased him!

Does the Djinn have a fucking death wish?

Did she not know who the fuck he was?

Malcolm's fist balled in anger on behalf of his former partner as Dallas revved his engine.

"Next time, lead with the killing part, why don't you?" he nipped as he sped off in the opposite direction.

It took Malcolm all of two seconds to sprint across the parking lot and crawl into his car, not even bothering to adjust the radio as he tore off after the motorcycle, with one sole focus.

17

"WHAT ARE WE looking for exactly?" Cleo asked as Alaric parked his BMW on the side of the road. The woods that flanked the concrete highway loomed like a dark fortress, and Cleo could not help the anticipation building in her body.

Rocky could be beyond those trees, she told herself, sliding her hand over the hilt of the blade pressed against her flesh behind her back.

Alaric glanced at her with the same steely gaze he always did, as if he were weighing what to say and how to say it.

How to sugarcoat it, she thought.

"Thomas should be beyond these coordinates," he said gruffly. "With some reinforcements in case things get..."

Cleo rounded the car, stopping in front of Alaric. She only barely came up to his chest, but she didn't let that stop her from looking up at him with her own bravery.

Perhaps I can channel that bravery into other things...

Alaric gazed down at her, his chest rising and falling with depth as he twisted his lips.

"Promise me if things get... messy... you'll take this fucking car and head back to the cabin."

Cleo could see the worry, the concern in his eyes. She could also *feel* his despair, his anxiety rippling off of him in waves. The reality was startling to her. After all, Alaric was an *alpha.* He did not worry about anything. But as his brows knit together, Cleo realized that maybe she didn't know the stoic, scary alpha as well as she thought she did. The instinct to argue, to fight his words, was undeniable. To tell him he needn't worry about her. But something else, a deeper feeling, something much more profound flowed through her, and she did not have the strength to fight its unrelenting pull.

"I promise," she said, nodding in response.

Alaric's jaw tensed as he pursed his lips, nodding in relief. "Good girl," Alaric said with the ghost of a smile. "To answer your question, one of the Mayfield wolves said they noticed some vamps in the forest."

Cleo cocked her head to the side as Alaric took a few steps ahead.

"What's so abnormal about that?" she asked as she followed suit. Together, they walked through the dark clearing, into the forest.

The sounds of night played like a symphony around them; crickets chirping, animals skittering in between the bushes and rustling the scattered leaves on the ground. Slivers of moonlight fell on Alaric's broad shoulders, lighting him up as he stalked through the night.

Cleo's insides twisted with heat as she watched his shoulder blades knit together, how he stealthily sauntered into the darkness. Her wolf was practically teeming with interest.

Now is not the time... she told herself, fighting back the desire to sneak up on the alpha in front of her and pounce.

Heat flushed through her veins as her wolf warred with her human brain, its instinct primal and deep.

Mate.

Cleo sighed, pushing her hair back over her shoulders.

Somewhere in the forest a twig

snapped, and Alaric stopped, his entire body rigid with alertness. He held his arm out, stopping Cleo from going any further.

"Cleo, get to the car, now," he said, his muscles cording, his spine straightening.

Cleo could practically feel the shifting energy rippling off of him, which should have alarmed her.

Alaric was right to want to protect her, but who would protect *him?*

Her mate?

Could she trust that the Mayfield pack would have her mate's back?

Not like I would.

"Alaric, what—"

The unmistakable scent of decay and blood was prevalent in the air as a howl tore through the silent forest, chilling Cleo's bones.

For she recognized that howl as a cry for *help.*

Alaric turned to look at her, his golden-hued eyes full of panic and concern, but he did not have time to argue with her.

Instead, he growled as his fangs pushed forth, as his body contorted and collapsed upon itself, wreaking the human visage she'd grown to... love.

Was love the right word?

Cleo wasn't sure, but what she was sure of was the vampires were near. But there was something else, a sweet citrus and spice scent that was damn near delectable that she couldn't place.

Alaric shifted in an instant, his thick thigh muscles now decorated with white fur, his shoulder blades now sharp, jaunting haunches. He threw back his giant head, howling in response as he took off through the woods like a bat out of hell.

Cleo tore off in a run after her mate, attempting to call her own shifting energy.

It started as it always did, but it felt... different.

She skidded to a halt as they approached the clearing, and she took in the sight in front of her.

And it was quite a sight.

Across the expanse was a generous field.

A field upon which an ominous, haunted house stood against the full moon.

The house from my dream... she realized with startling clarity.

Where Rocky is.

Somewhere deep in her bones, she knew it to be true even though she knew it was radical to believe such things because of a *dream*.

But the grounds were riddled with vampires, wolves, and...

Strange monsters with glowing blue eyes.

Cleo did not have time to soak it all in as a vampire charged her from the side. Though her reflexes and sense of hearing were quite good, and she instantly grabbed her knife, throwing her arm out to stab the vampire without a second thought.

The creature slid further down on her knife, it's dark, soulless eyes full of anger and wonder as he snapped his fangs at her.

Cleo's fangs pushed forth, but the energy felt... off. Less than normal. Still, she did not waste a moment as she bared her fangs, dragging her blade up through its chest. The gurgling and snapping of muscles sounded disgusting in her ears and her stomach roiled, wanting to expel whatever contents it had contained as blood splattered across her chest.

Cleo fought the inkling to wretch, tearing her teeth into the neck of the fanged creature who'd tried to hurt her. His blood tasted foul, like death and ash, and she removed her knife as the vampire crumbled to the ground.

She tried to call her power again, but it would not come.

And that was when she started to panic.

Why can't I shift?

Her fangs ached, pain shooting through her body as her wolf whimpered and whined, pushing against her frame.

But it was no use.

Cleo cried out in agony as she kept trying to force a shift, stabbing and defending herself as another set of vampires came at her.

"Cleo, watch out!" Malcolm's voice echoed across the way, and she turned just in time to land another deep blow to her impending attacker.

But Cleo would not have time to rejoice with her mate, not when she was frantically searching for the lumbering alpha and...

The scent of chocolate chip cookies invaded her senses, and she nearly dropped her knife.

Her wolf *salivated* at the scent, knowing its mate was near, her thighs already starting to moisten with an impending heat that was damn near consuming.

Mate.

Cleo searched as she fought, her gaze finally settling on the ominous house. With her eyesight as enhanced as it was, seeing great distances was not as much of an obstacle as it should have been.

Cleo's entire body heated like a flame as she set her gaze on familiar amber eyes.

There Rocky Thorne stood, his arms wrapped around someone else. A woman.

Jealousy and pain radiated through her as her fangs ached, her heat flaring as she tried a force shift once more, but she felt only *rage.*

Rage with no tangible outlet as her wolf protested, crying as she tried to force her spirit to do what she was born to do.

Fight.

Cleo roared in frustration, in anger, grabbing her blade, clutching it to her heart.

Had her mate betrayed her?

No, no, I would feel that... she thought, trying to still her wolf's anxieties and fears.

A flash of white jumped in front of her, pulling her attention as her energy sparked, dancing beneath her flesh as the scent of dark forests and thunderstorms etched with cedar and spice filled her pathways.

Alaric.

Cleo was caught between her mates, it would seem, on opposite ends of the spectrum.

Alaric needed her help, but so did Rocky. Malcolm was tangled with a vampire, but he was holding his own for the moment.

But Cleo would have no time to decide which mate to save.

Alaric shoved her aside, growling at her with ferocity. Cleo fell to the ground with a thud. As she moved to stand, a vampire jumped out at Alaric, it's fangs crashing down through his ivory hide, eliciting a deep roar.

"Alaric!" she called out, attempting to run after him, just as one of the blue-eyed creatures jumped in front, punching a second vampire away while the other screamed in agony as Alaric tore into the flesh of its neck.

Taking the hit for him… Cleo realized as she watched the towering monster who smelled of citrus and Moroccan oils, who made her vision *hazy* somehow, bared his own fangs and fought off the vampire. He glanced at Alaric, who had gotten up easily, black blood staining his white fur, dripping from his fangs.

But Cleo did not miss how he *faltered*

on his legs.

Alaric is hurt.

Cleo scrambled to her feet, heading toward her mate, just as the scent of burning fire erupted, howls of "retreat!" echoing in the air.

The great blue-eyed monsters fell back as the vampires hissed, and the wolves regrouped.

Nausea roiled in her stomach from the pungent smells surrounding her, and Cleo fell to the ground as Alaric's body started to shiver, as the shifting energy started to kick over once more, his great roar turning to one of human pain laced with cursing.

"Cleo! Al..." Malcolm's voice was heavy in the air as her ears rang, as the world around her thinned. She held one hand to her head, which was *throbbing* as she fought the will to throw up from the onslaught of sensory overload.

She felt as if she might pass out.

Cleo's entire body shook with spent energy, with frustration, desire and fear. The metallic scent was prevalent to her senses as Alaric's body fell back to human form, his golden-kissed skin marred with rivulets of blood.

So much blood.

"Shit, he's been bitten," Mal grumbled as he pulled off his flannel, ripping the sleeve off. "I have some anti-venom in the car, but I have no idea if it'll work on him since it's for... humans... but it's worth a shot," Mal said, his voice sounding far away as Cleo grit her teeth together, fighting the urge to spill her nerves and her insides.

What is wrong with me?

Cleo could only watch in horror as the world around her spun.

"Cleo..." Mal's voice echoed around her, but she couldn't move.

She could barely breathe.

Her gaze fell on the porch, now empty.

Had she imagined it?

Had she fabricated the sight of Rocky on that porch, *holding* someone else?

Her wolf whined as sadness, pain, and love festered within her like a hurricane.

"Cleo, baby, we gotta move. Come on." Mal's voice shook, and she did not miss the guilt, the anger, and the sadness in it. "We gotta get your boyfriend back to base."

Worry was a strange thing to hear in the hunter's voice. Especially given his disdain for the alpha in his arms.

Boyfriend?

Is that what Alaric was?

The word didn't sound right, but her insides twisted in longing nonetheless.

In *need.*

She blinked as she looked up to see a shirtless Malcolm, holding a naked Alaric, his arm tied off with Mal's ripped flannel sleeve.

And something about that sight

brought her back to the present.

Mates.

My mates need me.

Cleo stood though her legs were shaky and her head was splitting. She held her hand up to her lips, fighting to gain control of herself once more as Malcolm nodded.

"It's going to be okay," Malcolm said as he moved toward the edge of the woods, in the opposite direction.

Alaric groaned, but he followed as Malcolm led the way, his arms tight around the hunter, holding onto him for support.

Cleo could not speak, so she only nodded, following her mates into the darkness once more.

18

THE CAR RIDE back to the cabin was full of unsaid things.

Alaric leaned his head on Cleo's shoulder, his breaths labored and hot against her exposed skin. The blood on his chin was black as night, staining his golden skin like squid ink.

Cleo glanced down at his bloodied form, the debris of forest and remnants of vampire decorating his flesh like war markings.

His eyes were closed, his thick

eyelashes standing out against his complexion, his natural dark brown hair disheveled and damp from his brawl.

She reached out to softly push away some frenzied locks, catching Malcolm's gaze in the rear view mirror. She did not speak, and neither did he, the only sound between them the haunting vocals of Phil Collins singing about something in the air, echoing among them.

True to his word, Malcolm did have anti-venom. In fact, he had quite an array of vials and anti-potions in his leather carrying case that strangely reminded her of the one her mother kept her essential oils in.

She hadn't asked how he'd obtained it, or what the other potions did, despite her curiosity.

For all she could focus on was the sickness in her stomach, the anxiety in her blood as Alaric cried out in pain when Malcolm *stabbed* his thigh with the syringe.

"Rocky," Alaric's voice was gravelly and thick.

The man who lay against her had no fight. His body was relaxed, or rather exhausted against her as his system fought off the vampire's venom.

It was toxic to werewolves, after all, and she wasn't certain how much venom had actually spread before...

Alaric's lips brushed the skin of her neck as he gripped her thigh, causing a fresh wave of heat to traverse through her veins.

"What about Rocky?" Mal asked.

"Rocky's... Mayfields..." Alaric's words were slurred slightly as he grimaced, and Cleo could not resist sliding her hand over top of his.

They'd been here before, just like this. Over a year and a half ago.

Cleo's gaze drifted to Malcolm in the driver's seat, his dark eyes focused on the road.

"You saw him..." Cleo spoke softly, gazing down at Alaric. His amber eyes were open, staring up at her with a glassy sheen.

Alaric nodded. "With the Mayfield's omega," he grunted, trying to sit up.

"Hey now, don't you dare get vamp blood all over my fucking seat, Al."

Cleo couldn't help but laugh, though it sounded as if she'd gone insane.

How could anyone laugh at a time such as this?

"Fuck you, Crowley," Alaric snarled, coughing as he spit out some blood onto Malcolm's upholstery.

"Fucking asshole!" Mal nipped, sighing in annoyance.

"The Mayfield's Omega..." Cleo repeated the words, tasting them on her tongue.

"Yes. She's been gone for over a month. I came here to help Thomas rescue her. In return, he'd—"

"Help you build your army," Cleo said the words as if they were poison as reason befell her.

An eye for an eye and all that.

Malcolm turned up the hill to the cabin, the unspoken understanding between him and the alpha like a creature all its own.

Invisible, but so very present.

As the car came to a stop, Malcolm turned the engine off. But neither of them moved, the silence thick before he spoke.

"Djinn don't travel in packs," he said, turning to look at Cleo and Alaric in the backseat.

"What the fuck do they want? What's their connection to the vamps *here*?"

Alaric shifted his weight against Cleo, looking back at Malcolm.

"I don't know. They just showed up in town, and—"

"And what? Big Bad Wolf didn't tear

their throats out? Why?" Mal clicked his tongue. "It just seems... weird. It's like they were helping us."

Cleo did not miss the way Malcolm shivered, or the way his gaze dropped as his jaw tensed. He was keeping something to himself, but she did not have time to pry the secrets from her mate, not when every bone in her body ached for the mate who was not *here.*

Not when her inner wolf was pacing with worry, needing to *care* for the mate in her arms.

Malcolm opened the door, and Cleo expected him to walk away, to leave her and Alaric alone as he had the last time they'd been here. But Malcolm only opened Alaric's door, holding out his hand to the alpha as he pursed his lips.

Alaric glanced down at Malcolm's open palm warily.

"Come on, Al, don't make me come in there and fucking get you like a pansy,"

Mal smirked.

Alaric swatted at his hand, a deep growl escaping his throat.

Cleo's lips turned up in a smile.

That's my boy.

The words in her brain were not hers, and they startled her as she glanced back at Malcolm.

Warmth spread in her loins, her stomach, her heart.

Oops.

Sorry about that.

Cleo let out a small chuckle as Alaric pushed himself up, pushing Malcolm's arm out of the way.

"I am not your *boy*," he nipped, baring his teeth at Malcolm, who only had the audacity to smile.

"Right, I forgot. You prefer *Daddy*."

Alaric growled once more as he swung for Malcolm, who was lighter on his feet than a fabled fairy. He danced back and forth, baiting the alpha up the driveway.

"You little—"

Cleo stopped as she closed the door, watching as Alaric leapt into a jog, jaunting after Malcolm up the steps.

Her heart swelled with pride, with *love*.

He's okay.

My alpha is okay...

Cleo watched as Malcolm opened the door, sliding his arm around Alaric as he helped him inside. The jaunt up the steps had rendered him wobbly, it seemed.

Cleo stood for a moment, frozen.

The last year and a half converged on her all at once, making her feel nauseous.

Her arrival at the Thorne estate, sneaking out with Rocky.

Malcolm stirring her heat.

Alaric.

The thought of the Thorne alpha set a heat forging through her. It was almost as if they were right back where they started, but somehow...

Everything was different.

They hadn't changed. She was still the fiery Omega who refused to sit back and let things happen, and he was still the grumbling, stoic alpha who never stayed in one place.

Malcolm was still the same hunter, chasing monsters.

How had things gotten so complicated?

She set one foot in front of the other as she went up the steps, and the last bits of sickness faded from her body.

Too much stress will make anyone queasy, I suppose.

When she finally made it inside, she was surprised to see only Malcolm in the kitchen.

"Where is—"

"Big guy is going to need a fucking nap," Mal said nonchalantly. "Apparently he's a fucking baby, because he passed out when I stitched up his arm." Mal shrugged.

Cleo's eyebrows rose in alarm as Mal

took a drink of water. The amber light refracted off his skin, giving him an almost golden glow. If it wouldn't have been for the blood spatter, that was.

Though Cleo knew it was wrong, she couldn't help but think it made him more attractive.

Her inner omega salivated, wanting to lick it off him.

Some of that is probably Alaric's blood.

The thought froze her, but the heat did not diminish.

"He took a hell of a bite. I don't think I've ever seen—"

Malcolm's words were like ice water to her heat.

"Vampire bites are toxic for us," Cleo said softly, coming to stand in front of her mate. He stood shirtless in the kitchen, his naturally dark hair framing his deep eyes, the faint edges of facial hair shading his jaw. "Get bit by vampires a lot?" Cleo half-heartedly joked.

Malcolm's dark eyes caught her gaze, razing a fire in her blood as he smirked. "A little nibble here and there. Kind of hard to avoid fangs when you're up close with them." He shrugged. "I don't let anyone close enough to fucking claim my ass, though," he growled, and Cleo could see he was somewhere else.

The words hung in the air between them as her own fangs threatened to push through, his words igniting a wolfish instinct to bite him and remind him how much he liked her fangs in his neck.

Images of their tryst, memories of the taste of his blood as she claimed him, stirred her heat like a hurricane.

He gazed back at her for a moment, the unspoken words hanging between them, the threads of their bond taut and strong.

In the light of the kitchen, he looked breathtaking, even with the blood staining his chest. She followed the spatters, the rivulets down across his pecs, across his abdomen.

Across those delicious, sharp hipbones sticking out of his frayed, bloodied jeans.

Cleo found it hard to breathe when she looked at him, overwhelmed by desire and something else so much deeper than the euphoria of claiming a mate.

Love.

It ebbed between them, a resounding echo. Born out of circumstance, fighting like a demon. Even as Malcolm's gaze roved over her form, settling on her lips, she could feel his hesitation warring with his desire. In their bond, she could feel his need for love.

His fear of it.

It was undeniable.

She settled closer to him, pulled toward him like a magnet.

Malcolm Crowley was a black hole. She knew it to be true.

He would consume her until there was

nothing left if she let him.

Mal reached out lightly, brushing his thumb across her cheek. The pad of his thumb was rough, calloused. But the way he touched her, *gently*, caused a whine to escape her throat.

As volatile as Malcolm was, Cleo knew beneath the scars he was so much more than the blood and the fight.

"What were you doing there?" she asked, nuzzling her cheek in his palm. His touch ignited her heat, causing shockwaves through her core. She wanted to be wrapped up his arms, wanted him to never let go. She wanted to wrap him up in her nest and never let go of *him*, this man who stoked her fire.

Who taught her to fight.

Malcolm pursed his lips. "You know what I was doing."

"Hunting. For Dallas."

Malcolm stiffened at the very mention of his name.

"Hunting for monsters."

Cleo fell into Malcolm's space, closing the gap between them. His hand traced further back, finding the nape of her neck. He rubbed the sore muscles there, gripping her hair tight, then letting go.

The contrast of pain and pleasure as he did so elicited another whine from her Omega.

"Did you find what you were looking for?" she asked, gazing up at him. The words she truly longed to say were stuck in her throat.

Thank you.

I'm glad you're okay.

I love you.

Malcolm dropped his hand, turning away. "I need to go, Cleo." His voice was heavy, full of burden.

Please don't go.

Her thoughts were loud and clear.

I—

Cleo reached out, pulling Malcolm's

face back toward her, her gaze pleading with him.

"Stay. With me, please…"

With us.

Malcolm's eyes glazed with pain.

"Don't make me choose, Cleo. Don't put me in this fucking position."

"Why?" she mewled, tracing her nails along his cheek, the touch not at all gentle as her emotion swelled to anger, to frustration. "Why? Because you won't choose me?" she bit, her fangs pushing forth, her body hot like a flame. Her inner wolf raised its haunches, baring her teeth.

Malcolm grabbed her wrist, tearing it away from his face, his thumb brushing over her tight knuckle.

"No, because I *will.*" He growled in frustration. "Because I will throw away every fucking thing I've strived for because the only thing that matters is *you.*" His words were full of venom, and they stung her heart like a wasp on a summer day.

His grip was tight as he pressed his fingernails into her wrist. Where he touched her, blood flowed with renewed vigor.

"And you can't want that, right?" she whispered.

Blood rushed to the surface, where his fingernail met her flesh and he eased his grip, the pad of his finger stroking the sore spot gently, smearing her blood on his fingers, along her wrist.

"I want it more than you know," he said, leaning his forehead against her.

Cleo leaned in, brushing her lips against his.

Malcolm did not fight her.

He did not argue or fight, or push or try to run. He surrendered.

He fell into her like a stone, falling deep into the depths of a lake.

When they broke apart, he sighed.

"But I'm no good to you or Al, or...

anyone, Cleo, if my head isn't in the fucking game. Because that's when I make mistakes. That's when I lose people."

Cleo wished to tell the hunter he could never lose her. They were mates, after all. Their bond was well beyond the physical. But she also knew that she could not control Malcolm Crowley any more than she could control the lumbering alpha sleeping off a vampire bite in the other room.

And so, for the second time in her life, Cleo took a step back and let Malcolm Crowley go, hoping that she was doing the right thing. Hoping that he would come back to her; that when all was said and done, he'd come home.

Where he belonged.

***

Cleo stood in the doorway, gazing down at Alaric where he lay on a large, circular bed.

His naked body was golden in the light, his heavy chest rising steadily. Blood still covered parts of his golden body, and she could see the stitching along his shoulder where Malcolm had applied it.

She took a small step forward into the alpha's gravitational pull, gripping the blanket in her arms. Her insides warmed like a fire as she looked at him, the voice of her inner omega sounding one word over and over in her brain.

Mate.

The desire and instinct to care for her alpha was strong, embedded in her.

She approached the bed slowly, her gaze roving over his corded muscles, his thick eyelashes, the shape of his lips, the disheveled, long locks messily arranged across his fine features.

She liked the long hair look on him.

She had seen the man shirtless

countless times at the estate when he was there, but she'd never truly appreciated his form in all its beauty.

And he was *beautiful.* Naked, glowing like an Adonis, defined like a work of art.

Cleo shook out the blanket, fighting her curiosity.

It would be wrong to look while he was passed out, right?

She'd tried to be noble, but the heat was too tempting. The sight of his golden sun-kissed skin, of his defined form, not to mention his soft, steady breath, was practically spellbinding.

Her gaze traveled down his abs and she swallowed harshly as it continued along the dark smattering of hair beneath his navel.

Cleo bit her lip, her omega brain pushing all the right buttons.

She blushed, immediately tearing her gaze away as heat flourished through her at the sight of Alaric's cock. Even soft, it was rather sizable.

Her pupils dilated, her breath catching in her throat as her thighs tightened. Heat spread like a wildfire as her omega salivated at the sight.

But Cleo was more than just her animal instincts. She needed air.

So much had happened, and she needed space. Alaric needed to rest.

He'd seen Rocky too. With the Mayfield's omega. A rescue mission would most certainly commence now, and they would certainly need a plan. They'd need to talk to the Mayfield alpha, perhaps stake out the house, wait for...

Cleo shook her head.

You have no say in this, and you know that.

But it didn't stop her from wishing she did.

Cleo focused on giving Alaric ample coverage, her fingers tracing along the edges of his shoulder as she wrapped him in the blanket. Tiny shockwaves coursed through her, pulsing like electricity as they lit up her nerves, causing a fresh wetness to bloom between her thighs. She couldn't deny the depth of her attraction to the Thorne alpha.

But he also reminded her of someone else. Someone else with dark hair and amber eyes, who was far more lean, less muscular, and whose personality was like the sun compared to Alaric's moon.

Rocky.

Her omega *whined*, wanting, needing both the alpha in front of her as well as the one who was trapped.

Worry laced through her, compounded as if it were not her own.

She closed her eyes, wishing she could speak to Rocky the way she could with Mal or Alaric. But when she reached out in her mind, there was nothing.

Her heart ached, and tears threatened to fall, to drag her under to the depths of pain and despair.

We need him in our arms.

Cleo brushed the tear away quickly, stifling her sob. Emotionally, she was a wreck, and could not keep her feelings buried as she used to.

He's okay, she told herself.

We'll talk about it when he's awake. We'll make a plan.

A light grumble escaped his throat as she gently spread the blanket out over him and she stilled, worried she'd awakened him. The moment passed, and she turned to leave, knowing it was probably best.

But she could not set one foot in front of the other.

Not when the gravitational pull of Alaric Thorne weighed on her like the world on Atlas's shoulders.

"Cleo?" his gravelly, half-sleep voice caused goosebumps to prickle on her skin, caused a wave of heat to overtake her. It was as soothing as it was igniting.

She stifled a moan, biting her lip.

Now is not the time to get worked up!

She didn't answer him. She just stood there, frozen like a statue.

"Come here," he said, his voice stern and commanding, despite being laced in sleep and pain.

She could not deny his command, because it spoke to her on a deeper level than consciousness. Her omega obeyed without question, too tired to fight. She didn't want to admit she needed him.

But she did.

She turned around, focusing on her breath as she took slow steps toward him.

"Yes?" she asked, holding her head high, her hands placed in front of her. The heat rising off of her against her own palms was palpable.

She could not look at him, though. For she worried if she did, she would fall to the ground and the emotion, the pain, the turmoil, would release like a thunderstorm, and she would come undone.

Alaric shifted, sitting up on the bed. "Clementine, look at me," he commanded, and she fought the desire.

"I can't," she said, closing her eyes. The tears threatened to fall viciously. She grit her teeth together, her muscles tightening as she tried to hold onto her sanity. The remains of it, anyway.

Rain fell outside, softly pitter-pattering against the window. In the low light of the bedroom, it was rather... cozy.

Her omega paced, wanting nothing more than to settle into the nest before her.

Where her alpha lay, naked.

Warm fingers brushed her knuckle as he pulled at her hand, gently.

"Can't or won't?" he asked solidly. He tugged her hand, and she was powerless to fight his touch.

She fell against the edge of the bed, but she kept her eyes closed. Unfortunately, all her psyche could focus on was the stolen peek she'd taken moments ago.

What is wrong with you?

She huffed at her wolf.

Though she knew it was pointless to argue and fight with animal.

Cleo's voice cracked as she answered. "I can't." Darkness surrounded her.

Alaric pulled her closer, enveloping her in his warmth. He wrapped his arms around her tightly, pulling her against his chest as he buried his face in her hair, breathing her in like she was his source of air.

And perhaps, she was.

Cleo brought her hand up, tracing her fingers over the back of his, and she broke.

Into a million pieces, shattered like glass, she fell apart with a gut-wrenching sob.

"Shhh…" he soothed, running his fingers through her hair, his breath warm on her skin.

"It's okay, Cleo." His voice was not stern or commanding, it was soft.

Like a bed full of stuffed animals.

Like a cozy fire on a rainy night.

Cleo opened her eyes as she wiped the tears away. "No it's not." She sniffed. "Rocky is stuck in that god-forsaken house, and you're hurt because of me, and—"

Alaric sighed in defeat. "I'm not hurt because of you, Cleo. I'm hurt because that's just part of the fucking job."

"You were bitten, Alaric. Wh-what if Mal hadn't given you the anti-venom?" Her heart caught in her throat. "What if I hadn't gone with you? You wouldn't have been distracted, you wouldn't have—"

Her unsaid words died in the air as Alaric gently turned her chin toward him.

His amber eyes blazed with the reflection of the fire in her blood.

"Is that what you're worried about? That I could have died?" he asked, licking his lips.

Something in his gaze shifted, and Cleo was powerless to fight the urge to touch him.

She ran her hand along his jaw, down his neck, until her palm rested on his chest. His heartbeat was steady beneath her fingertips.

He didn't stop her.

"Yes," she said with a whimper. Her omega whined in their shared space.

Alaric's lips turned up in a soft smile. "Well, maybe I should get bitten by vampires more often," he teased.

Cleo cried out, laughing at his attempt to be funny in such a dire situation. Usually, Malcolm was the sarcastic one.

She gently pushed him in the chest. "That's not funny," she said with a sob.

Alaric tilted her chin up, gazing down at her with a fire that was as hot as it was comforting.

All the pain, the sadness, the guilt, dissipated when he looked at her with such... adoration.

Like she was truly *his*.

All you have to do is ask.

Those were the words he'd told her so long ago, the ones she'd stuffed down into the depths of herself.

"I don't want to lose you," she breathed softly.

Alaric slid his thumb across her cheek, wiping her tears away.

And then he kissed her.

But this kiss wasn't like the others.

It was softer, almost as if he was afraid she would disappear.

Cleo melted from the tenderness, the reverence.

She slid her hands up his neck, gripping his hair. The feel of the silky locks in her grasp grounded her.

He's okay.

My alpha is okay.

He broke away for a moment, licking his lips as he caught his breath.

"You called me *your* alpha," he breathed. His hand settled on her hip, his palm heating her skin through the denim of her jeans. Alaric's voice shook as he looked at her with glassy eyes.

She could not deny the truth when he looked at her like *that.*

For Cleo hadn't known how deep her desire went for the Thorne alpha until that moment, as the thunder rumbled outside.

"You are my alpha," she said softly, her heart in her throat.

The next words out of her mouth were her own, but yet... there were more.

They were fate itself.

"And I am your omega. I always have been."

Alaric crushed his lips against hers with hunger that went well beyond anything Cleo had ever experienced. He pulled her by her hips, his hand settling at her back as his lips moved with ferocity, and Cleo's entire body became Jell-O.

She was spineless, boneless, and nothing but *his.*

Instinct dominated all thought, all reason as she whined into his kiss, threading her fingers through his smooth locks, grabbing onto them for dear life.

When he broke apart their kiss, he stared down at her and said, "I've been waiting to hear you say that since the day you arrived."

As she looked up at him, she was acutely aware of his weight pressed against her, of the heat in her core.

Of the *need* running through her.

"So... you accept?" she asked shakily.

Alaric grinned, and the sight was

damn near orgasmic on its own.

She'd never seen him smile like that. He arched himself over top of her, pressing her body into the mattress as the blanket fell further down his body, resting across his hips.

"Yes," he said as slid his hand over her hip, slipping his palm beneath the hem of her tank top.

It was a blur of heat as shifting energy coursed through Cleo.

Her body boiled like molten lava and she fought Alaric's weight, needing to be cooled off. She needed air, she needed...

I know what you need, baby. But I want to hear you say it.

His voice in her head wasn't stern or commanding, nor was it gentle.

It taunted her. It baited her.

Cleo arched her back as the heat caused her to sweat, caused her insides to throb.

"I'm burning up," she said as she

nearly ripped her tank top off. "Please…"

Alaric laid his lips on her neck, sucking softly as he pressed himself against her, slamming her body back into the mattress like a weighted blanket.

Cleo writhed beneath him. The pressure was lovely, but she was still hot as hell.

Alaric nipped her skin with his fangs and Cleo moaned in response. His hands traced slow lines up her hips until he'd found her breasts. He freed her breasts from the cups of her bra, and she winced as his fingers grazed over her sensitive nipples. For some reason, they were a tad bit sore.

I should probably look into getting a sports bra in the future if I'm going to be beating down monsters on a regular basis.

"Say it," he murmured against her skin.

Cleo's eyelashes fluttered as he pinched her nipples, making her squirm.

"Alaric..." she whined, her thoughts hazy and disjointed as her wolf went haywire.

In fact, every part of Cleo was pure chaos as her mind, body, and soul tried to process the sensations coursing through her.

"I need *you...*" she whispered, the words sweet on her tongue.

The blanket between them did not hide the way his body responded to her words.

Alaric groaned as her words constricted in her throat.

Alaric's hands traveled across the waistband of her jeans, hovering for a moment before he took her lips once more. Slowly, he popped the button on her jeans, sliding his hand against her heat. The thin fabric of her panties separated them, and the heat flared like a fire in her core. Alaric pressed his fingers against her, taunting her.

Cleo wriggled against his weight,

arching her back as she sought his touch, needing to feel his friction.

She felt like she might combust into sparks if she did not find relief.

He grinned wickedly as he slid the side of her panties over just enough to tease her.

His fingertips slipped through her slick folds until he'd taken her clit between his forefinger and thumb. He stroked it slowly, causing Cleo to whine.

"Please," she cried. The sensation, the desire, the heat...

It was so overwhelming.

Cleo was on the edge of a cliff. She bucked and writhed, trying to angle herself so she could feel his palm pressed against her as he torturously teased her clit, until she was seconds away from release.

He pulled his hand, his fingers away, and she growled.

Alaric chuckled. "Patience, baby. Good

things come to those who wait."

Cleo whined. "I don't want to fucking wait." She lunged forward, knocking him onto his back.

He sucked in a deep breath, and instantly she felt remorse.

I hurt you! I'm so sorry, I—

Cleo reached for him, but he took her by the waist and slammed her back down. His hands made quick work of removing her pants, leaving her in nothing but her undergarments.

The blanket fell to the floor, leaving him exposed.

Cleo's fangs pushed through of their own accord as she took in the sight of him before her.

Alaric palmed his length, his thumb brushing over a swollen, purple knot.

Cleo's omega panted, whimpering with need.

Her pupils dilated and the shifting energy returned, festering within her.

The flames in her body rose, and she felt like she was going to burn alive if she didn't get what she needed.

His knot.

Her breath came in heavy pants as she struggled to see straight.

The human in her had disappeared.

It was replaced by a monster.

Alaric positioned himself above her, pressing his weight against her stomach as he dragged the edge of his leaking, swollen, knotted cock against her heat.

"Is this what you want, Cleo?" he growled as she struggled beneath him to buck, to arch.

Her body raged with heat.

The initial heat she'd felt the last year was nothing compared to this.

Even when she'd given in to it recently, when she'd let Malcolm put out the fire, she hadn't been so *consumed.*

Somewhere in the back of her mind, she knew it was because Malcolm was not a monster.

Not like she and Alaric were.

Cleo hissed, her fangs aching to bite.

Alaric's eyes glowed with ferocity as he bared his fangs, letting out deep, undulating growl that shook the room.

Cleo felt the shifting energy in her, but it was stunted. She wanted to rake her claws along Alaric's golden skin, but her claws would not come. No matter how hard she tried.

Frustration laced through her. She ran her fingernails down his chest, applying pressure. Enough to draw blood, even if it wasn't the same.

Alaric growled as he crushed his lips to hers, his tongue caressing hers. He ground himself against her, tormenting her. His hand snaked around her back, unhooking her bra.

She wriggled out of it underneath his weight as he worked her panties down her thighs, the motion drawing her closer to his swollen knot.

The head of his swollen cock was warm and wet and made her breathless. Alaric pulled back, just out of her reach as he groaned in her mouth.

Cleo had had enough torment.

She locked her legs around him, pulling him closer.

And then she flipped him over.

Shocked by her movement, Alaric's mouth opened, his fangs on full display.

The sight of his golden eyes and his ferocious fangs called to the animal inside of her and Cleo pressed her own body against him. Her palm held him in place, and he looked up at her.

Cleo's gaze pinned the alpha beneath her. The fire in his eyes burned and he didn't look away.

Cleo sank herself down on his length, the stretch of his knot filling her, bringing her a relief that was damn near angelic.

Alaric's hand slid up her thigh, until

he found her sex, his thumb and forefinger once again toying with her clit like a kitten with a ball of yarn.

"You are so fucking beautiful right now," he growled, his voice tinged in darkness. Her omega purred with excitement, relishing in its alpha's praise.

She rocked her hips forward slowly, the motion causing him to hit part of her that made her spine tingle.

"That's it, baby," he drawled, his breaths heavy.

His voice was dark and thick with lust and it was like a drug.

Cleo threw her head back in ecstasy as he thrust himself up into her, a deep growl leaving him as she rolled her hips forward. His knot dragged over a bundle of nerves inside her, causing her to cry out in pleasure.

"Harder," she commanded, every nerve in her body standing at attention.

She bounced and thrust against his

thick knot, against his fingers, relishing in the sensation it brought to her and her wolf as he cursed and growled beneath her as he thrust himself upward with a grunt.

There was nothing except the wild sounds of primal pleasure echoing in the space between them as she took what she wanted from him, as she *commanded* him to bring her what she and her wolf needed.

Once upon a time, Rocky had told her she was in charge. She was in control of who she allowed in her nest, who she chose as a mate.

And she wanted to make that abundantly clear to Alaric.

He was at her mercy.

But Alaric would not let her remain top wolf for long. The ever present fight for dominance against the Thorne alpha would never die.

It would burn like the fire of their bond

for eternity.

And perhaps, she loved that.

He would never let her win. He would challenge her forever.

In life, in love, and in the bedroom.

Alaric shifted them both as he wrapped his arm around her, cradling her back as he lunged forward, slamming her down again with a growl before kissing her. The bed moved with a harsh thud from the weight.

"So fucking bossy," he bit out as his fangs pierced her bottom lip.

The tang of blood on her tongue caused her core to flutter. Cleo bit him back.

"You're going to take this cock like a good girl and I don't want to hear your fucking attitude." His voice was dark, edged with teasing as much as it was with lust.

He thrust into her with a force that made her omega whine, made her see stars behind her eyes.

"Such a fucking diva," she nipped as he bottomed out and she hooked her legs over his thighs. The taste of his blood in her mouth was sweet, like hot strawberry topping on a fresh waffle.

Complete with whip cream.

Alaric sank his teeth into her neck and Cleo came undone. Her entire body curled around Alaric as his thrusts came harder, faster. The sound of wet skin, of deep growls, and cursing echoed in the air.

"Fuck, Cleo," he growled as he kissed her. She could taste her blood in his mouth, and the familiar flutter returned to her core.

"Alaric..." she cried his name like an answered prayer.

And perhaps it was.

For in Alaric's hold, she knew she was safe.

Loved.

Cherished.

The bond thrummed with vibrancy as he roared against her neck and a familiar warmth filled her, spurring her into another orgasm. Her body clung to his pulsing cock, locked together by his exploding knot.

Cleo's entire body went numb as Alaric collapsed against her, panting.

The heat subsided, and in its wake there was a warmth she'd never known.

Alaric nuzzled his face in her neck, his hands tracing her skin softly as the rain stopped. His touch was reverent as he whined against her throat in complete and utter submission, and the realization warmed her from her head to her toes. Their bond vibrated with warmth and adoration, with euphoria and bliss. Cleo wrapped her arms around him, holding him tightly.

"Mine," she purred, their bodies entwined. As the heat dissipated, so did the thickness of the knot that tied them together.

When Alaric left her body, she felt *empty,* despite Alaric's release dripping out of her. Warm fingers softly pressed into her sensitive, soaked entrance, pushing the remains of their union back inside her as he purred against her.

Her omega preened with pride.

Alpha has bred us.

Cleo didn't have the heart or the energy to argue with something that felt so undeniably right. It settled something within her, to feel his praise, his adoration.

Something that went deeper than sex, deeper than attraction.

"Mine," he whispered, his free hand pulling her lips to his once more. His kiss was soft and warm, a contrast to the rough heat and the hard fucking.

Cleo was remiss to argue with him as he peppered her skin with kisses and praise. She glowed beneath his love.

"Yes, Alpha. I am yours."

19

WARMTH SURROUNDED ALARIC, soothing his aching muscles.

He wasn't sure if the pain was from the vampire's bite, the anti-venom doing its thing, or the way Cleo had thrown him around in the bedroom.

Naturally, he knew wolves were strong, and therefore, Cleo could hold her own against him, but it was still shocking to think the small omega was capable of throwing his two hundred and fifty pound frame down on the bed, let alone *keeping* him there.

Cleo slept soundly against him, her bronze hair splayed about her pale skin. She curled closer to him, burying her head into his chest, and his wolf beamed with pride.

He ran his fingers through her hair, appreciating the moment before it would inevitably disintegrate. For when Cleo was awake, she breathed trouble.

My omega, sleeping peacefully in my arms. In my bed. The way it should be.

The memories filled his brain, and he almost couldn't believe any of it was real.

The bite, the Djinn who saved him.

Had the blue-eyed Djinn not knocked the vamp off of him, perhaps he would have been a dead man. Perhaps, they would have spread their toxic venom further, past the point of no return.

Malcolm's anti-venom wasn't much, at least, not for the metabolism of a werewolf, but the gesture was not lost on him and it had helped.

The hunter had come to his aid, and Alaric was thankful.

But his first aid stitching could use some finesse.

I'm really going to have to thank that Djinn if I ever see him again.

As his fingers traced rhythmic lines in Cleo's hair, he thought about Malcolm and Thomas's assessment.

Djinn did not usually travel in packs, and they were technically on the Mayfield's territory. Yet Thomas or the other wolves did not attack the blue-eyed monsters, even in the fray.

He hadn't thought anything of it until the pain in the ass hunter said something.

His thoughts wandered to Malcolm, who'd shot him full of vamp anti-venom.

Who'd driven him back to base and stitched his arm, which had been split from his tumble in wolf form.

Alaric wasn't entirely sure what to make of Cleo's... *other mate.* The word made him uncomfortable as his inner wolf screamed, "We are her mate! Her only mate!"

But Alaric knew the truth was much more complicated than that.

Cleo purred sleepily against him as a familiar voice broke the silence.

"Guess you aren't the only one who slept well," Malcolm said nonchalantly, examining his cuticles.

Alaric's wolf snarled in his brain, baring its teeth. The need to protect what was his was overwhelming.

"Relax, Al. I'm not going to kill you. Cleo wouldn't like that very much."

Malcolm leaned against the doorframe, his gaze flashing to the omega in Alaric's arms.

"Thank you. For the anti-venom, and... not... killing me."

Malcolm smirked. "Don't mention it.

Like, ever," he said as he pushed off of the doorframe, turning on his heel.

Before he could get very far, Cleo stirred.

"Malcolm…" her sleepy voice drawled, and Alaric tensed.

His wolf howled in protest.

Malcolm froze. "Yeah, baby?"

Cleo sat up, rubbing her eyes, her bronze locks falling over her exposed breasts.

Alaric's cock twitched to life, and he grunted in protest.

Though the desire to show the pain in the ass hunter who Cleo truly belonged to was prevalent, he also knew they had bigger things to worry about.

"You came back," she sighed, and Alaric did not miss the smile that crossed her face.

Malcolm's gaze softened. "Yeah, well, I had to make sure the big baby made it through the night."

Alaric growled as Cleo laughed.

She left his arms, running naked toward the hunter. Though he wanted to lunge at the hunter who set his hands on her waist, he found himself frozen.

Cleo leaned up on her bare tiptoes and kissed him, and suddenly warmth spread within their bond.

Gone was the anger, the fury, the jealousy.

Malcolm removed his flannel shirt, wrapping it around Cleo as he kissed her back.

Love spread like wildfire in their bond.

This human loved her.

He was sure of it.

Though it defied logic and sense, he couldn't deny the emotion, the depth flowing through the bond.

Alaric watched them intently with a new interest.

Fucking perv.

Malcolm's voice taunted him in his

head, and Alaric rolled his eyes, letting out a dark laugh.

Fucking pain in my ass, he shot back.

Cleo broke their kiss, turning to shoot Alaric a glare. "I can hear both of you, you know," she scolded him.

Alaric caught her glare as he stood tall, naked as the day he was born.

He raised an eyebrow as he sauntered over toward his omega. His wolf paced with possessiveness as the bond flushed with *heat.* Cleo's cheeks reddened as he stopped in front of her, grabbing her chin, and looking at her with a smirk.

"I know," he said, kissing her chastely, smiling as Malcolm cursed under his breath. Malcolm's grip on her did not relent.

Alaric let go of Cleo as he headed for the kitchen.

"Are you two coming, or are you just going to stand there and gawk?" he bit.

Malcolm's voice snapped back, "Maybe

if you put some fucking pants on!"

But Alaric did not miss the laugh in his omega's voice, and for that he could never be sorry.

He would torment the hunter a thousand times if it made her happy.

For she was *his omega.*

For her, he would fetch the moon.

Or more accurately, my baby brother.

***

Alaric fingered through his duffel bag in the living room, finding a clean pair of underwear and fresh pants. He'd just buckled the belt when he heard Cleo giggling, "Put me down!" from the hallway. His heart swelled at the sound of her happiness. A moment later, Malcolm's laugh echoed as he cursed.

He wasn't sure how he knew, but somewhere deep in the crevices of his soul, he knew the sound was a rarity.

Malcolm didn't seem the jovial type,

and a life spent hunting was surely quite depressing.

So Alaric said nothing as Malcolm and Cleo giggled, chasing one another down the hall. It reminded him of the way she was with Rocky.

Carefree.

Happy.

He'd been so jealous of her ease, her affection toward Rocky, blinded by his own obsession. But it was clear to see, even in hindsight, why she clung to Rocky as she did.

Because unlike him, Rocky was *free.*

Free of the responsibility Alaric was born into, free from the blistering heat of a full knot, free from judgment.

Everyone loved Rocky. It was hard not to. He was friendly, caring, and loyal. And he knew how to be fun.

How to make a prison feel like a home.

He'd always been the one instigating bouts of hide and seek and games when he was young. Alaric had always attributed it to his youth. There were eight years between them, after all.

Alaric's body tensed at the thought, the worry.

He didn't know how to be free and fun like Rocky, or even Malcolm. He only knew how to fight, how to lead.

But as he watched Malcolm wipe out, falling on his ass onto the hardwood floor as Cleo made her way into the kitchen, touting *"I win!"*, he vowed he would try to be more... fun. Once they'd completed their mission. Once he had his brother back home where he belonged, he would learn.

For Cleo, so I can make her laugh too.

"All right, I'm heading back. I've been awake all fucking night and my bed is calling my name."

Cleo sauntered over to where Alaric sat, wearing the fluffy robe from the bathroom he refused to touch, flashing him a pleading look.

He didn't have to have mindspeak to know what she was asking. He sighed, shaking his head as Malcolm made his way to the door.

Soon enough, they would embark on a rescue mission, and laughter would be far from their minds.

"You don't have to go, Malcolm," Alaric said, watching Cleo's eyes light up like fireworks on the fourth of July.

Malcolm's shoulders tensed as he froze, his hand on the handle of the door. He didn't look back, but he made no move, either.

"If you want to stay, you can stay."

Cleo whimpered, and the sound of her happiness warmed his heart.

Malcolm turned around, looking between the two of them. His gaze settled on Cleo, and he looked like he was struggling with what to say.

Alaric hadn't known the hunter long,

but he knew enough that the man never seemed to have a filter.

Anxiety flooded their bond as understanding befell him.

"You've earned it, Crowley," he said with a nod.

Malcolm dropped his hand, but he didn't move.

"Besides, Cleo wants you here." He waved nonchalantly.

That should be reason enough.

Malcolm's stony gaze met his.

"And what about you, Al? Do you want me here or am I cramping your broody alpha wolf style?"

Alaric looked at Cleo, her blue-green eyes sparkling with appreciation. He sighed, knowing resistance was futile. He nodded toward the hallway, toward the guest rooms.

"Go to bed, Malcolm. Get some rest."

Mal smirked. "That an order?"

Alaric growled. "Yes. You need to be at

your best, if you are to protect your mate."

Malcolm yawned as Cleo beamed with pride.

"You know what, I'm too fucking tired to argue with you about shit right now, so consider yourself lucky," Mal nipped as he sauntered toward the guest room at the other end of the hall.

"Thank you," Cleo whispered, throwing her arms around his neck. A warm wetness fell onto his shoulder as Cleo's terrycloth-covered breasts pressed against his chest. She purred in satisfaction, and his wolf forgot about the pain in the ass hunter.

"Of course," he whispered, kissing her cheek.

But their sweet moment would not last forever, it seemed.

His phone rang, making him nearly jump out of his skin. He grabbed it from the counter, knowing the familiar ringtone. He scowled, his voice hard and stern. All hints of teasing and love had diminished.

Cleo pulled away, her expression startled.

"I'm sorry, Cleo, I need to go," he said, feeling torn. Sawyer's ringtone echoed in the kitchen as she smiled softly.

"I know."

He silenced the call, sliding it into his pants pocket as he headed for the door.

"Try not to cause too much trouble while I'm gone?" He sighed, looking back down the hall. He could hear Malcolm's snores echoing in the hall.

"Where are you off to, exactly?" she asked, ignoring his words. His jaw tensed, but her bright eyes settled his anxious wolf.

"I need to find Thomas. Now that we *know* his wife is in their custody..." He swallowed harshly, flashing his own concerned gaze at her. "Now that we know

Rocky is with them as well, we need to consider all our options. We need a solid plan."

Cleo crossed her arms, nodding in agreement. "Right. Alphas know best."

Her words were true, but they lacked sincerity.

But Alaric did not have time to placate and soothe his omega, no matter how badly he wanted to.

So instead, he only leaned forward, kissing her sweetly, running his fingers through her hair as he whispered, "I'll come back, Clementine. I promise. And when I do, you can thank me later."

20

"HARDER," MALCOLM INSTRUCTED as he released Cleo from his grasp. Her glittering eyes were full of fire, her skin flush with heat and sweat.

Cleo fell back on her feet, bringing her knife—his knife—up in defense.

"We've been over this, baby. You don't *want* to hit me, but in the midst of a fucking attack, you can't hesitate. So don't hesitate with me."

He lunged forward and she dodged him, growling at him. Her natural green-blue eyes flashed with gold. She was trying to shift.

He grabbed her by the back of the wrist, spinning her around until he held her with one hand, his knife at her throat with the other.

His blood rushed, the movements familiar.

Fighting was all he knew. It was a constant in his life. Whenever Malcolm Crowley felt afraid, whenever he felt out of control, he fought.

He killed.

Cleo's waves bristled against his jaw as the scent of burning fire infiltrated him, filling his lungs. He breathed in, deep.

Knowing he could hold her, knowing she could destroy him in the blink of an eye was exhilarating.

She was a monster.

But she was *his* monster.

A deep growl escaped his throat as his cock twitched. He felt her pulse beneath his fingertips, the heat of her skin calling to his blood, singing one word over and over.

Mate.

Cleo writhed in his hold, growling as she dropped her knife.

Instantly, panic flooded him through their bond and he dropped his hold.

"Cleo?"

She broke free of him as she growled in frustration. "Why can't I fucking shift?" she cried.

Malcolm stood mere feet away as his gaze roved over the woman in front of him. She wore his red flannel shirt, the sleeves rolled up to the elbows tightly, her bronze waves pulled back in a high ponytail as opposed to the braid she usually wore. Two buttons on the front were popped, and she was not wearing a tank top underneath, her cleavage glistening with sweat.

The first time he'd laid eyes on her in

Howlers Bar, she'd been covered in layers, yet that didn't stop the werewolves in the bar from practically going feral when her heat came.

When you stirred her heat.

But now, the woman in front of him was not some small, shy, scared omega.

She'd undergone a transformation of sorts.

She was still small, but she was different.

When had she changed?

When had he?

Somewhere between the blood and the fight, between midnight phone calls and endless hunts, between sanity and insanity...

He had broken apart.

And only Clementine Srirocco was capable of stitching him back together.

Malcolm did not think twice about pulling her into his arms. "I'm sorry, I pushed too hard, I—"

Cleo pushed against him. "No, it's me. I can't shift. I tried the other night, when Alaric—" Her voice caught in her throat as she gently pushed away from him.

Malcolm collected their daggers from the ground, Alaric's name on her tongue stung like ice through his blood.

How he'd managed not to kill the alpha this morning, when he found him entangled—naked—around Cleo was a miracle.

Though he couldn't fault Cleo for having feelings for someone else. He'd stood in her driveway a year and a half ago, and told her he could not stay.

That he had a score to settle.

And even in the time between, despite his darkest wishes, he knew she would have to choose a Thorne to bind herself to. It was what her kind *did.*

Form packs, bonds.

So, why did the thought of her choosing the Thorne alpha hurt now?

Why did it make him want to scream "pick me!"?

They'd never promised to be exclusive, and he'd always told himself it was unfair to expect her to wait for him.

He wasn't sure why he came back to the cabin. After watching Dallas all night, with the other Djinn, he felt a mixture of emotion. He told himself he was waiting for the right moment to strike. But in the heat of the moment, during battle, he hadn't struck.

He'd pivoted.

He ran to Cleo, to Alaric.

His shoulders tensed as he slid his fingers along the blades in his hand, pressing the pad of his finger against the sharp tip, but stopped just short of drawing blood.

"Al seemed like he was doing just fine," he nipped.

Cleo's gaze pinned him underneath the hot sun. He didn't look at her, but he didn't have to. He could feel her ache, her pain in their bond.

"Because of you," she said softly.

Mal shook his head. "I didn't do it for him, you know," he said, sliding the tip of the blade into his skin.

The pain was a relief as blood pooled.

He swallowed, his heart in his throat.

"I know," she said. Her breath was warm on his skin, and he could feel the fire between them as she set her hand on his hip.

Her touch soothed his nerves and he hated it.

When he was around Cleo, he couldn't focus. Couldn't breathe.

Malcolm had spent so much of his life loving the kill, fighting against fate, against an endless string of monsters.

But he did not know how to fight this.

The spark inside of him that longed to be loved, cherished, and owned.

He did not know how to fight himself.

"You love him," he said the words solidly, breathing them into life.

It wasn't a question, but a truth.

Though they were less frightening than the declaration that threatened to slip out of his mouth of his own volition.

Pick me. Love me. Choose me.

Cleo's eyes sparkled as she looked up at him. "Malcolm..."

He turned away from her, taking one blade and striking the tree with it. Hard.

It seemed Cleo had done the impossible.

She'd broken through his sturdiest of walls.

Only hours ago, he'd walked into the room, the scent of sex and fire covering him like a thick fog.

He'd been exhausted, and therefore he blamed his stiff cock and mouthwatering lust on a lack of sleep.

It seemed easier than to admit the sight of his *mate* curled around the

Thorne alpha filled him with a hunger that was as savage as it was threatening.

After all, he didn't even like Alaric.

The man pissed him off, and he wanted to stab him every time he looked at Cleo.

Plus he'd gotten vamp blood all over the backseat of his car.

Malcolm vowed the next time he was in Alaric's swanky BMW he'd throw up. That way the alpha would never be able to get the smell out.

Fucking asshole.

"You can't tell me you don't. I can feel it in this fucking bond."

Jealousy was thick in his voice, and he hated that he couldn't hide it.

Hated that he didn't want to.

Cleo sighed. "Then you should be able to feel my love for *you.*"

The words struck him sharper than a thousand knives.

He growled again as he turned, holding

up his blade between them. "Don't do that," he said, his voice shaking.

Cleo raised an eyebrow at him. "Do what?"

"Don't fucking stand there like this shit is normal. That it's totally fine that I put aside my own shit—"

Cleo took a step closer, the tip of his blade kissing her ample cleavage. Her breasts seemed fuller, heavier, pressed together against his blade, and he wanted to see her blood rain down on her pale skin. Wanted to lick it off of her like a fucking animal. His cock throbbed at the idea.

"Stop messing with my fucking head."

And my heart.

And my cock.

Christ almighty.

Cleo settled her hand around the blade.

"Malcolm..." She tried to pull the knife down, but he held it with all his might.

For Malcolm feared if he dropped the knife, he'd perish.

Clementine would sink her claws into him, and she would tear him apart.

And he would relish the feel of her putting him back together, until he was whole again.

Images of Cleo and Alaric covered in blood flashed in his brain, and he had to stifle an angry growl. The memory of her fangs in his skin, *claiming* him, lapping at his own blood, only flared the fire coursing through him.

Did she bite Alaric while she fucked him?

Did she beg beneath him for release like she did when she was in *his* bed?

Had she done the same thing with Rocky?

The wolf she'd come to *him* for help rescuing?

The weight of it all on his shoulders was too much. He felt powerless against

Cleo's campfire scent, against her spellbinding blue-green eyes.

Against this *bond.*

So he attacked, like the animal he truly was.

"And what about your boy toy? Your damsel in fucking distress? Huh? You *love* him too, Cleo? Or is he just another fucktoy for you?"

Cleo's eyes glowed bright yellow as her fangs pushed through.

The sight made goosebumps rise on his skin, made his blood heat.

A mixture of killing desire and a need to surrender filled him.

It was a strange medley, and he wasn't sure which desire would win.

It was a startling reminder that Cleo was not some amorous human.

She was a monster.

"He is my *mate,*" she bit.

Malcolm scoffed. "Yeah, you seem to be collecting them like fucking Pokémon cards, so forgive me if I'm a little jaded about the term."

Cleo closed her hand around the blade, the scent of her blood filling the air. It made his mouth water, his cock twitch, and his heart beat faster.

He longed to lean in and kiss her. To steal her fire for himself, to soothe the storm inside of him that brewed, sucking in debris from everything in his proximity.

She pulled the knife from his hands, blood rushing down her wrist, down his. Her blood was warm and smelled like burning fire in the middle of an autumn day.

Cleo stabbed the tree, glaring at him.

"Fuck you, Malcolm," she nipped, turning her back on him.

His heart ached, his entire body tensing with apprehension.

Don't leave me.

Don't reject me.

I'm sorry.

I don't know how to do this.

I don't know how to be what you need.

The words he longed to say, to scream into the forest, would never escape his throat. Instead, he only grabbed the knives, throwing one at her feet.

"That's what I thought," he said as he turned around, heading back toward the hotel.

Back toward the mission.

Tears begged to free themselves from his amber eyes, but he would not give in.

So, he swallowed down his pain, his desires, and his truth. He had bigger monsters to fight, after all.

21

FUCKING MEN.

No, fucking hunters.

Cleo's entire body felt heated like a flame.

How could Malcolm go from carefree and fun to being a complete asshole in less than six hours?

It was like a long-needed nap had the opposite effect on him and turned him into someone else.

Though she couldn't really blame him. She knew he disliked Alaric, and she didn't need a bond to tell her that.

But for a sliver of a moment, when Alaric *kissed* her while she clung to Malcolm's arms, she dared to dream that maybe, just maybe, they could all exist in the same space without wanting to kill one another.

The omega inside of her purred and preened at the touch of her mates, and she hated that even the *thought* of both of them touching her, kissing her caused a moist heat to blossom in between her thighs.

What the fuck is wrong with me?

While she couldn't deny that Malcolm and Alaric were her mates, in the same way Rocky was, she also had to admit Malcolm was right.

It wasn't *normal* to have three mates, even by werewolf standards.

But the thought of losing any of them made her feel sick.

How could Malcolm be so dense?

Did he not feel the love in their bond?

The way her pulse raced when she looked at him?

The depth of her *need* to be his in every way possible?

Had he not remembered the moment she chose him as her mate?

When they'd made love in his hotel room and he called her such?

Had it been a lie?

Was he rejecting her all over again?

Tears bit at the edges of her eyes and she growled as shifting energy pulsed. Just like before, it did not fully kick over. Her claws would not come; her bones would not shift.

Her fangs were the only part of her she could shift.

She growled in frustration, picking up her pace through the woods, until a voice stopped her.

"Cleo? What are you doing out here?"

She stopped, her heart racing from her

run, and from the anger flowing through her over her *mate.*

But she could not deny the soothing, smooth sound of her alpha's voice, or how it relaxed her omega.

She closed her eyes, feeling overwhelmed.

By Malcolm, by the bond, by Rocky being so close, but yet so far away.

"I was training. With Malcolm," she said, biting her lip. She opened her eyes to see Alaric standing before her. "What are you doing out here? Shouldn't you be—"

"Mapping out vantage points," he said, as if it was obvious.

"Right, well, I wouldn't know because you don't tell me anything," she bit.

A part of her was angry from her argument with Malcolm, but she was also perturbed Alaric kept sidelining her. Rocky was her mate. She should be included in the plans to rescue him. Just because she was an Omega didn't mean she wasn't capable of helping.

She expected him to deflect, to tell her she wasn't capable of fighting. That her place was locked up in a nest, somewhere.

But Alaric's eyes softened. "Well, the last time I let you in, I ended up bitten."

She huffed in annoyance. "Well, you told me you could handle yourself."

Alaric raised an eyebrow. "We're not really talking about Rocky, are we?" he asked.

"Rocky is exactly what we *should* be talking about," she deflected.

Alaric hummed darkly. "Mhmm. Where is the hunter? Didn't you say you were—"

"I don't want to talk about it.," she said as she brushed past him.

Alaric grabbed her by the wrist. "I'm headed to the Badlands to meet with Thomas and the others in about an hour. Maybe we could... get something to eat beforehand? You've got to be starving."

Cleo relished the warmth of his touch, the silkiness of his voice.

It wasn't harsh or stern like usual.

And she could not deny that she was starving. She could not remember the last time she'd eaten. "I supposed I could use some sustenance."

Alaric smiled slyly. "Good girl."

The praise smoothed her rough edges, making her wolf preen.

***

The Badlands didn't open until four, but being as the Mayfields owned the place, they used it privately before it was open to the public. For the time being, it was only Alaric and Cleo, and of course, the staff.

Cleo sank her teeth into the juicy cheeseburger, groaning in relief.

"Oh my God, this is fucking amazing," she gushed, her eyes practically rolling back in her head. She couldn't remember the last time she had a cheeseburger with all the toppings. Howlers' burgers sucked.

The hot, melty cheese, the tart pickles, and even tomatoes—which she normally hated—tasted fantastic on her tongue.

Alaric cast her a sexy smirk as he tore into his buffalo chicken sandwich.

It didn't take Cleo long to polish off her burger and her fries. Though she was still hungry, she didn't want to make herself sick.

Alaric caught her gaze as it fixated on his fries. He gently pushed the plate toward her.

"Go ahead, I know you want them," he said with a grin.

"You are the best. Thanks," she purred happily, dredging his fries in the remains of her ketchup. Normally, anything with tomatoes made her run the other way but she was so hungry that she couldn't deny it tasted good.

"So what's the plan?" she asked, when

she'd finished his fries.

Alaric shrugged. "Thomas asked me to help map out the vantage points today. Now that we *know* where Ashley and Rocky are being held, we need a way in."

"They are being held by vamps, so can't we just walk in during the day and grab them?"

Alaric shook his head. The scent of fried chicken filled her lungs and made her mouth water.

He tore into the chicken with his teeth, before answering.

"I had Sawyer look into the property. I haven't told Thomas yet, but it's been Boracelli property since around the mid 1920s. Which, if the Boracellis are still using it, then we aren't dealing with regular vamps. Most of the vamps in their ranks are Daywalkers."

Great, so we're dealing with vamps with extra abilities.

Of course we are.

"They're still alive though, so that's good, right? Means they *need* them."

Alaric nodded. "Yeah, for now. But what happens when they don't?" Alaric's voice was heavy. "There's only so much blood they can take before…"

The silence was powerful, full of unspoken words.

"I know he's bait," she said softly. "But you can't ask me to just sit here. He's my *mate.*"

Alaric sighed in exasperation.

Cleo's stomach growled as Alaric raised another eyebrow.

"You want something else?"

Cleo peered at the dessert list, salivating over practically everything.

Was it weird to want one of everything?

Perhaps the stress really is catching up to me.

"I mean, I haven't eaten since I got here. I'm not sure how I'm still standing."

Alaric frowned. "You need to take

better care of yourself instead of running yourself ragged. You need to let me take care of you."

His words were clipped, but she could hear what he didn't say.

Running yourself ragged over things you have no control over.

Over Rocky.

Cleo shifted in her seat.

"I can't help it. My mate is my top priority. Nothing matters if—"

Alaric's gaze glazed over with shifting energy, his jaw tensing. "Yeah, and if something happens to you—your *mate* won't survive. Or maybe you've forgotten that, being as you've been so... distracted."

Cleo crossed her arms.

God, not you too.

"I have not been distracted," she lied.

Alaric chuckled. "Right. You always sneak out and steal my brother's car or fuck hunters when I'm not looking."

Cleo growled. "My sex life has nothing to do with rescuing my mate." She pouted.

Alaric laughed. "Cleo, your sex life has *everything* to do with your mates."

She looked away from him.

"It's the whole reason you have a mate bond." His voice fell, much more serious. "It's what omegas are literally *built for.*"

Sawyer's words echoed in her brain. *"It's all soft nests and hard dick for you."*

She huffed as she tried to push down the anger that those words caused her.

Alaric continued to press on. "While I'm not happy about your... bonds... outside of ours, I also understand. You gave in to your heat, with Malcolm it was bound to happen."

Cleo dared to look back at him as a silence befell them.

Alaric spoke cautiously. "Did you... have you..." He seemed to be struggling with his words as his cheeks flushed.

"Have you and my brother...."

Cleo tensed as embarrassment fell over her face. "Um, no. We have not."

Alaric's eyebrows furrowed as his jaw tensed. His expression was full of relief, but also worry.

"Why? What does that have to do with anything?"

Alaric sighed. "He accepted you, right?" His jaw tensed.

Cleo nodded. "Yes."

I think so...

"We have three days, then." He swallowed harshly.

"Three days for what?"

"Three days, the red moon will rise. You and Rocky need to... bond. Or it won't be pretty for either of you. An unbound bond will result in a severance. A severance that is extremely painful. On both parties."

Cleo felt a rush of concern flood her. "Then why are we sitting here? Why have we not—"

Alaric held a hand out, stopping her from getting up. "Because we can't afford distractions, Cleo. We need to be on all our fucking games."

Cleo huffed in annoyance. "I am on my game."

Alaric gazed at her with so much love she thought she might expire. "No, baby. You're not. You're a mess."

Cleo rose from her chair, readying to run. But she could not make her legs move.

Alaric was right. She was a mess.

She was emotional, starving, her entire body ached. She felt like a yo-yo, being pulled in several directions.

How had things gotten so complicated?

"Malcolm is a mess and he seems to do just fine," she bit.

Alaric laughed. "He is not fine. He's a fucking disaster. Honestly, I don't get what you see in him."

"You aren't any better," she growled. "You push me and pull me and it's exhausting."

Alaric rose from his chair as the Mayfield pack walked through the doors.

He looked between Cleo and Thomas, between his mate and the pack he was aiding.

"You're right. I am a mess too. But I know how to separate myself from the mission. I know what I am fighting for. Does he? Do you?"

Cleo whined at his words. Of course, she knew what she was fighting for.

Love.

Acceptance.

Family.

Images pushed through her mind of what those things meant.

Images of a frightened hunter in need of love.

Of a strong, demanding alpha surrendering under her gaze, her touch.

Of a sweet, loyal mate who'd shown her a softer side, who'd protected her and showed her how deep a mate bond could be.

Family.

The word hung in her throat, making her mouth run dry, her heart beat faster.

She'd always known one day she'd be given to a pack, that was expected. It was no secret her ability as an omega was coveted, and what her future would be.

But it wasn't until that moment as she looked at Alaric, she understood that the three of men—the pain in the ass hunter, the brooding alpha, and her protector—were more than just *her* pack.

They were *all* her mates, her future.

But they were fractured by singular bonds and jealousy, stifled by age-old roles and conceptions.

And at that moment, Cleo understood she wasn't just fighting to save Rocky.

She was fighting for what she wanted

more than anything.

A pack of her own. A family.

"Of course, I do," she said, her voice catching in her throat.

"Alaric, we need to talk," Thomas Mayfield said, stopping just shy of them. His pack flanked his side.

"About?"

"We have a plan. And some new allies to consider," Thomas said, his gaze flashing to Cleo. "But this is official pack business."

The implication was clear. Cleo was not allowed to be privy to this information, and she hated it. She wanted to shift, to show Thomas she was more than capable of being in the same room.

She was not some weak omega.

Why should he be allowed to decide how to save *his* mate, when she was not allowed to have a say about her own?

But the shifting energy did not come, which only frustrated her more.

Alaric reached out, tracing his hand up and down her arm. The touch instantly soothed her anxious wolf. She hated that he had such a profound effect on her.

"Understood," Alaric said sternly.

Please, Cleo.

His voice in her head pleaded with her, a stark contrast to his alpha stance, his commanding tone.

Stand down.

We'll talk about this later.

She did not want to listen. She was tired of being left out. Tired of waiting.

But the sudden rush of nausea and body aches made it hard to ignore his pleas.

Perhaps I shouldn't have had that last plate of fries.

She sighed deeply.

Fine.

"I suppose I'll leave you to it then," she said coldly as she brushed past him toward the cabin.

***

As Cleo climbed the last step, she felt the undeniable urge to wretch. She'd barely made it into the cabin, her entire body heating like a flame as she ran toward the ensuite bathroom.

Her muscles tensed as she heaved, the foul taste of acid and ketchup in the back of her throat throwing her into another convulsion. But it seemed nothing else would come up.

She banged her forehead against the cool ceramic of the toilet, cursing Alaric and her insistence of finishing his fries.

It's probably all the grease.

I definitely need to make healthier choices.

When she was finally certain the wave of nausea had passed, she rose from the ground. Padding through the cabin, she found her backpack—Rocky's backpack—

and fished out her toothbrush and some toothpaste.

She was glad she'd packed enough necessities for a week, though she had hoped by this point she would have had Rocky in her arms.

Where he belongs.

Her heart ached at the thought of the youngest Thorne, and she let out a whine.

There was no one else in the cabin, and knowing so only added to the loneliness she felt. She hadn't been alone in quite some time, and the feeling was unnerving.

The last year and a half she'd spent nearly every day with Rocky. Even Malcolm called frequently enough. And then she'd shown up in Mayfield, and hadn't spent a moment alone since. She was either tied up with Malcolm or Alaric, or fighting a bloody battle.

Cleo shoved her toothbrush in her mouth as she tried to push away the thoughts pervading her brain. Another wave of sickness came and went as she spit out her toothpaste foam.

"Maybe Alaric is right. Maybe I just need a fucking shower and a nap," she grumbled aloud to herself, turning on the shower. The hot water steamed up the room fast, and she did not waste a moment.

The heat was a familiar friend. She'd lived with it for a year and a half, after all. She thought giving in would take it away, but it didn't.

In fact, the heat felt *stronger* in the presence of Malcolm and Alaric. But it was undeniably the strongest when they were both in the room.

When they both *looked* at her like she was *theirs.*

Cleo shoved the tempting thoughts down, deep in her soul.

She could not voice such things aloud.

Her cheeks blushed as her wolf

salivated.

Don't get your hopes up.

That's never going to happen.

She lathered her hair with shampoo, massaging her scalp. The smell was spicy, like cinnamon and chocolate.

Like warm cookies.

It reminded her of Rocky.

Her wolf whined, her voice echoing the loss.

Seeing him with the Mayfield omega had done something to her. She understood he was likely one of many prisoners, and as such, he'd try to help any way he could. No doubt, he was protecting her as he had protected Cleo.

Realistically, she knew that. But intrinsically, the thought of Rocky touching anyone else, especially another omega made her seethe with jealousy.

The water tinkled against the tile like an echoing bell, and she was powerless to fight the memory that pushed forth.

Of the rain as it fell around them, as he looked down upon her.

As he kissed her.

And for a moment, Cleo could have sworn she could still *feel* his lips on hers.

Rocky kissed her with a tenderness, a passion, that stirred more than just heat.

It was sincere, reverent.

In that one kiss, Cleo submitted.

Rocky may not have been an alpha, but he had commanded her heart, her lips, like he was one.

A soft whimper escaped her throat as her hands slid down her warm, wet skin. The heat in her core returned, and she mewled in defeat.

Would it ever end?

This agonizing heat?

You know when it will end, her wolf said.

Cleo pushed the animalistic instinct, the truth back into the depths of her soul, where she locked everything else.

Despite the constant sex, she hadn't given much thought to whether or not she would end up being successfully bred.

There were bigger things to worry about.

Like rescuing my mate.

She turned the water off, towel-drying her achy body.

The heat was soothing against her muscles, but the towel dragging against her chilled nipples made her wince in pain. The scratchy fabric aggravated her and her wolf.

She looked at the clock on the nightstand. It was four pm. She set her alarm for an hour, settling on the thought that when she awakened, if Alaric was not back, she would find him at the Badlands.

She would not wait around for him any longer. Thomas Mayfield would just have to deal with it.

Exhaustion overcame her as she

yawned, dropping the towel. She fingered through the backpack for a clean pair of underwear and a shirt, when her fingers brushed against something much softer than her usual cotton tees and tanks. Beneath the fringey kimono, was something that felt familiar.

Flannel.

She pulled out the blue-checkered print shirt, her fingers sliding through the warm fabric as she realized Rocky had left it in his backpack.

Without thinking she pulled it up to her face, burying her nose in his scent.

Campfires and dozens of chocolate chip cookies filled her lungs. Her wolf was soothed by the scent of its mate, and she hugged the soft fabric close.

The memories that pushed forth were irrefutable.

Running the fields, chasing after him.

Smashing cookie batter on his cheek while they helped the Thorne pack kids bake Christmas cookies.

Curling up on the couch watching movies together.

Rocky made life at the Thorne estate bearable.

More than bearable.

He made it home.

Somewhere along the way, when they'd been pretending...

They'd stopped pretending.

She clutched his flannel close, like a stuffed animal, as she lay down, naked in the midst of upturned sheets and pillows, closing her eyes. And as his scent filled her lungs, she dared to dream.

The door was open, the amber light casting shadows on the walls.

Everyone had gone to sleep, but Cleo wasn't tired.

She curled next to Rocky as the light from the television bathed them both.

Rocky yawned, stretching behind her.

When his arm fell on top of the

cushions, she shifted her weight against him, causing his arm to fall.

He smirked as she looked up at him.

"You don't have to stay up with me, you know. You can go to bed. I know we tired you out today," she said.

"Nonsense," he said with a grin. "You just have boring tastes in movies," he taunted her.

She smirked at him. "Typical man. You can't handle a movie if there's romance."

Rocky shifted his weight, the motion causing her to sink further into the plush couch, her head falling against his chest.

He smelled like fire and cinnamon, like chocolate chip cookies with a hint of hazelnut. Likely from the cookies they'd baked earlier for his youngest cousin's birthday.

Firelight danced off of his skin, reflecting in his amber eyes.

Cleo's wolf paced with anxiety, her tongue practically hanging out of her mouth.

She was suddenly very hungry.

And hot.

As if he could sense her shift in mood, he shifted her lightly, putting distance between them.

"Maybe we should both go to bed," he said, his voice tinged in a darkness she had never heard before. He licked his lips, but his gaze remained solid, unwavering. He reached for the remote.

Though something was different. In her memory, Cleo knew what had happened.

She'd agreed, and he'd shut the television off.

She lay in bed that night, the heat driving her to the point of madness. Only her touch kept it at bay.

The need to give in to her heat, to choose a mate, grew stronger every day.

But as Cleo replayed the scene, she saw it with new understanding.

Remembered the wet, hot heat that formed between her legs, remembered the hunger, the desire to give in.

To Rocky.

"I don't want to go to bed," she said, removing the remote from his hand.

"Cleo..." he whispered, his voice soft and full of want.

Her fingers slid over his smooth skin, relishing in the feel. His hands were different from Alaric's or Sawyer's.

They were not calloused or rough. They were smooth and warm. Where Sawyer's touch was always deliberate and lingered too long, Rocky's touch was always quick, always careful.

Cleo threw the remote on the coffee table as she crawled closer to him, backing him into the couch.

"Yes, Rocky?" she purred, setting her hand on his hip, leaning into him. Her heartbeat was like a freight train in her chest, loud and heavy.

"I—" he swallowed nervously. "You don't want this," he said, dropping his gaze, adjusting his cock in his jeans. "You don't want me. You want him."

Her heart broke. Of course, Rocky had been her confidant, her friend, her sounding board for the last year and a half. He'd covered for her the night Malcolm stirred her heat, and he'd kept up her lie. He'd listened to her whine and pine for a man who she never saw, who she was never certain she'd see again.

But couldn't he see that she wanted him too?

She looked forward to seeing him every day. To running with him, to playing with him and the Thorne pack children. She looked forward to clandestine movie showings late at night, curled up on the couch.

Because she was deeply in love with Rocky Thorne.

She hadn't known it then, but she

knew it at that moment, as she dreamed.

Of what could have been.

What she was fighting for.

Cleo hovered her hand above his for a moment. Her gaze flashed at him with a fire of her own.

"I do want you, Rocky. I think I've wanted you a lot longer than I realized," she whispered, bringing her lips to his.

The fire crackled, and he melted under her kiss.

She pulled herself closer, straddling his lap as he rested his hands on her hips.

"Cleo..." he whispered her name with sincerity, with adoration.

When he breathed her name, it was like a prayer.

"I want to wake up and make pancakes with you every day for breakfast. I want to run with you until our legs are weak. I want to laugh with you, and play with you and the kids. I want your warmth, your heart. I want your scent to cover me like a blanket, and I want everyone in the pack to know you're mine. That I choose you."

Rocky tensed as she traced her hand over his prominent bulge.

"I'm a virgin," he squeaked. "I can't… You're an omega, and I'm a twenty-three year old fucking virgin." His cheeks reddened like tomatoes.

So tempting, and quite satisfying.

"I'm aware," she said with a soft smile.

Cleo smirked, rubbing her palm over his rigid cock, softly purring in contentment as she finally settled her hand on his hip once more.

Somewhere inside of her she relished in the knowledge that he had been untouched by anyone other than himself, but she did not want to push him.

He continued. "And I'm not an alpha. I don't have a knot, so I can't—" The words were lost in the air as he looked away, ashamed. "I'm not a beta or a hunter, or… If you choose me, there's nothing I can offer you."

"Yes, there is," she said, kissing his lips softly.

He returned her kiss with a heat that rivaled the temperature in Mayfield.

Cleo slowly popped the button on his jeans, unzipping his zipper.

"You can give me your heart." Her fingers gently toyed with the edges of his jeans as she gazed at him. "You can give me your consent." She kissed him softy and he melted like chocolate underneath her touch.

"Do you accept me, Rocky?"

He gazed down at her, the fire reflecting in his eyes, his lips swollen from her kiss. The sight was quite possibly the sexiest look she'd ever seen on his face.

"Yes." He swallowed harshly, his voice thick with lust. He leaned forward, kissing her deeply as he grabbed her wrist, sliding it beneath his jeans.

Her hands cupped his rigid warmth, noting the wetness against her fingertips.

Rocky's head fell back against the cushions as she stroked his velveteen shaft and watched his eyes fall shut.

She moved him back against the cushions, taking her time as she freed his cock.

"Look at you, you are perfect. Just as you are," she said, taking in the sight of his sizeable cock, gleaming with precum. "I don't want you to be some Cassanova or have a knot. What I need, is you. I need my savior. My loyal, protector. Just the way you are."

She could not help herself as she licked the fresh bead off his tip, relishing in the salty sweetness of his taste.

He tasted like cinnamon and vanilla cream.

Like sweet mate.

"I need you, Rocky."

He groaned as she dove in for another taste, wasting no time.

"Oh my God, Cleo..." His voice was strained.

She popped off of him, licking her lips as she giggled.

"So fucking perfect. This cock belongs to me, and only me," she said with pride.

Rocky looked down at her, his pupils blown, gold shifting energy glittering around his iris. "Yes," he breathed, dark and husky. "I'm all yours, Cleo. If you'll have me."

Cleo pushed his legs apart as she devoured him whole, taking him into the back of her mouth with an eagerness that was addicting.

Rocky's hand slid in her hair, gripping the locks softly as he gently thrust his hips up. The movement was slow, new.

Uncharted territory for the both of them.

"Oh God, your mouth feels so fucking

good," he cried, the fire blazing between them.

Cleo circled her tongue around him, her fingernails gripping his thighs as he hit the back of her throat.

"Fuck, I'm coming," he sighed, his cock pulsing as he groaned, his pleasure a soft cry in the quiet, dark living room as she swallowed his release.

When she removed herself, she could see the heat in his eyes as he adjusted his cock, stuffing himself back in his underwear. The sight as he knelt in front of her, his lean muscles glinting in the light, was breathtaking. And knowing she'd just tasted him, knowing his pleasure was hers and hers alone, sent a shockwave straight to her core.

Mine.

When he'd settled himself, he shifted his stance, grabbing her by her thighs as he pushed her back into the couch. She giggled with excitement from the shift in his demeanor. Rocky was usually so reserved, so patient.

His movements were graceful, yet somehow predatory.

He kissed her lips hurriedly, pushing up her dress as his tongue danced with hers, and she groaned in response.

"You taste so fucking good," she groaned as his fingers traced her panties. She was hot, consumed by heat. By the fire between them, around them.

The fire in her blood, the fire that ignited her wolf.

It was true, Rocky did not have a knot.

But the desire to be bred by the Thorne wolf was more than evident as the word reverberated in her brain.

Mate.

His fingers teased her through her lace, gently torturing her. His touch reminded her of someone else.

Someone else who favored torment. Perhaps it was an inherited trait.

"Tell me what you want from me, Cleo," he whispered against her lips. "Teach me how to please you."

His voice was soft, but full of desire. Full of love.

Cleo looked in his eyes, seeing the unspeakable truth. Her pleasure outweighed his own. Her needs, her safety. For Rocky, Cleo came first. In all things.

No one had ever truly asked her what she liked. As an omega, it was just understood that sex was enjoyable, but it was an omega's duty to provide heirs.

Interest and satisfaction were not paramount to being part of the equation.

Cleo looked at Rocky with her own pleading eyes as she licked her lips.

The world around her disintegrated into ash, until the warmth of the living room disappeared.

"Rocky..." she called, turning around in a panic. The walls were dark and the air smelled of blood, of death.

Vampires.

"Rocky!" she called out, but he did not answer.

The familiar scent of campfire and chocolate chip cookies filled her senses and she breathed a sigh of relief. His breath on her skin was warm, as he whispered in her ear.

"I'm here, Cleo. I'm not going anywhere."

She turned to see him standing there, his eyes sullen, and his skin pale.

The harsh truth.

His neck had two large bruised bites.

"They hurt you." It wasn't a question.

Rocky covered his bites, his eyes glassy. "I can handle it."

"But the venom..."

"They aren't turning us, so they aren't spreading the venom. They're just... feeding. Better me than Ashley or the kids."

Cleo's blood chilled. "Kids?"

Rocky coughed, his chest heaving. He looked thin. Thinner than usual.

She hated to see him so mistreated.

He needed to be safe, in the living room of the Thorne estate.

Wrapped in her nest.

"Yeah. They are hybrids. It's like Children of the Corn, but scarier. One's a Djinn hybrid, one's a wolf hybrid... and the other two I have no clue what they are."

A strange, maternal instinct overrode her brain. Children. Four of them.

The vampires hadn't just taken an omega, or an omega's mate.

They'd taken children.

"We're coming for you. All of you I promise." she said.

Rocky swallowed harshly. "I know, Clementine. I know." He gave her a half smile, and just like the remains of her sanity, he disappeared into the darkness.

22

ROCKY WOKE UP with his skin coated in a thick sweat. The sounds of breathing were faint; everyone was asleep across the hall. His cock throbbed beneath his clothing and the thin covers. He'd been sequestered to a much smaller, dirtier room since he offered himself to the vampires earlier.

Instinctively, he grabbed himself, trying to quiet the sudden disturbance.

The dream he'd had had been far too intense.

Remembering the night he and Cleo had watched *Serendipity*, when they'd *cuddled* on the couch had filled his brain.

For a moment, it had felt like they were... together. Just a wolf and his mate, snuggling on the couch, watching a movie.

He'd wanted to kiss her then. To reach out, pull her lips to his, and tell her he loved her.

That he'd fallen deeply in love with her. But he did not wish to persuade her against her mate.

He knew who she loved. He'd helped her keep up her lies.

He'd told himself she couldn't want someone like him. A run of the mill wolf, a twenty-three year old virgin. Not to mention he wasn't as strong or built as his brothers. There was no for sure sign his injury would get better, which meant shifting was limited for him, nor did he have any type of rank.

He was just simply not enough for an omega.

But in his dream, it had felt so real. It hadn't ended the way it did in reality.

In his dream, Cleo looked at him for all his shortcomings, and she said she wanted him, just as he was.

She wanted a *life* with him.

And he could not deny he wanted the same. He knew it was crazy to want the things he did. After all, he did not have a fabled knot and his sexual experience was quite limited.

But he wanted to give Clementine everything she deserved and then some.

Including an heir.

His cock twitched in response to the thought of being buried in Cleo, of her taking *his* virginity.

Of the fruit of their bond taking hold.

He vowed that when he finally escaped the vampire's nest, when he finally found Cleo, he would waste no more time on ifs, ands, or buts.

He would sweep Clementine *Thorne* up in his arms, and never let her go.

He would fight to be the man she needed.

Whatever that looked like, whatever she needed him to be. Even if it meant he wasn't the *only* one.

The door creaked open, bathing the dark room in a sliver of light. Rocky held his hand up, shielding the brightness as he tried to make out who was at the door. No one had set foot in yet but the door remained open.

"Come on, Trevor, just grab the wolf and let's go. I'm fucking starving."

Rocky tensed as he realized they were here for him. Again. He'd thrown himself on the chopping block to prevent the vampires from feeding on Ashley. She was looking worse by the minute, and Rocky knew from many assisted deliveries that stress was not good for the mother or the baby.

And as much nourishment as Ashley provided for Henry, she was not replenishing her nutrients. Between the vampires and the thirsty infant, she was being drained completely. It was only a matter of time before her blood and milk supply ran out.

He couldn't let that happen.

His cock throbbed as his bones ached. He was tired, sore, and he felt like literal death.

I suppose being a vampire's primary food source will do that to a person.

The vampire known as Trevor entered the room with a blue-haired woman who did not look like anything like a vampire.

For starters, she had glowing blue eyes and looked like a biker. Like the creatures that had been *attacking* on the field the other night.

The woman grabbed him by the neck, hissing as she licked her lips. Bright white fangs pushed through as the man held him still. Rocky fought, despite his pain. His leg had started to feel better, but he was not one hundred percent.

But despite the pain and the injuries, he fought a good fight.

But two vampires were better than one, he'd learned that the hard way.

Two sets of fangs pierced his skin and he cried out in pain. The female brushed herself against him, giggling. Her hand palmed his erection as Trevor groaned.

"Well, well, would you look at that? Looks like Balto here is hyped up on mate bond chemicals tonight."

Trevor groaned as he sucked at the fresh wound in his neck.

"Don't fucking touch me," he growled, smacking her hand away with claws.

This cock belongs to me and no one else.

Dream Cleo's words reverberated in his head, causing him to panic.

He didn't *want* anyone else's touch but hers. Certainly not a handsy monster's.

His own shifting energy kicked over as he growled, baring his fangs.

The woman laughed.

"Christ, Reby, what's so funny?" Trevor nipped, pulling up from his spot on Rocky's neck.

"Little wolf is feisty tonight."

Trevor held his arms back, his fingernails digging into Rocky's sweat-slicked skin.

"I can taste his desire. It's fucking potent."

The blue-haired vamp laughed insanely. "Oh God, I know. I'm so hot I don't know if I can stand it. His heartswish is fucking divine."

What the hell is a heartswish?

Trevor sank his fangs back in as Reby removed her shirt.

Rocky twisted in Trevor's grasp.

"Now I see why Eden's always going off

about these fucking bound wolves."

"Save some for me, will ya?" she said as she grabbed him from her cohort.

Trevor stumbled backward, his hand palming his tented erection. "Fuck, I don't think I've ever tasted a mate this sweet," he sighed. "I feel like I could fuck you for eternity," he growled.

The blue-haired monster woman giggled. "I'll hold you to that, baby."

"Although... we should probably save him for Eden," Trevor spat. "Boy is Grade A Wolf Meat."

Trevor cast him a smirk that made his skin crawl.

"How'd Octavius get so lucky? Hmm? How does he always find the juiciest steaks?"

Who's Eden?

The blue-haired vamp sank her teeth into him and he felt weak, his thoughts dispelled by the sudden flush of pain again as his blood rushed to the surface.

They were going to drain him.

He was sure of it.

He'd never get out.

Never see Cleo again.

That one name was the magic he needed.

The only drive, the only desire.

He used all his force to throw off the woman, who was stunned.

She fell into the man, knocking him down.

It was enough of a distraction as Rocky scrambled to the bathroom, locking himself in it.

"Eden always gets the good ones. Hasn't made a difference yet though, the bitch is still barren, so why not keep him for ourselves?" He could hear Reby bite between sucking. The sounds of crumpled clothes hitting the floor echoed in his sensitive hearing. He shuddered as a thud hit the floor.

"Because she would kill us. Besides,

we can't keep them from her. She'll smell them the second she sets foot in the house."

The panting, the breathing, the cursing continued as the sounds of sex filled the room next to him.

He hated how it spurred his own desire.

"Fuck, you are like an animal!" the woman cried out as Trevor roared. The sound was like something between a monster and a dying creature.

Blood traveled down Rocky's neck and his entire body felt as if it was hit by a truck after being dropped from an airplane. He leaned against the cold toilet seat, his hand on his cock as he tried to quiet the ache, the desire in his groin, tried to block out the sound of the vampires coming in the room next to him.

Cleo's image filled his psyche. Her bronze and gold hair cascading down her shoulders. Her bright, blue-green eyes.

Her perfect, pink lips, and her smile.

Her laugh.

Her kiss.

The memory of Cleo was so strong.

The desire to get back to his Omega's arms was stronger.

He cracked the bathroom door, if only to make sure the vampires had gone.

And only when he realized it was sunset, the time for the vampires to awaken and hunt, did he collapse into a heap, hoping his own healing would provide him with enough of a boost. Enough to possibly take down Reby and Trevor the next time they tried to feed on him.

If he could eliminate their main guards, perhaps they'd have a chance of actually escaping.

And a sliver of a chance was better than none.

23

THE BADLANDS WAS quite busy, bustling with townsfolk and visitors. And new "allies", as Thomas had called them.

Alaric wasn't entirely sure what to make of Thomas's declaration that he was working with a vampire. To fight another vampire.

A vampire who *controlled* an army of Djinn, which did not sit right with him.

Though it seemed for now, they had aligned.

Malcolm was right, the Djinn were

solitary creatures and rarely traveled in packs, if at all, and vampires... well, he knew firsthand they could not be trusted. Like his kind, the Djinn were natural born enemies of a vampire.

So why had a *pack* of them aligned themselves with the vampiress Amora Medici?

What was she lording over their heads to gain their alliance?

What was she lording over Thomas's?

Alaric felt like the world around him was slipping away, changing into something he no longer knew.

When he'd come to Mayfield, the mission was simple. Help Thomas rescue his wife, and in turn, he would provide Alaric with soliders to protect their mountain lands. To take back the vampire's territory and make it their own.

To bleed the bloodsuckers dry.

But now...

Now, everything had gone to hell.

Rocky was a hostage, Clementine was acting like a mad wolf, her moods and actions all over the place, and he knew he couldn't blame the heat. Not entirely.

And his allies were now working with enemies.

At least they could all agree the Boracellis should be exterminated.

A common goal, I suppose.

Alaric took another drink of his whiskey. The first had barely touched his nerves, his anxiety.

He was tired of the odds stacking against him. He wanted more than anything to dive into that house and pluck his brother and the Mayfield's omega from their prison and to go *home.*

But what was home, now?

He and Cleo had broken a barrier, that was true...

But when Rocky returned to her arms, would she forget about him?

Would they go back to the way things

were?

Where she attached herself to his baby brother like glue and left him to suffer in silence?

Would Rocky become territorial over his mate and challenge him?

And what about Malcolm?

Where did he fit into the equation?

Instead of answering the questions that plagued him, Alaric drank.

He lost his thoughts in the bitter liquid and the sounds of terrible karaoke as Thomas ordered another round. Small victories, and all.

The Mayfield alpha garnered the battle a victory. With the help of the Djinn, the vampires had retreated, and several had perished.

But Alaric knew vampires were like a hydra. Cutting off one head always spawned at least two more.

"Save some for me, why don't you boys?" A saccharine voice rang out and he looked up from his drink as Thomas rose from his seat at the head of the table. The Mayfield pack bristled in their seats, years of ingrained fear and natural instinct difficult to ignore in the presence of their natural born enemy. Even if she was breathtakingly beautiful.

Long, golden curls bounced halfway down her back. She was dressed in a soft pink sweater, and the color reminded him of Cleo's perfect lips. Her bright green eyes twinkled like jewels under the amber light of the bar. She looked barely legal, but he knew that was likely an act meant to entice men like him into death.

The innocent looking woman had likely killed hundreds, if not, thousands of men and women over the course of a century.

No, Amora Medici was a literal wolf in sheep's closing.

A deadly, venomous creature.

Who Thomas apparently trusts.

"Amora, so nice of you to join us,"

Thomas said with a mega-watt smile. The several rounds of drinks had obviously started to affect him.

"Well, we are celebrating a victory, are we not? A victory in which I have *aided* you."

The smile fell from his face as he swallowed nervously. The wolves at the table stilled, their shoulders tense.

This could go either way, Alaric knew that. He only prayed Amora swung in their favor, or it would be a brawl.

The group of Djinn hung behind her, like a pack.

Glowing green eyes fixed on him and the Mayfield pack, and it was unnerving. Alaric's wolf prepared to attack.

Thomas and Amora stared at each other for a moment. He pushed his whiskey toward her.

"We are."

Amora smiled wickedly. "Good boy. I see your intelligence proceeds you."

A low growl echoed from one of the wolves, but Thomas shrugged nonchalantly.

"What can I say? The enemy of my enemy is my friend."

"Have a seat, Amora. Celebrate this unprecedented victory with us."

Amora shrugged in response, flipping some silky blonde hair over her shoulder.

"Tempting, but I must refuse. I must tend to my Heartsgrave. You understand." She licked her fangs as she grinned. A waitress stopped to give her a glass of what looked like champagne.

Alaric gripped his glass tighter, watching the Djinn behind her.

"All I ask is that they refrain from killing my patrons," he said solidly, despite his drink.

Amora nodded. "We are not monsters, Thomas."

Thomas nodded in response. "Of course not."

And with that, Amora turned away, leaving with her drink, her voice loud enough for only our table to hear as she approached her Djinn, her *Heartsgrave.*

"Leave them alive. Or your deathwish will be mine." Her voice was soft, like a tinkling bell, but it carried a threat that was so much more frightening than if she'd simply bellowed like an alpha.

Alaric rose, needing another drink to deal with all of this.

Thomas rose with him. "Where you going, Al?"

Alaric grunted as he nodded toward the bar. "I need another drink."

"Me too," Thomas said, clapping him on the back. The two men walked slowly, dodging the ambling crowd until they reached the bar.

Behind them, the rest of the pack walked in.

Perhaps Thomas didn't trust the vampire or her Djinn army as much as he pretended to. Perhaps he'd called in reinforcements, just in case.

One could never be too careful.

Alaric scratched absentmindedly at a tear in his black shirt as Thomas stilled beside him at the bar.

"Well, well, well, what have we here..." he said darkly.

Alaric turned beside him, his blood chilling. Sitting at the bar next to him was a pretty Djinn woman dressed in a black leather jacket and jeans, her long, jet-black hair shimmering in the light.

The man beside her however, he would have recognized anywhere.

For starters, he was quite large for a Djinn, all rippling muscles and less angelic features. He looked like the equivalent of a bouncer rather than a Djinn.

He was the Djinn who had attacked the vamp that bit him.

The Djinn who had saved his life.

His attack had stopped the vamp from an attempted feeding, from draining him. If the vampire had latched any longer, they could have spread their venom. They could have killed him in an instant.

He'd been nonchalant with Cleo about the attack, only because he didn't want to alarm her, to worry her. He hated to see her sad or upset, and did not want to be the cause. But the reality that he'd been so close to death was not lost on him.

Perhaps that was why he'd stopped putting a fight when it came to the omega.

Death will put a lot of things in perspective for a man.

"We don't want any trouble," the woman said, her voice non-threatening. Her bright blue eyes implored them, and the world felt slightly hazy.

Alaric wasn't sure if it was his drink or something else. Some vicious attack on his soul by the creature in front of him.

Djinn prayed on your deepest wishes,

your darkest desires.

He tried to block any sort of poking and prodding, but he was not one hundred percent. His mind was not strong under the influence as it was.

"We're just here to enjoy ourselves a drink like everyone else," the man said, his tone cold and hard. His shoulders tensed as he stared down Thomas and Alaric.

Alaric's eyebrows furrowed as the scent of lemony vanilla spice perfumed the air. The man's eyes burned with threat.

Mine.

Alaric glanced between the woman and man, understanding befalling him.

He was protecting *her.*

Thomas smirked. "Not too often we see your kind in here," he said with a shrug.

The heroic Djinn grit his teeth, his eyes glowing with possession. He would attack if provoked, and the last thing Alaric wanted was a drunken brawl with their new "allies."

"And just exactly what *kind* are you referring to?" he sneered.

The woman's gaze pleaded silently with him.

"Oh, I think we both know what kind I'm referring to," Thomas said as he signaled the bartender.

Something about the way the woman looked at him, the haze that befell him, the deep understanding of connection between the two of them... Alaric's heart understood.

They may have been monsters, but they were not enemies. The man had proven that when he'd saved him.

"We don't want any trouble either, do we, Thomas?" Alaric said, setting his hand on Thomas's shoulder. His voice was stern, commanding.

Thomas opened his mouth as Alaric continued. "After all, this is the man who saved my life today."

Thomas raised his eyebrows as the man's face fell. He wore a look of shock.

Had he not realized?

"You…" he said with surprise.

Alaric extended his hand. "It's Alaric, actually. Alaric Thorne," he said sternly. He could feel Thomas's gaze on him, on them intently.

He bore his golden hued eyes at the Djinn, nodding to him with reassurance.

I owe you.

The man took it, shaking his hand firmly, with an immense amount of strength.

It was a cautious handshake, but it told Alaric this man was certainly not someone to piss off. If he was on your side, you were as good as gold.

Somewhere in his alcohol-induced brain, he felt a deeper connection to the man. Almost as if he'd known him for years despite the fact he'd only seen the man less than twenty-four hours ago.

"Thanks, man," he said, shaking in return with equal strength and measure.

"Don't mention it," the man grumbled, dropping his hand. Then he turned to his girlfriend and said, "We should get out of here."

"We just got here," she whined.

The bartender arrived and Thomas started to order his drink before nudging Alaric.

"At least let me buy you a drink?" Alaric offered, as the man and his girlfriend looked at him with surprise.

"Not every day I get my ass saved by a Djinn." It was the polite thing to do. Thomas may have been a stern alpha, but like many wolves, he was hotheaded.

And also drunk.

Alaric knew how to keep the peace, and had prided himself on such traits.

Drunk or sober, he had a command that went deeper than an alpha bark. He hated disharmony. Unfortunately, disharmony was a frequent issue for an alpha.

When the man's gaze flashed to Thomas, Alaric shook his head. "Don't worry about him, his bark is worse than his bite. It's an alpha thing."

Thomas scowled at him, but he did not say anything as the bartender waited for the man to respond.

"Fine." he said. "One drink."

***

"You've got to be kidding me!" Alaric barked as he slammed down his shot glass.

The woman, who'd learned was named Midnight, slammed her glass down next to his. He laughed as he started to count his bills. Despite the woman's size, she was a formidable drinking opponent.

Alaric couldn't remember the last time he'd let loose like this. As an alpha, he often had to uphold himself for stature and for his pack.

He was so tightly wound most of the time, he'd forgotten how good it felt to get shitfaced once in awhile.

Especially when the weight of the world was on your shoulders.

"Read 'em and weep, wolf," Midnight said smugly. Her boyfriend, Dallas—the man who'd save him—grinned with pride.

"Well earned, Miss Midnight," Alaric said as he slid a hundred dollars across the table. He breathed in deep as the room started to spin.

Midnight droned on about singing karaoke, and Thomas and the wolves around him droned on about something he couldn't understand.

He watched Midnight and Dallas bicker over singing, noting how the lumbering Djinn's brash nature collided with Midnight's softer energy.

It reminded him of himself, and Cleo.

Alaric didn't know how to be soft. He'd spent his entire life being primed to be tough, to command a room when he walked into it.

But for as soft as Cleo was due to her omega instincts, she was also quite commanding.

Under her spell, Alaric wanted to submit. He wanted to submit to her as much as he wanted to possess her in the way all alphas possessed their omegas.

Cleo...

He drained the remains of his whiskey as he wondered about her. A shot of arousal coursed through him as his thoughts drifted to the cabin, the memory of their tryst forming in his hazy brain.

It was then that he decided he needed to leave. He needed to find his omega. He needed to bury himself in her until he was nothing, until all the pain, the responsibility, and the ills of being an alpha disintegrated.

He slipped out of the Badlands without much notice. When he found himself under the darkened awning, he gave over to his wolf. His bones popped and rearranged, but he stumbled a bit on his wolfish legs from the heady mix of alcohol and shifting energy. He howled at the moon, the feeling of his wolf taking over.

There was no pain, no worry in this form. There was only animal instinct and desire, two singular focuses in his brain.

Protect the pack, and breed the omega.

Being a wolf for Alaric was simple. He preferred it to being in human form. Kill or be killed was easier to manage than the intricacies of pack politics and supernatural wars.

He ran like the wind up the hill to the cabin, adrenaline coursing through him.

It felt *good.*

The chill air, the beating of his heart, the magnetic pull that enveloped him as he tore up the hill, past the candy apple red Chevelle.

In his animal-alcohol induced state, he didn't see it.

He only saw *her.*

Her scent was thick as he approached the door, barely giving a shit that he was still in wolf form.

The door was unlocked and he pushed it in.

He roared at the sight he walked into.

A bloodied Malcolm had Cleo spread against the kitchen counter, her legs wrapped around his head, her fingers threaded through dark, matted hair.

The smell of blood mixed with omega arousal was intoxicating.

"Please," Cleo begged.

Alaric watched as Cleo unraveled, her voice full of lust. Her eyes glowed neon yellow, and he could tell she wanted to shift. Her gaze found him as his haunches rose, the instinct to attack mingling with the instinct to take what was *his.*

The sight caused him to shift of his own accord.

"Alaric..." Cleo breathed his name.

The world around him was spinning, the only clear sight, Malcolm bringing Cleo to a climax that echoed off the kitchen.

Malcolm slowly tore himself away as he turned to look at Alaric. His pupils were blown, his chin glistening with Cleo's arousal.

Alaric didn't think.

He couldn't.

Every nerve ending in his body snapped as instinct took over.

He strode over to Cleo and Malcolm, grabbing her from his grip. Stunned, Malcolm didn't fight him. Alaric threw her legs over his shoulders as he devoured her with a growl. He ran his tongue across her swollen clit, licking her clean until she was convulsing around his tongue.

"What the fuck…" Malcolm cursed breathlessly.

Alaric grabbed Cleo, slinging her over his shoulder as he carried her across the kitchen, not bothering to look back at Malcolm.

She was *his.*

And he was going to make sure the pain in the ass hunter knew it.

Mal's footsteps behind him were hurried as Alaric threw Cleo onto the round bed, growling as he fell onto the sheets, his brain complete mush.

The instinct to breed, the alcohol, and the deep-seated desire to exert his dominance was a heady cocktail.

"Alaric," Cleo's voice was a breathy prayer.

"Mine," he growled as Malcolm grabbed Cleo, pulling her back into his arms.

Cleo wriggled and writhed in Malcolm's arms.

"You belong to me," Malcolm growled

as Cleo threaded her arms around his neck.

She nodded, breathless. "Yes."

"Mine," Malcolm bit, his hand sliding between Cleo's thighs, his tone husky and slightly off-kilter. Alaric noted he smelled heavily of tobacco and whiskey.

Alaric growled as he moved Malcolm's hand away, his lips accosting Cleo's neck.

She whined. "Yours," she panted as his fingers slipped into her heat. She was soaked from the combination of saliva, arousal, and sweat. He slid a second finger in and she bucked her hips against him.

Cleo tore her right arm away from Alaric, grabbing Mal by his chin, gazing up at him.

"Both of yours."

The words echoed in Alaric's brain and made him absolutely feral.

He was not a man nor an animal.

He was *hers.*

"Are you sure?" Mal asked, his voice thick with lust.

Cleo nodded as she kissed him. "I'm sure. You are my *mates.*"

Malcolm groaned into her mouth as Alaric brought his lips back to her wet sex. He was starving and she tasted like a buffet of cake. All for him.

"Al, can you focus for like, two seconds?" Malcolm bit.

Alaric growled as he tore his lips away from Cleo's sweet pussy. Licking his lips of her sweet nectar.

"You on board or... with that?" Malcolm's voice was strangely sarcastic and humorous, but Alaric could not laugh.

He could only focus on Malcolm's fingers pinching Cleo's nipples, on Cleo arching her back, pushing against Malcolm's bloody chest.

"What's the matter, Crowley? Worried you won't be able to keep up?" His hazy voice was full of sarcasm and lust.

Malcolm grunted. "Oh I can fucking keep it up, asshole. Trust me."

Heat thrummed through their bond, lighting them all up like a volcano.

"Please, make the heat go away," she begged.

Malcolm's hands smeared blood down her abdomen as he whispered something in her ear. His dark brown irises were a fire all of their own, his swollen lips parted as he deferred to Alaric.

Giving him the chance to change his mind.

But the sight of his omega, wet, needy, and begging was not something Alaric could resist even if he had been in his right mind.

"I'll make it go away, baby. I promise," he breathed as he pushed her into Malcolm, angling his swollen knot above her entrance.

"Back up just a little bit, Al, or I'm

gonna get crushed," Malcolm's voice was steady, but not fearful.

"Perhaps that wouldn't be so bad."

Malcolm's amber eyes lit with mischief. "Did you hear that, baby? I think the big bad wolf wants to eat me. What do you think about that?" Malcolm nipped the shell of her ear as he breathlessly stoked her fire.

Cleo whined.

"Lay down," Alaric bit.

Malcolm's eyes narrowed. "No." Malcolm shifted himself and Cleo, bending her over as he stared at Alaric with challenge.

Cleo moaned in pleasure as Alaric watched Malcolm enter her from behind, grabbing her hair in his fist. He was ready to attack, to draw his claws across Malcolm's chest and rip him from limb to limb, but the feel of Cleo's mouth on his swollen knot stopped him dead in his tracks.

His body loosened, his walls crumbling as she ran her soft fingers up and down his thick shaft.

He cursed in defeat as she moaned around his cock.

"Jesus Christ, Al, you going to live? Mal tormented him.

Alaric groaned in ecstatic defeat. "I think I'm already dead," he said, and Mal laughed.

"Did you hear that, baby? You're slaying him," Mal praised. "Better you than me."

Alaric removed himself from Cleo's mouth, gazing down at her with a golden gaze.

Instinct took over as he pushed her backward, driving her further back on Malcolm's cock.

Malcolm's back hit the headboard and he grunted out an, "Ow."

But Alaric didn't care about Malcolm's back. Not at the moment, anyway.

Alaric knelt on the bed, kissing Cleo, shoving his tongue into her mouth. He could taste the saltiness of his precum on her tongue, and he didn't dislike it.

In fact, as the taste of her arousal was still prevalent on his, he relished in the mixture of flavors.

He righted himself as he pushed her back, positioning himself against her slick opening, dragging his knot across her sensitive folds. Malcolm's arms held her still, his hand splayed just beneath her full breasts.

Alaric's fangs pierced her lip, her blood filling his mouth.

"So you can be restrained," he purred as his chest brushed against Malcolm's hands, which slid upward, covering her breasts, his fingers pinching and pulling at her nipples.

In his haze, Alaric thought they looked fuller, bigger than he last remembered.

Perhaps that had to do with Malcolm

smashing them together.

Cleo wriggled, writhed, and whined as Malcolm continued to grunt with each thrust. She wiggled her arms free, grabbing Alaric by the jaw, her eyes glowing brighter than any star.

"I'm burning up, Alaric," she sighed. "I don't know how much longer I can do this. I might explode into a million tiny pieces."

He braced himself against her, pushing the head of his swollen cock against her slick entrance until she stretched around his knot, thrusting into her with a ferocity that was addicting.

His walls crumbled as Cleo moaned in response, heat billowing between the three of them.

Alaric grazed his fangs over her heated flesh, biting her neck.

Malcolm cursed as the blood rushed to the surface, coating Alaric's tongue.

Cleo mewled in agony.

Sweet, blissful agony.

So he did it again.

Blood ran down her neck like a river.

Malcolm leaned closer, licking it off of her.

"Does that taste good, Crowley?" Alaric bit.

Malcolm's amber gaze held its own against the domineering alpha.

"Tastes like mine."

Alaric growled as he gripped Cleo's legs, hooking them over his hips.

She was so slick, there was no resistance to his thrust, knot and all.

He roared as Cleo's body turned soft and pliable. His hips rolled slowly as he found a torturous rhythm, contrasting with Malcolm's punishing thrusts.

"Mine," Cleo purred in ecstasy as she kissed him. When she turned to kiss Malcolm, Alaric sank his teeth into her collarbone.

Tastes like mine.

The contented purr of his omega threw him overboard. Alaric's claws came out as he dug them into her back, sinking the tips into Malcolm's chest. Malcolm groaned as he stilled, his breaths heavy, his voice strained.

"Oh fuck…" he bellowed.

Cleo cried out in her own euphoric ecstasy, her insides clenching Alaric as his entire body went limp and his swollen knot broke, filling her with all that he was.

Giving his mate everything she deserved.

His mind, his heart, his body, his soul.

The three of them fell into a heap, spent.

There was no fight, no biting words, no posturing.

Malcolm held Cleo to his back, burying his head in her hair, the only sound in the room their labored breaths, and his soft whisper. "My darling Clementine."

Love vibrated in their bond and it filled Alaric with a peace he'd never known.

Alaric felt more than spent. He felt whole.

He couldn't help the words that fell out of his mouth. For he felt too good, too wondrous to fight the truth for once.

His hazy gaze roved over Cleo's glowing face. "I love you, Cleo."

Cleo purred happily, the sound the most beautiful thing he'd ever heard.

"I love you too, my alpha."

Malcolm smirked. "I guess I won't kill you, Al."

Alaric chuckled as he twisted his leg in between Cleo's, burying his head in her chest, between her soft breasts.

"Guess I'll let you live, Crowley."

24

MALCOLM GROANED, HIS head splitting, his muscles achy and sore.

"Fuck me," he groaned in pain, rubbing his temple.

"You're not my type," a deep sleep-tinged voice boomed from beside him.

Mal's eyes widened as he turned his head with haste. Cleo was still pressed against his side, warming his skin, her back pressed to his front, but she was not alone.

A fiery amber gaze met his.

Alaric Thorne.

"God, you're still here?" Mal grumbled as Cleo shifted, her breaths deep. She was out like a fucking light.

"This is my cabin. I believe if anyone should be kicked out at dawn, it's you."

Mal rolled his eyes, the need to piss overrode his desire to punch the alpha werewolf and tell him to shut up. He was so... annoying. Always acting like he was better than him.

"I believe your words yesterday were, 'you can stay,' and then you proceeded to order me to go to fucking bed."

In her sleep, Cleo whined, almost as if she could hear them.

"That was yesterday. Today is a new day."

Mal chortled. "Are you always this pleasant in the morning?"

Alaric nipped, throwing a pillow at him. "God, you never shut up."

Mal swatted the pillow, tossing it back

at Alaric.

Cleo shifted, murmuring something incoherent, her backside brushing against Malcolm's solid erection.

"God, you never stop complaining about shit," Mal bit.

"Don't worry, I got shit to do. I'll be out of your hair soon enough, Al."He extracted himself from Cleo's warm body, taking a moment to appreciate the sight of her sleeping so peacefully.

Despite his aches and pains, he'd slept soundly too, a feat that did not go unnoticed. He hadn't even had a nightmare.

He walked slowly away, finding the ensuite bathroom. Relief flooded him as he relieved himself.

Alaric's voice carried from the bedroom. "I know why the Djinn are helping."

Mal's shoulders stiffened as he flushed. He sniffed his arm, realizing he smelled highly of fire and pine. He smelled like a werewolf. The realization both disgusted him and made his insides warm and tingly.

"Why?" Mal asked, coming to the door. He still felt a pang of vulnerability, despite the fact Alaric had seen him naked. He hung back, just beyond the door. Close enough he could hear him, but not watch him.

Cleo may have liked the alpha's touch, but Malcolm had mixed feelings.

He wasn't sure how he felt about what had happened, although he didn't regret it.

In fact, if he was being honest, he also kept his distance to refrain from giving into the spark of desire that taunted him to push his luck.

As much as he couldn't stand Alaric, he couldn't deny that drunk Alaric seemed like a lot of fun.

A lot more fun than stoic, pain in the

ass daytime Alaric, anyway.

Images flashed in his brain, of memories from another time, another life.

Dallas, Vinny, Tito, and Hunter.

On the road.

Drinking, singing, hunting.

Strangely enough, he could picture the alpha alongside the bar with him and the hunters as much as he could in the field.

"It seems that their ring leader, a vampire no doubt, has aligned themselves with the Mayfields."

Malcolm cursed under his breath, remembering the Djinn's words outside the badlands. He sighed in exasperation.

"This vampire wouldn't happen to be Vampire Barbie, would it?" he asked, closing his eyes, already knowing the answer.

"Vampire Barbie?" Alaric asked in confusion.

"Tiny, blonde, wears a lot of pink," Mal huffed.

"I don't know about vampire barbie, but her name is..."

"Amora Medici?" Mal asked with an exasperated sigh.

"You know her?" Cleo's sleepy voice sounded.

Mal smiled, though no one could see him. "Yeah, you could say that. We have history." History that involved the hunter being dropped into a labyrinth and chased by monsters. History that led to the death of his partner.

Well, perhaps not death, in the literal sense, as Malcolm knew Dallas was not six feet under where he should be. No he was waltzing around with a sharp-eyed Djinn woman, riding motorcycles like a man in his mid-life crisis.

Could you have a mid-life crisis at thirty-four?

Mal was unclear.

Do midlife crises include threesomes with monsters?

Malcolm turned the corner, looking at her. She sat up in bed, nestled against Alaric, who was stroking her arm smoothly, purring.

A strange sort of warmth ebbed in Malcolm's chest.

Watching Alaric and Cleo was quite confusing to the hunter, but like many things in his life, he didn't question it.

Malcolm rarely dwelled on anything.

His memories shifted as he recounted the prior night's events. He'd tracked Dallas enough, but yet he couldn't bring himself to knock on the man's door.

He'd been so close at the battle, if he hadn't been distracted...

It seemed there was a lot of that going around for Malcolm.

Distraction.

Shifting priorities.

He'd gone to the Badlands simply to have a drink to numb the ever present anxiety that ate at him anymore.

His fingers had hovered over Ava's phone number.

In all his years, he'd only ever confided in Dallas. The man knew him inside and out, the good, the bad, and the downright horrid.

The need inside of Mal to come clean nagged at him.

He wanted to tell her everything.

About their parents.

About Dallas.

About how he was falling in love with a werewolf.

But he told her nothing.

Instead, Malcolm did as he always did. He drank, and stuffed the annoying feelings down below, replacing the softer things with something much more familiar.

The need to kill.

After his third drink, he'd gone hunting.

There were many things in life Malcolm

Crowley was good at.

He could find vampire in any direction, ten feet away, drunk or sober.

And that night, he'd found two. Feeding on some poor woman behind the dumpster at the Badlands.

His kill was swift.

Black blood sprayed across his lips, across his face. But he didn't stop at one slash, no.

The emotions bubbling up inside of him spurred him like an addict. He'd carved the bloodsuckers up like a Thanksgiving turkey. Each slice of his blade severed a part of himself. Tears welled up in his eyes as agony overtook him.

Killing was easy.

Malcolm had faced monsters since he was twenty-six years old.

Seven years.

He'd been fighting for seven years.

But love... love was what terrified him

more than any monster.

He fell back on his ass as he pulled his knife up to his chest. The sounds of bar crawlers and loud music droned on, and he felt sick to his stomach.

He struck a match, lighting the mangled ticks on fire. As he watched the flames consume them, he remembered burning his parents bodies.

It had been their wish, to have a hunter's funeral, something he hadn't understood at the time when he was just a young man. But he'd done as they wished, despite the pain it caused him. He could still remember the scent of burning flesh.

He wasn't sure how long he'd remained behind the dumpster, afraid.

Afraid of the monster he'd become.

He'd become hardened by blood, by death. Training, killing, rescuing folks from the claws of supernatural death had taken its toll.

Performing with his fellow hunters in their band, Blood Of My Enemy, was the only time he felt like himself. Like he wasn't some fucked up asshole.

Until he'd met Clementine Srirocco.

That morning he'd swept her off her feet, chased her through the halls. She'd kissed him. Alaric had kissed her. Surprisingly, there was a warmth that made him feel safe as they all connected at that moment. A warmth that made him feel like for the first time, he didn't *want* to run away.

He blamed it on sleep deprivation, on being spent from seven years of fighting.

But the truth was, Clementine Srirocco did not see Malcolm as a hunter.

She saw him as a man, and a man deserving of good things.

Not blood, not death.

But laughter, warmth, and love.

And at the first sign of a test, he'd done what he always did.

He deflected.

He'd viciously barked at her, kicking her below the belt as he *judged* her for her mate selection.

Because he was jealous.

He wanted to be Cleo's one and only. Because for him, she was it.

He knew it the moment he left her a year and a half ago. When he begged Hunter to find her number.

When he sank himself inside of her in the midst of her heat.

When he called her *mate.*

There would never be anyone else in the world for Malcolm Crowley.

"I fucked up," he cursed through his own choked sob. The scent of garbage lingered in the air, making him feel worse.

"Then fix it," a voice called from beside him. He turned to see a man in a black apron, smoking.

"Think you can spare one of those?" he asked. The man, who reeked of burning fire, took a step toward him and offered him a cigarette.

Mal mentally noted he'd have to get another pack, as he seemed to be going through them at a ridiculous rate since Cleo showed up.

She'll be the death of me if these things don't kill me first.

He sucked in the familiar toxins, blowing them out in the air as he said, "I don't fucking know how to fix it."

Because I'm fucking broken.

The wolf staff blew his own smoke in the air.

"You get up off your ass, and you grovel." He shrugged. "Works for me."

Mal took another hit, the embers burning through the paper with the crisp sound of ash.

"What if groveling doesn't work?" he asked, putting his cigarette out.

The wolf cast him a raised eyebrow. "You ain't never gonna know if you don't try, now will you?"

Mal swallowed, blinking away the thoughts as Cleo looked at him.

It all happened so fast. Showing up at the cabin, a bloody mess. He ran his hand over his body. He was still a bloody mess, the dried lines and spatter making his skin itch.

He'd told her he was sorry.

That he was an asshole.

That he didn't know how to navigate the bond that was between her and him.

Between her and Alaric.

Cleo kissed him, and he said he was sorry.

Then one kiss turned to a bite, and a bite turned into a mind-melting heat, and suddenly, he was groveling with his tongue in her pussy, begging for forgiveness in the only way he truly knew how.

And then Alaric showed up, and...

Mal looked away. "I need a fucking

shower." He spun on his heel, starting the shower and turning the knob to the left, setting the temperature as hot as he could stand it.

Underneath the water, Malcolm relaxed. The hot steam was soothing to his muscles, but he was not alone for long. The familiar grunt of Alaric alerted him, as did the steady stream of piss.

"Amora and Thomas have a plan. To draw out the vamps." Alaric's voice was steady, unwavering.

Malcolm scrubbed at the blood on his body until his skin was pink.

"Oh yeah? What's that? You gonna drop me in a fucking maze? Let the vamps chase me?" he nipped.

Alaric grunted. "No, why on earth—"

"Doesn't matter," Mal bit, soaping up his hair.

"The vamps are dwindling in numbers. They can't stave off feeding forever. They're saving the hostages for the bigger tick."

Mal slicked back his hair as he contemplated his words. "How do you know there's a bigger tick?"

Alaric shrugged, turning on the sink. "Call it a hunch, but the vamps have been after omegas for a while. They can't procreate like they used to. And queens need heirs to stay on the throne."

"The vamps with siring powers are dwindling too," Mal said, turning off the water. "They're running out of options," Mal said, but he didn't open the door.

Alaric's words made sense, but Mal couldn't shake his own concerns about mating vamps. Particularly one vampire who was too close for comfort.

"Can you hand me a—"

"Here. Pain in my ass," Alaric nipped, but there was no venom in his voice. It was almost like they were friends.

That would be weird though, right?

Alaric shoved a towel in his face.

The familiar warmth ebbed in the threads of their bond.

Yeah, that would be weird. We're totally not friends. Allies maybe.

Just two guys who happen to have a mutual werewolf girlfriend.

Totally normal.

"Thanks, Daddy," he drawled sarcastically.

Alaric scoffed. "Fuck you, Mal."

Mal wrapped his towel around his waist before opening the shower door. He smirked at Alaric who was shaking his head.

"You're not my type," he said as he stuck his tongue out. Before Alaric could bite back, before Mal could bust his balls again, he looked up, noticing Cleo in the doorway, watching them both with interest. Her blue-green eyes glittered with excitement, her lips curved into a perfect, pink grin. Her hair fell over her pale breasts, sticking out in messy waves.

The bite marks and claw marks were all fresh and pink, the blood dried and dark.

She smirked at him, and his heart skipped a beat.

Malcolm felt his cock twitch, rising to the occasion as if the appendage itself had committed their drunken fuckfest to memory. But he knew now was not the time. His head pounded, reminding him he was indeed thirty-four and not twenty-two, along with his back.

"So how do they plan on drawing out the vamps then?" she asked.

"Carnival," Alaric said, looking between them. "Mayfields are headed to the fairgrounds today to start setting up. The whole town will be in attendance, which means..."

"The ticks will likely show up because it's a fucking buffet." Mal nodded in approval.

"Which means the house will be empty or severely understaffed." Cleo smiled.

Alaric shot her a glare. "Cleo, you and Malcolm are not to be part of this."

Cleo and Mal both barked out curses of resistance.

"Like Hell! I ain't going sit here and—"

"This isn't negotiable. Yes, their defenses will be down, but it's still dangerous." Alaric craned his neck at Cleo. "I can't afford to let one of those fuckers bite you, baby. Not now. Not ever."

Alaric flashed his gaze at Mal. "And if something happens to *you,* she'll kill me. Not to mention, losing a mate... it's... it's fucking torture. I can't let that happen to my omega. I will not let anyone or anything *hurt* her."

Cleo met Mal's gaze. It was full of unsaid things, of promise.

Mal did not break his gaze as he nodded at Alaric, a silent understanding passing between him and his mate.

"Promise me, *both of you,* that you will

let me fucking handle this, so it goes smoothly."

Mal put on his best poker face. "Sure thing, Daddy. We'll be good, won't we baby?" His tone was clipped, full of sarcasm and mischief.

He didn't have to do shit. One drunken night sharing Cleo did not make Alaric the boss of him. He wasn't a werewolf. He was a hunter. He played by his own rules.

Cleo smiled innocently. "Of course."

Mal brushed past Alaric, toward Cleo, setting his hand on her hip. He gently kissed her as he whispered. "I'll be back later. I promise."

The sound of the shower rang out once more, the sliding of the door echoing in the space.

Cleo nodded as she pressed her full breasts against his warm, moist chest. Her fingernails traced his facial hair.

"Don't get yourself killed, okay?"

Mal smirked, kissing her sweetly.

"Promise."

***

The Mayfield wolves and the Djinn erected the bones of a pop up carnival rather quickly.

Malcolm casually patrolled the woods on the outskirts of the fairgrounds.

He knew Jake Dallas better than most. Hunting a former hunter was much more difficult than hunting a monster.

His former partner was now both.

Malcolm steeled himself to do what he must. Despite the aid the Djinn provided, his own moral compass, the law of the hunt ate at him.

Finish the job.

It had been over a week since he'd tracked his former partner to Mayfield, and he'd fucked up.

The stars aligned on the battlefield, but Malcolm's priorities had been elsewhere.

But he would not make the same mistake twice. Ever since, he'd carefully stalked his prey, waiting for the moment he could get him alone, away from the Djinn he'd attached himself to.

Sooner or later, Dallas would slip up. He would fall into old habits. He would become distracted.

Malcolm skirted the edge of the fairgrounds, the sound of heavy pants and curses telling him he had found his target.

Sure enough, through the clearing he could see Dallas, pinning his new fascination up against a storage shed.

Malcolm's jaw tensed.

He'd never given much thought to his former partner's sex life. They'd both had their fair share of one-night stands and strange beds on the road.

But he couldn't deny the sight angered him.

Barely a week ago they'd been fighting

together, and then Dallas had been attacked. Left for dead.

And the secrets he and Ava had kept had come to light.

Brotherly instinct flared within him. He knew Ava was more than capable of making her own decisions and leading her own life, but her taste in men had always been skewed.

And despite whatever feelings—if there were feelings at all—Dallas had harbored for Malcolm's sister, he seemed to have forgotten Ava rather quickly.

Though a part of Malcolm was happy he hadn't circled back to poison his sister with his new fangs.

He had enough fanged creatures trying to weasel their way into his sister's pants and neck. The woman was practically a magnet for monsters.

Malcolm grunted with disdain, rustling against the trees.

Dallas stilled, his entire body tensing.

No doubt his hearing and sight would be enhanced with his new abilities, something Malcolm was counting on.

Dallas's gaze roved over the forest as Malcolm slipped further into the woods.

For as skilled as the former hunter was, he was never the brains of their little operation.

No, Jake Dallas was the muscle, and Malcolm Crowley was the brains.

Malcolm slinked between the trees, the sun blocked by the array of foliage. The heat was sweltering, but the forest itself was cool from the shade. It made his skin prickle with goosebumps.

Dallas sauntered into the darkness, his gaze roving around the clearing, looking, waiting.

Hunting.

Though Malcolm could not deny the ease in which Dallas fell into his web. It was almost pathetic that he could bait him so easily.

Malcolm was not a large man by any means. Where Dallas and Alaric were practically ninety-nine percent muscle and brawn, Malcolm was lucky to keep a faint six pack, especially the older he got. But his wiry, leaner frame made him lighter on his feet than most of the men he knew, and therefore he was a master of sneaking up on just about anyone.

He slid out from behind a tree, unsheathing his blade.

Dallas froze, his entire body locking up.

"Give me one good fucking reason not to put this blade in your heart," Malcolm said with the utmost bravery. It was one thing to see the man from a distance, to stalk him through cyber espionage. It was another to be standing mere feet away from a man who was no longer a man.

Dallas's natural blue eyes were brighter now, with Djinn DNA. They glowed like aquamarines buried beneath rich, dark soil.

He stood in his tank top, biceps bulging, his jaw set.

Though he could have easily attacked Malcolm where he stood, he remained in place, only raising an eyebrow at Malcolm in jest.

"Because if you wanted me fucking dead, Mal, you would've stabbed me already."

His voice was the same rough, direct voice he'd always known. The faintest curl of his lips was familiar, and for a moment, Malcolm wanted to slide back into old habits too.

He wanted to drop his dagger, throw his arms around his friend and cry.

He is alive.

His best friend had lived.

The ache inside of Malcolm was unnerving, the desire to fall apart and tell his best friend just how complicated things had gotten, how lost he felt.

He hated that just being within mere feet of the man made him feel as if nothing had changed, when in actuality, *everything* had changed.

His hunter instinct told him not to flinch. To drive the knife in and carve up this monster until there was nothing left so he could not poison anyone else.

So that he could not *take* from innocent victims.

Dallas smirked, sliding his hands into his pockets.

From his vantage point, Mal could see his tribal sun tattoo.

The one that was supposed to protect him from being possessed.

Lot of good that did.

Malcolm's body shivered, his hunter instincts high with alarm. "Hands where I can fucking see them!" Tears begged to fall, but he could not let them. He had to do what he needed to do to protect himself, to protect everyone else.

Ava, the hunters.

Cleo, Alaric.

Strangers.

So why did his body betray him?

Why couldn't he move?

Why couldn't he finish the job as he was supposed to?

Dallas's voice fell. "Take it easy, Mal."

But Mal could not take it easy as seven years of memories, of car rides and gigs, of blood and ash resurfaced.

Of Dallas picking his wasted ass up off the floor, taking care of him.

Of drinking.

So much fucking drinking.

And commiserating. Of having someone in his corner. Someone who understood loss, who understood what it meant to be broken.

His stomach turned, his hands shaking as he gripped his blade tighter.

"You're a fucking monster, Jake. Give me a reason to *not* fucking kill you."

He was slipping.

He was weak.

Malcolm Crowley had been running, hunting, and killing for too long. Seven years of blood and death had caught up to him as he stared at Dallas, his resolve so close to cracking, it was painful.

He had his reasons to end Jake Dallas.

But he couldn't bring himself to do it.

He loved the man like he was his own blood.

"Because I'm still me," Dallas said softly. His voice was not harsh or evil. It was sympathetic, understanding.

It made Malcolm want to combust into ash, if only to escape the truth bubbling in his gut.

"Give me a reason not to kill you where you stand."

Dallas raised an eyebrow, shifting his casual stance. "You know if I wanted to hurt you, I could. You wouldn't be standing if I *wanted* to kill you. I'm stronger now, better. I'm—"

The truth rang in the air between them as Mal bit, "You are not fucking better. You're a—"

"Monster? Yeah, we've established that. Now put the fucking knife down and maybe we can talk this out," Dallas said smoothly.

As if he was talking to a rabid, wild animal.

Mal's arm flexed as he regarded Dallas's stance. In his aquamarine gaze, he could see a softness, an understanding that hadn't existed when he was... human.

The sight beckoned Mal to trust him.

"Since when do you want to talk about your fucking feelings?"

Dallas smirked as Mal slowly dropped his knife.

The sigh of relief that left Dallas's chest was more than noticeable as his shoulders relaxed.

At that moment, Mal realized Dallas was afraid of *him.*

And something about that knowledge, caused Malcolm to feel like an asshole.

"Because we have bigger problems than me being a fucking monster. A vamp problem, a hostage problem."

Mal slipped his knife into the side of his jeans. He didn't want it too far from his grasp. "I'm aware," he said.

Dallas slowly ambled around the edge of the perimeter, his gaze fixed on Mal. Though Dallas's gaze was not predatory. It was familiar.

They'd played this game before, plenty of times, usually when they were trying to figure out the puzzle.

"You on a hunt?" Dallas asked.

Mal crossed his arms, holding Dallas's steely blue gaze. The bright color on him was unnerving. "Something like that."

Dallas nodded. "Then maybe we could work together. Like old times."

Mal considered his words. They eased his soul in a way that he couldn't explain, despite his brain telling him to be wary.

"How do you know about the wolves?" Dallas asked, surprised.

Malcolm held his gaze, shrugging. "I told you, you aren't the only one on a hunt, D."

Dallas sauntered closer, slowly, like a true creature of the night. "Maybe I don't trust the wolves the way I trust you," he said solidly. He stood inches away from Malcolm.

It would be so easy, Malcolm thought, his blade hot against his skin beneath his jeans. He stared up at the towering Djinn, his steely blue eyes piercing and vast.

Malcolm sighed, running his hands over his face. "You shouldn't fucking trust me, not for a second," he sighed.

Dallas crossed his arms, his voice returning to its usual roughness. "You're right. I shouldn't. Given you lured me here to fucking stab me."

Something about his words settled something in Malcolm. They weren't antagonistic. They were factual, but yet full of familiar sarcastic bite. Malcolm's shoulders fell as he turned away. Looking at Dallas was overwhelming his fractured resolve.

"You've always had my back, Mal, and I've always had yours. Rule number one."

Dallas was right. They'd always had one another's backs. Because they were more than just partners on the road.

They were *family.*

The word stirred a hurricane in Malcolm. He'd felt so alone until he'd met Jake, until he'd found Vinny, Hunter, and even terrifying Tito. Ava was his blood, but the band, the boys... they were his family. His brothers in arms.

Thoughts of Cleo and Alaric threatened to upend him.

Were they part of his family too?

He wasn't sure.

He wasn't sure about anything, anymore. So, Malcolm did what he always did when the world got too heavy, when emotion was too unsettling.

Mal turned, biting out in return, "What about your new band of brothers, huh? You got their backs too now? They your new *family*?"

Like the ever present force he was, Jake Dallas did not flinch at his words. Instead, he fixed his steely gaze on Malcolm, his voice a deep rumble of truth, challenging Malcolm.

"No. Some bonds are stronger than blood, Mal." His words rang in the air between them, the weight of them irrefutable.

Dallas was right.

Bonds were forged in many ways, and family wasn't always what you were born with. He knew that, and the undeniable truth cracked his broken heart further.

"Meet me back here at midnight. If you're really serious, come alone," Malcolm said definitively.

He trusted that if Dallas was truly serious about teaming up, if he really felt their bond ran deeper than blood, perhaps there was a ray of hope.

Perhaps he wouldn't have to kill his best friend.

Perhaps, for once, things would work out in his favor.

"Midnight it is," Dallas said as he sauntered off toward the clearing, leaving Malcolm alone once more.

When he'd gone, only then did Malcolm breathe a sigh of relief.

25

MAL PARKED HIMSELF outside of the Badlands, lighting a fresh cigarette. His run in with Dallas had given him much to consider. The man was certainly a formidable partner when he'd been mortal, and Malcolm couldn't deny his new abilities could come in handy.

But could Malcolm assist a monster?

Did he even see him as a monster?

For a moment, in the woods, he had wanted to cave in and spill his woes to the Djinn.

To his friend.

Mal put out his cigarette, his stomach growling. Usually, he took better care of his appetite, but since showing up in Mayfield, he'd forgone a regular food schedule, trading greasy burgers and barbecue for nicotine and whiskey.

And sex.

Malcolm's cock twitched as he sighed in exasperation. He'd never been one to shy away from a good fuck, but it seemed like ever since he'd tasted Cleo's sweet nectar, he couldn't get enough.

Being away from her was maddening.

He adjusted his cock, dispelling thoughts of his beautiful mate, naked, spread eagle on the round bed with his face between her legs.

Now is not the time.

He pushed the doors open, knowing that despite the "closed" sign, the wolves and their allies were inside. Not only could he hear their voices carrying, but he knew from Alaric that the Mayfields had their own rules.

When he entered the doors, he wished he hadn't. For the room was filled with Djinn and wolves, including Cleo and Alaric. Who were speaking with a slender woman, draped in pink, with shimmering blonde hair, and vicious green eyes.

Amora fucking Medici.

Malcolm could not move fast enough as he swooped in next to Cleo, pulling her away from the vampiress.

"Malcolm, what—"

"Get the fuck away from my mate," he bit.

Amora only had the audacity to look bemused by his actions.

Alaric spun to shoot Mal a glare. "When the hell—"

"Nice to see you, too, Malcolm." Amora smirked. "But do not worry, I am not here to prey on your... mate, did you say?"

All at once, Malcolm realized the err of

his ways. He'd just given Amora information.

Information that could put Cleo in danger.

Amora pursed her lips. "Do not worry, I have no need for omega blood. I've got enough children of my own, and being a single mother is not all its cracked up to be."

Malcolm's eyes widened as he looked from Amora to Cleo, to Alaric.

What in the actual fuck?

Before he could open his mouth, at the amount of revelations tumbling out of Amora's mouth, Thomas Mayfield spoke up.

"That's why they took Ashley…"

Malcolm opened his mouth to ask as Cleo stopped him. "She's the omega trapped with Rocky."

Mal shut his mouth and nodded, trying to process all the information thrown at him.

He'd woken up tangled with his mate and her other mate, had a run in with his best friend turned monster ally, and now the very vampire who'd stuck him in a labyrinth like a common mouse to be chased was spouting bullshit about having *children* and was apparently corralling an army of Djinn and they were all one big Brady Bunch.

He slipped his hand into his back pocket, grabbing another cigarette.

"You can't smoke in here," Thomas nipped as Mal shook his match.

He breathed deep, letting the toxins infiltrate his lung, seeking relief.

"Fucking try me right now, wolf, I swear to fucking God..."

Amora laughed and the sound was like nails on a chalkboard. "I would not fear this one, Thomas. He is all bark and no bite, I assure you. Just your *average* hunter. Nothing to worry about."

Bullshit.

Malcolm didn't think. He only acted as he slipped his blade out of his jeans, lunging forth and grabbing Amora, cigarette hanging out of his mouth like a wild animal.

"What the fuck, Mal?" Alaric hollered as he pushed Cleo aside, wrapping his arms around Malcolm who had grabbed Amora, his knife pressed to her throat.

"You fucking bitch," he spit.

Amora rolled her eyes. "You think a little knife in the hands of a antsy hunter is enough to terrify me? Please," she hissed, baring her fangs at him as she pressed her neck against the tip of his blade.

Black blood dripped down his blade, down her neck and he longed to slit her throat, but Alaric's grip on his hand was firm and tight. He couldn't budge.

"Take it easy, Crowley. She's on our side." His voice was stern, commanding, and full of venom.

Malcolm struggled in the alpha's grasp. All at once, the world converged on Malcolm Crowley's shoulders.

"You fucking knew," he said, his voice and body shaking.

Amora grabbed his knife, grinning wickedly.

"You knew who he was, and you—"

"Helped a poor unfortunate soul? Yes, I did. I gave him what you and your little band of misfits couldn't."

"That's enough, Mal," Alaric growled in his ear.

Cleo stared at him with concern.

Alaric overpowered him, pulling his hand away from Amora's throat, forcing his fingers open and the knife to fall to the ground. Malcolm felt the onslaught of tears begging to be freed again.

He never cried.

Not even when he'd buried his parents bodies.

So why all of a sudden did he feel like

a dam, which at any moment may break?

Alaric wrenched Mal's body away from Amora, his hold strong.

Mal hated it, but he also appreciated that the alpha knew he was a much bigger threat than Amora claimed him to be.

He could fucking end her, if he wanted.

But with a million Djinn and werewolves watching him, with Cleo watching...

He knew he needed to stowe his bloodlust. For the moment, anyway.

His amber gaze fixed on Amora, who wiped her blood off on her pastel pink sweater like it was nothing more than ketchup.

The black stain permeated the soft blush fabric like ink.

"Fucking let me go, Al," he bit, pulling the cigarette from his lips with his free hand.

Alaric gripped him tighter. "Not until you get a hold of yourself," he bit back. His lips pressed against Malcolm's ear, whispering to him. "You're making yourself look like a total ass in front of your mate, you know. This is not the time to be picking fights."

Mal hated the alpha for many reasons, among them being the fact he was right.

Cleo's brows furrowed with worry, and Malcolm's entire body loosened, his chest shaking as he rode out the anger, the frustration.

God, I need to fucking stake something before I go mad.

"As I was saying, before Malcolm so rudely interrupted us," Amora said, sashaying over to Thomas, flipping her hair over her shoulder as if nothing had happened.

"Let me go," Malcolm whispered.

Alaric loosened his grip. "Promise you won't be a fucking idiot."

Mal nodded. He wasn't promising shit, though. When Alaric let go, he stood, rubbing his sore arms, and Cleo's shoulders loosened. She softly smiled at him, understanding flourishing in their bond.

I'm sorry. I just—

I know, she thought, her voice echoing in his brain.

Mal felt suddenly flush. He looked at the ground.

"The daywalkers will not be able to resist the plethora of people in one small, enclosed space. It will be like shooting fish in a barrel," Amora continued.

"But vampires aren't stupid, they aren't going to attack in plain daylight," Alaric said.

Cleo sidled closer to Mal, nudging him. Her touch, though small and simple, sent waves of relief through him.

"You're right, they won't. They'll use their thrall to lure the victims away to a secluded place."

Thomas perked up. "Somewhere like an abandoned funhouse?"

Amora grinned. "Exactly." She looked like a proud graduate student, blonde curls bouncing, eyes sparkling.

Malcolm didn't care much for vampires, but he couldn't deny Amora was beautiful. Though the memory of her words, her admission of having children, made him uneasy.

In fact, children altogether made him uneasy, but monstrous children...

Cleo slid her hand in his, rubbing his palm with her thumb.

His nerves settled for a moment, the touch hypnotic.

"It is in our nature to be solitary with our prey. Feeding is an... intimate thing. Empty and secluded is just as good as a neon sign for a vampire."

Malcolm shuddered, thinking about his own entrapment. Nearly two years ago when he'd been kidnapped by succubi, dragged to their empty and secluded nest.

He did not often think of the circumstances he'd found himself in over the years. He was always focused on moving, on the next hunt.

But Amora's words dredged up the memories once more.

One would think being used by beautiful sex demons would be pleasureful, but it wasn't. He'd been pushed past his limits physically, and he'd nearly died. They'd kept him trussed up in chains while they used him, accessing his mind, dressed themselves in his deepest desires. Appearing to him as a certain bronze haired, teal-eyed wolf, whispering words he longed to hear. Touching him places he longed to be touched.

Succubi needed a male host to transition into an Incubus capable of spreading their seed.

It was a miracle he'd escaped. That he'd somehow manipulated the succubi into releasing him, on the premise that he wanted to touch her.

He'd wanted to give in to the fantasy before him. Cleo in his arms, her body pressed against him.

Yes, feeding was quite intimate for a number of monsters, it seemed.

As if she could sense his spiral, Cleo squeezed his hand.

"So, we'll staff wolves and Djinn at all empty shacks? When the vampires steal their prey, we attack?" Thomas asked.

The room nodded and Amora smiled.

"I can't promise they won't have some form of security at the house. The Boracellis are not stupid. However, if we can take out the daywalkers, we will have a better chance of infiltrating the house."

Thomas nodded. "What's in it for you?"

Amora looked out at the crowd of Djinn and wolves, her gaze falling on

Malcolm as she said, "I want the property. What belongs to the Boracellis will become *ours*," she said solidly. "My Heartsgrave."

Malcolm couldn't help but notice the darkness in her voice as she hung on that name. *Boracelli.*

It seemed the Boracellis were everyone's blessed enemy.

Thomas nodded. "Understood. We will move forward with the carnival. Finish our construction, get the word out. Then we lay our trap."

The room sounded in approval.

"Let the circus commence."

***

"What the fuck was that all about?" Alaric sneered as they entered the cabin.

Cleo stepped in between them. "Please, Alaric, just—"

"No! I'm sick and tired of your fucking bullshit, Crowley. You need to listen when

I tell you to—"

"I don't have to do shit you tell me to, Al. I—"

"Stop!" Cleo cried. But the boys would not listen to her.

"You don't know what she's fucking capable of!" Mal bit as he stormed off down the hall.

Alaric did not let him get very far. He grabbed him by the back of the neck.

"My fucking brother is in there! You think I *want* to trust a vampire? I have no choice! My ally makes the calls, not me. I—"

"Yeah, and what do you need his help for, anyway, huh? Is the big bad wolf so fucking weak that he needs someone else to fight his battles?" Mal snarled, the anger, the pain, and the heaviness of his burdens fueling him.

Alaric roared. "What the fuck did you say, *hunter*?" He bared his fangs.

"I said stop!" Cleo's voice rang through

the air as her hands pushed at Malcolm's chest, throwing him up against the wall.

Before he knew it, her mouth was on his, and every nerve, every muscle, every bit of him ceased to fight. Mal slumped against the wall, Cleo's body pressing him into it with startling strength.

When she broke apart, he gazed down at her, her precious blue-green irises shimmering with understanding and love.

"This isn't about Amora, is it?" she said softly.

Alaric stood, frozen inches away.

"Yes it is," he said, his voice shaking.

Cleo slid her hands down his front, resting her fingertips on his hips. "I can't help you, Mal, if you don't talk to me," she said softly.

Malcolm breathed a heavy sigh, and it was no use. Love flooded him through the bond, and her touch was a weapon he was powerless against.

"I can't do this..." he said, his voice

shaking.

Alaric took a step closer.

Cleo stroked his skin underneath his shirt, burying her head in his neck.

"I can't fucking do this shit anymore," he said as the first tear hit.

"Do what shit?" Alaric asked softly.

Mal's chest heaved as answered. "I'm tired. I'm sick of fucking wars, and unanswered questions. I'm sick of the blood and the games, and no leads on how to cure Ava, and the death, and worrying I'm going to fucking lose everyone I fucking love."

Cleo kissed his throat, and he closed his eyes. His tears fell like raindrops on an old, tin roof.

Warmth surrounded him as Alaric pulled him and Cleo into a warm embrace.

"I'm tired too, Crowley. Tired of dealing with you and your stupid bullshit." His voice was not venomous, nor was it sarcastic. It was light, humorous, and Mal let out a laugh, wrenched in a sob.

Alaric's hold on them was strong, his body heat warming them both.

"I get it, though. For the record. I'm tired too."

Cleo held Malcolm tightly, her lips like silk against his flesh. He longed to feel her fangs sink into his skin, to bleed him of all the pain.

Take the fucking pain away, please.

I can't stand it.

Cleo pulled his face toward her, kissing with sincerity.

Let me, she said, answering his thoughts.

Malcolm was powerless to resist her. He sank into her kiss, her hold with ease, falling to the floor. Dragging Cleo and Alaric with him. For a moment they all just lay there, backs against the wall, a crumpled heap.

"I got your back, Crowley, don't worry,"

Alaric said. "I'm not going to let anyone hurt you or our girl."

Mal closed his eyes, his thick eyelashes heavy with tears. If he hadn't been at his limit, he would have nipped, snapped, or said some sarcastic comment to Alaric about his words.

Our girl.

But somehow the words brought him a feeling of peace, of serenity.

For the first time in a long time, Malcolm Crowley felt safe.

And he was too tired to fight.

He nodded, as he breathed through the pain, the sadness, the guilt. "Promise?" he asked as he swallowed harshly, riding out the euphoria of letting go. He trusted he wasn't making a mistake, letting them in.

Cleo kissed his neck once more, softly, reverently.

Mal looked up at Alaric, and in his eyes he could see his own fear.

Alaric nodded sternly, his gaze sympathetic. Understanding. "I promise," he said seriously. And within a flash, the sincerity and depth were replaced by something much more familiar. "Now get your shit together, we have fucking work to do. Christ."

Cleo wiped his tears as he nodded, laughing.

"Fuck yeah, we do. We have people to save."

Cleo held him tight as she uttered, "And vamps to kill."

Alaric rose first, holding his hand out to Malcolm.

"You ready to spill some blood, Crowley?" He didn't smile, but his voice was full of excitement.

Mal set his hand in Alaric's and let the man help him up.

"I thought you'd never ask."

26

ROCKY SHIVERED, DESPITE the sweltering heat. His skin was clammy, his eyes heavy. It was only a matter of time before Trevor and Rebel returned.

There was talk among the bloodsuckers about the arrival of their queen.

Across the hall, Rocky could hear Octavius's regal voice, like a breath of hope.

"And just where the hell do you want us to move them? What about Eden?"

another voice said.

"You let me worry about Eden. Move them south. Eden despises the heat, and they will be easier to harvest. The children have taken to the omega. Keep them together."

Rocky swallowed harshly as another wave of nausea hit him. He was feeling quite sick lately.

It must be the bond.

Because I'm getting closer to death.

"And what about the man? The other omega's mate? What should we do with him?"

Octavius laughed sinisterly. "I think I would prefer to keep him on ice. I hear his blood is quite exquisite. My sister is not the only one who likes shiny, wicked little playthings. The throne needs an heir, after all."

"But you have no queen, Octavius. Not anymore, how—"

Octavius's hiss echoed in the hall.

"Enough. When the imbeciles take to the carnival, we will make our move. You will not question me, about this, Jennings. You will do as I tell you to do. Your loyalty is to me, not Eden. Or do you need to be reminded?"

Rocky closed his eyes, breathing deep.

It was a sliver of a chance, but a chance nonetheless.

He crawled across the floor, his stomach curling into dry heaving. His head was pounding and he had the strangest hankering for a thick, juicy burger. Complete with melted cheese, pickles and lots of ketchup. He couldn't remember the last time he'd eaten more than the menial meals the vampires delivered to him and Ashley.

A sense of concern laced through him, tinged with fear. He hadn't seen any of the children, apart from Henry *eat*. The vampires did not bring them dry bread and cold chicken.

"Daddy, please, no! I don't want to go!" Emma's voice carried through the halls, causing Rocky to tense. He pushed himself up off the ground, cracking the door. Emma twisted in her father's grasp.

Rocky's blood chilled as his stomach turned in disgust.

The man she spoke to, the man she called father...

Was the very man who sank his teeth in Rocky's neck continuously, for no other reason than to get high off his mate bond chemicals and screw his fellow bloodsucker for hours.

Blood and sex were two sides of the same coin for a vampire, after all.

But they'd gotten carried away, last night. They'd only stopped because Octavius arrived, announcing the news of the town carnival. Which he seemed to think was a trap, but the rest of the vamps disagreed. It was however, an enticing food option. So many mortals in one place… they could sate themselves for far longer.

Which meant he had a chance of making it out alive with Ashley and the kids.

Ashley's gaze caught his across the hallway. The skin under her eyes was sunken in, and she looked as pale as the full moon. They were draining her too.

Their gaze met, and a silent understanding passed between them. They'd only get one shot to make it out alive, and they needed to pull all their reserves.

Trevor grabbed Emma as Daniel cried. "You need to eat, Emma. You know this."

Emma's eyes welled with tears. "Please, no. I don't want to—"

"You are coming with me, and that is final!" Trevor roared, grabbing her with a ferocity a grown man should never inflict on a child.

Rocky roared, "Let her go, asshole!" as

he stood tall against the doorframe. He felt like death, and he relished he probably looked like it too, but for the moment he channeled enough shifting energy to make Trevor's gaze falter.

He hissed at the man as he dug his fingers into Emma's wrist. "Get back in your cage, where you belong, dog," he hissed.

Rocky attempted to lunge toward the vampire, but he was not sufficiently healed.

Far from it.

Emma cried as her crimson eyes glowed with the faintest of gold light around her iris.

Rocky yelped as he fell to the ground hard.

Trevor hoisted Emma up into his arms, the child kicking and screaming.

"If you don't settle the fuck down, Emma, your little lapdog will meet his end. And it will be because of you." He sneered.

Emma tensed, tears pooling in her eyes, but she did not let them fall. She stiffened in her father's grasp as Daniel set his tiny hand on Rocky.

"And if you're a good little girl for Daddy, then I'll take you to the carnival."

"Carnival?" Emma's little voice lifted.

"Yes. A carnival. But I ain't taking you unless you settle your ass down right now and do as I say."

Taryn's pristine green eyes glowed in the darkness across the room.

Ashley cradled her belly, breathing deep.

Emma quieted down, whispering to the air, "I've never been to a carnival before."

Rocky's heart broke for the girl. She deserved a hundred carnivals. A father who didn't force her be the monster she clearly didn't want to be.

The strangest sort of desire bloomed in him, mingling with fantasies that he feared would never come true. Of cotton candy and stuffed animals and ferris wheel kisses, of laughter, and love. Stuffing his face with funnel cake and sharing it with Clementine and *their* kids.

The thought was a spark for Rocky. A fire that refused to burn out.

It gave him strength.

"If anyone else would like to argue, now is your chance," Trevor nipped, hissing at a shivering Daniel.

Warmth radiated from the boy's palm where it lay on Rocky's leg. An influx of tranquility filled him, and it was pure *bliss*. Rocky wanted to close his eyes, and give in to the peace. As his eyelashes fluttered, he remembered his dream.

Along with every other stolen moment. The quiet moments of respite, watching movies or reading together in the same proximity. Dining out at Howlers and singing karaoke.

It was a tempting trance to fall victim

to, and Rocky wanted more than anything to succumb.

He realized as Trevor carried Emma away, as Daniel removed his tiny palm, that the boy was using his *powers*. The power to manipulate emotion, to feast on ones *wishes*. He was a hybrid child, a crossbreed of vampire and Djinn.

Rocky looked at him softly, mouthing thank you, even though the reality terrified him. For a moment, the blissful fantasy had made him feel better, even if it was only for a fraction of a moment.

Taryn slowly made her way across the room as Ashley winced in pain.

"Are you okay, Ashley?" Taryn asked quietly.

Rocky held Daniel close, trying to show the sweet boy his appreciation, while also holding on to hope.

"I'm fine, baby. Just a little tired," she said, her gaze flashing to Rocky.

He understood what the children could

not, in that one look.

Ashley was running out of time.

She'd lost too much blood, and Henry's feedings were becoming more prominent.

They needed to escape.

Or they would both perish, never to see their mates again.

Daniel curled against Rocky, dozing off. Ashley's soft snores were not far behind. Even Henry slept peacefully in his room despite everything.

Tiny pulses of warmth emanated from Daniel, where he touched Rocky, and soon Rocky himself had succumbed to Daniel's Sandman powers.

Until he awakened to the sound of a large, lumbering body being thrown into his room nearly two days later.

"What the—"

The man before him was large and muscular, and passed out. He had dark hair, wore a tank top and jeans, and looked like he could bench press Alaric.

Taryn squeaked as she scrambled against Ashley, who stirred.

"Great, we've got a new guy," Rocky drawled.

The man groaned as he stirred. Before Rocky could get a word out, the man lunged for him, as if he was stuck in fight or flight.

Rocky's muscles ached, but he felt warmer, which he took to be an improvement. He still felt horrid, but no longer like he was five seconds from death.

I'll take it.

"Where am I?" the man bit.

"You're in the Boracelli estate. A prisoner like the rest of us."

"Where's Emma?" the man asked, shifting himself up. He blinked furiously, cursing under his breath.

"How do you know Emma?" Ashley asked between coughing.

"The daddy took her," Taryn squeaked.

"How long have I been out..." Rocky panicked.

Ashley sucked in a breath. "Two days." She squinted and looked like hell.

Rocky's gaze drifted over her and he could see the sweat had soaked her clothes.

She looked feverish and pale.

"Her mother sent me," the man bit. "But I fucked up, and—"

"Watch your language, there are children present," Rocky said as he stood up, stretching his leg. Daniel clung to him. He looked around the room.

"Where are the vamps?"

Daniel tugged at his leg. "The scary ones left. It's just Jennings and his buddies."

Rocky sucked in a breath as he looked out the window. The sun was still out, but it looked to be golden hour. They didn't have much time.

He offered the man his hand.

The man looked as if he wanted to bite it off. "And what are you, the parental ratings unit?"

Rocky raised his eyebrows. "You look familiar, have we met?"

The man appraised Rocky with a steady gaze. "Can't say that we have, but you're right. You do look familiar."

"What's your name?" the man asked, standing. His legs were shaky, and he rubbed his eyes. "F—I mean snickerdoodles, I can't see worth... squat."

Ashley breathed deeply, her face pained. Rocky's instincts told him something was very wrong.

"Rocky. Rocky Thorne. You?"

The man grumbled, "Jake. Most people call me Dallas though. Or... Viper."

Taryn giggled. "You don't look like a snake!"

The man's worried brows softened as he shot a smile at the tiny redheaded hybrid.

"What's your name, sweetheart?"

She smiled brightly. "Taryn. Taryn Aurelia."

The man's face fell. "Your dad's not... fu—I mean Cassius, is it?"

Taryn cocked her head. "No, I don't know who that is."

Dallas blew out a breath. "Thank God."

"You're Djinn, right? Were you bitten?" Ashley asked.

The man nodded. "Fu—I mean, that very *unpleasant* lady happened to think I was a threat. Because I figured out she had Emma."

"You know my sister?" Daniel said with awe.

"Sister? Midnight didn't say anything about more than one..."

"Half-sister." Ashley coughed.

"All right, Dallas. I know you just got here, and you're probably working off the vamp venom, but we don't have much time. The vamps will be back soon enough, and they want to move us. It's our only shot at getting the hell out of here."

Ashley cried out in pain, diverting all their attention.

Rocky paled as understanding took.

Her steady breaths. The focus, and the sweat.

The pain she was desperately trying to hide.

"Ashley… how far apart are your contractions?" he asked, his voice shaky.

Ashley's gaze met his, the orbs filled with sadness. "They're getting closer. I think… I think the last one was a minute and a half."

"You've gotta be fucking kidding me."

"Language!" Taryn nipped, as Dallas ran his hands over his face.

"I swear to God…"

Rocky rolled up his sleeves as instinct took over. "Taryn, Daniel, I need you two to go watch Henry for a little bit, okay?"

His voice was stern, steady.

Daniel took Taryn's hand. "Okay," he said with a grin.

When they were out of sight, Rocky slid up Ashley's dress, imploring Dallas with fiery amber eyes.

"You ever deliver a baby before, Jake?"

Dallas paled, his eyes going vacant.

"I'll take that as a no," Rocky said, as Ashley cried out in pain once more.

"This is really not the time... wait... have you delivered a damn baby before?"

Ashley cried out in agony.

Rocky nodded. "Yeah, sort of. I mean, I've assisted my aunts and cousins when they had their kids, so..."

Dallas cursed. "And they say hell doesn't exist."

Rocky ignored Dallas's words.

"Ashley, I need you to breathe, okay? We're going to get through this, I promise. You're doing so good already, I just need you to hang in there, okay?"

Ashley's tear filled eyes gazed back at him. "I don't know if I can, Rocky."

Something must have clicked, because Dallas slid to the floor, bracing his arms around her as he held her tight.

"Yes, you can. One breath at a time."

Ashley nodded, the sounds of Daniel and Taryn giggling and playing echoing behind them.

"You can, and you will. Ashley. And when Thomas sees you and Petunia, this will only be a memory."

Ashley cried. "It's too early."

A grave expression passed between Rocky and Ashley, but he refused to give up hope. He held the omega's gaze with the courage and bravery of an alpha.

"When I tell you to push, push."

27

CLEO GROANED WITH satisfaction as the cotton candy hit her tongue. "Oh my goodness, this is amazing."

Mal raised an eyebrow at her. "I can't believe you've never had cotton candy before."

Cleo shrugged, waving some in his face.

Malcolm smiled, stealing a puff.

"Not a lot of carnivals in Mahoning. Not much of anything in Mahoning, if I'm being honest."

Mal licked his lips, and Cleo's insides twisted at the sight.

The hunter had the prettiest mouth, and she loved all the wicked things that came from it. The way he drawled when he was being sarcastic, or the rumble in his dirty praise.

The smooth, silky feel of his kiss.

The way his whispers sounded in her ear when he told her he loved her.

Her inner wolf swooned along with her.

Despite the ongoing turmoil of their situation, this was the most time she'd ever spent with the hunter in the flesh, and she feared the inevitable moment in which he would leave.

Because despite Malcolm's unprecedented breakdown in the cabin days ago, she knew his fight, his mission, was not over.

It wouldn't be over until he found a cure for his sister, until he found the vampire who had killed his parents.

And she could not blame him.

"Remember, we had a deal. I get you some fairground goodies and then I take your sweet ass back to the cabin."

Cleo rolled her eyes. The sun was shining, the smells of the carnival filled the air deliciously, and she felt better than she had in days, at least physically.

But that may have had something to do with the burger smothered in ketchup, the fries, and the strawberry milkshake, and cotton candy she'd consumed.

She'd gone from little appetite to damn near ravenous in a matter of a few days.

Cleo smirked at Mal, and he shook his head.

"No," she said, as Mal groaned.

He kept looking at his phone incessantly, and if she had known any better, she would have worried he'd been waiting on some poor girl's text or something.

But Cleo knew in the depths of her

soul Malcolm was hers.

Plus, he talked in his sleep.

Something she'd begged Alaric not to mention, which he'd only agreed because he found it could be useful.

Yeah, useful for his own blackmail.

Cleo sighed, taking another bite of sugary goodness. "What's wrong?" she asked.

Mal looked at her in question.

"You've been staring at your phone for like ten minutes."

Mal cleared his throat, but he did not look away. The sounds of Selena Gomez filled the air as she crooned about running with wolves, and Cleo smirked at the haunting lyrics.

A group of children ran past them, laughing.

"It's nothing," he said as he slipped his phone back into his pocket. "Old habits die hard, I guess."

Their bond thrummed with anxiety

and worry.

Cleo raised an eyebrow. "Mhmm. This wouldn't have anything to do with your friend, would it? The one you've been hunting?"

Mal froze at her words. His forearms tensed. He wasn't wearing his signature flannel, being as the last remaining one he had had been ripped to shreds after Alaric's claws mangled it the night prior.

Cleo blushed at the memory.

It had been an accident, but she couldn't deny the sight of her mate's claws sinking into the hunter's arm from tangled proximity made her heart race.

He promised to buy the hunter a new one, a sentiment Malcolm did not take kindly to.

Thankfully, Malcolm had taken out his frustrations on Cleo instead, in a much healthier, much more pleasant way.

But Cleo could not deny the sight of Malcolm Crowley, with a scratchy beard, and his tribal hunter tattoos visible on his pale skin, was absolutely delicious.

"Maybe," he said, twisting his lips. He tapped his fingers anxiously on the picnic table.

"You don't have to do it alone, you know. I can help."

Malcolm chortled, tracing his fingers over her knuckles smoothly.

The touch still sent little shockwaves through her entire body. Even after all this time, after all they'd been through.

She hoped it would never disappear.

He sighed, rubbing her skin. "I know, my darling Clementine. But there are some things I just have to do on my own," he said.

Cleo understood his sentiments, but she didn't agree with him.

They were a pack.

But Malcolm was not ready to give up being a lone wolf. Not yet, anyway.

Before Cleo could speak, two women

came crashing through the edge of the forest, bustling through the crowds. She and Mal stood instantly, his entire body shifting, tensing.

Preparing for a fight, she realized.

"Vampires?" he asked, his voice changing to a much more direct, stern voice.

Gone was the man who opened up, who let Cleo in to see his vulnerability, his need.

With her, and only her, he was not a hunter. He was just Malcolm, her *mate.*

It was still strange to see him put on his hunter armor in person.

The women in front of them were clearly Djinn, both had those telling bright blue eyes, fair skin, and penchant for black. The only difference between them was the one who was bleeding had long, silky jet-black hair, and the one carrying her had short, clipped blue hair.

Malcolm shot Cleo a glare.

"They attacked first."

Cleo stilled, knowing what he would say next, but she would not listen, no.

"I'm not—"

"Get out of here Cleo, go home. I'm not risking it. I can't risk them hurting you. I don't have enough anti-venom."

Cleo steeled her own resolve, feeling quite brave thanks to her sudden spurt of feeling full and better. She watched as he pulled the woman into his arms, supporting her as she clung to him. Her inner wolf growled, disliking this woman, this Djinn touching her mate.

She did not want anyone touching Malcolm, but her. Especially creatures who prayed on blood and wishes...

The blue-haired woman spoke. "We should retaliate."

His words pulled her from her thoughts. "Clementine, this isn't a discussion. I—"

Cleo shook off the weird energy

befalling her. "You seem to forget, Malcolm, that no one tells me what to do. Not anymore."

Her implication was clear, and as long as Malcolm was in the presence of the beautiful Djinn women, she would not leave his side.

Something about them felt off to Cleo.

The blue-haired woman took a step forward, as if to pull her friend back.

Mal's arms tightened his grip as the bleeding Djinn breathed heavily in his arms.

"I'll take it from here," the blue-haired woman said, her aquamarine irises glowing.

Malcolm shifted the woman in his arms. "I got her from here. " He looked to Cleo. "Go home, Cleo."

The blue-haired woman pursed her lips, looking back and forth as if she wanted to argue.

"Stand your post. We'll inform Mayfield

and make sure your friend is all right."

Cleo set her hand on Mal's shoulder, hoping he could hear her.

She's lying.

Cleo wasn't sure how she knew, but she knew the blue-haired Djinn was not to be trusted.

Not everything was as it seemed.

Mal turned to her with worried eyes.

I'm better with you than in a fucking tower, Mal. Let me help.

Mal's jaw tightened along with the muscles in his arms.

Fucking hell, Cleo, Alaric is going to have my ass if something happens to you.

Cleo watched as he took another step toward the untrustworthy Djinn.

"I'm sorry, I didn't catch your name," she said.

"It's Malcolm. Malcolm Crowley."

The woman in his arms uttered his name with relief. "Malcolm..." Her voice was soft, not harsh and bold as the blue-haired woman. It was...kind, despite the pain etched in it.

Malcolm's gaze flashed to her as she swallowed harshly.

"Dallas needs you."

Malcolm's body froze and Cleo felt like time was moving in slow motion.

"How the fuck do you know Dallas?"

The woman in his arms lolled her head on his shoulder as she winced in pain.

"Mate," she whispered the word as she passed out in his arms, and Malcolm cursed.

Cleo's blood ran cold.

28

MALCOLM RACED UP the road with Cleo and the Djinn in the backseat.

Cleo held the woman upright, her dark hair spilling over Cleo's shoulders as she winced in pain.

"What's your name?" Cleo asked.

"My crew calls me Midnight," she said, her voice strained.

This close, Cleo could smell her signature Djinn scent; lemony citrus mixed with vanilla and musky spice. But beneath it there was the scent of something else.

Something her omega whimpered and whined at.

Cleo's gaze fell on Midnight's abdomen where she clutched herself.

"Can you tell me what happened?" Malcolm asked, his voice as strong and commanding as Alaric's.

"I think Dallas is in trouble…" she said as Cleo held her tighter. "He spoke to me, through… our bond." Midnight breathed deeply. "All he said was find Malcolm Crowley."

Malcolm cursed. "I should have known he wouldn't stand me up."

Midnight cried out in a shot of pain, as Malcolm pulled past the hotel.

Cleo focused on her own mindlink, trying to reach out to Alaric.

Are you hurt? He felt her immediately, it seemed.

Not me. One of the Djinn. Her name is Midnight. She's… bonded. Another Djinn brought her to us, said the vampires attacked...

Malcolm looked at Cleo in the rearview mirror, and she wondered if he could hear her and Alaric. She hadn't reached out to Malcolm.

Where are you?

Cleo answered, and Malcolm turned up the road toward the cabin.

We'll be there as soon as we can, baby. Please, just stay there... Stay with Malcolm, okay?

Malcolm threw the car in park. He opened the back door, pulling Midnight into his arms.

She lolled her head to the side.

"Stay with me, okay, Midnight? Just a little longer..."

Cleo ran ahead, opening the door to let them in.

That was when she saw three individuals traipsing up the driveway. Alaric, Amora, and an older gentleman wearing biker gear.

"Cleo." Alaric tore off up the steps with Amora and the strange man behind him. "What were you doing at the carnival? I told you—"

"Now is not the time for fighting, Alaric. We have a Djinn to take care of," she said as she slipped away.

Midnight cried out, clutching her stomach. "It fucking hurts," she cried.

"I don't have any anti-venom left, but I do have tranqs," Malcolm said as he opened his case.

Amora stepped forth, wrinkling her nose. She looked to Cleo then back at Midnight.

"It's not a vampire bite that's ailing her," Amora said nonchalantly.

"But the blue-haired Djinn said—"

"Blue-haired Djinn?" Boo questioned. "Rebel disappeared, I thought—"

Amora stepped over to Midnight, rolling her over onto her back on the couch.

"Vampires didn't do this, did they Midnight?" she asked softly.

Midnight shook her head. "Rebel... Rebel isn't—"

Amora pulled Midnight's hand away from her clutching abdomen. "Rebel isn't who she seems, I know," Amora said.

Malcolm fumed. "What the fuck do you mean, you know?"

Cleo watched as Amora brushed her thumb over Midnight's wrist.

"Malcolm, stand down," Alaric ordered.

Amora smiled. "Yes, Alaric, keep your mangy little mutt at bay, please. I do detest ankle biters bitching up a storm when I'm trying to *help* people."

Malcolm shouted as Cleo wrapped her arms around him.

"Please, Malcolm... don't make this worse."

Her words must have settled something, for the hunter stilled.

"I've known Rebel was a spy for quite some time. I had hoped, she would have provided me with more intel though, before she retaliated on her own."

Alaric glanced between them all. "You knew you had a defector and you offered us aid?"

Thomas cursed as he arrived at the doorway, walking in at just the right time.

Amora continued to stroke Midnight's skin, and Midnight's eyes glazed over.

Cleo realized all at once as the scent of sweet vanilla and flowers filled the room that Amora was *thralling* the Djinn.

But Midnight still cried, tears streaming down her face as her body shook.

"She works for the Boracellis. I had hoped she would have given us a more... direct path, but she always was a wildcard."

Amora turned toward Midnight.

Cleo gripped Malcolm tighter. His

hands brushed the back of hers, and suddenly she was not the one holding *him.*

It's okay, you're safe, baby.

I won't let Vampire Barbie near you.

"Your mate bond is what is causing you distress. Likely Rebel knew that you would be in excruciating pain the further away you and your mate are from one another. She probably counted on it. Buy her enough time to disappear."

"Dallas," Malcolm said aloud. "You said Dallas needs me. Midnight... where is he?"

Midnight closed her eyes, tears falling as she answered.

"Rebel... I think... I think she took him..."

Thomas cursed. "Back to the base."

Malcolm nodded. "What the fuck do they want with him?" he looked at Amora.

She shrugged nonchalantly. "Probably the same thing I do. He's a hell of a beast.

Good defense is hard to come by these days."

Malcolm twisted out of Cleo's grip.

Cleo watched, frozen as the hunter approached the vampiress in front of him.

"Let's get one fucking thing straight here, Amora. Dallas is not a monster for hire."

Amora smirked. "Careful, Mr. Crowley. You are outnumbered in this room."

Malcolm sneered as Alaric grabbed him by the arm.

Malcolm fumed angrily.

"I can take some of the pain away, Midnight. Enough perhaps that you can tell us what you know, to diagnose the root of your ailment, but I need your permission, darling."

Midnight looked up at Amora with glassy eyes, nodding. "Anything, Ami. Please."

"Don't you fucking dare!" Malcolm snipped, as Alaric lifted him off the ground.

Cleo watched in horror as Amora sank her teeth into the Djinn, the smell of blood permeating the air.

Her omega instincts flared with maternal rage.

The scent of Djinn tangled with thrall. With the blood tainting the air, Cleo could taste what she hadn't been able to put her finger on.

Suddenly, it all made sense.

The pain of the bond ransacked Midnight because her mate was far away, but it was compounded because there were more than simple mate bond chemicals in her system.

Midnight was carrying the fruit of a bond.

Amora's gaze met Cleo's as she drank from Midnight's arms.

She knows.

"Get him out of here, Alaric," Thomas hissed as the biker man fell to his knees, holding Midnight's free hand.

He did not seem scared of the vampire, despite the fact she was drinking his friend.

Cleo blinked as Alaric lifted an angry Malcolm out the door.

Amora stopped, wiping her mouth.

Malcolm cursed in the bedroom and Alaric roared.

"How long have you been bonded, Midnight?" Amora asked.

Alaric came back in the room, as a disgruntled Malcolm hung in the doorway. But he made no move.

"A few days, why?"

"Because, my dear, I hate to be the bearer of bad news, but you are pregnant. That is why your bond is trying to kill you from the inside out. Lest you find your mate and remain attached to his damn hip."

Silence befell them all, as Midnight swallowed, her skin paling.

Cleo's heartbeat slowed as Amora spoke what she knew.

Her omega could sense the extra life force in her blood.

"But… it's only been a couple days, how—"

Amora shrugged, her gaze vacant. "What does a djinn pray on, Midnight? Blood and wishes. Nothing is stronger than a heartswish, and a heartswish from *bound mates*? One of you, or both of you, wished for this. And your bond solidified it."

Cleo felt nauseous.

"But that still doesn't explain how it happened so fast… if she's only been bound for a couple of days," Boo said, taking her hand.

Amora sighed. "Much like the omega—" She pointed to Cleo. " —mate bond chemicals force them to breed, Djinn bond chemicals are tied to your wish fulfillment. Call it… manifesting. All they need is to simply *wish* it into existence, and if the bond is strong enough... it becomes reality."

"Fucking hell, Dallas..." Malcolm's voice carried across the tense room, shaky and full of heartache. "Fucking hell."

Midnight looked up at Cleo with a sympathetic gaze that made Cleo's own stomach flip with unease.

"Well, we can't just stand here. We need to rescue him, and the others. Or it'll only get worse, right?" Mal asked solidly as he looked at Thomas and Cleo. "You all have mates locked up too. How much longer do you think you can stand it before you go batshit like Biker Lara Croft over here?"

Midnight shot him a scathing look.

"What? D's always had a thing for Tomb Raider, it's a compliment!"

Midnight huffed in annoyance.

"Not to mention, Cleo... your mate

bond isn't solidified." He looked at Midnight, Cleo following his gaze.

"We're out of fucking time. We need to move."

Amora smiled, licking her lips.

"I have to agree with the hunter. The carnival will only last so long, and our window of time is dwindling. We need to move up the attack and rescue."

Alaric nodded as Thomas agreed.

"And what do you suggest?" Thomas asked.

Amora looked at Cleo and Midnight.

"Why, I say we give the vampires exactly what they want, and when the Boracellis think they've won, we fucking rip their throats out."

"Absolutely not," Alaric said, standing in front of Cleo.

The world around her was spinning.

She held onto him, finding strength.

Pain ebbed inside her chest, and she knew Malcolm was right. Time was of the essence.

"No, it's what needs to be done," she said.

"I am not using you as bait, baby. We talked about this."

Cleo stepped out from behind him, her gaze catching Malcolm's.

"I can take care of myself. I can fight, and I will fight. I will do whatever it takes to make sure Rocky is back where he belongs. And Ashley, and Dallas too."

Alaric's eyes filled with tears and his jaw tensed.

A pale hand with long pink nails settled on his shoulder.

Cleo looked to Amora.

"I will back them up."

Malcolm stiffened as Amora looked at him.

"I know you don't trust me, but you have no choice, Mr. Crowley. If you want to be part of this mission, you will do as I say."

Malcolm looked at Cleo with pleading eyes.

"She's right. Draw out the remaining vamps, rescue the hostages. Theoretically, it will be a piece of cake if we can all work together," Thomas said.

"I'm in," Midnight said. "My daughter and my mate are in that house. I will be damned if any of you ask me to sit here and wait on *you*."

Amora's smile was soft. "I would never."

Midnight smiled back at her. "Besides, I trusted Rebel. That was my mistake. I won't let her get away with what she's done."

Cleo found strength in Midnight's words. "My mate is in there, and he needs me and our bond."

Thomas nodded as Alaric grunted in approval along with Malcolm's heavy words.

"Then what are we waiting for? Let's

kill some fucking ticks."

29

"COME ON, ASHLEY, you're almost there," Rocky said, keeping his voice as calm as he could. His insides ached, and the pain had started to crawl up his back. His wolf growled and snarled inside of him, fighting against his own self-preservation.

Ashley was not his omega, but he would be damned if something happened to her or her baby on his watch.

"Well, well, look what we have here." Rebel's voice carried as a tiny wolf came barreling up the staircase.

"No, please…" Ashley cried out.

Rocky's hands were covered up to his elbows in blood.

Ashley was losing far too much, and she had been so drained to begin with…

Rebel took one step into the room as Trevor hollered, running after the wolf.

"Fuck," he stumbled into the wall, just as Ashley cried out, shifting energy coursing through her.

But it died in her eyes, for she could not shift on account of the transformation.

It was rare that Omegas could not shift fully while pregnant, but Rocky knew even if Ashley could have, it would have been dire. Her accelerated healing would not be able to replenish the blood she'd lost, and shifting at this moment could hurt her and her child.

Ashley raked her half shifted claws into the floorboards as a deep growl echoed in the room.

In the distance Henry cried, the door to his room opening.

Taryn and Daniel stood there, eyes glowing as Trevor fought off the small white wolf.

Trevor kicked it into the corner, and it whimpered.

The haze in his eyes was imminent.

Rebel licked her lips.

Dallas lumbered to the front as the tiny wolf shifted into a tiny child.

A tiny child crying in pain.

"You want to try that shit with someone your own size, asshole?" Dallas hissed.

Emma looked up at him.

"Who are you?" she asked, through a whimper.

"My name is Jake, and I'm here to bring you home, kiddo."

Rebel rolled her eyes.

"Oh please, save your family reunion

bullshit for someone who cares." She stepped toward Ashley.

Daniel stepped in front of her. "Mom, please... don't hurt her."

Trevor bared his fangs. "Listen to your mother, Danny Boy. This doesn't concern you."

Dallas grabbed Trevor by the throat, throttling him against the wall. "Don't you even fucking look at them, you piece of shit."

Trevor hissed, baring his fangs at Dallas. "What the fuck, Reby?"

Dallas pressed his fingers tight against Trevor's throat, his face turning pink.

Rebel shrugged, completely unbothered. "More for me. I'm going to dine on omega blood tonight, and then I'll leach some of those sweet, sweet mate bond chemicals from my favorite little toy."

Pain shot up through Rocky's stomach and made him cry out. His bones creaked and cracked as if they were being controlled by a machine. The desire to shift was heavy on his heart and body. His wolf was terrified.

Something was wrong.

"Ashley, you're almost there, I know you can do this," he said as he settled his hands in front of her opening, his fingers slipping in blood.

Rebel hissed as she crumpled to the ground.

In his peripheral vision, Daniel had set his hand on her, while Taryn stood with a glowing green aura, her eyes vacant, mumbling something in an ancient tongue.

Rebel twisted on the floor, her limbs frozen with green haze.

Guess we know what she is. A witch.

"Push!" Rocky hollered as shifting energy coursed through him, forcing him to the ground. His bones wished to snap, to bend, and he had to fight it.

A crash sounded downstairs, along with ample hissing and curses.

Dallas cursed, Trevor kicking, punching, and snapping his fangs.

The vampires were back, and they were not alone.

Dallas roared behind him in pain as Trevor landed a punch, knocking the stocky Djinn off for enough of a moment to sink his fangs into him.

They fought as Dallas punched him, stumbling on his feet, likely feeling the effects of the vampire venom.

It was toxic to wolves, but Rocky couldn't be certain how it affected other creatures. He only prayed that it did not kill the lumbering Djinn who was more than helping to keep the fray away from Ashley.

Still, despite the bite he'd endured, Dallas fought.

Emma cried as Trevor reached for her, but she kicked him away, now fully shifted into her small, human form.

"Don't you hide from me, you little shit!" Trevor hollered.

"I can't!" Ashley sobbed. "I c—can't..." A startling scream ripped through her as Rocky leaned up.

"I see the head, Ashley. Couple more pushes and you'll be there. It's almost over." He fought to keep his voice steady as another shock of energy ripped at his body, his wolf angry and in pain. His legs were numb, his hips snapping as his wolf tried to force a shift.

The scent of Omega blood was thick and smelled good to him.

It made him and his wolf long for their unbound mate.

The bones in his legs cracked and popped as he grit his teeth, trying to stave off the inevitable.

A tiny shoulder made its entrance as Rocky cradled the soft head.

"Come on, Ash. You're almost there,

one more big one and you got this."

The sounds of screams echoed in the house as footsteps fell faster.

Ashley screamed, her agonizing voice full of pain and anguish as the rest of the baby made its way into Rocky's bloodied arms. Its piercing wail was strong.

Rocky looked down at the small, blood-covered creature, feeling an immense sort of pride that despite everything, the baby was okay. Petunia had made it, and apparently, had quite the set of lungs.

Instinct kicked in, in a way it had never before for the youngest Thorne as he looked at the tiny mass of limbs and curled fists. At the cord still attached. His fangs pushed forth, and he tore into it, severing it.

Ashley's blood in his mouth was bitter. Sadness welled in him that Ashley's alpha should have been the one to deliver such an intimate bite.

His body started to shift of its own

accord, recognizing both his unclaimed bond, and a deep primal instinct to protect one's offspring.

He settled the tiny, crying baby in its mother's arms. Ashley was pale and cold.

"You did good, Mama," he said softly as the pain made its way up to his chest. He wiped his mouth, spitting out the unsavory blood onto the floor, away from her.

His heart ached, and he ground his fangs as tears prickled the edge of his eyes.

Ashley's faded gaze fell on her child.

"Welcome to the world, Petunia," she said as a deep voice echoed in the hallway.

"Well, well, what have we here?" Jennings sneered.

30

SEVERAL VAMPIRES ARRIVED just as Malcolm and the rest of the crew did, on return from their distraction, which made for a rather entertaining brawl on the porch.

The vampires targeted Midnight and Cleo nearly immediately, just as Amora had predicted, drawn to the aura of their bonds.

Surprisingly enough, Cleo and Midnight held their own against the vampires.

Claws, fangs, knives, and hands tore into throats and chests as vampires screamed in terror.

Malcolm had never been more proud as he watched Clementine sink her blade into a vampire and light him on fire.

Though when they reached the inside of the house, whilst Thomas and Alaric continued to fight the vampires in the foyer, the screams were much more potent.

Alaric and Thomas stilled for a moment as a bloodcurdling scream echoed in the house.

"Ashley," Thomas snarled, nearly going feral with shifting energy.

Alaric transformed instantly, shedding his clothes and transitioning into a giant wolf.

Cleo sniffed the air, a deep growl leaving her chest.

"Rocky!" Cleo dropped her knife, tearing off up the stairs after Thomas.

Amora watched as Malcolm struck his match.

"You got something to say?" he nipped, the vampire in front of them going up in flames. "Because if you do, I got another fucking match."

Amora did not look amused. "Just try not to burn the house down, Mr. Crowley," she murmured, as Midnight ran up the steps.

It was just him in the front, holding down the fort as planned.

All he had to do was stand guard for any returning ticks while Alaric, Thomas, Amora, Midnight, and Cleo rescued the hostages.

It wasn't long before he heard a familiar scream.

Cleo's scream.

Malcolm did not waste a moment as he tore up the steps, to find a tall, dark-haired vampire with Cleo in his arms, his fangs inches from her neck. Alaric was frozen, trying to move, but it was as if a force field prevented him from doing so. Him, and everyone else in the room, which was quite a sight.

A woman lying in a puddle of blood, with a newborn laying next to Thomas, a panting naked child covered in blood, two creepy *children* who glowed with green and blue auras, and a naked little girl wrapped up in Dallas's arms, his fangs glistening with blood.

Amora faced off against the vampire who held Cleo, and Malcolm didn't think.

He ran, but was stopped, mid-run. His entire body *frozen.*

What the hell?

"Put her down, Jennings," Amora called. "And let my friends go."

"Give me one good reason, Amora." Jenning's voice was deep, rich.

Amora's voice purred. "Perhaps we could come to a bargain. You give me the girl, walk away from us, and I give you what you really want."

Thrall encompassed Malcolm like velvet chains and he wanted to give in.

For under the thrall of a powerful vampire, resistance was difficult. He searched and searched his mind, trying to find the familiar agonizing memories that always fueled him.

His parent's cold, dead eyes.

His sister's bite marks.

Dallas's death...

But they were not strong enough. Whoever this vampire was, he was powerful. Likely older than any he'd encountered before.

"Oh yeah, and what's that?" the vampire bit.

"Higher rank, for one. The Boracellis don't appreciate all the hard work you do, do they?" Her voice was saccharine.

"Octavius knows my worth. He trusted me with moving the wolves because he knows I'm capable. But a mated pair?

That'll get me my rank. I'll go above Octavius."

Amora chuckled. "You think Eden will reward you? You are sorely mistaken. She will take your prize and she will bleed you dry, Jennings. Siphon off all those fertile omega chemicals, fuck you, then kill you. In that order. You don't stand a chance with her."

The thought of Cleo being drained was enough for Malcolm to channel his rage, his anger.

No one would touch her. Not on his watch.

He broke free of his thrall as he raced toward the vampire, stabbing him in the neck with his blessed blade. Dallas flanked him, the little brown-haired girl no longer attached to him, but cradled in Midnight's arms, wearing his tank top.

A small, brown wolf joined them, baring its teeth, along with a much larger white wolf. Malcolm didn't have to see their eyes to know who they were.

His... pack?

Cleo's mates.

The stab was enough of a distraction, and the vampire dropped Cleo.

Amora sauntered forward, pushing the vampire up against the wall. She hissed, her fingernails digging into his skin.

Malcolm pulled Cleo into his grasp as the wolves circled them, protecting them, baring their vicious fangs.

The air smelled of blood, of death, and burning vampires.

"Please... Amora..." He swallowed, begging. "Please, don't kill me..."

Amora laughed, the sound like bells. "Kill you? Oh heavens no. Jennings, sweetheart, my name's not Eden." She let him go and he crumpled to the floor. "I think you can still be rather useful," she purred. "You're going to tell Octavius that this land is Medici property now. You understand?"

Cleo nuzzled Malcolm's neck, blood spreading on his skin. He pulled her away, looking her over for bites.

"Did he bite you?" he asked in a rush. His hands shook as he ran them over her body.

Cleo shook her head. "No, I'm okay," she said. Her hand slipped down his waist, settling in the hair of a dark-furred wolf's head. The wolf whined instantly. The large white wolf brushed himself between their legs, separating them a hair, a low growl escaping it.

Malcolm would recognize that growl anywhere.

Alaric.

"I have my mates," she purred, tears falling down her face against Malcolm's heated neck. "Nothing else matters."

Jennings scrambled back, slipping on the puddle of blood on the floor.

"U–understood, Your Highness."

Amora smiled haughtily. "Such a good

boy you can be with the right motivation. I'm so glad. Run along now, Jennings. Don't forget what we talked about."

Jennings ran off like the cockroach he was.

Malcolm took in the sight once more, his arms still wrapped tightly around Cleo.

Dallas stood with his own arms around Midnight, who was shielding a child in her arms from the gruesome sights before them.

One dead body, and a very, very ill woman who'd just given birth.

His gaze met Dallas's as the Djinn in his arms buried herself into his chest, sobbing as she clutched the little girl and Dallas.

"Ashley going to be okay?" a tiny voice called.

Malcolm looked down to see a small redheaded child with bright green eyes being hugged by a small boy. They flanked Dallas and Midnight between their legs.

He could clearly see the boy's bright blue eyes, his pale complexion and features telling. He was a Djinn, or at least, part Djinn.

The girl didn't look like a monster, but he knew in his heart she wasn't as innocent as she looked. She smelled like death.

Like a vampire or even a... necromancer?

He'd only met one in his time hunting, so he couldn't be sure, but the smell of death, of graveyard dirt, was one he'd never forget. The little girl smelled similar.

Malcolm knew he should kill them. They were monsters, after all, abominations in their own right. But they were in this house too. They were prisoners, just as Rocky and Dallas were.

And they were just... children.

Malcolm's insides twisted, his eyes

filling with tears.

Leaving them unchecked could be dangerous.

Dallas met his gaze, shaking his head, his blue eyes pleading and soft.

Malcolm felt the faint beginnings of his own turmoil, unshed tears threatening to bubble up.

He knew better than anyone the things Dallas had lost, the life that was taken from him.

Malcolm's throat was tight as Dallas held Midnight and the children close. Protecting them.

"Is Mommy coming back?" the little boy asked, tugging on Dallas's tank top, attached to the girl in Midnight's arms. Her daughter, Mal realized.

She'd said they had her daughter.

The little girl with red-rimmed eyes shook her head.

"I don't think so, Daniel. Not now that Daddy's gone," the little girl in Midnight's arms spoke.

A baby wailed in the distance, and the woman coughed, deeply as she clutched her own baby.

"Henry..." she sighed.

Cleo left Mal to stand between the wolves, heading toward the sound.

The world around them was quiet, save for the sounds of crying infants and children.

When Cleo came back, she held a small child in her arms, rocking them back and forth.

Malcolm fell to his knees with fatigue as the reality settled in. The large white wolf nudged him, while the brown wolf lay down with a whimper. Cleo rubbed the baby's back smoothly, her gaze falling on Malcolm.

She looked sad and tired but also... content.

Malcolm had long parted with the idea of ever having children. In his line of work, there was only pain and death. His parents had tried to escape fate, giving up hunting to raise him and his sister, Ava. And it had worked, for a while.

Until his parents had been slaughtered seven years ago.

Malcolm's cold heart twitched as Cleo turned her attention to the child in her arms, who stared back at him with red eyes.

He had never felt a war so strong inside of him than he did at that moment.

The children in front of him, the baby Cleo held... they were monsters.

But as he looked at Cleo cuddling the red-eyed baby, the little girl in Midnight's arms, the little Djinn boy tugging at her leg, and the little necromancer who was staring at him intently with knowing emerald eyes, he felt a kinship with the tiny creatures.

For he knew what it was to lose his parents. To be thrown into a dark world full of monsters and evil things.

And so Malcolm Crowley simply rose from the ground, turned around, and walked out of the room, down the stairs, and out the door.

When he lit his cigarette, he closed his eyes, breathing in the toxins once more.

31

ROCKY STARED AT his reflection in the bathroom mirror of the cabin. His skin was pale, dark circles rimmed underneath his naturally amber eyes. His frame looked smaller, thinner than usual, and he was covered in blood and bite marks in various stages of healing.

The forced shift had helped heal some of his injuries he'd sustained, but it was painful. His leg throbbed from the shift, pain radiating through his back. His wolf pushed against his body, needing to express its dominance.

Somewhere in his bones, he knew what was happening. The bond was starting to sever. Every step, into Malcolm's car, up the steps, into the cabin, felt as if he was walking on shards of glass.

By midnight, the pain would be unbearable if he did not bond with his mate.

Even in his mortal form, his entire body ached fiercely. The only comfort he had was Cleo.

Burrowing next to her in the car had been the closest thing he'd had to bliss in days.

In another time, another place, he would have fought the desire to curl against her. But when the mere *touch* of her fingers through his fur sent pulses of comfort through his entire being, it was hard to ignore.

Alaric held her close, his hands resting

in Rocky's fur as well the entire ride back to the cabin.

Thomas had called for his pack doctors immediately, and rightfully so. Ashley may have been alive, but she was not well, and a premature birth on top of everything else was bound to have some complications.

But as far as Rocky knew, little Petunia was safe and healthy as could be, given the circumstances.

He stared at his image in the mirror, remembering the horror of the moment.

In all the years he'd assisted in pack births, he'd never seen a delivery such as Ashley's. There were several moments he had not been certain she would make it, and he was terrified.

But he could not let her see his terror. He had to be strong, so she could fight.

"Everyone's gone." Cleo's voice was soft in the space, pulling him from his thoughts.

He closed his eyes, relief flooding him as his shoulders fell. The sound of her voice was cathartic in a way he couldn't resist. He nodded.

"Dallas?"

Cleo took a step closer, into the bathroom, stopping as if she too were afraid of the fragility of the moment that lay between them.

As if she were afraid he too, would disappear at any moment.

"Amora took him and Midnight back to the hotel with the kids, and the other Djinn. Guess they're going to have to figure something out with those poor kids."

"Alaric? Malcolm?" he asked.

"Alaric and Mal went to the bar." She laughed. "Guess they needed a drink after everything. Can't say I blame them. It's been... crazy."

Rocky turned to look at her. Her smile was soft, but she was covered in vampire blood, her hair a disheveled wavy mess of bronze and gold. Her bright eyes were full of excitement and happiness as he took a step closer, hoping this wasn't some Djinn fantasy, or a sleep deprived hallucination.

"So... you and Mal... looks like you finally chose your mate," he said.

Cleo took another step forward, their bodies only inches apart.

"Alaric too," she said as she reached out, trailing her fingertip down his cheek. He didn't miss the way her cheeks blushed when she said his brother's name.

I suppose that was inevitable, but two mates...

God, the pack and mom and dad will have a field day with that.

His entire body thrummed with heat, with desire. His wolf was hungry to taste what it knew it needed.

Mate.

But she made her choice.

I'm not it.

A tear slid down his cheek as he said, "Oh."

Cleo gazed up at him through her eyelashes. "And you."

She gently caressed his jaw with her fingertips, turning him by his chin, as she closed the gap between them. Her warmth enveloped him and he couldn't resist touching her.

He needed her attention, her touch, like he needed air.

He blushed at her words, feeling on the spot.

"You think you can just get kidnapped by vampires to get away from me?" she teased him, but the levity of love in her voice was unmistakable, though Rocky remembered their last conversation vividly.

"I would never run away from you."

"So you accept me? Accept *this*?"

She ran her fingers through his hair

softly at the nape of his neck, and he set his hand on her hip, letting his forehead fall against hers.

"Of course I accept you. The question is do you accept *me*?"

Rocky gazed into her shimmering eyes, his wolf whining beneath the surface, begging to be chosen.

It was tradition and instinct for an omega to present herself to her mate. To ask their alpha or beta if they *accepted* them. Rejection was difficult for an omega.

But it was not in the nature of an alpha or beta to be rejected by an omega, and it certainly wasn't natural for a wolf of lower standing to be propositioned, let alone *accepted* by an omega.

In every way that mattered, Cleo outranked him. Yet, she stood in the rain on the terrace, over a week prior, and asked Rocky if he was rejecting *her*.

He'd told her he could never do such a

thing, and he meant it with every fiber of his being then, before the vampires showed up.

But so much had changed, time had passed, and the severance had already started.

Cleo sighed, letting her fingers twist in his dark brown locks. She looked at him with an awe that made him blush, made his insides warm like a cozy fire.

"Oh, Rocky. I could never reject you. Ever," she whispered as she kissed him.

Fire bloomed between them, rising high. The pain started to subside.

His cock twitched against her and he groaned into her mouth as a million images, a million memories, assaulted him.

Cleo pushed her tongue into his mouth as she purred. A smile graced her lips as she let out a soft chuckle.

"I stole your car," she said with a smile. "I hope you don't mind."

Rocky kissed her once more, his hands sliding over her exposed skin, slipping beneath her tank top.

"What did Alaric have to say about that?" he asked, his voice tinged with darkness. He knew the answer, but relished in the familiarity of such a discussion. It was almost as if nothing had changed, even though everything had changed.

Cleo broke away for a moment, flashing her bright eyes at him. "I suppose he wasn't too pleased, but I told him if he wasn't going to save you, I was. With Malcolm's help, of course."

She sauntered away from him, turning on the shower. He watched as she removed her shirt, then her jeans. The sight of her standing in just her bra and panties, her pale skin spattered with blood and healing claw marks, caused his cock to twitch once more.

He took a step forward, then another,

watching as she held his gaze while removing her bra.

"What are you doing, Cleo?" he asked, his voice full of unsaid things.

Cleo slid her body against his, her hands settling on his hips as she whispered, "I think we both could use a shower."

She pulled him toward the shower and he followed her relentlessly. Her touch was invigorating, like sunshine.

The hot water burned his skin, but it wasn't painful. It was soothing.

Cleo massaged shower gel into a lather, kneading his back muscles, working her way down his shoulders. His knee throbbed as he leaned forward, cursing.

"What's wrong? Did I hurt you, I—"

"My knee. I've put it through the ringer. It hasn't... been the same since Malcolm hit me."

Cleo stopped her motions turning him

around. "Why didn't you say something? All that training, I thought—"

"What was I going to say, Cleo? I didn't want to accept it either. Doctors told me I shouldn't shift until it healed, but it's been a year and a half and—"

"You attacked those vampires, knowing you were hurt! And when I found you... you were in shifted form."

Rocky pushed back against her, angling her against the wall. The touch wasn't harsh or malicious, but the pressure wasn't soft. He leaned on his good side.

"And I'd do it again, Cleo. If it meant you would be safe."

Cleo still faltered under his weight, a whine leaving her throat.

Rocky didn't miss the way her pupils dilated.

The sight only flared his and his wolf's desire.

To close their bond and bind them

together.

"You should have told me," she said, licking her lips.

Rocky's gaze dipped to her lips. "I didn't want to worry you."

He ran his fingers through her hair, washing out the shampoo.

"Is there anything else I should know?" she asked, her breath heavy as she looked up at him.

His fingers traced her cheek, down her slender neck, across her clavicle.

"Ashley said I only had a matter of days to complete our bond. Earlier... when I shifted... I... " He licked his lips. "The vampires, they... they drained a lot of me. Their venom, it should have killed me. I'm not as strong as you think I am." He dropped his gaze.

Cleo ran her fingers through his wet hair, her eyes glassy. Steam billowed around them as he felt his own tears begging to be freed.

He leaned his forehead against hers, the words rushing out of him with the utmost sincerity.

"I am not an alpha, or a beta... or even a skilled hunter. I'm just a wolf. A broken, drained wolf on the edge of crumbling into a million pieces. I failed you, Cleo. In so many ways."

Cleo's fingers traced down his cheeks as she shook her head. "Oh, Rocky... you have never failed me." Tears slid down her cheeks along the hot steam and water surrounding them. "You are not broken."

He closed his eyes as she held him close, whispering.

"You are perfect. Just the way you are. I don't need you to be like Malcolm, or Alaric. I just need you. My partner in crime."

He smiled softly as her words settled the ache inside his heart. "Like Bonnie and Clyde. Sneaking out and wreaking havoc."

A soft sob echoed between them. "Stealing cars, starting fights. A regular pastime for us."

His amber gaze held hers as he washed the water over her skin, running his hands through her hair.

Her eyes fluttered closed, her pouty lips parted as she groaned in ecstasy.

He loved the sight of her like this, relaxed.

Responsive to *his* touch.

He sighed. "You are my top priority, Clementine. You always have been, since the day you showed up. And not just because you're my pack, but—"

He licked his lips, his heart in his throat. He looked down at her face, her bright eyes opening as she looked up at him. Steam curled between them as the water rained down on them both. He was well aware of his hardness pressed against her, and he didn't miss how she arched her back, her fingernails on one hand finding the edges of his jaw while the other hand carefully, softly, stroked his cock. He closed his eyes, his jaw tensing as shockwaves of electricity pulsed through him, breathing new life into him.

Her touch was like a cure for all of life's ailments.

"But what, Rocky?"

Her voice breathing his name was the sweetest sound he'd ever heard.

"Because I love you." His own eyes were glassy as the truth blossomed between them. He kissed her softly. "You accept me."

She crushed her lips to his. "I love you too, Rocky. I was yours from the start, I just didn't know it."

Rocky felt his heart swell along with his cock. Cleo wrapped her hand around his thickness, and he couldn't help but groan. Her touch was like silk, warm and smooth. She stroked him slowly, her fingers running over his swollen head.

"And then I came into heat, after Malcolm stirred it, and you were just... The only time it was truly bearable, was when I was with you," she said softly, her eyes glistening with truth.

Alaric had avoided Cleo at all costs when he was home, not to mention he was constantly running out on "pack business." Malcolm hadn't come back in over a year, and though he knew the hunter still had her heart, he dared to hope, to wish that Cleo would see him as more than just a confidant or a friend. But he'd pushed that all aside, to be what she needed, to make her feel at home in the estate in the absence of his brother and the hunter.

"Oh, Cleo," he murmured, pressing his cock into her hand as he kissed her passionately, with fire and love, with animal instinct. He explored her warm, wet skin like an uncharted map, committing every inch, every curve to memory with his hands.

The dip of her shoulder, the thickness of her eyelashes, the swell of her breasts, the way her perfect lips looked swollen from his kiss, the stiff peaks of her nipples.

The slick, warm wetness of her sex.

Cleo grabbed his wrist, guiding him to the swollen, sensitive bud of her heat, her fingers rhythmically moving his.

Rocky smirked, realizing that she was showing him, telling him without words what it was she wanted.

He pulled her clit between his thumb and forefinger slowly, massaging it as he gazed down at her.

"You like that?" he asked, his voice much darker than he intended.

Cleo's thumb ran over his wet slit as she nodded. Her irises were rimmed in gold, shifting energy hovering just beneath the surface.

"Yes," she said, as he slid a finger inside her warm, wet walls, committing the feel to memory.

Gone was the insecurity, the guilt, the worry.

Her eyelashes fluttered as she bit her lip, her chest rising and falling, rivulets of water running down her breasts.

Invigorated by her response to his touch, he slowly slid another finger inside of her while continuing to rub her clit.

He felt an immense sort of pride from his wolf to his heart as he watched her ecstasy, emboldened that he *could* bring her the pleasure she sought.

He was a fast learner, and more than eager to learn all the things that she liked. The ache in his muscles dulled as sensation overtook him, as severed bonds stitched themselves back together.

Cleo was right.

He was *not* broken.

Not anymore. Not with her.

"I thought about you every day, in there. You, our bond, were what kept me alive. Kept me fighting. Even as it tore me apart to be away from you."

Cleo ran her fingernails down his chest, tightening her grip on his hips as he pressed her against the wall, bracing his free hand on the tile.

"Oh, Rocky, you have no idea how strong you are, do you?" She sighed. "You might not be an alpha, or a beta, or even a hunter, but Rocky, you... you are the *foundation* of my castle. Alaric, Mal... they may be pillars, but you.. Rocky, without you there is no house, there is no *home*."

Cleo looked at him with awe and love, and warmth blossomed all throughout him.

He slid his hands underneath her thighs, lifting her up, and she let go of him. Water fell around them as she wrapped her legs around him, kissing him.

Her fingers gripped his hair as blood pooled, tangled in the water that circled the drain, their skin cleansed of the violence they'd endured.

"You are my home, Cleo," He whispered as he kissed her. Her kiss, her admission, her love healed the fractures with him, breathing new life into him. Her lips pulled into a smile as she kissed him once more, her fangs grazing the bottom of his lip. He rotated his hips, pressing her against the wall as a low growl escaped his throat.

He was one with the feel of her body, with his wolf.

With his *mate.*

Cleo thrust herself against his leaking cock, her pupils blown, golden shifting energy dancing in them like pixies.

"You are my hero, Rocky Thorne," she breathed against his neck, her fangs grazing his skin.

He traced his fingers through her wet

hair as she ground against him, whimpering.

"Please," she begged, her hands sliding down his arm. "I need you."

Her words, whispered breathlessly, were like a drug, and he could not resist. Not when she sounded so perfect, when she called him a hero, when she rubbed herself against him, seeking his friction.

He didn't want to fight Cleo anymore. He pressed her into the tile, slipping one hand between them as he rubbed her slick folds, letting her arousal coat his fingertips. Her eyelashes fluttered.

"Tell me what you want," he purred against her neck. His body warmed with heat as Cleo thrust herself against his fingers. Her gaze was heavy-lidded as she breathed heavily, her lips swollen from his kiss. His fangs pushed forth as the desire to bite, to taste her blood pushed against him with renewed vigor.

"*I* want to complete our bond," she

whispered, looking up at him. "But this isn't just about me, Rocky." She sighed. "And as bad as I want you to breed me up against this shower right now, I also want to do this right. I want... I want this to be good *for you.*"

The weight of her words were heavy in the air.

They hadn't talked about his virginity, and he wondered about his strange dream.

Did she know?

Had Alaric said something?

Would he have even cared to say something?

Rocky blushed as she rested her hand on his neck, turning his face toward hers.

His silence was enough of a confirmation. Cleo slid down his legs and his cock bounced free between them as she turned off the shower.

"I can assure you, Cleo, no matter what, it's going to be good for me," he said with a shy smile as she looked at him over her shoulder. "I mean, I don't have any basis for comparison, and you're..." He swallowed harshly at the gaze upon her gleaming flesh, her full breasts, glowing eyes and wet waves.

She was stunning, and she wanted *him.*

The reality was irrefutable.

"God, you are so beautiful."

She smirked as she opened the shower door, casually strolling backward toward the bedroom.

"Come here," she said, fluttering her eyelashes at him coyly as she sauntered out of the shower toward the bedroom.

He followed her, both of them not bothering to towel off. Rocky followed her slowly, his wolf rising to the forefront of his being, incited by her sweet playfulness.

He'd never *stalked* anyone before, nor had he the desire. It wasn't in his nature.

But as Cleo became smaller, as he backed her up against the bed, he couldn't deny he liked the feeling.

Cleo leaned back against the bed, gazing up at him with bright irises rimmed in gold. "Closer," she licked her lips as he nudged her legs apart with his good knee.

Though he noticed the bad one still hurt, the pain was now a dull ache. In fact, his entire body felt better than it had in days. He felt almost normal.

Cleo wrapped her arms around him as she pulled him down into the sheets, with a giggle, her long hair spilling over the pillows.

He fell on top of her, bracing himself against the soft mattress as several scents hit him all at once.

Rocky stopped for a moment. The scent of arousal mixed with hunter and a most familiar Thorne alpha's scent, told him Cleo most certainly had claimed her other mates in this very bed.

It should have bothered him that she wanted him to make love to her in the same nest she shared with the hunter and his brother, but it didn't. Not in the way it should have.

It only solidified his desire, his understanding that Cleo truly did see him as an equal counterpart. As a worthy mate, or even a breeding partner.

She saw him as part of her pack, and as he crawled over to her, sliding his knee between her legs, bracing against the soft sheets and mattress, he embraced this new beginning, this new part of him he'd been dying to set free.

You are my hero, Rocky.

He would give her anything 'she desired. He would give her his heart and soul.

"Your wish is my command, Clementine."

Cleo purred with praise as the world

fell away around them.

Rocky kissed her softly, and he did not waste a moment as he slid into her with ease. He let out a shaky breath at the overwhelming feeling as animal instinct warred with human desire, dancing together in unison.

He parted his lips, and Cleo bit his bottom lip, licking at the faint prick of blood.

Cleo kissed him back reverently, hooking her legs around his hips, pulling him closer until he was buried within her completely.

For a moment, they lay still as he gazed down at her with adoration, love, and truth.

She was all there ever was, and all there ever would be for him.

He was hers, forever.

Her blue-green eyes implored him wordlessly as he rolled his hips, thrusting into her and pulling out slowly. Rocky kissed her neck, letting his fangs graze her skin, and he did not miss the way her insides clenched him as he did so. The feeling made him dizzy.

"Does that feel good, sweetheart?" he breathed darkly, emblazoned by every sensation, every movement, every touch.

"Yes," she praised.

Rocky smiled against her neck, rolling his hips slowly, repeating the motions, eliciting soft moans from his mate that made his wolf nearly feral.

But Rocky did not want to rush, no.

He wanted to savor every sound, every touch, every sensation that he drew out of his mate. He wanted the moment to last forever, the way he knew his love undoubtedly would.

He sank his fangs into her neck quickly, retracting almost as fast as he'd bitten her. With his tongue, he lapped at the fresh spot of blood and Cleo groaned.

Her breaths were short and erratic,

and he could feel a levity in between them, almost as if she was as overwhelmed as he was.

Her want, her need.

He bit and sucked at her tender flesh.

Bite, suck, thrust. Repeat.

They moved in tandem, heartbeats and thrusts in sync with one another.

Rocky's breath shook as he buried his face in Cleo's hair, letting her sweet scent surround him as the world around them dissolved into nothing. There was only the bliss of the their bond.

Clementine Thorne was perfect in every sense of the word.

His wolf preened with pride as the animalistic need to *breed* his mate tangled with his human desire to give this woman everything he was.

Slow and steady, he kissed her, rocking her into oblivion.

Cleo met him thrust for thrust, never breaking his hold or gaze when he looked at her.

"Mine," she said as she kissed him, her walls pulsing as she groaned into his mouth.

Rocky's tongue caressed hers as his breath hitched, his entire body locking up with tension as his balls tightened, his cock pulsing with release. He devoured Cleo's mouth, his fingers twisting in her locks as he whispered, "Mine."

His wolf was on cloud nine, knowing he'd just successfully bred *his* omega, as his human brain turned to mush with fresh mate bond toxins. The high of his own orgasm spiked as well as the pride that he'd brought Cleo the pleasure she deserved.

Perhaps there was something to be said that he'd waited so long to have this moment.

Looking at Cleo, his heart swelled with pride and joy. His mate would be his first and only, until the end of time, and the knowledge filled him with warmth and bliss. He would always belong to Clementine Thorne as long as he lived.

The pain in his body dispersed, giving way to a euphoria he'd never known, as the remaining sutures were drawn across their bond, across his injuries, and his fast-beating heart.

He and Cleo were *bound* together. In body, mind, and spirit.

But just as he thought for sure he would come back to earth, that he would wake up from this heat induced dream, Cleo rolled him over on his side. His cock was warm inside of her, and she made no motions to remove it. She gazed at him with love and awe.

The heat is gone.

Her voice in his head was heaven. For Rocky knew, it was the unspeakable truth that their bond was solid. They would never be severed.

Life started *now.*

They were mates.

And for the moment, that was all that mattered.

32

THE SMELL OF sizzling bacon roused Cleo awake. Warmth surrounded her and she blinked through her sleepy haze, her gaze settling on the sweetest sight.

Rocky's dark hair fell in his amber eyes, his sweet smile lifting her heart as the golden sun shone down on him.

"Good morning, beautiful." His grin made her heart flutter.

"What the fuck, Al? I told you to spray the fucking pan or shit was going to stick!" Malcolm's voice carried with annoyance as a growl echoed in the cabin.

"I know how to make fucking pancakes, Crowley."

Mal huffed. "Clearly you don't. Move it, dickface."

Cleo sighed as Rocky laughed and the sound was infectious.

"We should probably break them up before one of them gets hurt." Rocky laughed.

Cleo pulled herself closer, burying her head against Rocky's chest.

"You're probably right. I just... wish we could stay here, in this bubble a little longer."

Rocky held her close, kissing her forehead.

"Watch the bacon!" Malcolm yelled as another crash and growl sounded.

Cleo groaned as she removed herself from Rocky's arms, slinking away to the chair in the corner, where a soft, white robe laid untouched, a small

Squishmallow cow sitting on top of it.

Her heart lifted, knowing it was from Alaric.

She set the animal aside, dressing as she made her way out to the kitchen.

For a moment, she stood in silence. Rocky settled his hand on her hip, and she took in the sight of Alaric, bare-chested, mixing a fresh bowl of batter, while Malcolm—dressed in his usual ripped jeans and a flannel—manned the stove.

It was hard for her to believe, given the circumstances, that they were all here, at this moment.

Alive, together.

"Well, aren't you a sight for sore eyes," Alaric said as he caught her gaze. He gave her a small smile and she slowly sauntered into his arms. His alpha scent surrounded her, making her stomach flip as he purred against her ear, his chest vibrating against her.

"Good morning to you too," she said with a wide grin.

"No one says good morning to me, and I'm the man making the fucking breakfast," Mal grumbled and Cleo laughed.

"Well, depends on how good your breakfast is," she taunted him.

He turned, clutching his heart. "That hurts, Cleo," he said with puppy dog eyes. "Just for that, I'm not sharing the bacon."

Cleo shook her head as she headed over to where the hunter stood, hip-checking him as she stole a piece of bacon from the pan. He didn't say a word, just cast her a devilish look.

"I hope you slept... okay..." Alaric said, looking at Cleo, then shooting an uncomfortable gaze at his brother.

Cleo's entire body warmed as she looked between both of them. While they shared similar features, their distinctions were quite vast.

For one, Alaric was larger, darker in complexion from his long exposure outdoors, and his grown out hair and facial hair made him look every bit the thirty-one year old alpha, whereas the younger Thorne was much paler in complexion, leaner in frame, and softer in his features. There was eight years between them, after all. But the fiery amber gaze and perfect bone structure was most certainly an inherited trait.

"Like a baby," Rocky said, reaching behind his head, stretching his long, lean arms.

"Thanks for, uh, giving us the room." His cheeks reddened as he looked to the ground, as Malcolm huffed indignantly.

"Don't mention it. Like, ever."

Cleo stole another piece of bacon, batting her eyelashes at Malcolm in appreciation.

Rocky sidled over to steal a piece as well and Malcolm smacked his hand.

"What the fuck? Were you guys born in a literal barn? Paws off! There ain't going to be anything left for me!"

Cleo wrapped her arms around Malcolm's midsection as Rocky laughed, chomping down another piece.

She leaned up on her tiptoes to give him a kiss, and he melted against her like butter in the skillet.

"I've got a meeting with Thomas at noon, mostly just a debrief. After that, we should be good to head back home."

Home.

The word filled Cleo's heart with joy, but also fear.

Malcolm turned the stove off, slipping the remaining pieces of bacon onto a paper towel lined plate.

"I can't wait to sleep in my own bed again," Rocky sighed.

"You and me both," Alaric grunted as he settled his gaze on Cleo. "Although, I'm sure we're going to have to make some...

arrangements. Typically, the nest is meant to house two people, but…" Alaric flitted his gaze between Cleo and Rocky, and Cleo blushed in understanding.

Then Alaric turned to the hunter who seemed to be busying himself with traying up a plate of pancakes, his back to everyone.

"I suppose we can make some modifications."

Malcolm turned, looking between all of them.

"What?" he said, swallowing harshly.

Panic and anxiety flooded their bond as Cleo approached him.

"Are you coming with us?" she asked softly.

Malcolm's shoulders fell as he breathed a deep sigh.

You know I can't.

Cleo sighed, her hand settling on his hip lightly as she implored his gaze.

"You have monsters to hunt, right?"

She smiled, but it did not reach her eyes.

Alaric and Rocky casually grabbed the trayed up plates, moving them across the kitchen to the dining room, giving Cleo and Malcolm space. She knew they could feel the anxious energies in the bond too.

Malcolm reached out, tucking some wavy bedhead strands behind her ear. "Something like that," he said, his eyes full of wishful hope.

Cleo nodded. "I understand."

Mal traced his fingers along her cheek. "My sister... she... she was claimed, by a vampire, but not just any vamp. He's a pretty powerful one, and he's got a bit of an obsession with her. She's... she's the only biological family I have left."

Cleo's heart ached for Malcolm. He didn't talk about his family often. She knew he loved his sister fiercely and felt a responsibility for her.

"I might... I might have a lead on a cure."

Alaric spoke, pulling their attention. "If there's anything we can do…"

Mal dropped his gaze. "There is one thing."

Rocky came beside Cleo, and the warmth of the wolves surrounding Cleo and Mal was like a soft blanket.

"Anything." Alaric's voice was stern and solid, the unmistakable tone of an alpha.

Malcolm looked up at the towering alpha. "Take care of our girl. And learn how to make some fucking pancakes."

Rocky laughed as Cleo wiped a fresh tear from her eyes.

She half expected Alaric to growl and argue, but he only nodded and said, "Done."

Mal nodded as he pulled Cleo in for a kiss.

It wasn't hurried or rushed like usual. It was soft, hopeful, and full of promise. He also tasted like salty bacon, and her stomach growled with renewed hunger.

"We should eat before the food gets cold," she whispered against his lips.

Malcolm snickered darkly. "Can't hit the road on an empty stomach, I suppose. I did *slave* away in this kitchen all morning." He grinned.

"Bullshit," Alaric nipped as he turned from them, heading into the dining room.

Cleo slipped her hand in Malcolm's as Rocky clapped him on the shoulder.

"Welcome to the pack," Rocky said as he left Cleo and Mal to follow.

Malcolm didn't argue. He only looked at Cleo, his lips turning up in a smirk that melted her heart.

"I promise I'll come back, baby. As soon as I can."

Cleo squeezed his hand. "I know you will."

And as they sat in the dining room, eating, laughing, and taunting one another, Cleo couldn't help but smile. For she knew no matter how unorthodox their pack was, the truth was irrefutable.

The seer was right. The moment she moved to Thorne estate, her life changed, and despite all the turmoil, the blood, and the obstacles in their way, she knew when she looked at her three mates, there was no storm they could not weather.

33

MALCOLM CLOSED THE trunk of his car, nearly jumping six feet off the ground when he saw Dallas pull up in the spot next to him on his motorcycle.

"Jesus Christ, D, you scared the piss out of me."

Dallas laughed, popping the kickstand.

Malcolm's gaze roved over the bike, the Old English font spelling out the word *viper* in bright blue.

He raised an eyebrow. "Viper? Seems a little on the nose, don't you think?" he drawled.

Dallas crossed his arms, shrugging. "Wasn't my idea. Boo did while I was—" He cracked a smile, his white fangs showcased in the sunlight, making Malcolm uneasy.

"Don't finish that sentence, I don't want to fucking know," Mal said as he leaned against his passenger door, sliding his hand into his back pocket. He procured a lighter and cigarette as Dallas chortled.

"Those things are going to kill you, you know."

Mal breathed in the sweet chemicals, letting them settle his nerves.

"If the fucking monsters don't get me first," he said, cracking a grin.

Dallas chuckled. "Touché."

A pregnant pause passed between them as Dallas's grin fell, and Mal puffed out a circle of smoke.

"So, what's next?" Dallas asked

cautiously.

Mal took another hit, relishing in the crackle of the fire as it burned.

"I don't know, you tell me, Daddy," he said, his tone rich with sarcasm.

Dallas's eyebrows shot up in alarm.

"You know?"

Malcolm rolled his eyes. "Of course I fucking know. Amora broadcasted it all over the fucking room when we were trying to figure out why Midnight was like... practically dying of separation anxiety."

Dallas's jaw set tightly.

Mal hit his cigarette again, tapping off the ash.

"Kinda crazy after all these years I get a second chance." Dallas's voice was full of emotion as he leaned against the Chevelle, next to Malcolm. For a moment, it was as if nothing had changed.

As if they were still Mal and Dallas, hunting monsters, saving people. Fucking shit up.

Dallas held his hand out, and Mal passed him the cigarette. He watched as his friend breathed it in easily, blowing smoke out in the coolest way possible.

"Yeah, crazy right?" Mal shook his head. "What's going to happen to the... kids?" His voice was cautious.

Dallas turned to face him. "Amora secured the land, and Thomas plans to develop it. Add some more houses for the Heartsgrave. Even a school."

Mal flicked his ash. "So, all the Djinn just... what? Hang up their bike helmets and go full on suburbia?"

Dallas shrugged. "Something like that."

Mallas chuckled. "Fuck, that sounds *awful*. Like, can you imagine, just... settling down and shit. Putting down roots."

Dallas raised an eyebrow. "Yeah. That's exactly what I'm doing. With

Midnight and four kids."

Mal shook his head. "Five."

Dallas laughed. "Right. Five." He knocked Malcolm in the shoulder. The birds chirped and the sun was shining bright like there was nothing terrible waiting for him.

Not that day, anyway.

"I should kill you, you know," he said the words carefully, looking up into his best friend's aquamarine eyes.

Dallas's smile fell. "I know. But if you wanted me dead, you would have killed me in that forest."

Mal shrugged as he leaned off of his car. "Can't kill someone who's already dead."

Dallas grabbed him, pulling him into a hard, heavy hug.

Malcolm couldn't resist wrapping his arms around Dallas's tree trunk body.

"If you ever need me, Mal, you know where to find me."

Malcolm hugged him, the tears coming freely to his eyes. He seemed to be doing an awful lot of crying lately.

"Have a good life, D. You fucking deserve it."

Dallas let go of him and he headed back to his motorcycle. As Malcolm opened his driver door, he shouted, "So do you, Malcolm. So do you."

Mal waved him off as he climbed into his driver's seat, turning on the radio.

The familiar sounds of Kansas's *Carry On My Wayward Son* filled his speakers as he watched Dallas fire up his bike, and ride off to wherever it was he needed to be.

And as Malcolm pulled out of the parking lot, he vowed never to tell a soul about the monsters he let live.

***

The Paradigm Motel wasn't the most comfortable hotel he'd ever stayed in, and he was sorely missing the round nest-bed of the Mayfield's guest cabin.

He tossed his duffel on the bed, the silence deafening.

For the last week and a half, his days had been filled with blood and hunting, but they had also been filled with so much more. He looked at the single bed, cracking a smile at the thought of him, Cleo, and Alaric trying to fit on the thing together. They'd never make it.

His heart ached as he realized he missed the stupid, lumbering alpha.

But he'd never admit it.

His cell phone rang, disturbing the silence. He slid it out of his back pocket.

"Yeah, Hunter?" he drawled, leaning back onto the creaky bed.

"I might have a case, if you're ready to jump back into the fray."

Malcolm closed his eyes, sighing. As far as his sister and his fellow hunters knew, he was taking a well-needed break to get Dallas's affairs in order. They hadn't known it had taken him all of two days to process ownership of Dallas's former life. There wasn't much the man owned, save for a few bikes and the cottage he'd bought with his wife when they'd first married. When Jake Dallas turned to vengeance, to hunting, he'd given up a normal life.

But he still managed to find his happily ever after, even after all the loss.

Malcolm nodded, though no one could see him. "Yeah, Hunter. I think a case is just what I need."

34

Three months later...

AMORA TOUSLED HER blonde hair, separating her curls. The woman who gazed back at her in the mirror was one she knew well.

She opened her lipstick, a bright watermelon pink gloss, and carefully applied it to her lips, smacking them together. Set against her ivory skin, it was a dramatic contrast.

She tossed some curls over her

shoulder, drawing attention to the long, silvery chain she wore that dipped between her breasts, down to her navel.

The silver, slinky dress she wore clung to her lithe frame like a second skin, the sequins glittering in the low light of the suite.

She set her lipstick into her rhinestone purse, looking over her shoulder at the man who lay handcuffed to the bed, half-drained, but still breathing.

She hated fast food, but she was too far away from any of her own properties and safe houses.

As she slipped through the velvet curtains, back into the shadows of the Coliseum, the latest blood den on the market, she felt better, at least in appetite.

Though she always detested blood dens, ever since her late ex-husband, Marcellus Medici, had been a prominent patron.

"Everything to your liking this evening, Amora?" A familiar voice pulled her from her unsavory thoughts.

Thinking of her ex-husband always made her sour.

She put on her best smile as she approached the tall, studious vampire in the midst of the dungeon. His glasses glinted in the red light.

He stood next to a cage bearing a woman who looked a lot like a woman she'd once known, who worked at Leon's blood den in Paris.

Marguerite.

She had the same wispy white-blonde hair and ballerina frame that the vampires in Paris loved. Though the woman in front of her was not mortal like the one of her past. Her succubus eyes were vacant as she stared into the shadowed abyss at Amora.

Amora sighed, as thinking about Marguerite made her think about Cassius

Aurelia, her ex-lover slash heartbreaker, who was just as sour a topic as her late ex-husband.

She forced a smile as she answered. "Yes, Leon, of course. But I wouldn't expect any less of a man as accomplished as you."

Leon chuckled as he offered her his arm. "Shall we?"

She took it gingerly, letting him lead her through the dungeon. It was filled with cages bearing plenty of monsters, from female Djinn to succubi, to the rarest of all, sirens.

The ever-present red glow permeated the otherwise opulent black design, mixing with violet backlight. She had to appreciate Leon's penchant for design aesthetics. He did gothic seduction rather well, and it made her long for her own dissolved endeavors, such as her beautiful masquerade, the Marquis.

"What brings you out to these parts? I

thought you were traveling and collecting real estate?" he asked sweetly. "Word has it you conquered one of the Boracelli's properties in Kentucky, recently."

Amora shrugged, giving him no confirmation. As much as she trusted Leon, she had left her Heartsgrave in Mayfield for a reason. She'd always planned on finding them a place to rest, to build their lives from the ashes, anew. Amora did not have the luxury of settling down. In her experience, comfortability led to upheaval.

No, if she kept moving, the monsters that chased her could not capture her or distinguish her.

"What can I say, I'm restless."

Leon smiled knowingly. You are running again. Who has broken your heart this time?"

The blonde look-alike reached for her ankle as she walked past, and Amora hissed, kicking her back into the cage.

Leon purred. "Ah... so, I take it you have seen him."

Amora hissed at Leon. "I do not know who you are referring to," she bit.

Leon shook his head as he led her up the stairs. "I think we both know that is a lie."

Amora focused on the light above the stairs. "I did not come to this god-forsaken den to talk about your prodigal son, Cassius," she hissed.

Leon chuckled. "Of course you didn't. So why did you come?"

They arrived at the top of the steps and he let her go. On the upper floor, the room was packed with mortals and supernaturals alike. Though the mortals had no inkling they were among beasts and monsters.

Just as it should be.

"Perhaps, Leon, I am on a hunt for some blood of my own."

Leon slid his hands into his pockets.

"Imagine that, a vampire, hungry for blood."

Amora stopped, her gaze settling on a familiar face she most certainly did not expect to see. Her lips curled up in the corner.

She turned to Leon, flashing her thick eyelashes. "Yes, imagine that," she said as she nodded at him. "Now, if you will excuse me, I will feed your rumor mill no more. A woman's work is never done, as you know."

Leon smiled as he nodded at her. "Should you need my assistance in any way, Your Majesty, do not hesitate to call."

She giggled sweetly. "Oh, Leon, I thought you retired from a life of meddlesome vampires and monsters."

Leon chuckled darkly. "We must keep our brains stimulated in our old age, Amora."

"I will not hesitate to call if I need you."

She smiled and it was genuine.

Despite their bloody history, she'd always considered Leon a formidable ally. The man was sharper then a tack, and knew more of their history and law than anyone. But he'd left the world of the High Covens, just as Cassius had, just as she had.

When Cassius left Eden, everything crumbled, including her own Medici throne. Eden had stolen it out from underneath her, claiming she was not a proper heiress.

Even in death, the snake of a woman coveted that which did not belong to her.

No, Cassius had left Eden, and in retaliation the vicious vampire sought to dismantle the entirety of the High Covens.

Cassius had no idea how integral he was to the foundation of the High Covens. He did not understand that he was *born* for rule.

If he did, he would find some way to

ruin it further.

Probably take a mortal as his queen and make a mockery of us all.

Amora shook off the thoughts of her former lover and his mortal fascinations, instead, setting her sights on a much more volatile mortal sitting at the bar.

Perhaps this hunt would not be so difficult after all.

"I'll have a glass prosecco, please, and my friend here, will have a whiskey on the rocks. Your finest whiskey, of course."

Malcolm turned to her with fire in his eyes. "What the fuck do you want?"

She pulled up the bar stool next to him, flipping her hair over her shoulder. She beamed her bright green eyes at him.

"Now, is that any way to greet an old friend?" she said, pouting at him like a teenage social media influencer.

To be fair, she was perpetually twenty, but her features often gave her a much more youthful look.

It had been a formidable weapon all her life.

Amora Medici was used to getting what she wanted, except when it came to matters of the heart.

"We are not friends. Not in the slightest," Malcolm said as the bartender slid his drink to him, placing hers in front of her.

"Disgruntled co-workers then?" Amora asked as she sipped her drink.

Malcolm narrowed his gaze. "What the fuck do you want?"

Amora smacked her lips, tasting the fizzy sweetness.

It was too sweet for her liking. Perhaps she should suggest some better bottles to Leon.

"I have a proposition for you," she said, crossing her long, slim legs.

True to his bonded nature, Malcolm did not tear his gaze away from her eyes.

Pity he's bonded.

He is rather spicy.

I bet his blood tastes divine.

But Amora knew Malcolm's mate also came with two other wolves, in which she rationed that would be more trouble than it was worth.

Though the hunter was quite a livewire and he had garnered a reputation among the remaining silent covens, among the monster she waltzed with.

Malcolm Crowley was a killer.

A ruthless one.

"And why the fuck would I agree to do anything for you?"

Amora spoke plainly. "Well, I did save your mate from the hands of certain death once. I believe that means you owe me a favor."

Malcolm pressed his lips together, a deep growl rumbling from his chest.

He gritted his teeth. "Depends on what the fucking favor is."

Amora smiled sinfully. "Let's just say

that you and I have a mutual enemy.”

Malcolm sipped his drink. “Oh yeah? Who?”

Amora sipped her fizzy drink, relishing in the sensation on her tongue.

“Her name is Eden Boracelli, and she is the current sitting queen of the Boracelli coven. She is the one who has been kidnapping omegas, and other… supernatural oddities.”

Mal raised an eyebrow with interest. “What did she do to you?” he asked seriously.

Amora breathed heavily as centuries of unrest threatened to spill out of her.

“Does it really matter?”

She ruined my fucking life and took everything I wanted.

My husband.

My lover.

My fucking throne.

Mal shrugged. “Guess not.” He held the glass near his lips. “I do this for you, we're even." It wasn't a question, it was a downright solid statement.

Amora held her glass up. "Deal, Mr. Crowley."

As their glasses clinked, Amora smiled with genuine satisfaction.

Because there was nothing Amora desired more than revenge.

And with Malcolm Crowley's help, she was going to get it.

Amora, Leon, Malcolm, and the rest of the Goon Squad will return!
Watch for Blood Of My Heart: The Hunter Games #4.

If you enjoyed this book, please return to your favorite retailer and leave a review. Even a few words could mean the world to an author.

OTHER BOOKS BY ARIEL DAWN

Blackthorn Academy for Supernaturals

Monster's Spell

The Hunter Games

Blood Of My Enemy

Blood Of The Lost

Thorne Of Blood

Speed Dating with the Denizens of the Underworld Series

Hecate

Hades

Orion

Athena

Spike

Ava Crowley, Vampire Slayer

Blood & Bones

Blood & Lust

Blood & Ash

Ava Crowley, Vampire Slayer Series

Omnibus

Lost Souls

Heaven Knows

Hell Everlasting

Monsters Of Ashwood

Voices In The Dark

Whispers In The Woods

Sign up for Ariel Dawn's newsletter and

claim your sweet treat!

https://view.flodesk.com/pages/64b2b6e

fe181ddda00ff2a1e

CONNECT WITH ARIEL DAWN

Website

http://www.ariel-dawn.com/

Goodreads:

http://www.goodreads.com/authorarieldawn

Bookbub:

http://www.bookbub.com/authors/ariel-

dawn

Facebook:

http://www.facebook.com/authorarieldawn

Twitter:

https://twitter.com/ArielDawn10

Join Dusk Chasers—Ariel Dawn's Official
Readers Group for access to exclusive
content!
https://www.facebook.com/groups/6891673
88350361

ABOUT ARIEL DAWN

USA TODAY BESTSELLING AUTHOR Ariel Dawn grew up as an avid reader and is a creative soul.

What started out as writing reviews for indie romance authors led to featuring quirky, stereotypical, and weird covers on her Instagram Wrong Turn Romance, which gave her the courage to finally decide to live her dream and become an author.

Ariel writes plot driven paranormal romance and hopes to venture into fantasy and rom-com in the future. When she isn't writing, she can be found cosplaying, attending conventions, creating all sorts of artwork in her studio, or editing photos for her photography business.

A self-professed geek and foodie, she loves hanging out with family and friends and playing video games and board games with her retro gamer husband.